Going Home

ALSO BY JAMES D. SHIPMAN

Constantinopolis

Going Home

a novel of the Civil War

JAMES D.
SHIPMAN

LAKE UNION
PUBLISHING

This is a work of fiction. Names, characters, organizations, places, events, and incidents are either products of the author's imagination or are used fictitiously.

Published by Lake Union Publishing, Seattle

www.apub.com

ISBN-13: 9781503944190
ISBN-10: 1503944190

Cover design by Megan Haggerty

Printed in the United States of America

This book is dedicated to my father, James C. Shipman: community leader, historian, fireman, funeral director, husband, father, and grandfather. Thank you for giving me my love of life and history.

August 7, 1941–October 31, 2013

BASED ON A TRUE STORY

CHAPTER 1

Company D, 186th New York Volunteers

In the Trenches near the Military Railroad and Jerusalem Road

Petersburg, Virginia

Saturday, January 2, 1865

Joseph woke to the high-pitched shrieking of the rebel yell. His heart nearly pounded out of his chest while he groped for his rifle in the rain and the mud. He grasped wood and steel, releasing his breath as he found his weapon. The screaming drew closer. He heard panicked shouting from the trenches of officers trying desperately to rouse the men. He peeked his head over the lip of the trench but could see nothing, not even a few feet in front of him. It had to be the middle of the night. Something was terribly wrong, but he couldn't focus.

The screaming thundered. A flash. Forms emerged in the blackness mere yards away. He heard scattered firing along the trench. He lifted his rifle and aimed at a figure emerging out of the darkness. He had only an instant. He pulled the trigger. Nothing—unloaded. He could make out the man now, a monster with red hair in tattered brown clothing clutching a rifle with both hands across his chest. The attacker screamed, and his crazed eyes met Joseph's and locked on him.

Joseph stepped back, kneeling to give himself a fraction of additional space. He grabbed the stock of his rifle with both hands and jabbed the barrel into the stomach of the rebel, just as the enemy started to leap into the trench. The move caught the Confederate by surprise, and he was unable to dodge the lunge. The attacker's own momentum drove the blunt end of the barrel into his stomach with enough force to pierce the skin. He screamed in pain and surprise as he landed hard on top of Joseph, blood spilling out of the wound.

Joseph's rifle stock shattered into pieces from the impact. The weight of the Confederate pressed him hard into the mud at the bottom of the trench, and warm blood spattered as the rebel writhed and screamed on top of him. Joseph tried to shove the man away, but the reb was incredibly heavy, and the slippery mud prevented him from finding a toehold. Finally, Joseph was able to draw a boot in and press hard against the trench wall. With a heavy lurch, he threw the Confederate off with enough force that the rebel crashed against the far side of the trench.

Joseph gasped for breath, his heart beating out of his chest as his eyes strained to see in the darkness. Rifle fire flashed in the night like lightning. He was shocked to make out what looked like scores of the enemy overrunning the trenches. Many were already over the edge and locked in hand-to-hand combat while others peered down, rifles raised, searching for targets.

Joseph groped in the darkness for a weapon. For agonizing seconds, he tried to find anything to fight back with. His rifle was useless, and he had lost his bayonet. He crawled through the mud, trying to keep his body low. Eventually, he came across something soft, and as he ran his hand along it, he realized it was wet cloth. He grasped a handful and pulled himself over until he realized he was lying on top of his recent attacker. He couldn't tell if the rebel was dead or just badly wounded, but the reb wasn't putting up a fight anymore.

Joseph fumbled over the man's shirt and belt, searching for anything he could use as a weapon. He felt cold steel, a barrel, and he pulled, trying to release the rifle. It was trapped under the body so he had to jerk and lift at the same time, but eventually the weapon broke free. He examined it with both hands. He had been mistaken; the circular steel was not the barrel of a pistol but rather the handle of a small, blunt shovel. It would have to serve as a weapon until he could find something better.

Joseph grasped the shovel and kept his body low, crouching behind the Confederate. Flashes of musket fire continued, and the bursts of light allowed him to see dimly through the smoke and the night. He could make out the trench line again. The fighting continued. Several members of his company were only a few feet away, locked in combat with their attackers. In the blackness he couldn't make out individuals. Where was David? His friend had been asleep right next to him. Where was he now? Joseph had to find him.

A flash. A Union soldier and a Confederate were fighting not more than two yards away. He pulled himself up and waited for the next burst of light. Another flash. He leapt out of the darkness, landing heavily against the enemy. He grabbed the Confederate by the neck with his left hand, and with his right, he brought the shovel down hard where he judged the head would be. He heard a wet thud and the body went limp. He pulled back on the shirt collar, dragging the body for a moment and then hurling the rebel against the wall of the trench.

Joseph felt a hand in the darkness, grasping his arm hard and threatening to pull him down. He turned to strike with the shovel as another flash rent the night. He stopped midmotion, realizing he was about to hit his best friend. In the brief flicker of light, he saw recognition in David's eyes as well, and the hand relaxed.

Joseph grasped his friend by the forearm and pulled him close, dragging him down against the trench wall. He held David tightly for a moment, giving them both strength and a moment of rest.

"Are you okay?" he whispered.

"Yes," answered David.

"Where did they come from?"

"I don't know. I woke up to screaming and gunfire. The next thing I knew I was fighting with someone. I didn't even know who. He was getting the better of me and I thought I'd had it. Then he let go. I pulled my bayonet out and was going to get 'em, but when the light flashed again, he was gone and it was you."

"I killed him. Do you still have your bayonet?"

"It's right here."

"What about your rifle?"

"I don't know. It was next to me when I fell asleep but I haven't seen it. It happened too quickly."

The din of battle was beginning to die down. Joseph struggled to see in the dark, but he could make out nothing. "We have to get out of here. I think we've lost this trench. Do you remember the connecting trench to our left? The one that leads back away from the front? If we can make it there, I think we could sneak out and get help."

David stepped closer to Joseph and searched from left to right.

"This whole trench must be crawling with rebs. How are we going to make it all the way there? Can't we just climb up the back of the trench and escape?"

"The lip is too high. And with all the mud, it's too slippery. Even if we made it out, they would see us for sure with all the musket fire. We have to try the side trench." Joseph grabbed his friend's hand, holding it tight for a moment.

"Okay, but I don't know where I'm going."

"I know the way. We'll use the flashes of light to see. I'll take the lead. Stay down and keep quiet."

Joseph closed his eyes for a moment and tried to imagine the distance to the connecting trench. He knew it was at least twenty yards away. If they kept low and were lucky, they should make it. He groped in the darkness around David, searching for his rifle. He found nothing; it must have been picked up or kicked away in the fighting. He would have to do without a musket. He grasped the shovel in his right hand and took David's hand with his left, then slowly crawled forward, leaning against the trench with his left shoulder as he tried to orient himself.

His luck held for several minutes. The sound of battle was fading now to almost nothing, replaced by murmuring in Southern accents. There were fewer flashes, which made the going more difficult, but Joseph knew they were getting closer to their goal, and the darkness might save them now. He crawled forward, keeping a firm hand on David and feeling for the opening in the trench. He was prepared to fight. Even if they were able to make it to the connecting trench, Confederates would almost certainly be guarding the entrance. If only he had his rifle.

From the darkness, new flashes emerged: matches. The Confederates were beginning to light their lucifers in the trench. Joseph pulled hard on David's hand and struggled forward, trying to reach the side trench before the lanterns revealed them. Several were fully lit, but fortunately they were farther down. The dim light had the advantage of allowing Joseph to see at least vague shapes. He was terrified to discover what looked like a hundred rebels milling around the long ditch. Lower to the floor there were bodies, some Union and some Confederate. He could also see the entrance to the side tunnel on his left only a few yards ahead. Surprisingly, it was unguarded.

"Look, David. We're almost there. I don't think they've seen us. Just keep quiet, stay low, and keep going."

David nodded silently and squeezed his hand in gratitude. Joseph turned and crawled forward. A few more feet and they would be there. A flash burst right in front of him. A Confederate standing directly behind the entrance of the side trench had struck a match. His head was down as he concentrated on putting the match in the opening of his lantern. Joseph tightened his grip on the shovel and slid forward, pressing as close to the trench wall as possible.

Finally, he reached the opening. The rebel had successfully lit his surroundings and was blinking, trying to adjust to the light. Joseph only had moments. He turned the corner, keeping his body low and against the left wall. He pulled himself forward a foot or two and then tugged on David's hand to follow him. They were going to make it.

"Hey! There's live Yanks out here!"

Joseph cringed at the shout. He turned and saw the rebel with the lantern staring openmouthed at them and pointing.

"Run!" Joseph screamed. He pulled hard on David, jerking him past and pushing him forward down the side trench. Joseph gripped the shovel more tightly in his hand, and threw it at the Confederate with all his strength. The shovel spun through the air and caught the rebel hard on the head, knocking him back against the far trench wall and sending the lantern flying. Joseph turned and struggled to his feet, following David down into the darkness of the side trench.

Joseph crashed hard into an object in the black night. He started to fall backward and reached out, grasping at the form he had run into. He felt arms and fabric—it was a man. Pulling himself up, Joseph tried to regain his bearings. He heard a low moan that he recognized. The voice was David's. He was holding on to his friend.

"David?" he whispered.

Silence. Joseph, grabbing with all his strength, tried to keep David up as his body began to slump.

A match lit up the darkness. Four Confederates stood lined up across the trench. The left center rebel held his rifle with both hands. Joseph looked down in horror and saw the rifle extended out, the bayonet buried in the middle of David's chest. Blood pumped out of the wound, covering the front of the musket and spreading a crimson stain across his friend's uniform. Joseph cried out in anguish.

"Don't move a muscle, Yank!" ordered another Confederate who Joseph recognized as a lieutenant.

Joseph couldn't follow that command. He had to try to help David, but he did so very slowly with deliberate motions. As the rebels watched closely, Joseph took a step back, slowly pulling David off the bayonet and gently laying him down on the muddy trench floor. He then rose even more slowly, keeping his hands visible, and moved them over his head in surrender.

"You moved," noted the lieutenant.

"He sure did," said the rebel holding the rifle.

A flash. Joseph felt a terrible ripping pain in his left shoulder and chest. He was blown backward by the impact. His head hit the mud of the trench. A fire pulsed in his shoulder. He tried to reach up and feel the wound, but he couldn't move his hands. He fought to stay conscious but his mind was drawn into the darkness. His last thought was of home.

Union Military Hospital Camp, near the Jerusalem Road
Petersburg, Virginia
Sunday, January 3, 1865

Nurse Rebecca Walker held the wounded Union soldier by both shoulders, pressing with all her weight to keep him from jerking off the table. The man stared up at her with wild terror, biting down hard on a dirty cloth. Doctor Thomas Johnston stood at the lower end of the table, his left hand holding down the soldier's ankle while he sawed purposefully through the left leg, just below the knee. The saw made a wet, ripping sound as it tore through flesh and bone. The wounded man jerked upward, his torso coming off the table.

"Damn it! Hold him!"

"I'm trying," responded Rebecca. She pushed down again, looking into the soldier's eyes and trying to impart compassion and mercy. His eyes looked past her.

She had administered chloroform on a rag before the operation. The patient had initially lost consciousness, but as often happened, he had woken up thrashing even though he was still under the effects of the drug and not truly aware. He moaned and stirred, his head moving back and forth, but fortunately, after the first thrashing jerk, she was able to keep him down and in control.

The doctor cut the rest of the way through the leg, blood spattering his already-stained and dirty shirt. He casually tossed away the foot and calf onto a pile of other limbs in the corner of the tent. He then motioned Nurse Walker over to him, and together they set to work tying off the arteries with thread. When they were finished, the doctor ground down the end of the bones with a file to assure no sharp protrusion would later stick out of the skin. Finally, he pulled the skin over the bone and sewed the stump of the leg shut, leaving a hole for drainage. The entire operation took less than twenty minutes.

Two orderlies pulled the soldier off the table and carried him on a stretcher to the recovery area while two more brought another wounded Union soldier onto the table. Rebecca quickly washed the instruments and sponges in cold water. The water was already bloody from a dozen previous operations, but she did her best to clean the tools before they started the next procedure. She brought the tray back to the table.

"Where are all these wounded coming from?" asked the doctor.

"An orderly told me the Confederates overran one of our trenches," said Rebecca. "The position was retaken but there were many killed and wounded, mostly from some New York regiment."

"That certainly explains the wounded. I haven't seen this many casualties since The Crater. But I wonder why they would bother attacking a trench? We have them boxed in; they aren't going anywhere."

She shuddered. She remembered The Crater very well. She had just arrived at the front in mid-July of 1864. After only a couple of weeks at the hospital, on July 30, the Union attempted to break the siege at Petersburg by exploding a huge underground mine beneath the Confederate trenches. The attack was a fiasco, and thousands of Union soldiers were killed inside the crater left by the explosion when they rushed in to try to take over the line.

Rebecca had spent three solid days assisting surgeries in an almost never-ending line of wounded. Hundreds died waiting their turn. The burned bodies were the worst. She could never get used to the sweet, cloying smell of burned flesh. She still woke up screaming when she dreamed of them.

She prayed quickly that the soldier would survive. She used to pray many times a day, but she found herself doing so less and less. Perhaps it was the mind-numbing horrors she had witnessed. She was trying to keep her faith, but she struggled to understand God's part in all this.

Orderlies set the next soldier down. She wondered why they had even bothered. Chest wound. Blood covered his chest and upward to his left shoulder. The bloodstain continued all the way down to his belt. She was surprised he was even alive, but she could see his chest heaving with labored breath. Doctor Johnston stared for a moment and shook his head.

"I'm going to have a pipe. There's nothing I can do for this man. Try to find any personal information to pass on, and in a few minutes we'll start on the next one."

She stared after him as he walked away, words halting on her lips. She could protest, but there was no point. She always wanted to struggle for their lives, even with the impossible patients. Doctor Johnston would walk away from what he considered hopeless cases. The doctor wasn't a bad man or a bad doctor, but he was jaded after a year of endless amputations, a year of death. After his experience, he knew at a glance when he would be wasting his time. She had difficulty feeling the same detachment. She wanted to try to save a person as long as they had breath; she wanted to fight death until the battle was lost.

She wondered if anyone had fought to save her husband, a young lieutenant killed by a sniper on the White Oak Road, only a few miles away. Less than a month ago now, it seemed like a year.

That wasn't her first personal tragedy. She remembered a different doctor two years ago, a lifetime ago, trying desperately to save their baby girl. He had fought hard, fought to the end, but she had died. First their daughter and now her husband. All her dreams were gone. Her future had faded until she only had the present to cling to.

Her grief swelled up again. It always came in waves, out of nowhere, crushing her. She couldn't breathe. She put her hands down on the end of the table and began to shake, trying to control herself. Eventually, she felt both the panic and the pain fade. As she calmed, she heard the breathing of the soldier slowing down. He was dying.

The wave of grief passed. She reached down and began unbuttoning his coat, the single row of thick, brass buttons slick with blood. As she opened his uniform and pulled aside the undershirt below, she saw the wound was not in the middle chest as she had thought, but in the left collar below the bone. Blood continued to spurt from the wound, pouring out in frothy bursts with each beat of his heart. Farther down, she saw a paper pinned to the inside of his shirt, the white splotched with blood. The man had tagged his personal information on the inside of his shirt, as veterans often did. The paper said "Joseph Forsyth, Macomb, New York."

She pulled at the paper, tugging until it ripped off the pins, when she saw something beneath it. She removed the object and examined it: a letter. The envelope was soaked through with blood. She hesitated, then opened it and quickly read the letter within. Her heart burned and tears flowed down her face. She was awash in emotion again, experiencing the love of another husband for his wife, his desire to get home to her.

She looked down again with fresh eyes at the corporal on the table. After she read his letter, he became more than flesh to her: he was a man, a husband, a father. She couldn't let this man die without even trying. She could hear the doctor's objections in her mind before she even asked him, but she would fight the doctor. She would fight for this man's life, no matter the odds. He would surely die, but she would have done everything she could for him. She squared her shoulders and prepared for the confrontation.

After a few minutes, Doctor Johnston returned to the tent, taking a moment to notice the soldier still on the operating table. His face showed surprise and then irritation.

"Why is he still here? Were you able to find out who he is?"

"Yes, he is Joseph Forsyth from New York."

"Good, give the information to the clerk and we will at least be able to let the poor devil's family know he died here. Let's get him to a cot and move on to the next one."

"No. I want to try to save him."

"There's no point and no time." He motioned for the orderlies.

"No, Doctor. I want you to operate on him."

Johnston looked up at her and chuckled. "My, aren't we becoming the feisty one? I told you he's dead. I need to save the living." He turned again toward the orderlies and raised his hand.

"No." Nurse Walker grabbed his wrist and pulled him back around, looking into his eyes. "I want to save him. He is not dead yet. We have to try."

"*Nurse*, we've worked together a long time. You know he's gone. We have a dozen people waiting. Would you let them die while we waste time with this one?"

"Please. I'm asking you to try. I need to try." She knew she was pushing hard. She had worked with Doctor Johnston for months, but in many ways, she hardly knew him. He was distant, and their relationship had been distant as well. There were times when she had hated him. He always made it very clear that *he* was the doctor and she was but a nurse. Challenging him now was risky. He could simply order her out of the operating tent or, if he was upset enough, recommend her dismissal. She could see his face flush.

"I told you he's a dead man. I have dozens of wounded waiting. They have a chance to live. He doesn't. Are you questioning my judgment? Perhaps I need a new assistant."

"Please, Thomas, don't." She held on to his arm for dear life. "Please, I need this. I'm begging you. I looked at his wound. It's not a chest wound. He has a chance. I found a letter . . . his name is Forsyth and his wife is waiting at home for him."

The doctor watched her for a second and she saw his eyes soften. "You can't bring him back. Nothing we do here can save him. You know that, right?"

"Please, Thomas. Please, can we try?"

He looked at her again and then over his shoulder in the direction of the waiting wounded. "This is a waste of our time. But as you wish. If you want to try, we better get to it."

She felt a surge of joy and she gave his arm a final squeeze before she let go. "I have all the instruments ready. We can begin immediately."

Doctor Johnston examined the patient with new interest, assessing the injury. He picked up a sponge and began dabbing the damaged area, attempting to clear the blood away so he could see the wound more clearly. After a few minutes, he stood and wiped his brow. "You're right. It's not a chest wound. If the ball missed the arteries and the bone, there might be a slight chance he'll survive."

He went back to work. Nurse Walker moved closer with another sponge, helping to pull away tissue and dab, attempting to stem the constant flow of blood. The soldier's face turned gray as his breathing became shallower. They had to hurry.

Thomas continued to poke and prod. "He's incredibly lucky. The ball passed through his chest and out his back without hitting the bone. If we can stop the bleeding, we might be able to keep him alive, at least for a few hours."

Rebecca shuddered as she thought of the minié ball, actually more of a conical shape with a pointed end than an actual ball. Almost all the wounds they saw were from this soft, lead bullet used as rifle ammunition by both sides. The minié ball would expand when it hit a person, tearing bones and exploding arteries. The wounds were devastating.

Almost all wounds to the chest, stomach, and head were fatal; only soldiers hit in a limb could hope to survive, and usually the damage was so significant that amputation above the wound was required. Only about fifty percent of the wounded survived the operation and the risk of infection afterward. Torso wounds like this were almost always fatal.

Thomas finished his initial examination, then glanced around the tent, squinting in the dim light. "Let's move him outside. I can't see properly in here."

During the daytime, Doctor Johnston, like most surgeons, typically operated outside, when possible, where the lighting was better. He did not like the audience this often created, but the surgery tents were too dark to see in, particularly when precision was needed. Nurse Walker motioned orderlies over and they carried the soldier, table, and all outside. She followed quickly behind, squinting in the early morning light, her eyes adjusting slowly after hours in the dim light of the tent.

Thomas set to work again immediately. Rebecca watched him, impressed as always by his intensity and skill. He had come this past year to the front with no surgical experience at all, but he had learned quickly and become very adept. He had a quick and steady hand. She looked up to study his face as she sometimes did. He was of average height and slender with pale skin and blond hair—handsome man, although prematurely aged by the stresses of war. He was thin but strong with wiry muscles. If he had not been married, he would have been attractive to her, but of course, he was, and such thoughts were a sin. She turned her mind away from them as she always did, harshly reminding herself of her obligations as a widow and chastising herself for allowing her mind to wander from the job at hand.

Doctor Johnston instructed Rebecca to keep sponging the area around the wound as he probed the tissue, occasionally pulling out a fragment of cloth. He then asked Rebecca to roll Forsyth on his side so he could clean the exit wound in the same manner. He was sweating from the effort, but he kept going as quickly as he was able. After assuring as best he could that he'd removed all foreign objects, he set to work closing the holes with a large needle and wax-coated thread. He sewed up the exit wound first, covered it with a cloth bandage, and then set to work on the front. Finally, he was finished and he wiped his brow. The procedure had taken ninety minutes. Forsyth was still alive, although his chest was rising and falling in shallow breaths.

Doctor Johnston stepped away and leaned against a nearby wagon, resting from the intense exertion of the operation. "Well, I've done everything I can, and he's still alive, at least for now." He looked a little sternly at Rebecca. "To be honest, I'm torn about this decision. Why does he have more of a right than everyone who is waiting? He probably won't survive as it is. How many have died while we wasted this time?"

Rebecca felt ashamed but grateful to Thomas. "Thank you for trying to save him. You're right. He probably won't survive and I know we risked others. I needed this. I needed to know that we are doing our best for him. When I found that letter, I was overcome. Maybe I'm being selfish, but I just imagined his wife sitting at home for months with no word—then finally hearing he is gone. She deserves to know we did our best, no matter what the result."

Thomas watched Rebecca for a moment and started to speak, then hesitated as if changing his mind. "Perhaps she does. Perhaps she deserves that. Perhaps every woman deserves to know her husband was given every chance to survive."

Rebecca knew what he was really saying. She felt a new warmth for Thomas. He had always been distant and gruff. At times they argued, and his haughtiness upset her nearly every day. She had considered asking for a transfer, but he was a skilled surgeon and she enjoyed working with him as a nurse, if not as a woman. She was surprised by his reaction now. He had never shown her any real sympathy or compassion before. Maybe he was thinking about how his own wife back in Pennsylvania would react if she found out he had been killed. Whatever the reason, she was grateful.

The orderlies moved Forsyth away and brought the next wounded soldier—another leg wound. Her thoughts returned to the immediate task. They continued surgery outside all day and into the early evening, then returned to the tent and proceeded through the night. They were finally finished as dawn broke on yet another day. She was exhausted and barely able to keep on her feet. She cleaned herself up, washing the blood and dirt from her hands, and found some coffee and salted beef for breakfast before falling exhausted onto her cot for a few hours' sleep.

Rebecca woke to darkness. She was startled. She had slept all day and into the night. She had missed her rounds. Doctor Johnston must have ordered that she not be disturbed—another surprise. She stretched, feeling better than she had in days. Then it hit her. *My husband is dead.* The grief washed over her again.

She craved that moment of awakening each time she slept, that instant when everything was all right, before she remembered that her husband was gone forever.

Why did God take him away from her? Why did He take their child? Was she to be left with nothing? She felt guilty with these thoughts. Everyone was suffering in this war. She was no different; she had no right to feel sorry for herself. But knowing that others also suffered did not help her. She felt her own pain intensely, and that's all that seemed to matter.

She reached into a small satchel she kept near her cot and pulled out a stack of letters bundled neatly away. They were so similar to the one she had found yesterday, except for the blood.

Yesterday! She thought of that soldier. What was his name? Joseph? There had been so many others after him. She realized with regret how foolish she had been. She had allowed her own emotion, her own grief, to interfere with her job. They had let patients in need wait while they spent precious time trying to save someone with little chance of survival. All for nothing, poor Joseph likely did not live out the day.

Then she remembered Thomas, and how different and kind he had been yesterday. He had let her do what she wanted. She had acted irrational and childish. Regardless, he had given in, for her. She must thank him, and she must apologize. She must never let herself lose control again. She would seek him out, but first, she would check on her patients.

She made her way out into the darkness lit only by a small oil lamp she carried with her. She noticed the lamp was smeared with blood. What a mess! She must have been exhausted when she used it in the early hours of the morning. She would normally never pick up something without first washing her hands.

Rebecca made her way into the hospital tent. The "hospital" was actually three large tents, each with a different purpose. One tent was used for sorting out the incoming wounded. Another tent was utilized for surgery. She headed for the final and largest tent, which contained the recovering wounded. She opened the flap and entered, nodding to another nurse who was walking among the soldiers, checking their bandages.

Rebecca moved around the enclosure, trying to remember those she had worked on the day before. Here was a leg amputation she remembered. The young Union soldier had a boyish face with freckles and sandy-blond hair. He was sleeping fitfully. She checked the bandages and the wound below. The wound was seeping some blood but so far had not turned septic.

The greatest risk with amputations was infection. Many soldiers endured the amputation just to die a few days later. She wished there were some action she could take to prevent infection, but they could only do their best with surgery. They tried to amputate as far from the torso as possible. The farther from the body the amputation occurred, the higher the chance the patient would ultimately survive.

Rebecca checked several more patients and realized she was hungry. She could come back in an hour or so and finish. She wondered where Doctor Johnston was. She would like to talk to him about yesterday. Near the tent entrance, she stopped in surprise. Joseph Forsyth! There he was, stretched out on a cot. She knelt down. He was breathing. She couldn't believe it. She was sure he would have died by now. She checked his bandages and all looked normal. Was it possible he might survive? What a miracle that would be.

She looked at him more closely, as if for the first time. When Doctor Johnston was operating, she had so little time to behold a patient's features. Normally, she tried to avoid that altogether. She couldn't survive emotionally if she looked at each patient as a person with family and a life back home. She was haunted enough already.

He was in his thirties or at least his late twenties, a little older than the average soldier. He looked about six feet tall with brown hair and skin burned red by the sun. He had a long, faint scar in a half-moon pattern extending down his left eyelid to his cheek. She wondered what could have caused that. He looked peaceful as he slept, and she was delighted to see his chest moving up and down in regular, strong breaths.

Rebecca left a few minutes later, smiling with tears running down her face, her appetite forgotten. She went to find Doctor Johnston to share the news. She heard her husband's voice in her mind, telling her she had done the right thing. She had fought for this life and at least, for now, she had saved him.

CHAPTER 2

Moneymore Village

County Derry, Ireland

Wednesday, May 23, 1849

Eleven-year-old Joseph Forsyth stared out the window of his family cottage for the last time. The bags were packed and they were leaving Moneymore, the village where he had lived his entire life, forever. He was afraid of his uncertain future, afraid of the ocean and ships, things he had never seen. Why couldn't they simply stay here? Why were his parents making him depart his home and leave behind everything he had ever known?

Joseph was tall for his age with pale skin and blue eyes. Brown hair rested in an unruly mop on his head. He was thin, too thin. There was never enough food, but he knew it could be worse. He knew people who had starved, whole families. Others had left for America before them until the village seemed like a ghost town. They had been lucky; his grandparents on his mother's side had helped, bringing food and money when they were their most desperate. His father did his best, but there was never enough work, and he was always losing his jobs.

Joseph was old enough to help out and had been for several years. When there was work, he would join his father in the fields at the Conyngham Manor, and they brought home food and a little money. He was proud to help his mother and father.

Now they were leaving everything to go to America. Da had talked about America for years. He said there would be land there and their own farm instead of always having to rent. In America, there was always work and plenty to eat. His mother didn't want to leave Moneymore, and he had often heard them arguing late at night, sometimes for hours. He hated it but he loved them. He would eventually get up and brave a beating to try to break up the fighting. He wanted peace. He wanted home.

"Joseph boy, are you ready to leave?" asked his father.

"Yes, Da."

"Good lad. Get the rest of the baggage and load it in the wagon, will you?"

Joseph moved through the three rooms of the small cottage, collecting a few bags and loading them on the rickety wagon waiting outside. His ma was nowhere to be seen. He looked at the pitifully small collection of things in the back of the wagon. They could only take a few small possessions, clothes mostly. The furniture would all remain behind. He didn't understand why they had to leave everything—why they had to leave at all.

He looked through the cottage one last time but couldn't find anything they had forgotten. His da sat at the table, quiet as he so often was at home; he sipped whiskey out of a cup, his eyes lost in the distance. Joseph knew better than to disturb him when he was like this. His father's anger could come quickly like a violent storm. Joseph still bore the crescent scar of a mug thrown at him during a particularly stormy outburst. His da had apologized for that, but the scar remained.

He heard another voice, a pleasant voice. "Joseph, what are you doing there?"

He smiled, turning to see his ma. His mother was the center of his life. She was so kind and sweet. She always took care of his every need. She encouraged him and protected him from the worst of his da's fits. He was almost as tall as she was now. She smiled with her eyes, the same blue eyes Joseph had. Her face was weathered by the years of hard work and the years of worry, but her eyes were still young and joyful, and she was still beautiful to Joseph.

"Have you packed everything up in the wagon?"

"I think so, Ma. Will you look with me?"

"Yes, let's look one more time." They walked through the cottage together in silence, checking in drawers and under the beds. His mother picked up a few more items here and there, stuffing them into an extra bag she had found in a drawer by her bed. Finally, she was done and she shrugged her shoulders and sighed.

"Well I guess that is everything. Are you ready to go?"

"No, Ma. Why do we have to leave? I don't want to go. I want to stay here forever."

She watched him for a moment, a look of pain in her eyes. "I know this is hard, Joseph, but we are going to a better place. Your father will be able to find work there. We can buy land. We will finally have the things we have always wanted. Your da will finally be happy."

"Will Da be able to find a job that will keep him?"

She looked at Joseph for a moment before she answered. "I hope so, my dear. I certainly hope so." She smiled again. "These are not the worries for a young boy. We have a great adventure before us—a whole sea to cross. I want you to enjoy yourself, my dear. Leave the worrying to us. Everything will be well by and by. Now give me a moment to get your da."

Joseph went to the wagon and pulled himself up into the seat. The morning was fine and sunny and already a little warm. He kept his eyes on his home, trying to memorize every detail. He wanted to run away, hide in the village, and stay forever. He knew he couldn't. He would simply delay things for a day or two and he would face a terrible beating. Nothing he could do would stop this. He felt powerless.

Joseph's ma and da soon came out of the cottage. His da helped his ma up into the rickety wagon and then pulled himself in after her, gathering the reins. There was just barely enough room for the three of them to sit abreast on the hard, wooden seat. His father started their mule with some clicks of his tongue and a snap of the reins, and soon, they were bumping down the worn cobblestones of the village. Joseph kept his eyes on the cottage as it slowly shrank away and eventually faded entirely from view. He knew he would never see his home again.

Hours passed. The sun climbed in the sky until they traveled under the midday heat. The day was especially warm for May. The road was dusty and bumpy, jarring them along until they were all sore and exhausted. Still they went on for hours before they found an inn. They had to travel to Derry on the coast to catch their ship, a three-day trip by wagon. Joseph had never been this far away from home and he looked around with great curiosity at the unfamiliar farms and villages.

After what seemed an eternity, they finally arrived at a small inn. Joseph helped his ma with the baggage while his da took care of the mule and the wagon. They met in the common room and ate a meager meal of stale bread and cheese before retiring to a dingy room upstairs. The fire below heated the room uncomfortably and the mattresses were lumpy and smelled of mildew. Joseph's da remained downstairs with a pint of ale.

Joseph was exhausted from the day. His body ached from the constant jarring of the wagon. He missed his home and his friends. He was terrified by what the future might bring. His ma put him to bed and sat next to him, running her fingers through his hair.

"Ma, I don't like this. I want to go home. Can't we just turn around?"

"I know, my dear, but we don't have a choice. We need a new start. Your da needs a new start. We'll be fine once we settle in. You'll see."

"I love you, Ma."

"I love you, Joseph boy."

He tossed and turned on the mattress, trying to find a comfortable position. Eventually, he felt himself drifting away to sleep.

He woke with a start in the darkness. He could hear his da and ma talking in whispered tones.

"You've been in the drink again."

"Bah! I just had a bit of a nip. I've the right."

"You promised me you would be done."

"I will, I will. I promised I would quit the drink *when we arrived in America*. We aren't there yet, are we? I'm in Ireland and I'll act like a proper Irishman while I'm on me own soil."

"I can't go with you if you are going to break your word to me. Think of your boy."

"Quiet, woman. I'll do as I wish. I've made me promise to quit the drink in the new country. Now *you* quit your carry-on and go to bed. We've a hard day tomorrow, and harder days to come on the ship."

The room fell quiet. Joseph lay in the darkness with a pit in his stomach. His ma and da fought so much and always about the same thing. Always about his da's drinking. Why did ma have to make him so mad? She would make him run away someday and they would be all alone. His da worked hard. It wasn't his fault that his jobs were taken away. Why was she asking him not to drink? Drinking was a nightly ritual among the working men. They gathered each night at the local pub for a pint or two before they headed home. She had no right to ask him to quit something that made him a man. Still, drinking made his father angry. All the terrible things happened when he was drunk. Joseph was confused. He tried not to think anymore, but the thoughts flew through his mind. Finally, he faded back to sleep.

He was awakened early. He felt sand in his head after the restless night. He stumbled out of bed and ate a cheerless and cold breakfast with his ma while his da slept on. After breakfast he brought the mule and wagon around and then loaded the baggage alone. His ma remained in the room, trying to get his da out of bed. He waited patiently for what seemed forever. Finally, they came out and climbed up into the wagon to depart. The sun was already halfway up in the sky before they began.

The next two days followed the same pattern, with the wagon creeping closer to the coast each day, except his da did not linger in the common room after dinner at night but rather came straight up to bed with them. How long would that last? This too followed a familiar pattern. A blowup between his folks, followed by Da changing his behavior for a few days, but he always returned to the drink.

In the midmorning of the fourth day, they sighted the walls of Derry. Joseph stared openmouthed; he had never seen anything so big and grand in all his life. A stone wall surrounded a large portion of the town with houses spilling out past it on both sides. The town led down right to the water itself, and Joseph looked in awe at his first view of the mighty sea. He was amazed at its tranquil beauty, and terrified at the endless horizon.

"That's the sea, lad," his da said, giving his arm a gentle squeeze. "Six weeks or more we'll be on a ship to get to the other side of it. Be a brave lad now and let's get to it."

They rode through the narrow streets of Derry, eventually making their way to the waterfront. Joseph had never seen so many people or buildings. He saw black, shiny carriages with fine horses pulling them, the passengers dressed in the finest clothing. A market they passed was filled with more food and articles for sale than he could have imagined existed. They rode past row after row of red-bricked homes with white windows, dazzling in the morning sun. He spotted a huge building with a spire climbing to the sky. Eventually, the wagon crossed a stone bridge, a river flowing below.

Joseph's da pointed the river out to him. "That's the Foyle, lad, the gateway to the sea."

Eventually, they made their way to the waterfront. There, Joseph was in for another shock when they found their ship.

The ship was huge, rising well above eye level at the dock. Tall masts covered with ropes and mounds of fabric rose into the sky. The ship crawled with sailors packing in supplies and also with families standing at the rail, more passengers for the New World who had already gone aboard. The ship's name was *Leander*. Joseph sounded out the letters on the side of the ship. He prided himself on his reading. His mother had taught him even before the lessons at school. He loved books and study, and took every chance to learn something new.

Joseph unloaded the baggage with his ma while his da turned the wagon over to a man who handed him a small bag of coin. Soon he was back and he picked up an armload of the bags and led them up the gangway and onto the deck of the *Leander*.

A tall sailor greeted them and examined some paperwork offered by Joseph's da. He then led them down into the hold of the ship. Joseph was assaulted by an overpowering stench as soon as they stepped into the hold. The smell was a combination of tar, fish, and urine. The heat was stifling and the air was thick. The hold was dimly lit by a couple of lanterns. Dozens of people stared out from wooden bunks with straw mattresses. Joseph could hear coughing and the cries of several babies. He had never seen anything so miserable in his life. How could they last here for a day, let alone for six weeks or more?

The sailor led them to a corner where a single bottom bunk was available. He pointed at the bunk.

"Here's your berth for the voyage."

"We can't all stay in this bunk. There's hardly room for two and no way for three," said Da.

The sailor reached out and grabbed Joseph's da by the shirt, pulling him hard toward the bunk.

"That's what there is and that's what you'll take, or you can take that bitch and brat right off the ship and stay ashore."

His da balled up a fist as if to strike the sailor. Joseph watched and waited for the fight. His da wouldn't back down from a fight, even now, where he was a head shorter than the sailor.

"Don't, Robert. Leave it be," said Joseph's ma.

Robert stood for a moment, red faced, his breathing rapid. Then he stepped back and let his hands relax.

"Good," said the sailor. "Now get your baggage stowed and your bed made. We set sail today." The sailor turned and walked away.

Joseph watched his da stare after the man and then look around silently at the small bunk. Finally, he motioned to Joseph and they shoved the baggage beneath the wooden frame. When they were done, Robert introduced himself to the other families and talked to a group of the men. They described the conditions on the ship for the past several days. The sailors treated them like scum and the food was of poor quality and in limited amount. The heat and stench were unbearable. Still, they were all looking forward to beginning the voyage to the New World.

Robert pulled himself onto the bunk without talking to them. He drew out a flask and took a deep drink, staring ahead without speaking. Joseph's ma stood with Joseph nearby, her hands on his shoulders, trying to adjust to this hell they must live through.

As terrible as conditions had been as the ship was moored at the dock, it was nothing compared to the ship at sea. Joseph had felt the sickness in his stomach after only an hour or two at sail from the terrible rolling of the ship back and forth, sometimes gentle and sometimes harsh. He didn't throw up, but many did, the vomit mixing with the urine and all the other smells. Some were stricken with such terrible seasickness that they could only lay in their bunks, moaning and crying for hours on end.

Food was served twice a day. The sailors took the best and left the rest for the poor families below: brackish water and slimy pork so salty it left one burning for thirst. Stale bread became worse each day, and soon even that was gone, leaving only the pork and water. The sailors occasionally had fruit, but when the families in steerage asked about it, they were told it was for the working crew only. They must get by on what they were given and pray for the better days ahead.

Two weeks in they woke to find a person dead below. One of the mothers had died. She'd had a fever for days. The first mate conducted a short funeral ceremony and then her body was pitched overboard. She wasn't much older than Joseph's own ma. Another died a week later, an old man traveling with his daughter's family.

Joseph tried his best to keep himself busy. There were several other boys and girls near his age and they invented games to pass the time. Sometimes they were allowed above deck and Joseph would run around with his friends until they were shooed below again. The time passed slowly as the *Leander* edged ever closer to America.

Joseph's da passed his time in his flask, and after that was exhausted, he passed it with a group of Irishmen who sat in a far corner of the hold on some makeshift chairs, using a barrel as a table. They played endless hands of cards and passed bottles among themselves. Joseph remembered his father's promise to his mother; of course they weren't to America yet. At night, his parents would sometimes argue, and he was sure they were fighting about his da's drinking.

A larger-than-life character would join in the nightly card games. Michael O'Dwyer was a well-dressed Irishman about fifty years old with balding, brown hair and skin reddened by too much drinking. He claimed he was a guest of the captain, although nobody had seen his sleeping arrangements. It was true that he did not sleep below, and would only come down in the evenings to play cards.

Mr. O'Dwyer was a printer with a shop in Quebec City. He had come to the New World as a young man and apprenticed in the printing business. He had then opened up his own shop and done very well for himself, or so he bragged after the drink was in him. He was also Catholic and made no attempt to hide his disdain for the Protestant families from Ulster who made up the immigrants in the hold, including Joseph's. Despite his bragging and his constant jibes, he was popular with the other men, primarily because he brought a new bottle down each night and shared it freely. O'Dwyer had traveled back to Ireland to settle some financial affairs after the death of his father. The other travelers were in awe that anyone would have the money to make this trip more than once in a lifetime.

Joseph would often sneak over and sit quietly in a corner, watching the men play cards and share the bottle and stories of the Old World and the new one. His ma did not approve and would scold him when she caught him. He stopped trying to watch in the early evenings and instead would wait for his ma to fall asleep before he would quietly sneak out of the bunk and cross the hold to watch the men.

Tonight was no different. They sat on the deck of the hold as a family, gagging down a bit of salted pork for supper. The pork portions were becoming fouler and smaller as the trip went on. They had all lost weight and were constantly thirsty and hungry. The family ate in silence. Robert didn't like to talk at meals. He kept looking over in the direction of the card table.

"Don't worry, your boys will be there soon enough. I wouldn't want to trouble you with a few minutes with the family," said Joseph's ma.

"Now then, Lydia, don't go running your mouth off in front of the boy. I see where he's getting his cheek after all. I've made my promises to you and I'll follow them through . . ."

". . . we aren't in the New World yet," she finished for him.

"Exactly true. And you'll be remembering your place. I'm the head of this family, so stop your blather. Now off to bed with the both of you. I'm going to spend a little time with the boys before I sleep."

Robert rose and dusted himself off. He stretched and walked to the other side of the hold. Soon, he was sitting with four other men, and shortly after, Mr. O'Dwyer made his way down the stairs with his bottle and his loud, booming voice. Joseph remained near the bunk by his ma but kept an eye on his da across the ship.

"How are you doing, Joseph boy?" asked his ma. "I know this has been hard on you. It's no place for a boy cramped up like this. Soon enough you'll have streets to run in, or better yet, a farm. And it will be school for you again as well. You need to keep up your learning."

"I'm fine, Ma. I've found my things to do by and by. I worry more about you and Da. I hear you yelling at night when you think I'm asleep. I want you to be happy, Ma. I want Da to be happy."

She looked at him for a moment. "We are happy, Joseph. When you're older, you'll understand. Mothers and fathers aren't happy every second. Life comes along and gets in the way sometimes. You have to take the good with the bad."

"Like Da and the bottle?"

Joseph saw his ma's face flush red. "You've no place to say such a thing. Your da brought you into this world, and he tries as hard as any man I know. He's put food on your table and clothes on your back all these years."

"But you made him promise to stop drinking."

Joseph could see his mother's face redden. "Go to bed! I won't hear any more of this. You'll stop listening to things that don't concern you. And you'll keep your mouth quiet too, or I'll tell your da what you said and surely you'll see the strap." Her voice softened. "We have a new life in front of us, Joseph. A new chance. Your da knows that too. Things will be different. We will have food and land and a life there. Everything is better in America."

Joseph crawled into the bunk and closed his eyes to think. He was surprised by his ma's words. She so rarely was mad at him. She was right though. He had no place asking what his da was doing. His da was a man, and he should make his own decisions in the world. Joseph thought of America again. He tried to imagine what it would be like. Were there truly open fields and land to be had for everyone? He had heard stories of heaping plates of food, of fat cattle and ripe crops bent down with vegetables and fruit. Could such a place really exist? He prayed it did. He prayed they would be there soon and that his father would give up the bottle. He prayed his ma and da would never fight again. Whatever his ma said, he knew his life was different from others. He hadn't heard any other people fighting in hushed tones in the night. He prayed everything would change in America and that they would live forever in happiness.

Joseph awoke in the darkness. He could hear his mother's soft breathing next to him. Farther away, he could make out the laughter of the men as they drank and talked. He felt wide awake. He decided to get up. Joseph climbed quietly out of the bunk, carefully watching his mother's breath to make sure he didn't wake her. He finally made his way out and then tiptoed through the darkness of the hold until he eventually made it to his favorite spot, a crate tucked in among some baggage in a darkened corner. He was close enough to hear and see what was going on, but he would not call attention to himself if he remained still and quiet. The men were engaged in a loud discussion, with Mr. O'Dwyer, as usual, creating a commotion.

"Come on now, lads. You only left the church because your English landlords made you. Except for you Scots in disguise like Robert here. Forsyth is no Irish name and that's the Lord's truth."

Joseph watched his father bristle but contain himself. "Now, now, Michael, let's keep a civil tongue. You're knee-deep in Protestants here. And as for my background, it might be true my ancestors came from Scotland but that was an age ago. I'm as Irish as you and yours."

"Scotland to Ireland to America. Your family does get along, doesn't it?"

"And you're different, are you? I don't care about your fine clothes. You left Ireland same as us."

"No, not the same as you, Robert. I'm not going to America in rags without a shilling to my name. I've already made it in the New World. Not such an easy task either, I'll tell you, but you'll learn it soon enough."

"I'm not broke. I've money to buy land with. You don't know all you think, O'Dwyer."

Michael laughed. "I didn't realize we were sitting with a landed gentleman. Forgive me, your honor." He doffed his hat to the laughter of the others. "If you're so rich, maybe you'd like a real hand of cards. For some real money."

Robert took a deep drink from a bottle he was holding, then looked at Michael with hard eyes. "Aye, I'll play your game. Let's see if you have any money or you're just running off your mouth."

"That's settled then. We'll play for a hundred pounds."

There were gasps. Joseph had never even heard of such a number. There was no way his da had a hundred pounds to play with.

"Fine, a hundred pounds it is."

One of the men took the cards and slowly dealt five to each of them. Joseph could see his da's cards. He didn't fully understand poker, but he saw Robert had a pair, a good hand.

"Oh tsk, tsk," said Michael. "I don't know if I can win with these cards." He smiled at Robert. "Perhaps you'd like to double the wager?"

Robert looked around from person to person. His face was red and getting redder. He took another drink. "It's a wager."

"Ah bad choice, boyo, you may need help from your false religion."

Robert put down his cards. "I have a pair of tens. And I fancy I'm two hundred pounds the richer."

Michael looked at the cards for a second and then laid down his own cards. "Two pair, lad. Bad luck for you. I'll see your money now."

Robert went white. He looked around at the other men but they were avoiding his eyes. "I . . . I don't have two hundred pounds in my pocket. I have it in my baggage, well hidden. I'll get the money and have it for you in the morning. I don't want to wake my wife."

"Quit acting the maggot, Robert. I'll take my money now." Michael rose and drew a knife from his belt.

"Are you calling me a liar or a thief? I'll have your God-cursed money." Robert rose with fists clenched.

One of the other men intervened. It was Patrick, one of Robert's friends. "Come on now, lads. There's no need for fighting. We're on a ship. Nobody is going anywhere. Robert can get the money to you in the morning. We were all witnesses and we know what is owed."

Michael paused and then sheathed his knife. "I won't be cheated out of the money. I expect my two hundred pounds at first light or you'll answer to the captain and spend the rest of this voyage in irons." He walked swiftly to the stairs and up out of the hold.

The other men watched Robert in silence, avoiding his eyes. Patrick put a hand on Robert's shoulder. "It will be all right. Just get the money together and pay it, and the sooner it's out of your mind. I'll stand with you in the morning to make sure there's no funny business about."

"Cop on, Patrick. Do you think I have two hundred pounds?"

"Why'd you go bet that then, Robert? God alive. You've sunk yourself and your family."

"I need to sleep and think about things. There's always a way out, boyo. I have some money. I can't look at all sides gee-eyed and tired."

"Best of luck to you, Robert. I'll be there in the morning."

Robert shook his hand. "Thanks to you."

Robert stumbled away from the table and looked up, seeing Joseph for the first time.

"What are you doing up, lad? What did you hear? What did you see?"

"I saw everything, Da."

Robert came closer and stared at Joseph for a moment, then he slapped him hard across the face. Joseph felt the pain and his head explode with bright lights.

"Let me tell you something, lad. You're going to keep your mouth shut. If you breathe a word of this to your ma, you won't live out the day. I need to think, do you understand? Now go to bed before I give you another hand."

Joseph ran through the darkness to the bunk. He crawled in and moved close to his ma, who was still sleeping. He lay in the darkness, tears streaming down his cheek and his face throbbing. What would become of them now? There would be no New World for them. Da would be thrown in prison. They had nobody and nothing. Joseph tossed and turned for the rest of the night without sleep, dreading the dawn.

CHAPTER 3

Aboard the *Leander*

Friday, July 6, 1849

Joseph woke early the next morning. His mother was still asleep. His father was not in the bunk. He climbed out and put on his shoes, fumbling with the laces in the dim light of the hold. He rose, stretched, and went out to try to find his da.

He finally located him above deck. He was standing near the rail, silent, watching the early morning calm of the ocean. The day was bright and peaceful. A beautiful day.

Robert turned and saw Joseph. "Ah, morning, lad. Is your mother up?"

"No, she's not, Da."

"You haven't spoken to her?" Robert stared hard at Joseph.

"No, Da, she's not woken this morning yet."

"Good lad." He ran his hands through Joseph's hair. "I don't want you to worry, Joseph. I've thought things through and we'll be fine. I just need to sort things out with your ma. I want you to stay above deck here. I need to talk to her alone."

"Yes, Da."

Robert turned and climbed down into the hold. Joseph waited a minute and then followed. He climbed carefully down into the dim light and then kept to the shadows until he was close enough to their bunk to hear. He felt guilty he was disobeying his da and also terrified of getting caught, but he had to know what was going to happen. His father always had a plan, a way to fix things. As he watched, Robert gently nudged his mother, waking her. She stretched and yawned, then rolled over to face Robert.

"Good morning, dear," he said.

"Good morning. Where's Joseph?"

"He's above deck. How are you feeling this morning?"

"I'm fine. Is everything all right?"

Robert hesitated. "I need to talk to you, dear. We've had a bit of a setback."

She sat up, looking at Robert with searching eyes. "What do you mean?"

He took her hand. "I . . . I don't quite know how to begin. I was playing cards last night and that bastard O'Dwyer was shooting his mouth off again. His lies are as bad as his poker playing and I saw a chance to make some real money. I bet him a hundred pounds and then doubled it. With that kind of money, dear, we could buy our own land right now. We wouldn't have to work and wait for it. It was the chance of a lifetime."

"How could you do such a thing, Robert? What happened?" Joseph could see the fear in his mother's eyes.

"Somehow the bastard beat me. I had the cards to win. He must have a pact with the devil, the Catholic arse."

"Jesus, Joseph, and Mary. We don't have two hundred pounds, Robert. Good Lord, we don't have a pound to our name! You've ruined us! You've ruined our lives!" She pushed him away from her and tried to rise, but he put his hand on her shoulder and held her down.

"You just settle down now, lass. I've thought all night and I've a way to fix the problem. We won't have to pay the man tuppence—we might even make a few pounds out of the deal."

"How can that be, Robert? What are you talking about? We don't have anything to bargain with. We wouldn't have had the money to make the voyage without the help of my family. You don't have any money. You don't have any skills."

Joseph could see Robert bristle. "You shut your mouth now. I'm tired of hearing about your high-and-mighty family. You're not part of your family anymore. You're part of mine. I'm the head. I've told you I have a plan."

"What plan, Robert? What's your new plan to save us all?" she asked defiantly.

Robert raised his hand to strike her but then hesitated. He looked around and lowered it. Joseph could see that others were watching the commotion in the cramped quarters.

"Now you've to listen to the whole thing. You have to trust me. All this will be for the best." Robert looked around again and then moved his head closer and whispered into her ear.

"No!" She pushed him away. "Are you mad! I won't agree. You drunken bastard, you've destroyed our lives!"

He slapped her hard across the face and reached back to strike her again.

Joseph ran out of the darkness and grabbed his father's hand. "No!" he shouted. "Leave her alone!"

Robert turned, angry. "I told you to stay on deck, boy. You've disobeyed me and you'll feel the strap for it."

"Leave him be!" demanded Lydia. "Just leave him alone! You've done enough already!"

"Get out, Joseph! Get out right now! I'm not done talking with your ma. I'll deal with you later."

Joseph turned and ran, tears streaming down his face. He broke out on deck into what now seemed a harsh and bitter light. What was going to happen to them? What could his da have told her that made her so upset? He found a quiet place on deck and sat, his head buried in his hands.

After a long time, he saw his mother come slowly above deck. She was bowed down as if she carried a deep burden. Her eyes were red from weeping. She rubbed them, trying to adjust to the bright light. Eventually, she began looking around until she spotted Joseph. She stared at him for a moment and then walked slowly over. He could feel his skin crawling. Something was wrong. He had never seen his mother look like this, or rather he had never seen her look *this* bad.

"Ma, what's wrong?"

She started to cry again and kneeled, embracing him and holding him so hard he thought his breath would be crushed out of him. She sobbed with her head buried in his shoulder. Finally, she looked up at him with her tear-streaked eyes.

"Oh, Joseph. Joseph."

"It'll be all right, Ma, come what may."

"I don't know, Joseph. I don't know. Your father has made a bargain with Mr. O'Dwyer. A bargain you will have to suffer for."

"What do you mean?"

"I mean you're going to go with Mr. O'Dwyer. He's a fine man and a printer. He's going to teach you a trade, you . . ." Her voice broke and she couldn't continue.

Joseph tried to follow what she was saying. What did she mean? "Will I have to travel far from where we live to Mr. O'Dwyer's?"

"Oh, Joseph! You don't understand. We won't be coming with you. You will live with Mr. O'Dwyer, and you'll do what he says."

"What do you mean? I'm coming with you! You promised! Da promised! You told me we would have land. We'd have cows and chickens and pigs and crops to grow. You lied to me!" Joseph pulled himself away from his mother, rising. He felt the anger and confusion welling inside him. He almost felt he could strike her.

"Joseph, I'm so sorry. I didn't want this. We don't have a choice. Do you understand? We have to do this."

"Because Da lost that money?"

She hesitated. "No, that's not the reason. We . . . we paid that back, but your da thought this would be best for you."

"No, Ma. No! Don't do this to me! Don't leave me! You're lying to me! This is Da's fault! This is your fault!"

Tears streamed down her face and he could see the anguish. "Please don't cry, Joseph. My heart will break inside me. I need you to be strong for me. Please, darling. It's only for a little while. Only until you're a man. Then you can return to us a strong printer with a trade. You can open a shop. You'll make us so proud. Here, take this. Your father wanted you to have it." Turning her face away, unable to even look at him, she handed him a small leather necklace with a wooden cross.

He was sure his ma had lied to him. Why would they let this happen? How could they let this Mr. O'Dwyer take him away? Didn't they love him anymore?

He felt the tears welling up. He nearly fell to the deck. He rushed forward, grabbing his mother's arm and holding on for dear life. "Please, Ma, don't leave me! Don't leave me!"

He held her for the longest time, sobbing, begging, and pleading with her. She wouldn't answer him, but she kept repeating over and over "*Beidh grá agam duit go deo,* I will love you forever."

The *Leander* came into sight of land later that day and docked at New York harbor before the morning. Joseph hugged his mother good-bye, refusing to let go. Finally, she pulled away. She turned and walked down the gangway, unable to even look back. Robert mussed his hair, gave him an encouraging farewell, and followed her away.

The *Leander* set sail again the following day, heading up the coast and eventually turning into the Gulf of Saint Lawrence and then down the Saint Lawrence River. Joseph stayed below deck in his family's bunk, refusing to speak to Mr. O'Dwyer or anyone else, barely eating and unable to sleep. As the days passed, he tried to understand what had happened, how his family could have deserted him. He was so scared and alone in the world. Finally, the *Leander* docked at its destination and all the remaining families were shooed above deck and then down the gangway and onto the dock. Joseph could hear their excited murmurs, their shouts of joy at reaching their new home. Everyone was excited except for him.

Hours later, Joseph followed Mr. O'Dwyer through the winding streets of Quebec City. He carried a small bag of his own clothes and several bags for his new master. The streets were cobbled and rising up from the harbor. They were walking along a large street called the *Rue Saint-Jean*. He caught snippets of a language he had never heard before.

"Move along now, lad!" ordered Mr. O'Dwyer. "We're nearly there."

"What words are they speaking?"

O'Dwyer turned. "You'll call me sir, and don't forget it."

Joseph cringed. He bowed his head slightly. "Sorry, sir."

"That's better. They speak French, lad, the whole town's full of 'em, except an Irishman here and there and an Englishman tucked in for good measure. You'll get used to it and even learn a bit. I can't say as I speak it well, but I can make myself understood by and by. Mrs. O'Dwyer is French, but I've learned her to speak proper over time."

"What is French?"

"Well I see you know nothing, lad. We shall soon remedy that. You'll be learning my trade and more for the bargain. I need all your wits, not just your muscles. We'll be home soon and you'll meet your *maman*—your new mother. Mrs. O'Dwyer and I will look after you from now on."

"But my ma said I'd only be gone a little while."

"Hah! If seven years is a little while, then she spoke the truth. Forget your old family, lad. You've everything here you'll ever need. Your ma and da scurried off the ship like rats. You won't be seeing them again I'll wager."

What was he saying? Joseph stopped. He started to shake. His mother and father were gone? Gone forever? Had they lied to him even about that? He felt the hot tears welling up again.

"Now stop your crying, boy. It'll do you no good."

Joseph felt strong hands on his arm as Mr. O'Dwyer jerked him up to look him in the face.

"Your kin are gone. You're here to work for me and mine. In seven years, you can do as you wish, but for now you'll do as you're told. If you keep your crying up, you'll work without food. I have taken on quite a burden here with you. Forget your folks. This is your new life. My wife and I are the only parents you'll ever have again. So stop your bellyaching and pick up those bags."

Joseph obeyed, terrified. He was still whimpering, but he tried to be quiet as he hustled to keep up with Mr. O'Dwyer. They walked for at least another half hour. His arms ached and his feet were worn down when they finally arrived at a storefront in the middle of the street down a narrow alleyway off the *Rue Saint-Jean*.

They entered the building. Inside, there was a desk near the entryway and then bookshelf after bookshelf stacked with all kinds of paper. On one wall there was a display of different kinds of paper and printing from newspapers to large announcements. Most of the documents were unreadable, and Joseph, who could read at least a little, assumed they must be in French.

In the back of the building, there was a narrow staircase. Mr. O'Dwyer led him up the dimly lit stairs to a door at the top. O'Dwyer reached in his pocket again and drew out his keys, fumbling until he found the right one. He jiggled it in the keyhole and eventually the door swung open. They were home.

The upstairs apartment was small with a front room connecting directly to a kitchen. Two tiny rooms with narrow doorways branched off from the main area. Joseph could see a bed through one of the doors. In the middle of the main area sat a small wooden table with four chairs and two side tables with lamps. There were two large carpets on the floor, one under the table and one in the middle area toward the kitchen. They were brightly decorated and looked very expensive. Joseph had never seen anything so fine as the rugs.

Mr. O'Dwyer's wife was short with brown hair and a mousy look to her. She was much younger than him and seemed no older than twenty-five or so. She embraced her husband but kept an eye on Joseph, then turned her head and whispered into Mr. O'Dwyer's ear.

He turned to Joseph. "The missus wants to know who you are. Mrs. O'Dwyer, this is Joseph Forsyth. I won him in a game of poker, so to speak. He's going to be my apprentice, and more if he behaves himself."

She looked at Mr. O'Dwyer with a questioning glance and then turned to Joseph. "Good day." She had a thick accent and Joseph could barely understand what she said.

"Now as I told you, lad, the missus is one of these Frenchies, but you pay that no mind. You'll understand her soon enough. Now let me show you where you'll be staying."

He led Joseph to one of the small doorways and opened the door. Inside was a cramped room with stacks of paper and boxes. There was no bed, and hardly any space to even walk inside.

"Now I know it doesn't look like much, but you'll get it in top shape soon enough. Your first job will be straightening things up. I'll get you some blankets and a bit of straw to make you comfortable.

Now get started on this now while I talk to the missus. You'll need to hurry, we have Mass tonight before dinner."

"What . . . ? What do you mean Mass?"

"Mass, boyo. You know, the Lord's service and the taking of the Communion? Are you dumber than I thought? Hurry now, we've no time for your questions."

Joseph didn't know what to say. He was so confused by all of this, and the most scared of what Mr. O'Dwyer had just told him.

"Sir, I . . . I can't go to Mass. I'm not Catholic. Mass is a . . . it's a sin, sir."

O'Dwyer frowned, looking at him a moment. "I forgot your cursed family's a batch of heretics. I told you, boy, you have a new family now. We celebrate the Lord proper. I'm saving your soul along with your life. Now get this cleaned up and I'll come get you after a while."

"Sir, I'm sorry. I . . . I can't go." How could he ask that he go to Mass? Everything Joseph had ever heard and learned screamed out against this. He needed his mother. He could feel his eyes welling up again.

O'Dwyer's face reddened. "Listen, lad: I'm not used to being argued with, not by a boy for sure. You'll do as you're told or you'll pay the price. Now be a good lad. I'm giving you a new life. Good for you. Good for me. Now get going." He reached down and grabbed Joseph's arm as if to force him to begin cleaning.

Joseph pulled away and backed farther into the room. "Please, sir, don't do this to me. I want my ma! I want my da! I don't want to be here. I want to go home!" He started sobbing, the tears streaming down his face. He had never felt more terrified in his life, more lost. Everything was gone.

"Enough! I told you your ma and da left you and they won't be coming back. You seemed a smarter lad on the ship, but one way or another you're going to listen to me, boyo. I guess I have to show you the hard way."

O'Dwyer reached down to his waist and unbuckled his belt. He drew the belt out of his trousers and snapped it together, the leather cracking. He advanced on Joseph and grabbed him by the head with his left hand. He pulled his head down and held it against one of the boxes. He then brought his right hand down hard, lashing the belt against the boy's back. Pain erupted up and down his torso. Joseph could hardly stand it. He tried to break free, but he couldn't. He had never felt such pain. His father would hit him now and again, but he had never hit him this hard.

The belt struck again on his lower back. Then again. Joseph was crying out from the pain, but O'Dwyer wouldn't stop. Again. Again. He kept raining down the blows on Joseph's back and backside. Joseph fell to his knees. He could feel darkness overwhelming him. His mind spun.

Finally, O'Dwyer stopped. Joseph stayed down on all fours, his breathing heavy, his back throbbing. He felt he would die.

"Now, boyo. I don't want to have to do that to you. But you have to listen when I tell you, don't you know? I'll let you think long and hard on that. You can stay here tonight in the dark, without Mass, without dinner, without water. I'll see in the morning if you've changed your mind. When you're ready to do as you're told, you let me know. Until then, you stay here, and you think good and hard about it."

O'Dwyer left the room, taking the only lantern with him. Joseph heard the door slam shut and felt the blackness cover him. He could see the dimmest pinprick of light through the keyhole and nothing else. He was wretched. His parents had abandoned him. He was going to lose his soul if he was forced to go to Mass. He had heard such terrible things about the Catholics. He needed his mother. He lay down on the hard wooden floor among the musty boxes of paper, shivering and in deep pain. He prayed to God to take him away from all this horror. He would do anything God wanted. He prayed and prayed until he was exhausted and sleep overwhelmed him.

Joseph woke hours later. He wasn't sure whether it was morning or still night. The sharp pain on his back from the night before had been replaced by a dull ache. He was exhausted and sore from sleeping on the hard, wooden floor. The dim light emitting from the keyhole remained the same, telling him nothing.

He crawled to his knees. He was so weak. His throat burned with a terrible thirst, and his stomach rumbled with hunger. He crawled slowly over to the keyhole and tried to peer through. He could make out a lower corner of the table in the middle of the room and an edge of one of the chairs. He couldn't see anyone. He turned his head and put his ear to the door, straining to hear anything. Silence. He had to do something; he couldn't stay like this. He felt panic. He raised his arm to the door and knocked. After waiting a few moments, he knocked again, a little louder. Still silence. His panic grew. He was locked in the darkness, alone and in pain. He beat on the door and shouted, calling for help, calling for anyone.

Finally, he heard a jingle of keys. The light disappeared for a moment and then the door swung open. He was bathed in bright light and he squinted his eyes and turned away for a moment. He heard a voice. A voice he dreaded.

"Well now, lad. Did you pass a restful night? It's morning and time for work. *Mass* and then work. Are you ready to obey me?"

What could he do? He couldn't go to Catholic Mass. What kind of nightmare was this? Where were his ma and da? He was so tired and in so much pain. He was terrified of O'Dwyer.

"I . . . I can't. Please, Mr. O'Dwyer. Don't make me go to Mass. I'll work hard for you. I'll do anything else you ask. But I can't do that."

O'Dwyer looked at him in disgust. "Little bastard, who do you think you are? You won't bargain with me. I'm your master and you'll do as you're told. It looks like another day in here for you." He slammed the door shut.

Joseph cried out in anguish and lunged for the door. "Wait! Wait, please!" He cried. It was too late. O'Dwyer had left or was ignoring him. "Please! Please at least give me some water!" His throat was burning. His voice was hoarse from crying out.

He fell down again in exhaustion. He was so weak, so tired. Why had God allowed him to be here with this terrible man? Why had his parents abandoned him? He closed his eyes again and fell into a fitful sleep.

The hours passed in an endless, tortuous ordeal. He rolled back and forth on the hard floor as the pain became unendurable. His back continued to throb in waves of aching agony. He dreamed of food and water. He went through his mother's dinners one by one, longing for each bite. Corned beef and mashed potatoes, sausages and gravy, shepherd's pie. He could smell and taste them in his torment. It felt like days, even weeks had passed. Soon, he was so thirsty that even his hunger seemed to fade away. His tongue lay heavy and dry in his mouth. He wondered how long he would take to die. He didn't even care anymore, so long as the torment ended.

Finally, when he thought he could endure no more, he heard the jingle of the keys again and the door opened. This time he didn't have the strength to rise.

"Well, lad, you've had another day to think about things. Another fine morning has risen. Are you ready to go to Mass and do some work?"

Joseph nodded his head, his eyes still closed.

"That's me boy. Come on then." Joseph felt hands on him. He was pulled up and half dragged, half carried out of the room. The light was blinding and he blinked his eyes in pain, trying to adjust to his surroundings. O'Dwyer pulled him over to a chair at the table and sat him down. There was already a cup of water at the table for him. He reached out a trembling hand and brought the water to his lips. He gulped the water greedily, his hands shaking so much he was barely able to hold the cup.

"Another," he whispered.

"You'll get no more with that sass, lad. You'll ask for what you get, and be happy for it."

"Another please, sir."

"That's better." Joseph saw Mrs. O'Dwyer enter the room. She brought him another cup of water that he downed as quickly as the first, then he sat silently while she prepared breakfast. Soon, he could smell the delicious aroma of frying meat. His mouth watered and his stomach ached.

After what seemed an eternity, she brought him a plate of sausages, boiled potatoes, and beans. Just like home. He dug in with a fork, shoveling the food in. He heard himself groaning with the pleasure of eating. He had never tasted anything better in his whole life; it was more delicious than he imagined food could be. His hand still shook but he kept it as steady as possible. He ate and ate until it felt like his stomach would burst.

"Good lad," said O'Dwyer. "You disobeyed me but you took your medicine like a man, and you've come around. I won't take you to work today or to Mass. You will clean that room up and make a bed. Otherwise, today you can rest and eat and recover your strength. Tomorrow you *will* go to Mass and tomorrow you *will* earn your bread."

Joseph nodded silently and helped himself to a second serving of food. After breakfast, he carried a lantern back to his room. He spent the morning organizing his room, stacking the boxes higher and clearing a space for his bed. Mrs. O'Dwyer brought him a giant flour sack stuffed with straw that he placed down as a bed. He ate a midday meal of potatoes and cabbage and then he slept. When he awoke, Mr. O'Dwyer was back and they shared an evening meal together. Joseph hadn't spoken a single word all day, and he didn't say anything at supper.

"Cat's got your tongue, has it? Well, many a lad's lived a good life without saying more than a few words. Maybe you're still angry, aye, boyo? Well, that will pass too. Blame your drunk father and that whore of a mother. If they had a proper life, you would still be with them. A proper life and a proper faith."

Mrs. O'Dwyer crossed herself when he mentioned faith.

"Still nothing to say even after that, aye? You do learn after all. Tomorrow we'll see if you can work as well. Remember the lesson I taught you, boy. You will obey me or you'll have more of the same. And one thing's more. I don't ever want you to mention your kin again. They're gone and as good as dead. You live here now and we're the only ma and pa you'll ever know. If you work hard and obey us, you'll have a good life and a good trade. More than most have and that's the truth of it."

Joseph nodded again silently. He felt much recovered after a day of rest. He helped Mrs. O'Dwyer clear the table and wash the dishes, then he nodded again to them and took a lantern to his room.

He closed the door and placed his lantern gently on the ground. He lay down on the mattress and pulled a woolen blanket over himself. Compared to a day before, he felt immeasurably better. In the silence, he finally considered the day. His parents had abandoned him. God had abandoned him. What did it matter if he attended Mass? If he worked hard and did what he was told, he would be warm and safe. He had nowhere to run, no family or friends to depend on. He was done with crying, done with begging. He had no choice. He would do what was necessary. He would survive.

CHAPTER 4

Union Military Hospital Camp, near the Jerusalem Road

Petersburg, Virginia

Tuesday, January 5, 1865

Rebecca knelt beside one of the wounded young men and ran the back of her hand over his forehead. He was burning up. So many died of infection from their wounds, and one of the signs was almost always a burning fever. She felt so helpless. Why couldn't she do more to assist them? Even if she worked in one of the big hospitals in Washington City, there would be little more she could do. Perhaps the rooms would be warmer and better lit there, maybe slightly cleaner. Still, there was nothing else that could be offered, no miracle drink or herb that would more effectively fight the infections that took so many lives.

She placed a cool cloth on the soldier's forehead and he stirred, his eyes opening. She grabbed his hand and squeezed it, smiling, trying to convey comfort and love. That was all she was really able to give: a small measure of love and comfort to ease the patients in their recovery, or in their passing.

He closed his eyes again and she did the same, taking a moment to remember. She saw her beautiful daughter lying in bed, as clearly as if it were happening now. Her fragile little body shivered, and sweat covered her forehead as she too burned with fever. Rebecca had stayed night and day by her side, helpless, praying and doing everything in her power to save her. She had begged and pleaded with God. She had implored the doctor who visited each day to do something, anything to save her. He had assured her it was in God's hands and that they must wait—they must keep her comfortable. The days passed slowly and her little girl faded until one morning Rebecca awoke to find her tiny chest had stopped moving and she was gone. She had faced it all on her own, her husband unable to obtain leave from the war.

She had wept and prayed but there was nothing she could do. She buried her little girl the next day, and on the following day, she had volunteered for training as a nurse. She would learn how to take care of the sick and the dying—how to save them if she could.

"How are your patients today, Nurse?"

Rebecca looked up in surprise, torn from the past. Doctor Johnston was standing over her, standing close. She felt an unexpected joy spring up inside her. Why was she so happy to see him? She scolded herself. *He is not for you.*

"How are the patients?" he repeated.

"They're . . . they're fine. I've only checked a few so far but no surprises."

"And your pet patient?"

She felt her face flush. "I haven't had time to see him yet."

"I would have thought you would see him first. After the fuss you made about him."

She didn't know how to read the doctor. He could be so distant at times. She searched his face to see if he was teasing her, but he was inscrutable. "I was just going to check on him," she said, trying to still her thoughts. She moved away from the patient she had been tending and a couple of cots down to where Joseph lay. Thomas followed her, still close behind her. She tried to concentrate but for some reason it was difficult to do so. She chastised herself. She was a professional and she needed to do her job.

She turned her attention to Joseph. The soldier was still unconscious. His face was pale and his breath still shallow, too shallow. She checked his bandages carefully. He continued to bleed from the chest wound slightly but there was no infection, which was the greatest danger at this point.

"How is he, Nurse?"

Why was he calling her "nurse"? Why so formal today when he had been so kind before? Again she looked up to see if he was teasing, but he was focused now on Joseph. She decided to bring up the recent incident herself, hoping he would open up to her.

"I'm sorry about the other day, Thomas. I know I overstepped my bounds. I know I pushed you and exceeded my authority, but I was overcome. I found a letter. A letter to his wife. He has a family at home. Somehow the letter made all of this more real. Made him more real to me."

She watched Thomas closely as she talked. He was facing her now, his eyes watching her intently as if he was searching for something. For a few moments he said nothing. Then she saw the light die in his eyes as his face grew stern.

"I have to talk to you about that incident. I understand you have been under a tremendous amount of pressure. I know you have experienced your own losses. That makes me a little more understanding of what happened. However, you can never let your emotions gain control over you like that again."

She hadn't expected this. He had been so kind and understanding the other day. "Thomas, please . . ."

"It's *Doctor* Johnston. I am the doctor and you are the nurse. I'm sorry, Rebecca, but I have to say this: If this insubordination happens again, I *will* have to replace you. I will have no choice in the matter. There are too many lives at stake. You put the lives of dozens of other wounded at risk over one soldier. You usurped my authority in front of the rest of the staff. You forced me to change my own procedures based on our working relationship. I can't have those kinds of feel . . . those kinds of decisions forced on me."

Rebecca felt her heart breaking inside. Why did he have to be so cold? "I didn't mean to . . ."

He took a step closer to her but then shoved his hands behind his back as if he was willing himself away.

"I'm sorry, Nurse. *I didn't mean to* isn't good enough. You may consider yourself on report. I don't have further time to spend on this. Do your job please and allow me to perform my own."

"I . . . I will," she heard herself say. "Now if you will please excuse me." She turned and walked slowly out of the hospital and across the camp yard. She felt the tears welling up, but she held herself together, nodding to several people along the way. Only when she finally reached her tent did she rush inside and throw herself on her cot, sobbing as quietly as possible into her pillow. She hated him, hated him more than ever. He didn't care about anyone or anything.

Her thoughts returned to her daughter. Her beautiful daughter and her loving husband, both gone to heaven. Why did God leave her here to suffer?

Why had she felt joy and excitement to see Thomas today? What a betrayal to her family, to God. Thankfully, he was sensible and had given her the chastisement she deserved. She was riddled with guilt and confusion. She prayed, asking that she be allowed to die. A shell could hit her in the tent. Nobody else would have to be hurt. She wanted to die, wanted to be away from all the pain.

She lay on her cot for a long time before she calmed down. There were patients to be attended to. She had selfishly thought of herself when others needed her attention. She breathed deeply, calming herself. She would take care of the wounded like she always had. She had a purpose here. She didn't need Doctor Johnston's friendship or kindness or anything else from him. She rose with new purpose and walked back to the hospital, losing herself in her duties.

CHAPTER 5

QUEBEC CITY

THURSDAY, MARCH 23, 1854

Joseph sat at the press, carefully reading the type and comparing it to the handwritten document resting on the bench near him. He selected the last three letters from a divided wooden box to his right. The box was three feet tall and two feet wide, and it contained a slot for each letter of the alphabet as well as numbers and common punctuation marks. Each part of the set was lead with a long, triangular back piece tapering down to the symbol at the end. Joseph carefully cleaned each type piece with a rag soaked in alcohol. He noticed that some of the letters were becoming worn and would have to be replaced soon, an expensive process. He remembered when he had first sat here five years before. The letters were almost new then. He had been a boy. Now he was sixteen and a young man.

As he placed the individual pieces in the press, he tightened them between wooden blocks on each side. He then very carefully reread the handwritten paper to make sure the typesetting was perfect. Any mistake could be extremely expensive, sometimes requiring that hundreds or even thousands of sheets be reprinted. Michael hated the cost of a reprint. Joseph had learned that lesson very clearly a number of times in his first year with beatings or confinement.

The cramped printing space in the back of the little shop was poorly lit and even more poorly heated. His fingers were frozen in the winter air. He frequently stopped to rub them together and blow on them with his hot breath. He had a hundred copies still to print today and it was already getting late. He hoped he would be able to finish in time for supper.

He placed a sheet in the middle of the square platform of the printer, then pulled the typesetting up into place. He made sure it was properly centered and checked the inkwell to make sure it was full. He then pushed down and pressed the type to the paper with a firm thrust and pulled it back as cleanly as possible. If he held the press too briefly, some of the words would not set to the paper or would be too faint. If he waited too long or moved the handle, the words would smear. He pulled the press back and examined his work. It was perfect. He had a knack for it.

Michael said he was a natural printer, the best he'd ever seen. Now that the test sheet was completed, Joseph pulled out more paper and started the printing in earnest. He worked methodically with great accuracy and speed, his wiry muscles rippling beneath a wool work shirt. In less than an hour, he had produced the full run without having to throw away any copies. He checked the documents carefully, placed them in a stack, covered them in a wrapping, and tied them with a brown waxed string. The whole process had taken half a day.

Joseph made sure the outside of the wrapper was properly marked, then he straightened the area, cleaned his press, and picked up his lantern, opening the door into the main part of the shop. Michael had already gone upstairs and was likely preparing for dinner. Joseph checked the store quickly to make sure everything was properly put away, then he turned and climbed the stairs to their apartment.

He opened the door to the smell of baked bread and roasted beef. His mouth watered at the savory fragrances. Aimée O'Dwyer was smiling at him as he came in. He nodded to her and then went to a bucket to run cold water over his hands and face. He spent some time on his fingers, doing his best to wash away the ink.

"Did you finish that run of announcements for Monsieur Belland?" asked Michael.

"I did. As long as Monsieur Belland's French was correct, everything is perfect; every page was just like the proof. However, I'm having trouble with some of the type. We may need to order new letters soon."

"Och. Now, lad, you let me worry about that. Those letters are mighty expensive. No use in spending money we don't have, aye? We'll get another season out of them, or more if you're careful."

Joseph didn't respond. He had learned that Michael was very tight with money. There was no use arguing the point. He would have to make do as he always did.

Aimée brought a heaping platter of beef over to the table. The meat and potatoes were mixed together with a gravy served on the side along with a coarse but tasty bread. They all sat down together and Michael said grace. They crossed themselves at the conclusion of the blessing, then O'Dwyer helped himself to a portion of the food and passed it along to his wife and then to Joseph.

Joseph had learned all the rites of the Catholic Church these past years. He had even been baptized and had his first communion, but he had never forgotten his true roots. He didn't know what to think about religion or about God. What God would take his family away from him so young? What God would allow the different churches to hate each other so much? There was nothing wrong with the Catholic faith. He had learned to enjoy the beauty of the ritual and the formal worship. But what had been wrong with his old church? Other than the forms, there was hardly a difference in the services or in the message. They all worshiped God, all believed in Jesus. Michael interrupted his thoughts.

"Well, boy, Mrs. O'Dwyer and I have been doing some talking and we have something we would like to discuss with you. You have been as good as a son to us for these past five years. God knows you were a stubborn lad at first, but you learned your place. What's more, I couldn't have asked for a better apprentice. You put in your hard day's work every day without complaint. Saints be praised you don't complain about anything or talk too much, in fact. But each to his own, and it's no sin to keep your thoughts to yourself."

"Go on, Michael, tell him what we talked about, *dépêche-toi*!" said Aimée.

"All right, I'm getting to it. Joseph, there's something we would like to ask you. We want you to be part of this family. We want you to take our name and become an O'Dwyer. If you agree, lad, then I'll cut your apprenticeship short. You can become a printer with regular wages at the shop. Someday the shop will be ours together, and then in the long run, yours."

Joseph looked back and forth at the two of them. Aimée had tears streaming down her face. They both leaned in, clearly nervous and waiting for an answer from him. What was he supposed to say? How to answer? He had so many thoughts swimming through his mind. He needed to consider their offer.

"That's very kind, very kind of you both. You know how much you've both meant to me all these years. You took care of me when my family let me go. You have been my mother and father these past years. I . . . I just need to think about this. May I answer you in the morning?"

Joseph could tell he had disappointed them, but Mr. O'Dwyer quickly recovered. He was used to Joseph taking his time with things.

"Of course, lad. You take your night to ponder. Just remember, we love you, boy. We want you to be part of our family. Truly part. I hope you have the right answer for us tomorrow."

Aimée came over and put her arms around him. "*Je t'aime, mon fils.*"

"I love you too."

Joseph looked down at his plate. He had been ravenous but now he had no appetite. He took a couple more bites then excused himself. He scraped his plate of the remaining crumbs, then washed it and went to his room to think.

As he closed his door, he looked around at his room, the only room he could clearly remember. He tried at times to recall his room back in Ireland, the old cottage in Moneymore, but he found he could hardly remember the details, as he could hardly remember his real ma and da.

He placed the lantern down on a small table he kept near his bed. Another bookshelf adorned the opposite wall, full of assorted possessions he had collected over the years and also a half dozen books. His books were his prized possessions. He had acquired them over the years by horse-trading printing products, laboring on the weekends for O'Dwyer's friends, and using the small wages O'Dwyer sometimes paid him.

He lay back on the bed and stared up at the ceiling, trying to sort out what to do. He wasn't surprised by what he had heard. He had been expecting them to make this request for some time. Certainly they had hinted enough, referring to him as their "son" or "the same as a son." The question was, should he accept them as parents?

They had been good caretakers. Without a doubt, things had not started well. Joseph still remembered the terrible beating and the starvation when he first arrived. That had not been the last beating, although it had been the worst. Still, would any father have acted differently toward his own rebellious son? Joseph had few friends because of his work, but he had heard similar stories throughout his life. Fathers were to be obeyed without question. He reached up and felt the half-moon scar above and below his eye. His own da had been no different.

They had certainly taken care of him. He hadn't been able to go to school because of his long hours in the print shop, but O'Dwyer had tutored him in math, reading, and writing. He had also taught Joseph how to run a business and, of course, everything to do with the craft of printing. Now Joseph had a trade that he could use for the rest of his life, no matter what he decided.

And they had loved him. He felt very close to Aimée. She had fed him day after day, washed his clothes, cared for him when he was sick. No, she did far more than that. She had laughed and sung with him. She had taught him some French. She had told him stories of her youth in a slum of Quebec City; how she had found Michael when she was little more than Joseph's age now; how they had starved together while Michael completed an apprenticeship just like the one Joseph was bound to.

She had also told him about their disappointment, the years of trying to have a child but failing. Joseph knew how much she had wanted a child. Then Michael had brought him home—finally a child for her to care for. She loved Joseph like a true mother. He knew it and he loved her in return. He felt some guilt about this love; as his memories of his own ma faded, he wondered if his love for Aimée was now stronger. What kind of son did that make him?

His feelings for Michael were more complex. He had watched O'Dwyer humiliate his father at cards. He knew that because of that loss, his father and mother had been forced to give him up for this bound apprenticeship. Mr. O'Dwyer had taken his family away from him. He was a hard man to love. He was a sharp dealer with customers, often charging different prices according to the financial circumstances of the buyer. He used cheap paper and kept every cost at a minimum, so he could reap as much financial benefit as possible.

What he did with all of this money, Joseph didn't know. He certainly didn't spend it on the shop or the apartment above. Everything looked almost the same as the day Joseph had come here, except for the used bed and furniture he had acquired for Joseph a year or so after he arrived. He was a hard man, but he had taught Joseph everything he knew about printing and about running the shop. In all the years together, Joseph had grown to have a certain companionship with Michael as they worked away together in the shop. Was it love? He wasn't sure he could go that far, but he certainly cared for his master.

What about his real family? Joseph felt his heart sink. He conjured up images of his parents in his mind. When he first came to Quebec, he would stay up late each night, quietly whimpering in bed, missing his family terribly. Over time, that feeling had lessened, replaced by anger and disbelief. They had never even bothered to write him. He had never heard another word from his ma or da. Why had they abandoned him so completely? If they had kept in touch, he could have shared so many things with them, and he would know how their lives were. Did they have new children, brothers and sisters for Joseph to help raise? Were they in good health? Had they found the land his da had always dreamed of? Were they living on a farm? Their own land?

But he didn't know. He feared they had been killed. He almost wished that were true. Anything was better than the truth he feared: that they didn't want him anymore.

He let those ideas drift through his head over and over. He would not make up his mind until the last minute. He would think about this until he couldn't stay awake and then he would think on it more in the morning. He had learned early to be silent, cautious, and deliberate. He would sleep on it and let the dawn decide.

The next morning Joseph woke early. He made his way in the cold out to the front room and lit the morning fire in the stove, rubbing his hands together and moving his feet as quietly as possible to keep warm until the stove began generating heat. Soon, he could hear stirring in the other bedroom and the O'Dwyers eventually made their way out. The atmosphere was awkward. He could tell they were waiting for him to broach yesterday's subject.

He looked at both of them, watching their eyes, trying to understand what was going on in their hearts and in his own. Finally, he was ready to decide.

"I've had time to think over what you said."

"Well, lad, what's your decision?"

"I want to do as you said. I've no family of my own anymore. You and Aimée have been the only family I've had for years now. I'll be your son. I'll take your name. I want to work in the shop with you as a true printer."

Aimée let out an exclamation of excitement and rushed forward. She jumped into Joseph's arms and embraced him. She was so tiny now, barely coming to his chin. He held her tight while Michael came over and patted him on the shoulder.

"Well you're family now, lad. I'll have papers drawn up right away to end your apprenticeship. You'll be a proper printer with a man's wage. After a few years, we'll talk about a partnership together."

Joseph held Aimée tightly, keeping his eyes away from Michael. He was happy but he felt a pit in his stomach at the same time. Had he betrayed his mother and father? Was he only doing this to finish his bound apprenticeship? Would this repay the O'Dwyers for taking care of him after his family abandoned him? Did he even care anymore? All of these thoughts wandered through his head. He did his best outwardly to keep his emotions in check. He hurried through breakfast, nodding now and again as O'Dwyer talked about the shop, and what plans they would make. He left the table early with the excuse that he had pressing work. Soon he was downstairs in the cramped printing office with the door closed. Only when he was alone did he feel peace again. Let them celebrate. He would guard his heart and see how things went.

A week passed. Life went on very much as it had before. Joseph had hoped his mind would clear, that he would better understand the choice he had faced. He did not. He still felt the nagging guilt of betraying his real family. He still felt ambiguous about his feelings for Michael. He still felt grateful and loving to Aimée.

One thing had changed: He was becoming excited about the future. Now that his apprenticeship was over, he would earn real wages. He would eventually earn enough to open his own print shop, perhaps in the country.

He would never partner with Michael. That was his secret. For now, he would stay and put in his time. He would let Michael further profit from his work until all of his debts were paid. In the long run, he would never agree to spend the rest of his life with Michael. When he had some money saved, he would move out a little way into the country and open a shop in a smaller town. He would visit the O'Dwyers. He would continue to be a part of their lives. But he would have his own life as well.

O'Dwyer interrupted his thoughts. It was near the end of the workday. "Well, boyo, it's off to Mass then dinnertime. After dinner I want to sit down and talk about the end of the apprenticeship. Then we can start talking wages. Don't think I'll be breaking the bank now! You'll have to work your way up just like I did." O'Dwyer slapped him on the back.

Joseph rose and stretched, his back muscles sore from another day sitting on his hard, wooden stool. He picked up his lantern and followed O'Dwyer up the stairs.

"Oh, darn it! I've left the money box downstairs. Mustn't leave the money where someone could find it, whether locked or no."

"I can get it," said Joseph.

O'Dwyer looked at him for a second with searching eyes. He had never allowed Joseph to open the cash drawer. Joseph was testing Michael. He wanted to see if maybe life was changing, if maybe O'Dwyer would truly treat him like a real son. The Irishman looked down at him for a few moments longer from the upper stair, then reached out and mussed his hair with his hand.

"All right then, son. If you're going to be me partner someday, you'll have to be trusted with the money. Here's the key. The money is in a wooden box inside the drawer. Hurry now!"

Joseph turned and ran down the stairs. He was inwardly excited. He had walked past this locked drawer for five years, but he'd never even had a glance at the contents inside. What might be hidden in there? He made his way to the front of the store where O'Dwyer's desk stood. He sat down and fumbled with the key until he was able to work it back and forth in the keyhole. He heard a click and he pulled the drawer back. He then pulled his lantern down and looked at the contents of the drawer. There was the wooden box on the right just where O'Dwyer said it would be. He reached in and pulled the box out. It was dusty and it jingled with coins as he removed it.

He started shutting the door when he paused, curiosity getting the better of him. What else was in the drawer? He looked up to see if he was being watched. O'Dwyer must have continued to the apartment. He held the lantern closer and quickly inspected the contents. He was disappointed. There was nothing of interest. A rusty watch sat next to a stack of receipts and other assorted paperwork. A rag rested in the upper right-hand corner, obviously for cleaning O'Dwyer's spectacles. He lifted the papers to see if anything was hidden below but there was nothing, just a stack of letters. He put the papers down and was closing the drawer when his heart sank. He opened the drawer again and pulled out one of the letters, holding it close to the lantern. It was addressed to him. He reached down to open it.

"Joseph, what are you doing down there? Let's go, boy!"

He stood up quickly, tucking the letter into the inside of his shirt. He quickly closed the drawer and locked it. His mind reeled and he fought hard to calm his emotions. He had to read the letter and then think about what to do. He was in agony. He would have to wait hours through Mass and dinner and the discussion with O'Dwyer before he would finally be alone.

The evening was the longest he could ever remember. He had to exert every ounce of strength to keep his composure. The worst part was the discussion about the end of his apprenticeship and the future. How could he think about the future when he had just learned the past was a terrible lie? He nodded and told O'Dwyer he would like to think about things. That was true to form. Thank God he was always quiet. He could get by so often because he didn't have to say how he felt.

Finally, he shook hands with Michael and made his way to his room. He closed the door and put the lantern on its familiar stand. He then removed the letter and slowly tore open the envelope, coughing to disguise the sound. He recognized immediately that the letter was written by his mother.

> *Dear Joseph,*
> *Why haven't we heard from you? I'm in the deepest anguish. I know you must be angry at father and me but we had no choice. Please forgive us. If I could only hear from you and know that you are all right I would feel so much better. I've written you over and over but with no reply. Please, you have to write us back. Your father worries so.*
>
> *We have found a small farm to rent near Macomb, New York. We tried to make a go of things near New York City but things did not work out with your father and our first landlord. He heard about cheap land to rent out west so we moved there. The good news is we are much closer to you now.*

Joseph dearest. Please forgive us. Please forgive me. I should have fought harder for you. We could have worked something else out with Mr. O'Dwyer. Anything to keep us together. Please know I will never forgive myself for what has happened. I beg you to write, my dear, even if you never speak to us again. Please just let me know you are safe.

Tears streamed down Joseph's face. He read the letter over and over, his hands shaking. His family didn't abandon him. O'Dwyer had intentionally lied to him, intentionally concealed the proof of his mother's love. He felt anger welling up inside him like nothing he had ever felt before. He would kill O'Dwyer. He was young and very strong from years of hard labor. O'Dwyer was old and had gone soft. He had given all of the hard jobs over to Joseph years ago. It would take but a moment and he would snap his neck. He found himself rising in his bed, ready to open the door.

He stopped himself. What about Aimée? Did she even know about this? She had always been so kind to him, so loving. Maybe Michael hadn't even told her the truth. What about his real family? If he committed murder, he would be hanged. He would never see them again. Worse, his real parents might even learn of the murder and he would bring terrible shame on his family. He must think on this. He could not afford to act rashly. He needed time to decide what to do. He carefully folded up the letter and placed it back inside his shirt near his heart. He then blew out his lantern and lay back in his bed, closing his eyes and trying to relax. He could feel his heart pumping blood through his body. His body wanted to act, didn't care what the consequences might be. He breathed deeply, willing himself to calm down. He thought to himself as he did so often, stopping himself from actions that would result in beatings and punishment. He would think on this. He would decide what to do.

The following morning, Joseph rose and dressed for work in silence. He had hardly slept the night before and he felt exhausted and devastated. He had been betrayed again. He felt he couldn't trust anyone. Who could he trust? The parents who bound him to an apprenticeship, or the O'Dwyers who had lied to him all these years? He hated everyone. There was no one he could turn to or depend on.

What about Aimée? The thought flashed again. What if she didn't know? What about his mother? She had written to him faithfully, hoping for an answer. She had acknowledged her mistake and begged his forgiveness. He shook his head, trying to drive the conflicting thoughts out of his mind.

He went through the morning routine in silence. He again thanked God he was so reserved, as he wasn't questioned about the silence. He excused himself from breakfast as soon as he could and went down to the print shop for work.

He kept himself as busy as possible the entire day even as his mind considered what to do. He struggled through the morning in exhaustion but his body perked up in the afternoon and he felt his mind could more clearly examine the problems he faced.

Finally, as he finished his workday, he knew what he would do. He was glad he had not acted rashly, had not responded with emotion when he first discovered the letters. Now, he had a plan, and that plan would determine his future.

He came upstairs with O'Dwyer's summons and washed his hands, then sat down for dinner.

"Well, lad, you've been more quiet today than usual. Cat got your tongue?"

Joseph turned and looked at Mrs. O'Dwyer, watching her closely. "I found the letters from my parents."

He watched her reaction. He saw surprise, which quickly turned to a look of shame, then to fear. She quickly recovered but he had seen the emotions as plain as day. He had his answer: She knew. She had always known. He felt his heart break a little more. He turned to O'Dwyer, who was stunned in silence.

"You broke me trust, boy! I told you to get the money box. You had no business snooping around in me private affairs."

"Your private affairs! Those are my letters! You told me my family forgot me! You told me they were probably dead! You lied to me all these years! How dare you!"

"We did it for your own good, Joseph," interjected Aimée.

"What do you mean? How could that be for my good?"

"You don't know your parents, Joseph. Your father is a no-good drunk. He would have gone from job to job with you in tow. You would be out on the street and starving. We saved you! We gave you a trade and a life. We want you as our own son. The son we could never have!"

"You lied to me! You kept my family from me! How could you expect me to be your son now!"

"Come now, lad. That was a long time ago," said O'Dwyer. "The missus speaks the truth. You're still too young to know these things, but your father is the kind of man who will cause you nothing but pain. I never really got to know your ma and I'm sure she's fine enough as they go, but your da was a ne'er-do-well if I've ever seen one. He would only bring you misery and shame. He would have ruined your life."

"Don't you say that about my da!" Joseph balled his fists. He was losing control. He willed himself to calm down, remembering why he had confronted them.

"It may be hard to hear, but it's the truth sure enough, me boy. Now that you know the truth, what will you do? I ask you for the missus's sake and for mine to forget them. They won't bring you nothing but heartache even if you seek them out. Your life's here, boyo. We've built a new life together, all of us. Won't you stay here?

I have such plans for us together. And you'll break the missus's heart if you leave."

"Please, Joseph. Michael speaks the truth. There's nothing for you there. If you go away, I'll die inside."

Joseph looked at them both, his head turning back and forth. He was silent for many minutes before he spoke again. "I will stay."

Aimée ran to him and embraced him. Tears fell down her face and she sobbed as she held him. "Oh, my boy. *Mon fils précieux. Merci! Merci!* I couldn't stand it if you left."

He held her tight, tears streaming down his face as well. He could feel O'Dwyer's hands on his back.

Joseph spent another long night awake, riddled with guilt and uncertainty. Had he made the right decision? What would happen now? Could he forgive himself?

The next day passed more quickly. He was so exhausted from another restless night that he worked half asleep. In the midafternoon, O'Dwyer knocked at the door of the back office and came in.

"How are things today, lad?"

Joseph nodded in return.

"I know all this is very difficult for you, but remember that we did this for your own good. We did it out of love and to save you anguish. I'm proud of you for bucking up and staying. You're a real man now, Joseph."

Joseph smiled and nodded again in return.

"I have to go up for a few minutes and talk to the missus. Keep an eye on the store while I'm gone."

Joseph nodded a third time and returned to his work. He listened for the footsteps on the stairs and the door closing above. He then stood and walked into the main store area. There were no customers present. He looked up again and then walked to O'Dwyer's desk. He pulled a long, thin piece of metal out of his pocket and wedged the tip into the drawer between the front and the main desk frame. He breathed in, then jerked the metal with all his strength. The drawer made an awful cracking sound and then tore open, the brass interior lock ripping out of the bracket and dangling loose on its hinge.

Joseph paused to see if the noise had alerted O'Dwyer. It had not. He reached into the drawer and lifted the papers. The letters were still there. He grabbed them all and put them into his pocket. He then picked up the money box and placed it on the top of the desk. He wedged the metal into the seam of the box and jerked again, cracking the box open. Inside were a few coins. He quickly scooped up the money and shoved it into his pocket.

He turned again and waited a moment. O'Dwyer was still upstairs. He hesitated, thinking of Aimée. His eyes welled with tears. He would miss her. Miss her terribly. He loved her. But she had known . . .

He turned and walked out the front door and was quickly lost in the busy afternoon street. He was going home.

CHAPTER 6

Union Military Hospital Camp, near the Jerusalem Road

Petersburg, Virginia

Wednesday, January 6, 1865

Rebecca Walker woke up late. She was surprised. She had slept through the night. Usually she woke up in the middle of the night and then lay awake for hours, tormented by thoughts of her husband and enveloped in grief. As a result she was always exhausted. Today she felt wonderful, rested, and refreshed. She remembered the confrontation yesterday and her despair. She was a little ashamed that she had lost control. She hated that about herself. But then she had regained her control and remembered her purpose. She was part of something much bigger than herself, an important part. She had set out to save lives after the death of her daughter, and she had succeeded. She had saved many lives. Fathers and brothers and sons were going home to their families because of her.

She stretched, her thin frame barely noticeable under the wool blankets. She had always been thin but had grown thinner in the past year under the stress of combat surgery. She was short, just over five feet, with olive skin and jet-black hair. She was beautiful, or so many men had told her. She used to care about such things before the war, before everything changed forever.

Rebecca rose and dressed quietly in her tent. *Her tent.* One of the great luxuries she possessed. As one of the few women in the camp, she was afforded the luxury of her own living area, although she yearned deeply for female company. The tent provided her with a few moments of privacy each day, regardless of how long she worked. She knew the soldiers had nothing of the kind. They were together each day, all day. They slept together in crowded tents and more recently in the muddy, disease-ridden trenches. They fought together and died together. The guilt rose again. She knew she was doing much for the cause, much for her country. But she faced little real risk. The men she treated risked everything. That was one of the reasons she tried to give them everything in return. That was her part to play in all of this. A small part, but at least she hoped she was able to give them something in return for their sacrifice.

She made her way to the mess tent. Another luxury. The hospital had its own mess with an actual cook. Most regiments in the field made do with a few unfortunate novices selected primarily because they were the most hopeless soldiers. Not that they had anything to cook with, in any event. The staple was salt pork and hardtack. She thought of the hardtack with distaste: the hard, flour biscuit baked to last—perhaps forever. Hardtack was like flint and could break the teeth of even young, healthy men if it wasn't boiled or otherwise softened ahead of time. Often, it was teeming with maggots. Rebecca was more fortunate. Because of the importance of the hospital and the relative stability of the location away from the front, they had at least periodic vegetables and fresh meat. They also had bread—fresh, warm bread daily. She sometimes brought extras to the hospital tent and shared her food with recovering soldiers.

The tent was nearly empty when she arrived. She was served a portion of salt pork and cornbread along with coffee, and she turned to find a place to sit at one of the long, vertical tables. She had grown to love coffee, its hot, rich aroma. Perhaps her favorite time of day now was in the morning, when she could peacefully sip a hot cup and close her eyes, searching for a little peace.

"Good morning."

She nearly dropped her plate. Doctor Johnston had come in behind her. Lately it seemed that he was always behind her, always standing close. She nodded to him and started to move away.

"May I join you?"

She was shocked. Thomas had never asked to sit with her before. How dare he do so after he treated her the way he had yesterday.

"No, thank you," she replied and started to walk away again. She felt a hand on her arm.

"Please, Rebecca. I need to talk to you."

"Didn't you say enough already? I understand you, Doctor. I won't make the same mistake again." She tried to turn but he didn't loosen his grip on her.

"*Please.*"

She hesitated for a moment. She was very conscious of his fingers gripping her arm. She felt the warmth of his hand. A dizziness came over her. She started to pull away and then finally relented. She nodded slightly and he released his grip. She walked over and set her plate down at a long wooden table. There were a few other people in the tent but none at that table, so they had relative privacy.

She had never sat with Thomas before. Although they had worked together constantly that past year, she still felt she did not know him. Their relationship had always been distant and professional.

"Another day has passed, is your miracle patient still alive?"

She felt a hot flush. She always checked her patients *before* she ate. "I haven't seen my patients yet this morning. Perhaps I should go now and come back for sustenance later."

"Please, Rebecca. Please sit. I . . . I have some things to say to you."

"You were right, Doctor. I did put lives in danger. I was thinking with my heart. I should not have contradicted you in front of others. I'm sorry."

"You don't have to apologize. I felt very badly about what I said yesterday. It is true that we must maintain our professional boundaries. *That is essential.* However I was too harsh with you. Perhaps it is not always the wrong decision to take a little extra time. Perhaps you have proved that to me. I was definitely not expecting that soldier to still be alive. I try not to think about what we could do if we had more time. If we had better conditions, I'm sure we could save some of the chest and stomach wounds, but not like this, not with dozens of others waiting who do have a better chance."

"I appreciate you indulging me. I promise not to lose control again. I just had this sudden feeling—this urge to try against all odds to save him because . . ."

"Because you hope in your heart that the doctor did everything he could to save your husband?"

She was surprised by such an empathetic response. "How did you know?"

"I didn't know, but I guessed. I guess or try to guess things about you now and again."

Rebecca felt the embarrassment wash over her and she knew her cheeks must be flushing. Where was this coming from? They had never had a significant friendship, or even a slight one. She wasn't aware he bothered to think about her at all, yet he seemed to know what was in her heart as if they had been close for years.

"I had no idea."

"I shouldn't be admitting it now . . . it's not proper. I just have felt so badly for you with the loss of your husband. You are a good woman, and a good nurse."

"I had no right to demand that we proceed with surgery on that patient. I was emotional and unprofessional and I'm sorry."

He stared at her for a moment. "You already apologized and I already told you that it was all right. If I didn't want to do that for you, I wouldn't have. God knows I certainly haven't had a difficult time telling you what to do this past year. But Rebecca, look at the result we achieved with Forsyth. Perhaps I should listen to you more often."

Now he was teasing her. She felt more warmth. Her mind reeled. She had felt only pain for so long, and now she felt a glimmer of happiness. Why? Because the cold, cynical doctor she had spent the past year with was showing her the tiniest bit of kindness? Obviously it was out of sympathy. She had to pull herself together. She rose from her seat, her breakfast hardly touched.

He rose too. "What's wrong? I've obviously upset you. Please, finish your breakfast."

"No, please stay and finish yours. I wasn't that hungry this morning." She placed her hand on his and squeezed for just a moment. "Thank you so much for talking to me and for your warm regard." She turned quickly and walked out of the tent, trying to hide the tears.

She was supposed to see her patients, but she had to compose herself first. She walked to her own tent. What was going on? She was a grieving widow. She was a grieving mother. She had always kept her emotions in check, always kept going. Now she was falling apart. First, she insisted on a surgery for no purpose at all. Never mind that the patient miraculously survived, she had put many others at risk who were waiting for treatment—patients with at least a decent chance to survive. Now she had lost her composure twice in as many days just because another man justly corrected her and then showed her a little compassion.

She breathed deeply. She would not let her life fall apart. She would see her patients. She would fill out her paperwork. She would keep her distance from the doctor. She would mourn her husband and her daughter. She would attend the chaplain services. She would keep her life together.

She reached her tent and went to her knees, praying, seeking the strength she had always found from her devotions before her grief. She felt nothing. God didn't seem to speak to her anymore. It was her fault, she knew. She had grown confused by the terrors of this war. She knew she couldn't understand God's plan, but how could He be allowing all of this to happen? How could He have allowed everything to happen to *her*?

She chastised herself again for the selfish thoughts. She knew she must continue in her faith, even without understanding. She nodded to herself, wiped her face clean with a cloth towel, and left the tent, marching with purpose to conduct her rounds.

She entered the hospital tent fully composed and with a sense of calm. She would not be dominated by weak emotions. She was a nurse and a Christian woman. When she walked over to check on Joseph, he was still unconscious, moving back and forth a little and groaning.

She moved closer and sucked in her breath. She knew immediately things had gone terribly wrong. He was covered in sweat. She reached a hand down and checked his forehead. He was on fire. She carefully pulled back the bandage and examined his injury. The wound area was covered in pus and blood, and most distressingly, a black splotch had spread out in each direction several inches from the bullet hole. The wound was septic, likely with pyemia. She felt pain wash over her again and she nearly fell over. Septic wounds were almost always fatal. There was nothing they could do. He would die after all, just like her husband.

CHAPTER 7

Quebec City

Wednesday, April 5, 1854

Joseph awoke shivering in the dark alleyway. He was asleep under a pile of boxes. For three days he had wandered through the city, figuring out the best way to find his parents. He had learned the location of Macomb, New York, from a mapmaking store. He had purchased a small map from them. He was fortunate, the town was in the upper part of New York, within thirty miles of the Saint Lawrence River. Quebec City was on the same river, only about two hundred and fifty miles away. The same kindly store owner told him he should be able to purchase passage on a ship. Unfortunately, the sum he named was far more money than Joseph had.

He decided to seek work so he could earn enough money for the voyage. He couldn't work in print shops as he had no papers and would immediately arouse suspicion. He tried at a lumber mill and also at several boat-loading companies. He had a very hard time communicating; he had learned only a little French from Aimée. After three days, he had been turned down dozens of times. He was dejected and uncertain about what to do next.

Joseph had acted quickly, perhaps too quickly. He had not formed a plan beyond immediate escape. With regret, he now realized that he should have bided his time, perhaps accepting O'Dwyer's proposal. Then he would have received his apprenticeship papers and he would have earned wages. Still, he didn't know how he could take another day with them. As careful and guarded as he could be, there were some emotions that he could not keep under control. He was afraid he might kill O'Dwyer.

No, it was best he had left regardless of his present situation. He just needed to sort out a way to get on one of the boats heading down toward the Great Lakes. He had spent hours at the docks over the past days, observing the loading of the boats, watching them depart and arrive from both north and south. There had to be a way to gain passage. He had even offered to work aboard a ship if they would let him travel with them. When it became clear he had no experience, he was quickly rebuffed.

The previous night, as he lay down in the alley, trying to find some warmth, he had decided he would try to sneak aboard one of the boats in the morning. He walked around in the early sunshine to try to warm up and bought a hot potato from a street vendor with the last of his money. He then made his way back to the docks.

He leaned against a wall across the *Boul Champlain* from the quay, observing the coming and going of the men loading the ships. He needed to wait for their lunch break, then he would sneak aboard one of the boats and hide below deck. He would reveal himself after the boat had set sail and offer to work for food and the cost of the voyage. He hoped that after the vessel was already under way, they would have no choice but to allow him to come with them.

The morning dragged on. There were six ships in his immediate field of vision. He was sure he would find a way onboard. He had to. He yawned. He was so tired, but he had to keep himself alert. He tried, but he soon found himself drifting off to sleep.

Joseph felt a rough hand on his arm. A policeman had snuck up on him, and behind the officer was O'Dwyer. He had been caught! He tried to break free, but the man was very strong. His heart sank. Joseph didn't understand the French O'Dwyer spoke to the policeman, but it sounded like he was confirming Joseph's identity.

Joseph was led away by the officer with O'Dwyer following closely behind. They walked away from the docks for several streets. Joseph looked around for some escape, but the policeman had too tight of a grip and there were no obvious places to hide. Soon they arrived at a building marked "*Gendarmerie.*"

He was pulled roughly inside by several gendarmes and brought into a small room with a wooden table. O'Dwyer followed him in and sat down. The policeman stood at the door. Joseph kept his head down, refusing to look in either man's eyes.

"Joseph, we've been worried to death. How could you leave us, lad? The missus hasn't stopped crying this entire time."

Joseph refused to answer.

"Come on now, boy. Do you realize the trouble you're in? You broke your bound apprenticeship. You could rot in a jail here for years. All I have to do is walk away from here and that will be the end of you. They don't take kindly to apprenticeship breakers."

"You told me I was done with the apprenticeship!"

"Yes, and you told me you were taking my name. That you would be our son. You lied to us, boyo. I don't owe you anything."

"I lied to you? How can you even say that? You kept letters from my family from me for years. You told me they were probably dead. You told me that they wanted nothing to do with me. Everything about our life for the last five years was a lie."

"I already explained why we did that. You're too young to understand, Joseph. Your family is no good. Your father's a fool and a drunk. With us, you had a future. You still do. I don't care what you did. Just come home. Come home to us now and I'll drop all of this. We can still do everything we talked about. Don't throw it all away.

You're going to learn in life nothing is as easy as it seems. Sometimes we have to make choices."

"Yes, you made a choice. A choice to lie to me. I've made my choice. I don't care what you do to me, what they do to me. I will never come back to you. I'm going home. I don't care how long it takes. My family didn't abandon me and I won't abandon them. You're nothing to me now."

O'Dwyer visibly flinched when he said that. Joseph could see his face flush with anger.

"Now listen here, you little bastard. There won't be another chance. If I walk out this door, you won't see or hear from me again. You'll be alone in this world—alone in jail. Terrible things happen in prisons. You might never see the light of day again. Don't throw it all away for a drunk and a whore like your ma and da."

Joseph rose out of his chair. He would have struck O'Dwyer if the policeman was not so close.

"I'll face the future, whatever it is. I don't want you in my life. You took me from my family. You beat and starved me. You lied to me. I don't want you."

O'Dwyer stared at him for a moment. "Don't say that, Joseph. I'm sorry. I didn't mean to . . ."

"Go!"

"So be it, lad. You're on your own." O'Dwyer stood up. He looked at Joseph for a second longer and then turned and walked out of the room.

Joseph sat at the table for a few minutes, refusing to look up. Finally, the policeman came back in and ordered Joseph to follow him. He was led down a hallway and through a wooden door to a row of cells. The cells were lined with wood and had large iron bars in the front. The policeman opened one of the cells and motioned Joseph inside. The cell was bare except for a bucket in one corner and some moldy straw spread out as a bed.

Joseph paced back and forth, wondering what he could do. By refusing O'Dwyer, he had consigned himself to prison. How long was a prison sentence for breaking an apprenticeship? Was it the remaining two years he owed? Was it the entire seven years? Longer? He had no idea. He had never known anyone who had been in jail. He felt his anger rising. O'Dwyer had done this. He had promised the apprenticeship would be over. No matter how terrible prison would be, he would never go back to O'Dwyer. Not after what he had done. What *she* had done.

After a few hours, the policeman returned. He opened the cell door and ordered Joseph to follow him. Where was he taking him now? Before a judge? He followed reluctantly down the hallway to the front door. The officer turned to him.

"*Prends celui-ci,*" he said in French. "Take this."

Joseph looked down. The policeman was holding an envelope. Joseph reached out and took it.

"I'm free to go?"

"*Oui.*"

"Just like that?"

"*Oui.*"

Joseph nodded and went out the front door. He turned to the right and hurried down the street as fast as he could, not looking to see if he was followed. Was this a trick? He didn't want to stick around to find out. After turning down multiple streets and making sure he wasn't being followed, he finally ducked into an alley and sat down against the wall. Looking around to make sure nobody was watching him, he tore open the envelope.

Inside he found his apprenticeship paperwork signed by O'Dwyer with a release. He was a free man. There were also ten coins—ten gold sovereigns—more money than Joseph had ever had in his entire life. It was enough for comfortable passage to Macomb and money left over. Inside too was a letter to Joseph. He sat down, leaning against a wall, and read.

> *Joseph boy:*
> *We've tried everything we could to keep you with us, but I see you are leaving no matter what. You've been a good lad, a hard worker. You've kept every bargain with me except the last. I can't blame you because of what you found. Again, I tell you we did what we did because we wanted you to be safe and sound. I hope you will come back to us, even if it is only years from now. Beware your father. He will bring you nothing but sorrow, lad. It would be a kindness if you would write the missus, she loves you so. Go with the blessings of the Lord and the Blessed Virgin.*

Joseph read the letter several times and then tucked it and the money into his pocket. He was thankful O'Dwyer had freed him and provided money for a safe journey, but he couldn't go back to them, not after what they had done. *Beware your father*. The words echoed in his mind. Who was Michael to tell him to beware after his betrayal? He climbed to his feet, clenching his fists a few times, then straightening his back and looking down the alley toward the river. He was a man now. He could make his own decisions. He would find his parents and judge for himself who they were, who he was. He would go to Macomb.

Saint Lawrence River
Saturday, April 8, 1854

Joseph looked out over the wooded shores on both sides of the Saint Lawrence River. He had booked passage on the *St. Charles*, a two-masted sailing vessel of a little over a hundred feet, a size limitation that Joseph learned was required to allow the ship to make it through the Second Welland Canal to Lake Erie below. The ship had departed the same day he was released from jail, and Joseph had spent the last three days as a passenger. The voyage reminded him somewhat of the passage to the New World. It brought back disturbing and complex memories. A ship had taken him away from his family, now another was bringing him back.

The similarity ended there. The trip from Quebec City down the Saint Lawrence toward the Great Lakes was the greatest adventure Joseph had ever known. Unlike the trip across the Atlantic, he was able to spend all of his waking hours above deck. He had to stay out of the way of the crew, but he was able to watch their work and watch the slow passage of the land going by, hour after hour and day by day. He was amazed at the huge waterway with the canals and the endless land drifting past. He spent half a day watching Montreal pass by on their right, a city larger than any he had ever seen. He enjoyed watching the lazy farms and the fields and woods, a whole wide landscape he had never seen before.

He was still unsure of his decision. The O'Dwyers were far from perfect, particularly Mr. O'Dwyer; however, they were the only family he really remembered. They had taken care of him, taught him a valuable trade, and offered to make him their own son. But they had also deceived him in the worst possible way by holding back letters from his true family.

They said they had done so for his own good. They said his father was a drunk. This haunted him. He still recalled his father losing that hand at poker. Had he been so drunk he'd gambled recklessly? He couldn't remember enough about his father. No, Mr. O'Dwyer must have lied to him again. He just wanted Joseph to stay with him and Mrs. O'Dwyer. O'Dwyer must have somehow cheated his father out of the money. He was a sharp businessman and a sharp card player. Joseph's father had been a simple Irish farmer and laborer. It must have been O'Dwyer's fault after all. Why then did he let him out of jail and pay his passage? He didn't know how to answer these questions. He didn't know who or what to think. All he knew was his mother was out there, assuming that he had refused to write her, believing he was gone forever. He had to find her, had to show her he still cared.

"Joseph, how are you today?"

Joseph looked up into the smiling face of Captain Jorgenson. The captain of the *St. Charles* was a redheaded and freckled man in his midforties. His skin was a burned red from constant exposure to the wind and sun. He had taken an instant liking to Joseph and stopped and visited with him whenever he had a chance.

"I'm fine today, sir. How are you?"

"Fine as can be. We're making good time and the weather is cooperating. We can't hope for more. You haven't seen the river in a storm, my boy. Not something you would enjoy, I can tell you."

"Thank you again for loaning me this book."

Jorgenson smiled. "Think nothing of it. A boy who reads is a treasure. I'm glad to give you something to do on this trip. We're not set up for visitors."

The *St. Charles* was hauling a load of wheat down to Cleveland. Captain Jorgenson was not intending to carry passengers and the ship was not set up for it. Joseph had talked to him at some length in order to convince the captain to allow him aboard. He slept on deck in a hammock he fashioned, and he was careful to stay out of the way of the sailors. He even pitched in with some of the chores, which endeared him to the crew and the captain.

"Say, boy, why don't you join me for dinner tonight? I eat pretty much the same as the rest here, but I have a bit of extra food for special occasions and it looks like you could use a full meal."

Joseph looked down. He had hardly been able to eat since he ran away. The stress of the escape and the whirl of uncertainty running through his mind had kept his appetite away. He had lost weight and probably looked haggard and frail. He paused for a moment to consider the request, then finally nodded his head in agreement. He could use some company and some good food.

Jorgenson clapped him on the back. "That's my boy. I'll come find you at suppertime. If you wouldn't mind between now and then, the crew could use some help with painting."

Joseph nodded again and rose, dusting himself off. He found some of the crew and grabbed a brush. Soon he was painting away at the rails, listening to the sailor gossip and to their songs. He knew they appreciated his help, but he also liked the hard work. When he was working, he didn't have time to brood over his past and his future. At the present, work was the only way he could find some peace. The quiet times were the worst of all, particularly at night when he lay down and was tormented by his decisions and the uncertain future.

A few hours passed and then Captain Jorgenson came and found him. Joseph cleaned up and followed the captain to his quarters. He had never been in Jorgenson's room before. The cabin was spacious and nicely decorated with wooden paneling. It contained a bed and a small wooden desk, as well as a table and four chairs closer to the door. The desk was covered with books and charts. Blankets and a heavy bearskin sat on the bed. Several muskets were stacked in a corner.

"Why are there guns in here?" Joseph asked.

"You never know what you will find on the river. Not many years ago, there was even an Indian attack or two. Best to be safe."

The table was already laid with a white tablecloth and white china dishes. A basket laden with different breads sat in the middle of the table along with a bottle of whiskey. A platter with a fully cooked chicken rested between two plates. The chicken was well browned and steam rose above it. The smell was delightful and Joseph's stomach growled. He hadn't eaten a hot sit-down meal since he'd escaped from the O'Dwyers.

Jorgenson motioned to a seat and Joseph took his place. The captain poured both of them some whiskey and then cut the chicken, placing a portion on each plate. He motioned to the breadbasket and Joseph took some brown bread, which was still warm. There was also butter and potatoes. Joseph set to work eating right away. He couldn't believe how hungry he was. He also lifted the whiskey curiously and smelled it. He had never tried any alcohol. He took a tiny sip and winced; the flavor was terrible and it burned his tongue and throat. Jorgenson laughed.

"First drink then is it, boy? I figured as much. But you're near a man and you have to start sometime."

"It's horrible."

"You get used to the taste. Give it time. Now, tell me your whole story from beginning to end."

Joseph was taken aback. What right did this man, who hardly knew him, have to ask? His instinct was to shake his head and then excuse himself, but he wasn't sure how that would be received. Besides, the captain had been nothing but kind to him. Before he knew it, he found himself opening up to Jorgenson in a way he had never done with the O'Dwyers or anyone else. He told the story of growing up in Ireland, or rather, what he could remember about it. He told about the passage to the New World and the fateful poker game. He described his first terrible days with the O'Dwyers, then his life with them. He told of the terrible betrayal of the letters and his escape, capture, and release. Finally, he finished. He asked the captain what he thought.

Jorgenson was thoughtful for a long while before he responded. "That's a tough riddle, my boy. And a sad story."

"I don't really know what to do." Joseph felt his defenses crumbling, the tears welling up. He forced his emotions down and tried to regain control.

"It's a difficult question without an easy answer. My gut tells me don't go back and don't go forward."

"What do you mean?"

"You didn't really say it outright, but it's clear you're torn between the two families. I would be cautious with both. The O'Dwyers treated you like a dog when you first came. You don't train a boy like that. Least ways no decent man would. Then they lied to you and withheld those letters. Whatever they say they feel for you, their actions have been poor at best.

"Then there's the matter of your true folks. Who would sell their very own son into slavery for seven years over his own damned debt? I don't think it matters if your da was drunk or not, although a drunk is no small thing. Your father made his own bed and he should have slept in it. Instead, he had you do the work for him. And your mother let it happen."

"That's my ma and da you're talking about!"

"I mean no disrespect, Joseph. Your love of your folks suits you well, but that doesn't change their actions. I'm worried for you, boy. You could be getting out of the frying pan and into the fire as they say."

Joseph was still upset about what Jorgenson had said about his parents, but a part of him knew that the concerns were fair. He also felt drawn to Jorgenson, who treated him like a man and seemed to care about his future.

"What would I do? I have nowhere to go."

"Why don't you stay aboard? The lads love you. You didn't have to help. You paid your way same as any passenger. But you have helped. And you stay silent and listen when others would flap their jaws. You put in a man's work and you act a man. We could use you.

I'll pay you a fair wage and you'll have another trade to go with the one you've already learnt."

Joseph was surprised. He had never really felt accepted by anyone. His own family had left him and the O'Dwyers more or less owned him like any chair or table. Captain Jorgenson was measuring Joseph on his own merits and so was the crew. They had watched him on their own, and on their own they wanted him to join them. He wanted to say yes, but he had learned to be cautious by nature.

"May I think things over?"

Jorgenson smiled. "Of course you may. I'm no bully like O'Dwyer. We have a few days until we would have to drop you off if you intend to seek out your family in Macomb. You spend the time as you like and you decide when you want."

They spent the rest of the evening in silence. Joseph did not drink any more of the whiskey. He didn't like the taste, but there was more to it than that. A part deep inside of him feared his father might be the drunk that O'Dwyer had painted him. If that were true, then Joseph would never allow himself to be the same. He vowed it quietly to himself as he finished his meal and excused himself from the cabin.

On deck again in the outside air, he breathed in the beauty of the night sky and the crisp wind. He made his way to his hammock stretched between two crates, and, balancing himself carefully, he lay back and relaxed. He had much to think about, but not tonight. Tonight, he would go to sleep knowing he was a part of something, even if it was just for a moment. He imagined himself traveling up and down the Saint Lawrence with Jorgenson, hard work, and companionship with the crew, and a real home, even a floating one.

Joseph spent the next few days working harder than ever. He had decided that no matter what, he would be a real crew member at least until it was time to decide. He rose with the men and worked the whole day. He ate with them and stood watch with them. He visited with Jorgenson each day. The captain was respectful and didn't press him on his decision.

Finally, one morning, the captain summoned him to his quarters again and he knew he would have to give his final answer. Jorgenson was sitting at his desk and looked up immediately when Joseph arrived.

"Well, boy, we will arrive at a dock just beyond Morristown no later than midafternoon. You've worked hard these past few days. I was right about you, Joseph, and make no mistake. It's time to make up your mind. Will you join us?"

Joseph had prepared for this moment, but it was still difficult. "I want to, but I won't. I thank you for everything. I've felt more at home here than I've ever felt anywhere. You may be right about my da, but I have to find out for myself. If he's as bad as O'Dwyer said he is, my ma will need me. I need to be there for her."

"Ah yes, mothers. It always comes down to mothers, doesn't it, boy? We men don't talk about it, but it's always there. I don't blame you, Joseph. I wish you had decided differently, but I was expecting this. The crew will be disappointed. You go, Joseph. You go out and find out about your folks. You save them if you can. They have a fine son, they do."

Jorgenson patted Joseph on the back and walked away, leaving him to stare out over the bow at the shore passing slowly on each side of them.

Had he made the right decision? He would never know. In some ways this was more difficult than leaving the O'Dwyers. He had always felt he was their servant. Even their request to adopt him seemed more to fill their void because they didn't have children and to assure the prosperity of the print shop. Jorgenson and the crew here had truly accepted him for who he was. They had no previous ties to him. Yet they wanted him to join them. Still, he couldn't abandon his family. He had to know what had become of them.

What they were really like. He had to help them if he could, particularly his mother. If his father was the drunk O'Dwyer said he was, then he would save his mother. He would make her life better.

He allowed himself to relax. He closed his eyes, imagining the homecoming. Imagining the happiness in his parents' eyes. He would work hard, earn some money, improve the farm they had purchased. They would all build a better life together.

He dozed off and woke several hours later. The sun was out and the day was getting warmer. In the distance on the left-hand shore, he saw a tall, wooden dock extending fifty yards out into the river. Huge pylons jutted out of the water to the top of the rickety wooden dock. Joseph heard Jorgenson shouting commands and the ship turned slightly to port, moving directly toward the dock. Gradually, the ship turned farther and slowly came to rest against the dock itself. Joseph was impressed by the skill with which the men handled the ship, bringing it in deftly against the side of the dock without crashing into it. Several men leapt ashore and tied huge ropes (the men called it "line") onto iron pegs fixed to the dock.

"Well, Joseph, this is your port. Are you sure you don't want to reconsider? We come by here at least every other month. You could stay aboard awhile and get off any time you wish. Why don't you go with us for one trip? I could show you the Great Lakes. They are mighty fine, so big you'll think you're in the ocean again. We would be back here in no time and drop you off on the return."

Joseph hesitated. He hadn't thought of that. No, if he did, he might never get off. He had to do this now. He shook his head. "I want to. I want to stay aboard. This voyage has given me some of my happiest times. But I have to go find my ma and da. I have to see if they are all right. Thank you for everything."

Jorgenson reached out a hand and shook Joseph's. He then gave him a cloth bundle.

"Here is some food and water. It's a bit of a jaunt from here to Macomb. You won't make it today. The woods should be safe around here, or you might find a place to stay, I don't know. Be safe, boy. Go find your destiny. If you decide you don't like what you discover, come back and camp by that dock. I'll keep a lookout every time I'm by. You'll always have a home here."

Joseph nodded again. He took the food. He wanted to say something, but he was afraid he would lose his composure. He just shook Jorgenson's hand again and gave it a squeeze. Then he stepped off the *St. Charles* and onto the dock. He turned and waved. He heard jokes and advice shouted from the crew. He would miss them all. He watched the *St. Charles* sail away. The ship headed farther downriver, slowly growing smaller until it was lost around a bend. He didn't move until the ship was gone. Jorgenson's last words echoed in his mind. *You'll always have a home here.*

Joseph turned and looked out at the countryside. Overgrown fields pulled gently away and eventually connected to forests full of oak, birch, cherry, and maple trees. He could hear the buzz of insects and the chirping of birds in the trees. The air was cold but the sun was out and felt hot. The air was still except for the breeze coming off the Saint Lawrence. For some reason he didn't want to start. He had to will his feet to move. Eventually, he pushed himself forward, walked down the long dock, and then stepped down. A dirt road extended directly at the foot of the dock both to the right and to the left. A rickety wooden sign listed a number of towns with pointed arrows. The arrow pointing to the right directed him toward Macomb. As he began walking down the road, he felt very alone. Although he was a quiet figure and often had worked for hours by himself, he realized he'd always had people around him. Now he was entirely alone on the road, a feeling that was a little unsettling for him. He hurried himself along in the already fading light.

Soon it was dark. He realized with regret that he had not brought anything to start a fire. He had forgotten to ask Jorgenson. He couldn't go any farther without the danger of wandering off the path. There were no towns or even houses in sight.

He ducked off the road about twenty yards and found a more or less comfortable patch of ground at the base of a tall oak tree. He leaned against the tree and undid the bundle, pulling out bread, some dried beef, and a canteen of water. He ate the meal in silence, then lay down and watched the stars. He wondered what tomorrow would bring. What would it be like to see his mother and father again? What was their farm like? He also worried whether he would even find them. The last letter from his ma was more than three years ago. They might have moved on. He might never find them. He might have left Jorgenson for no reason. The thoughts whirled around in his mind as he tried to calm himself. Finally, he drifted off into a fitful dream.

Joseph awoke shivering in the early predawn hours. The morning air was crisp. He rose as quickly as possible and walked back and forth, stomping his feet and rubbing his hands together. After fifteen minutes, he felt the shivering subside and he was warm enough to proceed. He grabbed the last two slices of bread and placed the remaining meat between them to take on the road. He also had an apple to eat later, but that was all the food he would have. He set out by the early dawn light. He had to make it to Macomb today if he could, or he would have to try to find a place to stay and some food. Fortunately, he still had money left.

He traveled down the road for a number of miles. The sun rose in the sky and he started to feel hot. He eventually came up on a large lake spreading out in front of him to the left and the right. The road wound to the left and he followed it just above the shore of the lake for several miles before the road wound again to the right. As he moved around the lake, he started to encounter lonely farms spread out far apart from each other. He had never seen so much open land in his whole life. He remembered the tiny farm holdings in Ireland. Truly, America was a world of endless land like he had been told.

Afternoon turned into late afternoon and Joseph was becoming weary. He started to worry he would be unable to reach the town before nightfall, but he rounded a bend and saw a small collection of houses and buildings about a mile or so down the road.

He felt renewed energy and excitement. This must be Macomb, where he would see his family soon. His heart and mind filled with uncertainty. There was always the possibility his family had moved on. Even if they were there, would they even want him? They had already abandoned him once. What would they be like? Would they accept him? Would they love him? He stopped and said a prayer.

He soon found himself passing the first houses and entering into the town itself. A sign said "Pope's Mill." So this wasn't Macomb after all. The town wasn't much, just a cluster of houses around a large sawmill, a schoolhouse, and a couple of stores. A few men and women, dressed in simple country clothing, made their way back and forth through the dirt-and-grass streets. Joseph headed to a store situated more or less in the center of the small town. He walked through the door to find a cramped interior with a musty smell. Rows of shelves contained scores of products like sugar, flour, rope, soap, and a wall of hardware. An older gentleman with gray hair and glasses stood behind the counter. He looked up from some paperwork and over Joseph, obviously not used to seeing strangers.

"May I help you?"

"Hello, sorry to disturb you, sir. I'm looking for my family. I'm trying to find Macomb and I thought I was there but the sign on the town said 'Pope's Mill.'"

"Pope's Mill is part of Macomb. What family are you looking for?"

"I'm Joseph Forsyth. I'm looking for Robert Forsyth. Do you know the family?"

Joseph thought he saw a strange look cross the man's face, but he quickly recovered. "Aye. I know the man and the family. Is he your father then?"

"Yes he is."

"He lives down yonder close to Old's Mill. You follow this road to the south. You can be there in a half hour or less. He is a tenant on a small farm that will be on the left side as you go. The farmhouse is two stories and painted red as I recall. I hate to say it, but it looks pretty ramshackle from the road."

Joseph's heart sank. A tenant? His family had come to the New World to buy land, not to just be tenants again. No matter, if they had come to hard times, they would need him even more. He was prepared for anything. He bought a loaf of bread, or rather tried to. The man looked in surprise at the gold coin and told him he couldn't make change for it. He handed Joseph the bread and told him to come back and pay him later.

"I'm Pete Patterson by the way. My family has owned this store since the town was founded."

"Thank you, Mr. Patterson."

"You can call me Pete. I have my own son about your age. Come back another day and I'll introduce you to him. His name's David."

He thanked the storekeeper and hurried out the door. He made his way through the small town and found a dirt road leading off to the south. He turned and quickly made his way down the road in the failing light. He walked past farms dotting the countryside on both sides now. None of them matched the description given by the storekeeper. The darkness was closing in and he was having a difficult time seeing the road in front of him, let alone the farmhouses.

Joseph began to worry that he would have to sleep outside again when he saw lights in the distance to his left. He hurried his pace and soon came to a side road turning up to the farmhouse. He couldn't make out any details from that distance, but he had a feeling it might be the right place, so he turned off and moved cautiously forward, not wanting to disturb the inhabitants if he was wrong.

As he approached, he could make out the color of the exterior of the farmhouse. It was red or brown, or rather had been. Paint was chipped off in many places. The house itself went well beyond the description of the storekeeper. The roof ran in an uneven line with parts of the house sagging. It looked as if the whole structure might fall down at any moment. A skinny cat with ribs showing sat on a dirty rail on the front porch, keeping a cautious eye on Joseph. He hesitated. His family couldn't possibly be living here, could they? What about all of his da's dreams of land and a big, fine house? He almost turned around, but he needed to know. He stepped up on the porch and walked up to a cracked and filthy front door. He knocked.

He could hear some shuffling within and the sound of a baby crying. Eventually, he heard the groan of a bolt shifting, and the door opened. A woman in her thirties holding a baby stared out at him. She was thin with dark hair and wide brown eyes. The baby was no more than six months old and was still whimpering as she held it against her. This was obviously the wrong home. He started to apologize when he heard a familiar voice behind her.

"Who is it, darling?" a slurred voice barked from the house.

Joseph froze. He recognized his father's bellow, although he had not heard it in half a decade. He stepped forward so he could see into the house. The interior was even more decrepit and dirty than the outside. A rickety table with two chairs stood in the middle of the room, the only furniture. A cracked and worn wooden floor stood without even a rug or any covering. A man sat at the table, a bottle of whiskey next to the remains of a dinner. His head bobbed around and he strained his eyes to see. It was Joseph's father, a little older, but it was him. He was very drunk.

"Who is it?" his father repeated, closing his eyes now as if concentrating on the answer.

"Da, it's me. It's your boy, Joseph." Joseph's voice cracked and his heart broke.

Robert opened his eyes and looked up at Joseph, trying to see him. He put both hands on the table and pushed himself up, taking a stumbling step forward.

"Joseph. Joseph, is it you? My boy Joseph." Robert fell to the floor and vomited, the filth splashing all over the ground. The stench hit Joseph immediately, overpowering him with the smell of raw spirits.

"Da, where is my ma? Where is Mother?"

Robert looked up, vomit still sticking to his lips.

"Your ma? Your ma is dead, boyo. Dead trying to make a little baby brother for you. This is your mother now." He raised a shaking hand at the woman holding the baby.

Joseph looked over at the woman who was staring back at him in surprise. She was keeping her distance, obviously afraid of him. He took a step toward her, but she backed away, fear in her eyes.

He felt the world crashing over him. His ma was dead. His wonderful mother, the center of his life, gone forever. The O'Dwyers had taken away his mother from him forever. He could have written her; he could have told her he was all right. Instead, she was gone and he would never see her again.

He looked over at the wretched man on the ground. His father. His da was a drunk and remarried. Joseph despaired. He had come back for nothing. He had given up the chance to stay with Jorgenson. Even the O'Dwyers' offer was better than this. There was nothing for him here, only his fool of a father and his wife, a stranger to him. He had no home.

CHAPTER 8

UNION MILITARY HOSPITAL CAMP NEAR THE JERUSALEM ROAD

FRIDAY, JANUARY 8, 1865

Rebecca sat on a hard stool in the dim candlelight trying desperately to stay awake. She wasn't sure how late it was, perhaps three or four in the morning. She stood and stretched, trying to work the stiffness out, then she reached down into a bucket and pulled out a wet sponge, drawing it up and placing it gently on Joseph's fevered forehead.

He was still alive. For two days she had stayed by his side, barely leaving to eat or catch short naps. She checked his bandages for the fifth time that night. The wound was horribly discolored and seeping with pus. The smell was overwhelming. He was dying. She knew it and there was nothing she could do about it. Why was she sitting here? She had asked herself the same question over and over for the past two days. She couldn't bring herself to leave him. She knew it was irrational. Fighting to save him in the first place had been a purely emotional decision brought on by fatigue and her grief over the death of her husband. Why was she still fighting for him now?

She knew there were answers, even if she didn't like them. For one, she had come to know this patient in a way she had never known any patient before. Even though he had never been conscious, she connected with him. She had read the letter he had written his wife over and over until she had memorized every word. She was struck deeply by the love he held for his wife, even as she wondered about the meaning of some of the words. It reminded her so much of her own letters to her husband. The letter was filled with hopes and dreams of the future. He was not able to share their present lives together, so he talked of what they would do when the war was over. Joseph had hidden things from his wife; Rebecca had no doubt. He hadn't written about the horror of their conditions, of the mud and the killing, the broken and dead bodies. He was protecting her. Rebecca wondered if her husband had done the same.

She was also here because she was stubborn. She always fought hard for her patients. Certainly, she had pushed harder with Doctor Johnston in this instance, and perhaps her reasons had been less than rational, but she always tried her best to save the wounded. Thomas had the ability to let go, to walk away from the wounded and conduct his off hours without the day dominating his emotions. She could not. She was haunted by the living and the dead. She cared about them and didn't know how to let her feelings go. She admired Thomas for his strength.

Her thoughts wandered to him again as they had more and more frequently. And this was the third and most selfish reason she sat by Joseph's side. Thomas had joined her in trying to save Joseph. He came by every few hours to check on Joseph's condition and to talk to Rebecca. Since she had insisted on his surgery, something had changed between them, a softening of their relationship she had never expected. Now she yearned to see him, to talk to him even for the briefest of time. This longing was wonderful and terrible at the same time. She was a widow in the infancy of her mourning period. He was a married man. What was she feeling? She had strived her entire life to live as a Christian woman and here she was with improper affection running through her heart and mind. Why was she so terribly weak now when she had always prided herself on her fortitude?

She must say something to him. Things could not possibly go on like this. She needed him to stay away or her heart would burst. She must find the power to send him away. She would care for Joseph on her own. Didn't Thomas understand how his kindness was crushing her even as she burned with joy? She closed her eyes in prayer, begging God to give her strength, pleading for the power to get through this.

She felt a gentle squeeze on her shoulder. Thomas. He had greeted her this way each time he came to check on Joseph, to check on her. His hand lingered just for a moment. She felt warmth surge through her. Her resolve melted away in an instant. She couldn't let him go. She needed him; she needed this. She had been in pain for so long. She turned and smiled, joyful in his presence.

"How's our patient doing?"

Was he speaking of Joseph or her? So much of what he had said the past few days seemed to have two meanings. "He's still alive. His infection is worse. But I've never seen anyone so strong. I thought he would be gone by now. It's a pity there isn't anything else we can do for him. I've kept the wound as clean as I can, but I can't get the infection to go away."

"You've done everything you could possibly do and more. If you hadn't fought for him in the first place, he would be long dead. This is in God's hands now."

In God's hands. She needed God's help desperately. She had to tell Thomas. She had to put an end to things. She avoided his eyes, gathering her strength to speak. "Thomas, you have been so kind to me these past few days . . ."

"I have to keep my nurse in good working order. I know you've been through a bit of a rough patch. Please, think nothing of it."

Thomas reached down past her and began examining Joseph, prodding the infection areas expertly with his fingers. Rebecca watched him carefully, admiring his skill, admiring him.

A thought troubled her. What did he mean, *think nothing of it*? Had she imagined a significant tenderness? Was he simply being kind? Was she an object of pity? She felt her heart sink.

Thomas frowned as he finished his examination. He turned to Rebecca, watching her intently for a moment. "He's very ill. His infection has grown worse and so has his fever. I fear he won't last much longer."

"I don't know what else to do."

He rested his hand on her arm again. "What can you do? Once the infection sets in, almost all of them die."

She was very conscious of his hand on her. She felt warmth coursing through her body. Her heart raced. He still watched her closely. What was he thinking? "I should have left him alone like you ordered. I've wasted your time."

"Nothing you do is a waste, Rebecca. I was glad to do it. To help him for you. I care for you—I care about what's important to you, I mean."

Had she heard him correctly? He cared for her? Did he mean that? Or did he just mean he cared about all the things that had happened to her? Why couldn't she read his expression?

His face darkened as if he realized he had somehow crossed a threshold. He moved his hand and rose to his feet. "Keep an eye on him please. I would like to know when he passes away. Don't forget your other duties."

She flushed. His voice had changed so suddenly. Now he was the stiff, cold doctor she had known this past year.

"I have only been here a moment. I will keep an eye on him, but I do have many other patients to see. I will attend to them immediately of course."

He nodded. “I wasn’t questioning your duty Rebecca. I just know you’ve been caught up in this patient. We have to try to keep perspective. I’ll check back in with you this evening.” Thomas turned and walked stiffly out of the tent.

Her mind reeled. She felt confusion, guilt, uncertainty. She moved to her next patient, castigating herself for her inattention and her sinful thoughts. She would focus on her duties. He was right; she was losing perspective. As she moved from patient to patient, she felt her control returning. She was a nurse among her patients, bringing comfort and care. As she worked, however, the words kept coming back to her, his soft voice whispering: *I care for you.*

CHAPTER 9

Macomb, New York

Friday, April 14, 1854

Joseph took in the scene again in disgust. His father was so drunk he couldn't get back up off the floor. He was covered in vomit and whimpering quietly while his new wife stood near him with her child in her arms, keeping an eye on Joseph. He saw a look he couldn't measure in her eyes. Was she afraid of him? Angry with him? Begging him to stay and save them? He couldn't tell. Robert was too drunk to deal with for the time being. Joseph needed to find out what was going on. He turned to Robert's wife.

"I'm Joseph."

"I'm Charlotte, Robert's new wife. This is our child, Jane." Her response was tentative, and she looked scared. She was afraid of him after all. He felt a little tug at his heart and some of the hardness seemed to fall away.

"What happened to my ma?"

"I . . . I don't know everything about it. She died in childbirth, Joseph. She was trying to give Robert another child. It wasn't anything bad or anything he did. She just didn't make it through the delivery."

"So you strolled in and took her place?" he asked accusingly. He wasn't being fair and he knew it. She winced and he regretted his comment.

"It wasn't like that, Joseph. I didn't know Robert at the time. I met him when I was working at a . . . in Macomb."

"Working where?"

"I'm not proud to say it, but I was working at a tavern. It's not easy finding work around here. Not for immigrants and all. My folks came from England, and even though I was born here, we still have had a hard go of it. Your father was so sad about your ma's death. He would come in and just sit at the bar every night, drinking his whiskey. I came to know him. He's a charming man, Joseph. He has great plans, great dreams. He's going to buy land someday. We married just a bare year ago and the little one came along right away. We're renting this land until Robert can save enough money. He's had a tough go of it too. They don't like Irish around here, less than English. He's had his share of jobs, but he keeps trying. He said he'll show them all. He'll have land of his own. We'll have land of *our* own.

"But things have gone from bad to worse. Robert lost his job again a few months ago and he hasn't been able to find another. Our crops didn't do as well as he had hoped either. We're desperately behind on our rent. Mr. Hastings, the owner, is threatening to evict us if we don't pay. We are running out of food and there's nothing for Jane to eat. I don't know what to do. Poor Robert has grown so much worse with all the bad news."

Joseph felt himself growing angry. Poor Robert. He had heard all of this before. Robert always promised a new and better life just over the horizon. His mother had lived by this dream, and now another Mrs. Forsyth was doing the same. He looked over at his father. How could they believe him? What if someday he ended up the same way? A drunk and a dreamer. Joseph wanted to walk out right now, walk out and never look back. But who would care for Charlotte and the child? Robert couldn't do it. Not like this. Robert did need him and so did Charlotte. This might not be his mother, but she was a woman in need and her child was his half sister. Could he walk out and leave them to their fate? What about his father? Could he walk out on his own blood? Maybe he could help him too? He looked down again at the pitiful man on the floor. What a mess.

"Let's get him up and get him to bed."

He saw the grateful look in Charlotte's eyes. She laid the baby down in a rickety wooden crib, then assisted Joseph in easing Robert back up to his knees. She took a cloth from the kitchen and wiped his front and face, cleaning him up as well as she could. Together they lifted him to his feet and then half carried, half dragged him to the bed. They laid him down as gently as possible and covered him with a blanket. His eyes opened and he looked up, smiling.

"Oh, Joseph, look how big and strong you are. You're a man now, no doubts about that. I'm so proud of you coming to find your da and helping him out. A little help is all I need now and again." He turned over and was asleep in moments, still mumbling, "Just a little help."

Charlotte thanked him again and then invited him to sit down while she made coffee. He watched her as she worked. She seemed so fragile, shy, and afraid. When she finished, she poured him a cup and brought him some bread and cheese. Joseph shook his head, remembering what she had said about their lack of money.

"No please, Joseph, I insist. I know you must be so upset about your mother and about Robert. Don't be too hard on him. He loves you so. He never stops talking about his boy, about how when you came back you would be a trained printer and you could open up a shop and also help him on the farm. All his plans include you, Joseph. Even though he hadn't heard from you, he always dreamed you would walk back through that door one day. Now that you're here, he has a real chance to get better. He will be so much happier." She looked at him closely. "Why didn't you ever write him?"

"That wasn't my fault. My master hid the letters from Ma and Da. He told me they abandoned me and that they were probably dead or good as dead. He told me my da was a no-good drunk . . ." Joseph's voice broke as he said it.

"He's not like this all the time, Joseph. Just when life gets him down. He's usually happy and full of laughter. I've never known a man as full of joy as your father. He's a good man. You have to give him a chance. Give us a chance. I know things will turn around now that you're here. He is going to be his old self again."

Joseph didn't answer. He needed to think about things. "I'm sorry to ask, but I am tired. I've been on the road all day. Do you have anywhere I could sleep?"

"Oh, of course. How rude of me. I've been so caught up in my own sorrow I forgot about yours. You must be exhausted. We have a spare bedroom with a bed upstairs. I'm afraid we haven't lit the fireplace and it is probably dreadfully cold."

"I can start a fire if you have some wood."

Charlotte helped Joseph gather some wood and kindling along with the end of a burning log from the downstairs hearth. Joseph carefully lit the fire in the spare bedroom. He blew hard and soon the flames were licking up through the gaps he had left. The light illuminated the plain room with worn wallpaper and a single lumpy bed. The bed didn't even have a headboard, but there were plenty of blankets. Joseph was shivering from the cold and climbed in. In a few minutes, he felt much better as the roaring fire warmed his face.

His mother was dead. The thought hit him hard as he lay there alone. He could only remember scattered images of her. She had always been so kind. She had cooked and cleaned and taken care of him and his father. Then she was taken away from him. For five long years when he wondered often why she hadn't even cared enough to write to him. Now she was truly gone. He had missed his chance to be with her. She had been closer to Joseph than anyone he had ever known and she was gone forever. He felt the grief washing over him. He pulled his pillow closer and buried his face, sobbing in anguish, trying to muffle the noise.

What did he have left? He had run away from the O'Dwyers. He didn't regret that decision. No matter what they had offered him, they had deceived him about his family. They had taken away his chance to share his life with his mother, even if only by letters. Now all that was left of his family was his father. What was he to do with Robert? He was every bit the fool O'Dwyer had described. But Charlotte's words echoed in his mind: *He's a good man*. A good man with many faults. His da needed help. More importantly, she needed help. Charlotte had a baby and she couldn't work outside the farm or earn enough money in employment to make a difference. They were in deep debt and they were going to lose the tenancy on the farm. The only person who could save them was Joseph.

But should he? There was another way for him, a carefree, happy life. Joseph thought of Captain Jorgenson. An easy life of friendship and adventure was his for the taking. All he had to do was sneak out the door and disappear forever. It would be so simple. What did he owe Robert? He already knew the answer. He didn't owe his father anything. He owed someone else, however. His mother. He had to honor the memory of her. His ma had stuck with Robert through thick and thin. He owed it to the memory of his mother and to this new half sibling to try to save his father. According to Charlotte, Robert wanted to share a farm with him. To have a real family. If he could save Robert, then he could truly have what he had always wanted: a home.

He would stay. He would stay and fight to keep the farm. He would help his father dig out of this debt and eventually save enough money to buy their own land. He would work harder than anyone until he had achieved his desire. Nothing would stop him.

Joseph fell asleep feeling peace now that he had made up his mind. That night he dreamed of his mother in heaven looking down on him from a golden sky. She was smiling, proud of the man he had become, proud he had finally made his way home.

Late in the afternoon on the following day, Joseph set out down the road farther south several miles to the home of the venerable Hastings family. When he reached the Hastings property, he stood for a moment in awe. In stark contrast to his father's ramshackle farm, the Hastings home was three stories of whitewashed perfection with a manicured lawn surrounded by vast acres of well-tended grains and staples. Joseph could see dozens of men and women tending the various crops in the fields and several gardeners working in the yard. He made his way up the drive and climbed the long front stairs toward the entryway. The porch itself extended the full length of the house and was covered by a roof with white columns extending in both directions. He had never seen anything so grand. He approached the front door and with some hesitation pulled back on the fine wrought-iron door ring before releasing it with a heavy thud.

Some time passed before the door opened. An older man with white hair, dressed in formal wear, looked at Joseph in puzzlement, and then spoke.

"Excuse me, but may I help you in some way?" His voice didn't sound particularly helpful.

"Yes, hello. I'm Joseph Forsyth. My father is Robert Forsyth. He is a tenant of Mr. Hastings. I've come to speak with him about the rent."

"Do you have an appointment?"

"No I don't."

"Mr. Hastings doesn't meet without appointments. Particularly with his tenants. You should arrange a time and come back another day. Better yet, send your father. I doubt he will want to meet with you at all." He started to close the door, but Joseph stepped forward and put his foot in the way, blocking him.

"I need to see Mr. Hastings and I need to see him today. I'll wait as long as need be."

The butler tried to force the door shut but gave up after a few moments when Joseph would not relent. He glared at Joseph and then finally exhaled sharply as if surrendering.

"Well you can come in and wait in the front entryway. You're probably wasting your time, but you may sit here all day if you like. I'll inform Mr. Hastings you are here when I have a spare moment." He motioned for Joseph to enter and then turned and abruptly left the front room.

Joseph found a chair and sat down to wait. He was amazed at the entryway. A red oriental carpet filled the center of the room. A rich brown and red wood table stood against the far wall with a porcelain vase and flowers. Above the table hung a large oil painting depicting a landscape and encased in an intricately adorned gilt frame. A wide staircase led up to a balcony above. He could also see through the door in front of him, which seemed to lead to a large dining room. He had never seen anything like this house before. He had delivered printing jobs to many homes and businesses in Quebec City, but even the wealthy homes were smaller townhomes and not as spacious or as grand.

He sat for hours in the room quietly observing the comings and goings of the staff members. They hurried along and spoke in hushed tones. The atmosphere in the house felt oppressive. He grew hungry, but he hadn't thought to bring anything to eat and certainly he was not likely to be offered anything from the staff, so he did his best to think of other things.

The afternoon turned to early evening. Finally, the butler returned. "You are exceptionally lucky, young man. Mr. Hastings has a few moments to speak with you, although he can't imagine why you would be here. I caution you to show only the greatest respect to Mr. Hastings or you will find that your interview will be cut short. Do you understand me?"

Joseph's blood boiled, but he was used to this kind of treatment. Instead of reacting, he merely nodded his head and stood to follow. He was led through the door to the dining room and quickly through to another room immediately adjacent. This room was filled with tall wooden bookcases and more rich carpets. A fire crackled in the fireplace, and at the far end of the room, there was a desk facing outward. Seated at the desk was a man Joseph assumed to be Mr. Hastings. He was in his mid to late forties with shortly cropped gray hair and a thin, chiseled face. He had a white beard and mustache, also closely cut and well groomed. Another man stood near him, a hand resting on the desk. He looked to be about twenty and was tall with black hair and a black mustache. He was dressed in a blue suit with a white shirt. He was clearly Mr. Hastings's son.

Mr. Hastings looked at Joseph with hard eyes, and he felt he was being sized up. "I understand you are Robert Forsyth's boy. I didn't know he even had a son. What can I do for you?"

"Mr. Hastings, sir. That is true, I'm Joseph Forsyth. I've come to speak to you about my father—about the rent."

"Well strange you should wish to do so since your father clearly won't. He has been avoiding me for months. Your father is very far behind on his rent. Out of the kindness of my heart, I have allowed him to stay on the property while he tried to get together the money he owes me. However, my patience is at an end. I have already served him notice of the eviction. He will have to be out by the end of the month. I need productive people on my land. I'm not sure what else I can say to you."

"I'm here to ask that you reconsider, Mr. Hastings. With my help, I know my da can pay you back. We just need some more time."

"Listen to the mick boy, Father," said Mr. Hastings's son. "What cheek the little rat has. They're all the same. Drunks and liars." He turned to Joseph. "Your dad is the drunkest Irishman I've ever seen, and the most useless. And trust me, boy, that's saying something."

"I'm not a boy, and I'm not your boy." Joseph was angry, so angry he felt himself losing control. He willed himself to calm down, to keep his emotions contained.

"From where I stand, you look a boy. A dumb, useless Irish boy like the rest of them."

"Enough, Warren." Mr. Hastings raised his hand and his son went silent. "I'm sorry. Joseph is it? I'm sorry, Joseph, but it's too late. I've already promised the property to another family. There is nothing I can do for you. You seem a decent enough boy, but this is a man's agreement. Your father, unfortunately, has chosen not to meet his obligations, and I have run out of patience."

"I could work for you. I'm a trained printer."

"What need would I have of a printer? I don't have equipment for that and there's hardly anyone around with money for printing. Not this side of Morristown."

"I could work for you then. Work for free until the debt is paid off. I'm a strong and hard worker."

"You're a drunk and a liar like your father," said Warren.

Mr. Hastings turned to his son. "I said to keep your mouth closed! If you can't keep your temper, then you won't sit with me for business. Get out, Warren!"

"But, Father . . ."

"I said out!"

Warren stared at his father for a moment and then turned to look at Joseph with anger in his eyes. He started to step toward him but then stopped. He turned abruptly and stormed out of the room.

Mr. Hastings turned back to Joseph. "Now, where were we? Oh yes, free labor. As I'm sure you saw, I already have plenty of workers here. How would it help me to have another? Even if you worked as hard as you say you would."

"I'll work dawn to dusk to pay the debt, sir. And I can pay some of the debt right now." Joseph reached into his pocket and pulled out his remaining gold sovereigns. He approached the desk slowly and placed them down on the surface. He had hoped to save this money for the future, but he had to do something to convince Mr. Hastings to let them stay.

Mr. Hastings stared at the coins for a moment and then at Joseph again, looking him up and down.

"You will pay this money now and you will work for me until the debts are paid? You will work for six months, six days a week, twelve hours a day. That will pay the debt. Do you agree?"

Six months. Another six months of his life. He had already worked five years for his father. Now he would have to give up another half year. He didn't know what else he could do. He had committed to saving them, to building a home.

"Agreed."

"If you don't live up to the obligation, your father will still be evicted and will still owe the full amount, regardless of how much work you have already done. Agreed?"

He had no choice. "Agreed."

"All right then, we have a bargain. Just remember, your father made a bargain with me too, and he didn't live up to it. You'll have to do far better. Do you understand?"

"I understand."

"You can start tomorrow. Report to the field foreman in the morning. You will find him in the barn or just ask around for him."

"Thank you very much, Mr. Hastings."

He waved a hand at Joseph to dismiss him. Joseph turned and walked back out to the waiting butler. He escorted Joseph briskly out of the house and the door was closed behind him.

He had done it. He was going to have to work hard, but he knew how to do that. He would catch up with the rent and they could keep the farm. In time, they would save up enough money to buy their own land. They would be a family.

He arrived back at the farm well after dark. Dinner was on the table and Charlotte greeted him warmly. Robert was sitting at the table and scarcely glanced at Joseph as he came in. He had a half bottle of whiskey with him.

"I've done it," said Joseph. "Mr. Hastings will let us stay."

"How wonderful, Joseph!" said Charlotte. "How did you manage that?"

"I'm going to work for Mr. Hastings for a few months, just until we catch everything up."

"You don't mean for free? Oh, Joseph, we can't let you do that. Can we, Robert?"

Robert looked up with bleary eyes, trying to catch up to the conversation. He waved his hand negligently.

"Of course we can, darling. He's my flesh and bone. What do you make children for if not to help you out of your troubles? That's a good lad, helping your father. See, dear? I told you everything would work out just fine." Robert turned back away and seemed to lose interest in the rest of the conversation.

Charlotte stepped forward and hugged Joseph, holding him tightly. "Oh what a dear boy you are. Or should I say man. You've been a man today, Joseph, and make no mistake. Your mother would be proud of you. I'm proud of you."

"Is my da proud of me?"

"He is, Joseph. He just can't show it."

Joseph sat silently through the rest of dinner. He was hurt that Robert had failed to show much appreciation. He didn't understand his father. It must be the drink. He just had to be patient. Charlotte had said that Robert got like this only when they fell on hard times. If Joseph pulled them out of it, he was sure to come around. He had plenty of time to wait for it. For now, he needed his rest. He had a long and weary road ahead.

CHAPTER 10

Macomb, New York
Oliver Hastings's Farm
Tuesday, September 12, 1854

Five slow months had passed. Joseph worked long days every day at the Hastings farm with only Sundays off. He had an hour walk both directions as well. In the evenings, he sometimes fell half asleep as he trudged along. In the late winter, he had worked primarily in the barn and the shop, feeding animals and repairing equipment. In the spring, he had spent extensive hours plowing acre after acre of fields and then planting the Mediterranean wheat that made up the majority of the cash crop on the Hastings property.

His work only allowed them to stay on their tenancy, not to eat. From his side jobs, Joseph managed to make enough money to buy food for the family, but he didn't know how much longer he could continue to work at this pace. Even at sixteen years old, he was exhausted and was working beyond his limit. He was getting closer to the six-month mark, however, and he willed himself to keep going, one day, one moment at a time. Soon, he would be done with his obligation to Mr. Hastings, and he could start working for true wages.

For now, the hardest work was in front of him. They were in the harvest and had to gather all of the crops as quickly as they were able. The days extended to sixteen hours. Joseph had to suspend his odd jobs, but at the same time he was now given food to eat each day and additional food to take home to the family.

Joseph had found the other laborers cold at first. There were a number of Irish, but they all seemed to know about Robert and treated Joseph with disdain. He was horrified to learn his family was considered worthless even among the poor immigrants in the community. His shock had turned to resolve: He would change all of that and he would save his father. He worked harder than ever, focusing every part of his will on doing the best job he could do consistently, over and over. He worked not only hard but also fast, with seemingly limitless energy.

In time, just like among the crew of the *St. Charles,* the attitude of the others had changed. His hard work and quiet nature endeared him to everyone around him.

Everyone except Warren. The owner's son seemed intent on harassing Joseph at every turn.

Warren was disliked but feared by virtually all of the workers on the Hastings farm. He did not work with the laborers, but would ride on his horse and issue orders. He loved to sneak around, waiting to catch a person resting or working too slowly. Then he would spring on them and castigate them loudly in front of everyone.

Warren reserved his special attention for Joseph, although he was never able to catch him at an idle moment. Warren made it a point to find Joseph and issue orders for the most difficult and dirty jobs, like carrying stones to repair a wall or mucking out all of the stalls in the barn. He would stand over Joseph and berate him, calling him a mick and a son of a worthless drunk. Joseph had learned from the others that Warren always had a special target, someone he bullied and tormented as much as possible. There was nothing to be done about it. Those who responded in kind were discharged from the farm. So Joseph held his tongue, telling himself he could take it and that the words didn't mean anything. He only had one month left. He had survived and he could make it a bit longer.

In stark contrast, everyone liked Lucy. The twelve-year-old daughter of Oliver and sister of Warren was always well dressed and smiling. She had long, curly black hair and blue eyes. She was like a doll, arriving by carriage with her nanny and quickly being whisked inside by the house servants. Lucy's mother had died in childbirth so she was always attended by her nanny. She loved to walk around the property, playing and laughing. Her laughter was bright and infectious. She would tease the workers and joke with them, but in a light and innocent manner. It seemed impossible that Warren and Lucy were related, although they looked remarkably alike.

Another month remained of servitude; Joseph could handle another month. In a few days, the harvest would be over and things would slow down as the weather turned colder. Before he knew it, his time would be up and he could finally find employment for wages and start saving money for the future.

Joseph began the day in the fields, assisting with the harvest. He was working extra hard that morning because Elias, one of the older hands, was ill with a fever and could barely shuffle along. Elias was another target of Warren, and Joseph knew he would delight in firing him if given half a chance.

"You're a saint," whispered Elias, leaning heavily on a shovel.

Joseph blushed. "Think nothing of it. You'd do the same for me. Just keep your head down and keep walking with me. Everything will be all right."

At noon, Joseph looked up and saw Lucy. She was moving along among the hands, handing out biscuits. A worker trailed behind her with a hand wagon full of milk.

"Good afternoon, Joseph," said Lucy, smiling at him.

"Good afternoon."

She handed him a couple biscuits and a large bottle of milk.

"How is the work today?"

"It's just fine, Miss Lucy." In fact it was backbreaking, particularly at double the speed. His shirt was soaked through and he already felt exhausted, but he had kept up the expected pace while Elias was still stumbling along with him.

Joseph heard a horse galloping near and turned to see Warren riding up, a slight grin on his face.

"What's going on here?" he demanded.

"I was just handing out some biscuits," said Lucy.

"They can relax on their own time at home. I don't have time for lazy good-for-nothings to take our money for half a day's wage."

"Lucy just arrived here a moment ago," explained Elias.

"I didn't ask your opinion!" Warren turned to the worker. "You are white as a sheet. Are you fit to work?"

"Yes sir, I am."

Warren looked shrewdly at Joseph. "I've another task for you. The stalls need mucking out. You come with me. Elias, I expect you to keep pace for both you *and Joseph* for the rest of the day. I'll be back soon to check your progress."

Elias looked to Joseph with begging eyes. There was nothing Joseph could do. Joseph looked meaningfully toward Lucy, hoping Elias would talk to her and see if she would intervene for him, then he turned and followed Warren to the barn.

Late in the day, Joseph leaned against his shovel, taking a quick break to catch his breath. He had been working in the barn for hours, mucking out the stalls and repairing some of the tack. He was almost done for the day and was already imagining the feast to come. Each day during the harvest, Mr. Hastings and the Hastings family would eat outside at long tables with the workers. The harvest feast was one of the best times of the year. The tables groaned under the weight of hams and turkeys, fresh bread, and pies still hot from the oven. Piles of corn and sweet potatoes were stacked near blocks of sweet butter made fresh each day. Everyone would visit and savor the feast, laughing and enjoying themselves. One of the workers would play the fiddle, and sometimes people even danced after the meal. His thoughts were interrupted by a familiar voice.

"This is the second time I've caught you shirking work today."

Joseph looked up to see Warren with a couple of his friends. They all stood menacingly at the entrance to the barn. As he stared at them, he heard the dinner bell ring. He started to leave but found that the men blocked him; he sensed trouble. They were carrying a bottle and laughing. Warren extended the bottle to Joseph.

"Do you want a drink, boy?"

"No, thank you."

Warren turned to his friends. "Well there's a change for you. An Irishman turning down a drink! And a Forsyth at that. Come on, Joseph, have a little sip. Maybe it will help you work. It didn't help Elias much. I hope his family saved up some money for the winter." His friends laughed. Joseph felt hot anger rising, but he kept his tongue. So all his efforts to save Elias had come to naught.

Warren stepped closer and flipped the end of the bottle; whiskey flew out and washed all over Joseph's shirt and down his trousers. Joseph balled his fists. He felt the anger rising up and knew he had to get out of there. The entrance was still blocked but he took a couple steps to the side, trying to ease closer to the large double doors.

Warren took a deep breath. "Smell that. Now you smell like a proper Irishman."

Joseph ignored him, repressing his rage and attempting an easy tone. "Come, Warren, you've had your fun. The dinner bell's rung. Let's to it."

"Oh the bell's rang for you all right, boy, but not the dinner bell. I've a score to settle with you. If you think I've forgotten that day in my father's office, you've another thing coming. You embarrassed me that day. What's more, I've watched you these many months—always chumming around when there's work to be done. Cock of the walk, are you? Who the hell do you think you are?"

"I haven't done anything to you, Warren. You embarrassed yourself that day in your father's office, and what friends I have I've earned. Now step aside so I can go."

"It won't be as easy as that, boy. As I said, you've a lesson to learn. What's more, we don't need your kind here. Drunken Irish coming and taking our jobs, and your father is the worst of the lot. That and his whore of a wife that died trying to bring another litter into the world."

Joseph exploded. He rushed forward and struck Warren in the face, knocking him off his feet. Warren hit the ground hard. Both his friends rushed forward, grabbing Joseph by the arms and holding him. Warren rose and dusted himself off; his face was red and blood flowed from a cut on his cheek. His eyes burned with hatred.

"How dare you strike me. You're finished now, Forsyth. After I'm done with you, I'll report this to my father. He will fire you and you'll lose your land. But for now, I still have that lesson to teach you." He stepped forward and struck Joseph hard in the face. Joseph felt the stinging pain but he held his feet. He felt the blood rush to his head, and his heart was beating out of his chest. He spat in Warren's face.

Blows rained down on him from every direction. He could feel the pain exploding in his head and body. He dropped to the ground and covered his head, trying to ward off the blows. He wanted to fight, but he couldn't take on all three of them at the same time.

"What is the meaning of this?" Joseph looked up through his swollen eyes and saw Mr. Hastings standing at the door, a pistol in his hand.

Warren turned and began dusting himself off. "Father, I caught Joseph with a bottle of whiskey. He was drunk on the job. I threatened to turn him in and he attacked me. We were trying to restrain him, but he's like a wild animal."

"Joseph! How dare you violate my trust like this. I've given you a home and honest work. You repay me with drunken conduct and you strike my son? You remember our agreement, don't you? You have violated it in the worst way. I could forgive many things, but I can't forgive this. You will leave this land tonight and your family will be off my property by nightfall tomorrow."

Joseph pulled himself to his feet. His face was throbbing and one eye was swollen shut. He ignored the pain and tried to explain. "Mr. Hastings, please! Your son is lying. He came in with these men and threatened me. He wouldn't let me leave. They were the ones who were drinking."

"You call my son a liar? How dare you! Look at you, covered in whiskey! You smell like a distillery! Joseph, I had such high hopes for you. You have worked hard. I thought of offering you a job when you had paid off your father's debts, but I see you have your father's weakness after all. Now get off my property before I call the sheriff!"

"He's not lying." Joseph was surprised to hear a girl's voice. It was Lucy. She had come into the barn at some point during the argument.

"What are you talking about, girl? This is no place for you. You should go back to the banquet. I'll be along in a few minutes."

"Joseph is not lying, Father. I overheard Warren and his friends walking by about a half hour ago. They had the bottle in their hands and they were looking for Joseph. They were laughing about him. I knew something was wrong and I tried to come find you, but I was too late."

Mr. Hastings turned to Lucy. "Dear, this is none of your concern. Now go back to the banquet like I said."

She hesitated, looking at Joseph, then turned and quickly left. Mr. Hastings turned to Warren. He was angrier now than Joseph had ever seen him. "So you're a liar after all, are you? Drinking with your friends during the harvest? You were supposed to be overseeing the work, Warren! I can't do everything on this farm, can I? I will deal with you later. Get out!"

"But, Father . . ."

"Get out, Warren!"

Warren and his friends left the barn. Mr. Hastings watched them for a few moments and then turned to Joseph.

"Well, Joseph, what do you have to say for yourself?"

Joseph was surprised. "What do you mean? You heard what Lucy said."

"I heard that Warren was drunk and came in to bother you. He isn't a perfect boy, that's true, but he's the son of your master. Did you strike him?"

"He had me cornered. They were going to attack me."

"Did you strike him?"

"Like I said, they had me surrounded."

"I asked you if you struck him."

"I did."

"Then I have no choice but to demand you leave my land. You will leave now."

"Mr. Hastings, that isn't fair. I've worked hard for you all these months. My time is almost up. You can't take it all away from me."

"I can do exactly that. You remember our agreement. If you broke the terms, then you must leave and your father still owes all the money. Assaulting my son certainly breaks those terms. Do you want me to take this to the sheriff and the judge? You'll be in jail and make no mistake."

"Please, sir. Please don't do that. There must be something I can do. Anything. I've worked so hard."

Mr. Hastings paused for a moment as if considering things. "Well, I suppose if you agree to extend your work until the first of the year, then I'll agree to let this pass."

Until the end of the year? "That's three more months, sir."

Mr. Hastings's face reddened. "And you should thank me for that! Do you want me to make it six more? You owe that much and interest! Do we have an agreement? I won't ask again."

Joseph froze. What could he do? He could try to fight Mr. Hastings, but who would the authorities back, a respected member and landowner of the community or the son of a drunken Irish immigrant? Besides the sheriff, who else could he turn to? To Lucy? He'd never spoken to her, and besides, she was a little girl and would certainly back her father however nice she seemed. He had no choice. He must either move out with his family or he must swallow his pride. He hated the lack of control. His entire life adults had taken what they wanted from him. For now there was nothing he could do.

"Well? What will it be, Forsyth?"

"Agreed."

"Good decision. You can go home now."

"What about the dinner? I don't have anything at home."

"You should have thought of that before you struck one of your betters. You go home hungry, boy, and you let that sink in real good. Next time I won't be so generous. You had better never disobey me again. Now get off my land."

Mr. Hastings turned and walked away. Joseph sat in the barn, shaking. He was sore all over from the beating. He could hear the laughter and the celebration just a few yards away. Finally, he stood up and dusted himself off. He arranged his clothes as best he could and walked straight back out of the barn. He turned without looking at the harvest celebration and he walked down the drive. As he left, he vowed to himself that he would fight. He would fight and work until he controlled his own life, until he could protect his family. He swore that nothing would ever stop him. As he gathered his jacket to leave, he noticed a lump inside. He opened the coat and found a bundle tied with a handkerchief. He untied it to find a warm loaf of bread and half a chicken. He smiled to himself. He knew who had put it there. At least there was one Hastings who didn't seem to come from the devil. He picked up the bundle and slowly walked away from the sounds of celebration and into the darkness.

CHAPTER 11

MACOMB, NEW YORK

THURSDAY, FEBRUARY 8, 1855

Joseph sat up late by the dim light of a candle going over the family accounts. Winter was almost over and with some luck, they were going to make it. He prayed silently for their miraculous survival. He had completed his commitment to Mr. Hastings in the early winter, but this left him no time to make any substantial improvements to their land or attempt to bring on any livestock. Worse, he had little knowledge of what he was doing. He had done some work on farms in Ireland as a boy but the past five years had been entirely devoted to learning the printing trade. Much of his prior knowledge had faded away and of course he had never managed a farm.

The months spent working for Hastings had helped him renew his skills at farming. However, he was limited to the work he was given, which often involved cleaning out horse stalls and other jobs reserved for a person at the bottom of the pecking order. He had used the time at the property to learn everything he could, and since his release of service, he had learned more, often staying up late to read almanacs and anything else about farming he could lay his hands on.

He also was able to glean some knowledge from Robert, although he was almost driven mad in the process of doing so. Robert was perpetually at least half drunk and, worse, his stories meandered about as he described the glory days in Ireland and his past and future prospects for wealth and renown.

With so little experience and no time to fix things before deep winter set in, Joseph had been afraid he had staved off eviction just to fall immediately into arrears again. He did the only thing he knew how to do: again he knocked on doors and offered his work to anyone who would listen. He had a difficult time securing employment but little by little he added small side jobs and soon he was able to work full days Monday through Saturday. He would rise well before dawn and do the morning chores of their farm by lantern light before setting out to other local farms to do work mending fences and other winter projects. He would then return in the evening, eat his dinner, and head out by lantern again for evening work on their property. Robert promised he would help, but five out of six days he remained in bed and claimed illness. Even without Robert's help, Joseph somehow made the rent each month. Little by little he had even saved some money.

Joseph was proud of what he had accomplished but he had grown to hate Robert. His father was lazy, a daydreamer, and a liar. He would have liked nothing more than to walk away and leave his father to his own problems. He would do it in a second without hesitation if it wasn't for Charlotte and for Jane. He had grown so close to his stepmother these past months. Charlotte appreciated and loved Joseph. She thanked him daily and he saw in her actions how much she cared for and needed him. He knew without his help she would be without a home, without food. She had become the mother he had lost, the mother he could hardly remember now.

Nobody had ever needed him before or depended on him this way. He would never let her down. He would protect her and Jane, and he would improve their life together one scrap at a time.

He felt a hand on his shoulder and he smiled. "I thought you were asleep," he said. Only one other person could be up this late; Robert would have passed out for good hours ago.

"I brought you some coffee," said Charlotte. She placed a mug down in front of him and then sat down. "You really should go to bed Joseph, you work far too hard."

"Who will take care of things if I don't? Your husband?"

"Please don't. I know he hasn't helped you very much. He wants to, Joseph, please understand that. He's just been down and out for so long. He tries to find work and he's rejected. Then he becomes angry. He drinks to try to forget. But the drink takes away his energy. He is ill too. You must see that, dear." She placed a hand on his.

"I don't see it. I see a drunk who won't work for himself or for his family. I knew it when I was young although I pretended I didn't. All those years working for O'Dwyer, I imagined the best about him. I tried to believe that my flashes of memory were wrong. I hoped and prayed when I saw him and Ma again they would be happy and successful, that Da would finally have the land he had dreamed of, that we had come to this country for. Instead when I came back it was worse than I even imagined." Joseph pushed back hard on his chair and stood, his fists clenched and his breathing rapid. He felt her hand take his again, squeezing it gently in a gesture of love and calm. He sat back down.

"How are we holding up?" she asked, clearly trying to divert the conversation.

He motioned toward their ledger. "Do you mean this? We are making it. I don't know how, but we are. But this month is the worst so far. The jobs have dried up with the snow. I've done as much of the winter work as folks seem to have, and I'm having to walk farther and farther afield to see if there is anything left to do. We are going to have to use what little I've saved and what eggs and milk we can sell to make it through February. Next month should be better, the weather will improve and spring work will begin. With luck we will make it."

"I'm so proud of you. You made this happen, Joseph, nobody else. I don't know where I would be without you. Where little Jane would be."

He felt the warmth of her love flow through him. He smiled and squeezed her hand in return. "Well, my dear, as I said we will make it with eggs and milk, but we won't succeed without work and there's still work left to do tonight. I have to leave the accounts for a bit and make sure everything is secure outside before I turn in for bed."

"Do you want some help?"

"You need to stay here in case Jane wakes up. I won't be more than a half hour."

Joseph rose and walked to the front door where he had kicked off his boots and overcoat. He pulled on his outside clothing and then lit an oil lantern and quietly left the farmhouse. The evening was bitter cold but beautiful, the moonlight illuminating the snow on the ground and in the trees. Joseph looked into the sky and saw thousands of stars, a sight he rarely saw in Quebec City because of the buildings and all of the streetlights. He looked out over the property, *his land*. He had fought for this farm and he had saved it. He alone.

He stomped out through the knee-deep snow to the chicken coop. He had repaired the structure over the summer and added extra space, gradually growing his brood to three dozen. He looked over the hens and made sure they were all safe and healthy. He also made sure the caging was secure and there were no signs of wild animals trying to get in. He smiled to himself again proudly. These chickens produced two dozen eggs or more per day. The family used six to ten eggs, and he was able to sell all of the rest in town.

He next headed to the sty. He had purchased six piglets in the late summer and had worked hard to raise them. One had died from illness but the other five were growing larger each month. In the spring he would be able to butcher or sell them; perhaps he would even breed them himself next year. Everything seemed to be in order so he walked last to the barn.

That's when he heard the noise—a strange moaning. He didn't recognize the sound and he rushed as quietly as he could to the barn door. Before entering, he looked around the entrance trying to find something he could use as a potential weapon. The sound could have been anything from a wild animal to a dangerous trespasser. He found an axe near the entryway and picked it up with his left hand, holding the lantern up with his right. He pressed against the barn door and pushed in slowly, trying to be as silent as possible.

The moaning grew louder and seemed to come from the back of the barn farthest from the door. He walked toward the sound cautiously, his hand gripping the axe, ready to strike. It seemed to take forever to cross the distance, but finally he was near the source of the noise. He took a deep breath and rushed forward, but halted abruptly, dropping the axe.

Before him, lying on the ground, was his only cow. Robert had owned the cow before he came, but Joseph had worked hard to buy the best feed and to fatten the animal up all summer until they had the best quality and quantity of milk. The beast now lay on its side, its hide mottled, a white froth surrounding its mouth. Joseph turned and ran back to the house to alert Charlotte before returning to the barn.

Joseph spent the rest of the night trying to save the cow, Charlotte and Robert standing behind him. He tried everything he knew but to no avail. Just before dawn the cow died and, with it, his supply of milk for the family and for sale. He knew there was no money to buy another cow and, worse, that without the milk for the family and what he made from selling the extra, they would never make it through the winter.

◆ ◆ ◆

A few weeks later, Joseph knocked on the door of the Snider farmhouse. Although it was midday, there was still snow on the ground and the temperature was freezing. He could feel the bone-chilling cold coming up through his boots. He had spent all morning as he had spent most of February, walking from farm to farm looking for any available work. He heard footsteps at the door and then the sound of a latch turning. The door opened. Mrs. Snider was there. She was a short gray-haired widow in her late middle age. She smiled and greeted Joseph. He had done odd jobs for her earlier in the winter.

"Oh, Joseph it's you," she said. "I was wondering who would be out in this terrible cold. Please come in." She motioned him in and he followed her into the simple farmhouse. She lived all alone although she had sons and their families nearby that kept an eye on her and made sure she was safe. Mrs. Snider poured Joseph some hot coffee and brought it to the table so they could visit.

"How are you doing, Joseph?"

"I'm fair, Mrs. Snider. I'm wondering if you have any work available? Anything at all?"

She looked at him for a moment, understanding and compassion in her eyes.

"Oh, I wish I did dear, but there simply isn't anything to do with the snows still here and the ground frozen solid. The boys have been over a few times this month and they've mended the fences and sharpened the plow for the spring. I could use your help setting in our crops once we have a good thaw."

He nodded politely, feeling the desperation creep over him again. The answer had been much the same all month. There simply wasn't any work to do in the dead of winter. He had picked up a few jobs here and there but not enough to cover the loss of his cow. He did not have the money to pay the March rent to Mr. Hastings. He didn't know what he could do.

She smiled at him and offered him some bread she had wrapped in cloth. "I'm sorry I can't help you, Joseph. I know you will find some work now that spring is near."

He smiled back as best he could, took the bread, and departed back into the snow. Only when he was down the road and out of sight did he allow himself to let go a little, tears streaming down his face. He stepped off the road to a nearby oak tree and leaned against the trunk, closing his eyes, his shoulders shaking. After a few minutes he stood up and composed himself. He would not stop. He would not quit. He would find the work and find the money no matter what. Charlotte and Jane depended on him. His father depended on him. He stomped his feet to gather a little warmth then returned to the road and headed up to the next farm.

Hours passed. He visited a dozen farms, receiving the same answer over and over. Always polite, always compassionate, but always no. What was he going to do? He knew there was an answer. He could go to Oliver Hastings. He could tell his landlord the situation and ask for his help. He knew Oliver would make a bargain. Hastings would set Joseph to work for the entire spring for free to make up the rent. Joseph would save the farm again but he would be no further ahead at the end of the labor, no closer to his plans to free the family from tenancy and gain their own land, their own future.

I won't do that until I have no other options left, he told himself. He walked the last couple of miles into Pope's Mill and trudged through the muddy snow to Patterson's. Charlotte needed some salt and flour, and Joseph promised he would pick it up when he was done looking for work that day. He scrambled with frozen fingers in his pocket, looking for a few coins to pay. This was the last of his money. He felt the panic again, the despair burning through him, but he had to control himself. He would worry about all of this tomorrow. There was still one more day.

"Joseph! How are you, boy? I haven't seen you in weeks!"

He recognized the voice of Pete Patterson and looked up to see the elderly gentleman standing at the store counter and smiling at him. Joseph felt his dark mood begin to slip away again. Mr. Patterson was always kind to him.

"Good afternoon, Mr. Patterson."

"Please, it's Pete. What can I do for you?"

"I need to purchase some flour and salt."

"Sure. How much do you need of each?"

"One hundred pounds of flour and two pounds of salt."

Pete looked at Joseph with appraising eyes. "And how are you going to get that flour home?"

"I'll manage," said Joseph, embarrassed that he didn't have a horse or a wagon.

"A one-hundred-pound bag of flour? You're going to carry it all the way home? That's nonsense." He turned around. "David, come out here."

Pete's son, David, entered from the back room. David and Joseph had said hello a couple of times in the past but never really talked. David was a little shorter than Joseph and much skinnier. He had brown hair and brown eyes and didn't look like Mr. Patterson much at all. David saw Joseph and raised his hand in greeting.

Pete waved his hand over to his son. "I need you to mind the store. I'm going to take a delivery to Joseph's house. I'll be gone a couple hours. Close the store down and help with dinner."

"Yes, sir."

Joseph nodded again and then walked into the storehouse behind the shop with Mr. Patterson. Pete found the flour and Joseph picked up a hundred-pound sack and followed the store owner out the back door. He waited for a few minutes, and then Pete arrived with the wagon. Pete helped Joseph load the flour and also a large sack of brown sugar and cornmeal along with the salt he had ordered. Soon they were headed down the road in the darkness lit only by a small lantern attached to the wagon.

Pete reached into his jacket and pulled out a brown paper package. He unwrapped the paper and pulled out some cooked bacon, handing some to Joseph.

"Please, sir, I couldn't."

"Eat up, boy," said Pete, kindness in his voice. "You look the death of cold and half starved to boot. What's going on over there at your place?"

"Nothing. Everything is fine."

"Fine my eye. It's a rudeness to lie to an elder, and a sin. Tell me the truth now."

"We've had a tough few months. There hasn't been much work and I wasn't able to save much up before winter set in. I thought we were going to make it but our cow died and I needed the milk money to pay the rent." He didn't know why he was telling Pete all of this.

"I heard about the cow." He looked shrewdly at Joseph. "What's your father doing about all this? It's not your job to keep the farm running, boy, it's his."

"He's . . . he's trying his best."

"Nonsense. He's doing nothing and what's more I'll wager he's drinking up the money you do make. I've seen some useless drunken Irish in my day boy, but your da wins the prize."

Joseph felt himself bristle. "Please don't say that about my da."

"That's the kindest thing I could say about him. But never mind. How do things sit with you now? From a money way I mean."

"I just used the last of it to buy that flour and salt. I've no money for rent this month. Don't worry, I'll go see Mr. Hastings. We'll work something out."

Pete spat into the darkness. "Oh, he'll work something out all right. That penny-pincher will work you to the bone at a third your value."

Joseph knew Pete was right, but what could he do? They rode along in silence for some time and eventually arrived at Robert's property. Pete turned up the lane and then jumped out to help Joseph unload the flour.

They brought the sack up to the porch along with the salt. Then Pete went back and pulled off the cornmeal and the sugar. "Take these too."

"I don't have any money for that, sir."

"You'll take it, boy. I insist. What's more, I'll expect you at my store first thing in the morning."

"What?"

"I've just hired you, boy. I'll pay your first month's wages to you in the morning. You can have the afternoon off to go pay that skinflint Hastings what he's due. After that I'll expect you at work each day."

Joseph was stunned. This was an answer to all his prayers. "You can't do that, Mr. Patterson. I'm not a charity case."

"You think I'm doing this for charity? You're the hardest worker around, Joseph. Everyone knows that. You might as well be paid a fair wage for it. Now go inside, get yourself a decent meal, and get to bed. They'll be plenty of work for you on the morrow."

Joseph stepped forward and shook Pete's hand, holding it for a moment with both of his. "Thank you so much, Mr. Patterson."

The storekeep looked back kindly for a moment and then smiled. "I told you, boy, it's Pete."

The following morning Joseph reported to work, arriving a half hour early. Pete, who was already inside stocking the shelves, greeted him. "Joseph boy, you're early." He could see that Pete was pleased. "The first thing I need to have you do each morning is check the back for new stock that's arrived. I usually get a shipment or two a week. We received a wagon load from Ogdensburg yesterday that needs unloading; you'll find David in the back."

Joseph walked back into the storage area and found a large pile of supplies. David was there already. He greeted David and was surprised to receive a grunt in reply. He watched Patterson's son for a few seconds but there was no further response, so he picked up a sack and went to work, bringing supplies into the store and then stacking the items where Pete directed.

In the early afternoon, Pete directed Joseph to load the wagon up with animal feed and a bundle of wire fencing. "You can take this to the Hastings property since you already need to go there. Make sure to have them inspect the goods and sign the receipt."

Joseph climbed up into the wagon and took the reins. Soon he was riding down the frozen dirt path. The sun had come out and although it was still very cold, the direct light felt wonderful. He felt so blessed by God for finding a way out of his troubles after such a difficult time.

Eventually he arrived at the Hastings'. Despite the snow, there were workers moving about on the property, shivering against the cold. As Joseph approached the house, he was surprised to see Lucy Hastings outside talking to one of the workers, an older woman who was sweeping the porch. The woman had set aside her broom and was holding a steaming mug of coffee between her hands.

"Good afternoon, Miss Lucy. Good afternoon ma'am."

He hadn't seen Lucy since he had paid off his debt. She had grown, even in those few months. She smiled up at him. "Good afternoon, Joseph. Why are you visiting our home?"

"I'm just paying the rent. What are you doing out in this cold?"

"This kind child was just bringing me something warm to drink," said the woman. "She's an angel on earth, I tell you."

Lucy giggled, turning red. "Joseph, when are you coming back to work here?"

"I'm working for Mr. Patterson now."

"That's too bad. We would love to have you here all the time."

Joseph smiled at Lucy. She was so kind. How could she be related to Oliver and, worse yet, Warren? She was too young to understand how difficult they were, what they were really like. *I pray she never learns it.* He smiled again and nodded, then turned away and went inside. He left his payment with the butler and then helped several of the workers unload the rest of the supplies. As he was preparing to leave, he saw Lucy again. She had brought him a cup of coffee and reached up to give it to him.

"Thank you, but I can't take that," he said. "I have to go, and I can't keep the cup."

"Just bring it next time you come," she said, blushing prettily. "That will give you a reason to hurry back."

He took the coffee and thanked her again, then flipped the reins and started the wagon moving. Such a kind girl.

He arrived back at the store as the sun was fading and twilight falling. He was freezing and took care of the horse and wagon as quickly as he could. When he finally returned to the store, David was the only one there.

"Where is Pete?"

"He's at the house preparing dinner."

"It's so cold out there," said Joseph, stamping his feet.

David grunted again. Joseph knew by reputation that Pete's son loved to laugh and was always joking. Something was wrong between them, but he didn't know what. He decided to confront him head on.

"Why don't you tell me what you are taking issue with?"

David looked up and hesitated before answering. "Nothing, I'm not taking issue with anything."

"Liar."

David's face reddened. "I'm no liar. I just don't understand something, that's all."

"What?"

"Why my pa hired you. He and I have handled this store for years. We didn't need someone else. Least ways we didn't need you. You come here, you Irish, and you take our jobs away."

Joseph felt his anger rising. He had been called names because he was Irish before, but he thought his hard work had earned him some respect in Macomb, except for people like Warren.

"I haven't taken anyone's job."

"Yes, you did. I asked pa about hiring Casey. He didn't answer me and the next thing I know he hires you instead. Casey is worth two of any mick."

Joseph had had enough. He stepped closer, standing a few inches from David's face. "You can complain all you want about Casey and the job, but you'll shut your mouth with the name-calling."

David shoved him and Joseph fell back, his frozen boots slipping on the wood floor. He hit his head hard and bright lights flashed. He rose to his feet and charged David, knocking him to the floor. The two rolled around on the hard ground, wrestling and beating each other.

"What in the name of God is going on in here?"

Pete shouted at them and then pulled Joseph off David. Joseph felt a numb pain under his eye and realized there was blood flowing down his face. David had a swollen cheek and a bloody lip.

"You, boy!" shouted Pete. "Get out of here. Get out of here right now."

"It's not my fault."

"I don't want to hear it. Get out!"

Joseph turned and walked dejectedly out of the store and into the darkness. Now things were worse. He had lost his job on the first day, and owed Mr. Patterson a full month's wages. Why couldn't he just keep his temper? Who cared what people called him; he knew who he was, and he should have known better than to let his temper get the best of him.

He arrived home after what seemed an eternity. His head ached. When he walked through the front door Charlotte gasped. "Joseph! What happened to you?"

He told her the terrible news. She brought him some snow wrapped in a cloth and held it to his face, her arm around him, holding him. "It will be all right," she said. "You'll take care of things. You'll take care of us. You always have." Fortunately, Robert was already asleep, probably from the drink. He couldn't face Robert's barbs tonight.

He heard a bang at the door. Charlotte answered and then called to Joseph. He turned. It was Pete and David. David was looking at the floor.

"Good evening, Charlotte, I'm sorry to disturb you. Joseph, I talked to David and he told me what happened. Well, *eventually* he told me. He has something to say to you."

David looked up for a second then back down again. "I'm sorry," he mumbled.

Pete grabbed him by the back of the hair and pulled his head up. "Do it proper, boy."

"I'm sorry."

"I'm sorry, too, Joseph. I didn't raise my boy to be a bigot. I had no idea he was mad about Casey. As if I'd hire that lazy ne'er-do-well. I hope you can forgive us, and I hope you'll be back to work tomorrow."

Joseph stared at David for a few moments. "Yes, I can forgive him. I understand about taking care of friends and family."

Charlotte smiled at him then invited Pete and David in out of the cold. She had made a pot of hot soup and the Pattersons stayed for dinner. David's mood improved with the soup and warm bread and soon they were all laughing and joking. Joseph came to work the next day as if nothing had ever happened.

CHAPTER 12

UNION MILITARY HOSPITAL CAMP NEAR THE JERUSALEM ROAD

SATURDAY, JANUARY 9, 1865

A shadowy figure crept into the darkness of the hospital tent. It was well past midnight and all was quiet except for the occasional moan of the wounded. The shadow passed through the rows of cots silently, pausing to look at each soldier as if searching for someone. Finally the figure found the right cot.

Doctor Johnston looked down at Joseph then quickly around again. No hospital staff was presently in the tent. He reached into his inner pocket and pulled out a bottle, slowly unscrewing the top. Thomas knelt and examined Joseph. The soldier's breathing was regular, but his forehead was hot with fever. The doctor peeled back his bandages. The wound was worse. Black streaks extended out like angry fingers from the center. A foul reek hit Thomas like a hammer, forcing his head away. He concentrated, willing himself to focus on the infection. He looked around again and then took the cap off the bottle, turning it over into a cloth in his hand until he felt the liquid spilling through. He applied it to the wound area, bathing the infections with the rag.

This technique was new and unproven. He had never seen it performed, only heard of it. He not only was cleaning the wound but also wiping away the "good" pus that, according to all science, was the only thing that would fight the infection. He hadn't discussed this action with anyone, including his commander. If he was caught he might well be dismissed. He was risking everything.

Why? Why was he putting his career, his future in jeopardy? For this soldier? He hadn't wanted to take the time to deal with Joseph in the first place. He had always thought it was hopeless to save him, and the infection merely confirmed his assessment.

No, he was doing this for Rebecca. Risking everything for her. He shook his head, trying to drive the thought from his mind.

He poured more of the liquid into the rag and continued bathing the wound. He was probably killing this patient. It didn't matter, he was dead already. *I've done my best for him, for her.*

She was so vulnerable. Even the first time he had met her she was fragile, broken. Yet within her pain and fragility she had such strength. She willed herself through her sorrow. She worked harder and with more determination than any nurse, any woman he had ever seen. He knew she often had left the hospital in tears, hurrying back to her tent, but she never displayed her emotions among the wounded or the staff.

They had worked like that, month after grueling month. He watched her from afar, his respect and admiration growing. *That's where it must stay*, he told himself. He had succeeded through his own considerable will. He kept his distance, showing her a mask of cold and cynical professionalism. He had watched her frustration and occasional anger. He felt badly, but he knew he had done the right thing.

Then disaster struck again. Rebecca received the news that her husband was dead. A husband gone to join their little girl. He watched her fall deeper into despair. His heart cried out to help her, but he knew he couldn't. If anything he became more distant. What else could he do?

Then came the night of the big battle. They were up to their arms in wounded. She had defied him by demanding they save Joseph. He had seen it in her eyes in an instant. She *needed* that. Not for Joseph, but for herself. He had given in and from that moment his resistance crumbled. Layer after layer fell away until he grasped desperately at the last barriers. He was losing his control. He knew it without a doubt. One step more and he would be gone.

He shook his head again, driving the thoughts from his mind. Plenty of time to think through those feelings. He poured the rest of the liquid directly into the wound, then patted the surface dry and replaced the bandages. He rose and snuck back out of the tent, returning to the darkness of the night.

◆ ◆ ◆

Rebecca knelt beside her cot in prayer. She begged for forgiveness. She felt hot guilt burning through her. Battling with her remorse was a glowing joy. *He cared for her.* She knew in her heart that's what he had meant. He didn't mean pity, he meant that he cared for her as a woman. She felt his hands on her again. She closed her eyes, pretending for a moment that they were alone together. She was in his arms; he was holding her tightly, kissing her, his strong hands drawing her to him.

Stop it, she commanded herself. *You are coveting him. What has happened to you? You are burying yourself in unforgiveable sin.* She thought of her husband again and hot tears flowed down her cheeks. She was losing control. She felt it, but she didn't know how she could stop herself from sinking into despair.

She began praying again, over and over. She pushed herself into the words and away from her thoughts. She had survived the loss of her daughter and husband and she would survive this.

She felt a tiny doubt. She may have misread everything in any event. The thought filled her with dread. What was she doing? She had lost focus again. *You will concentrate, Rebecca.* She resolved to remain awake all night in prayer. She would force all these thoughts from her mind and her heart. She was a child of God and she would never surrender. She arched her back with newfound resolution and launched into the Lord's Prayer. She repeated the words over and over, burning away the thoughts, burning away his touch. Soon she felt triumphant as the words gained power and she felt them deeply inside her. She rose at the dawn exhausted but with new strength.

CHAPTER 13

MACOMB, NEW YORK

MONDAY, AUGUST 13, 1860

Joseph hunched over the milking stool in the early morning, working his hands as he drew milk from one of his seven cows. He worked by lantern light in the predawn hours. He finished the task and carried the milk in a great jug back to the farmhouse, past the chickens and the pigs. Joseph looked up at the farmhouse with pride. Over the years, he had repaired and replaced the sagging roofline and painted the exterior. He had done the same to the barn and had slowly, agonizingly, built up the livestock on the farm. He now had dozens of eggs to sell each day, along with milk and pigs to slaughter for meat. He spent most of his daytime working on the farm now. After six years of hard labor, he still had been unable to save enough money to purchase a farm of his own, but he was well on his way. At night, he continued to help out at Mr. Patterson's store along with Pete's son, David. He also traveled to Morristown on Saturdays and put a full day in at the print shop.

He brought the milk into the house. He could smell breakfast already cooking. Charlotte was making eggs and bacon. There was fresh bread and a warm fire. The floor had been replaced the previous spring and Joseph had also found money to replace the kitchen table. Joseph's half sister, Jane, heard him come in and ran into his arms. Joseph hastily set down the jug and picked her up with both hands, twirling her around. She was nearly seven now with beautiful brown curls. She wore a new farm dress that Joseph had bought her at the market in July. He loved Jane like she was his own. Although he was gone long hours, he always tried to find time for her. She would sit on his lap, and he would read her stories out of his book collection. He spoiled her with candy and every year he bought her a doll out of the mail-order catalogue at Patterson's.

Charlotte watched them and smiled. Joseph smiled back. He was content. He had worked so hard and he was succeeding at building a life for his family. His muscles rippled beneath his work shirt as he lifted the milk jug up onto a shelf in the kitchen, and then he poured some coffee and took his seat at the table.

"What are you doing today?" Charlotte asked him.

"I'm going to deliver these eggs and some of the milk to the Bellingers and then I'm heading up to Pope's Mill to talk to Patterson and see if our grain delivery came in. Then I have to drop by the Hastings place and pay the rent."

"What a burden that we keep paying for nothing. Particularly lining the pocket of such a scoundrel. I'll never forgive him for what he did to you."

"That's water long under the bridge, dear. He's kept his word and allowed us to stay."

"Allowed us to stay? You've improved his property with your sweat and money. Of course he wants you to stay. You do twice the work of anyone else he has. You're a regular mule for him."

"I do what needs to be done for us, not for him. He doesn't own our livestock and he doesn't own our savings. When the time is right, I'll buy us our own piece of land. We're getting close."

"Getting close to what?"

Joseph looked up as Robert came in. His father had declined these past years. He had continued to drink no matter what Joseph and Charlotte said to him, or threatened, or begged him with. At some point they had stopped trying to make him stop. He claimed he would quit if he could only find a job, but he had hardly tried to look for employment for years. Most of the time, he lay in bed or sat at the kitchen table, talking to anyone who would listen about his glorious past in Ireland. At night, he often walked down to the tavern at Pope's Mill where he would sit with a group of Irishmen and sip whiskey until he fell to the floor or stumbled home. He didn't eat much anymore. He had become so thin. His face was ruddy with red veins mottling his nose and cheeks.

Joseph didn't know what to do about Robert. He knew from his own experience that there was work to be had if a person only put forth the effort. Still, his father was older and he was physically weak. It would be harder to find work in his father's condition. For the most part, he was harmless. He stayed out of the way and let Joseph take care of Charlotte and Jane. He would have loved his father's help, but he knew that was not going to happen, and he took great pride in caring for the family by his own effort and his effort alone.

"Well, boyo, what do you have planned today?"

Joseph repeated his plans to Robert.

"The Bellingers, there's a nasty lot. Old man Bellinger can't hold his tongue or his drink."

Joseph held *his* tongue. Tom Bellinger was a hardworking and respected member of Macomb. Robert had become bitter of late and had taken to insulting the other members of the township, often with wild statements that even he knew were not true.

Joseph finished his breakfast and brought the milk and eggs out to the porch. He walked to the barn and hitched up a wagon to his mule. His wagon was a great source of pride to him. Not everyone could afford their own working wagon. He had raised a small herd of beef cattle a few years back. When they were old enough, he sold them at market and used the money to buy his wagon brand-new. He kept it in perfect condition. He remembered the rickety wagon his father had owned in Ireland, the wheels wobbling and the bed chipped and full of splinters. He would never allow his wagon to fall into that condition.

He finished preparing the wagon, and brought it around and loaded up his goods. With a final hug for Charlotte and Jane, he jumped up onto the bench and soon he was on his way down the road toward Pope's Mill.

After delivering his goods to the Bellingers, he made his way farther up the road to Pope's Mill and stopped the wagon outside Patterson's. He walked into the store and received a warm welcome from Mr. Patterson. David was also present. David had grown to become Joseph's closest friend, as had David's first cousin Casey Ormsbee. All three were about the same age, though Casey was a couple of years younger, and often worked together on projects at their respective farms or joined together on side jobs when work was available.

"I see our confirmed bachelor has arrived," said David by way of greeting. "When are you going to marry and bring some hard-working Forsyths of your own into the world? You don't want to become an old maid after all."

Joseph laughed. He was constantly needled for not having married. He was almost twenty-three, well beyond the age that men married in Macomb. David had a wife and two young children, Isabelle and Grace, and Casey had married a young woman, Marie, from Morristown. They also had two daughters, Katherine and Lily.

"I've plenty of family to care for already, you know that. I don't need to add to my burdens."

"You'd have no burdens if things were in proper order," responded Pete.

Joseph grunted in return and then fell to silence. Robert's condition was a touchy subject that was rarely raised in Joseph's presence. He could see Mr. Patterson's face flush in embarrassment. Joseph changed the subject quickly.

"Where is Casey today? I thought he was going to come in and help us mend your fence?"

Casey lived on a quarter section of land farther up Black Lake. His father owned a small sawmill that Casey and his two older brothers helped run. He lived in a smaller house near the main house with his wife, their children, and his younger sister, Joy. He was the opposite of Joseph in every way. If there was a way out of work, then Casey Ormsbee would find it. He was also loud and always fooling around. Joseph loved him for all of it.

"It's a *surprise* that Casey is missing when work needs to be done," joked David.

"We will have to fix it without him. I have to get up to the Hastings place and pay the rent."

"Oh yes, your benevolent landlord. When are you going to buy that property you've always dreamed of?"

"Soon enough. I'm nearly there."

"As hard as you work, I'm surprised it's taken this long."

"Well, Irish labor comes at a discount in Macomb."

Joseph assisted David and Pete in repairing the white fence in front of their home in Macomb. The Pattersons had a fine old home on the outskirts of Pope's Mill, well maintained and elegant in its simplicity. Some of the individual pieces of their picket fence had rotted and needed to be removed and replaced. They pulled the boards out, sawed and sanded the replacement pieces, then nailed them into place. David would whitewash the replacement boards the following day.

Joseph bid his friends farewell and drove his wagon back down the road toward the Hastings property. He passed his own farm on the way, but didn't stop because the afternoon was already growing late.

After another half hour, he finally made his way to his landlord's farm and turned in on the long drive. The property had remained virtually unchanged in the past six years, except that the barn had been replaced with an even larger structure and there seemed to be more hands than ever on the property. Oliver Hastings had offered Joseph a job at the end of their agreement, but he had declined. He knew the measure of Mr. Hastings and wanted as little to do with him as possible.

Joseph walked up the stairs to the porch and rang the door. He was greeted by the butler (a new one as the previous butler had passed away a few years before), and he waited in the front entryway where he took a seat. He had his head down, looking at the carpet and thinking over some plans he had for the farm, when he heard a rustling sound. He looked up and saw Lucy.

Lucy Hastings was now eighteen years old. She was petite, with an elegant bearing that made her seem taller than she was. Her long, dark curls remained and tumbled down her shoulders and her back. Joseph hadn't seen her in years, as he paid his rent up front in six-month increments and so he rarely visited the property. He heard tales from his friends that Lucy was always the belle of the ball in their town's social circles, but he was stunned by Lucy's beauty in person.

"Good afternoon, Joseph," she said. Her voice was light and musical, and held a hint of amusement.

"How do you remember my name?"

"Everyone knows the famous Joseph Forsyth. The hardest worker in Macomb they say, with a father who's a dru—" She stopped herself, her face turning red.

"A drunk. No harm in saying it. He is what he is."

"I remember when you worked here too. I remember what my brother did to you. I remember . . ."

"That's old news and hardly news at that. Don't worry on it. I remember a certain little angel who snuck a delicious dinner into my jacket."

She blushed. "What brings you to our house, Mr. Forsyth?"

"I'm bringing your father's rent."

"That's right. You are still a tenant, aren't you? I'm surprised you would do business with my father at all."

Joseph didn't know how to answer that. He hesitated a moment, then changed the subject. "So what is Lucy Hastings up to?"

"Not much of anything except fighting off mindless young boys with their ridiculous babble trying to win my heart, and everything that goes with it."

"Yes . . . well I don't have much experience with that sort of thing."

She laughed. "I've heard that too. Serious Joseph Forsyth taking care of his father's problems with never a time for himself."

"I have to take care of my family. Who would do less?"

"Many would do less."

"So which of these ridiculous boys will you pick?"

They were interrupted by a house servant.

"Mr. Forsyth. I understand you have Mr. Hastings's payment. I am to take it."

"Yes, I do." Joseph handed him an envelope stuffed with bills.

"Thank you." The servant turned and left the room, a curious look on his face as he kept an eye on Lucy.

Joseph turned back to Lucy. "Well, my business here is done. It was a pleasure to see you again."

"You asked which boy I will pick. The answer is none of them. I want a man, not a boy." She looked in his eyes boldly when she said it, her gaze brimming with amusement. Women were a mystery to Joseph, except for Charlotte, who was a second mother to him. He felt himself blush. What was she trying to say?

"What man would that be then?" he heard himself ask.

"Well, he will have to wait for that." She smiled again and walked out of the room.

Joseph left the Hastings property and drove his wagon slowly home. He tried to consider his plans for the farm again, but his thoughts kept flitting back to a beautiful young woman with mystery in her eyes.

The following week, Joseph was working in the evening at Patterson's when he heard a familiar voice.

"Well look, it's Joseph Forsyth again."

He flushed. Lucy Hastings had come into the store. He had never seen her at Patterson's before. What was she doing here?

"Can I help you?"

She smiled that devastating smile she had. He felt that strange confusion welling up again. He tried to control every situation, to keep his head down and work his way through any problem that came his way. Only he couldn't work his way through Lucy.

"Oh yes, you can definitely help me, Joseph Forsyth. Let me see, what is it I was looking for today? I can't precisely remember." She wore pink silk gloves over her delicate hands and she walked slowly down the aisle, gently gliding her fingers over the various products. She turned and looked him in the eyes again.

"That's right. Now I remember. I'm looking for a real man."

What did she just say? He had never been more uncertain in his life. What did she want from him? He heard a chuckle and he knew Mr. Patterson, who was tending the counter, had heard her. He flushed even more.

"You said that the other day when I saw you. I don't know what you mean, but I don't think I can help you. Is there something from the store you would like?"

"Oh, I think you know exactly what I mean, Mr. Forsyth. I told you before I don't want one of these young, useless boys who have come courting. I want a real man. A hardworking man. In other words, I want you."

"What are you speaking of? You don't know me. You don't know anything about me. Your father and your brother would kill me or destroy me for even talking to you. You're playing a young girl's game with me and I don't have time for it." He turned away and went to the front of the store. He was upset and growing angry. He didn't even know why. He saw Mr. Patterson pretending to clean the counter with a rag. Pete was barely containing his laughter.

"All right, Joseph. You can ignore me today if you wish. But I won't go away. I know what I want and I'm going to get it."

She left the store as quickly as she had arrived.

"That's quite a woman right there, that is," said Patterson.

"She's a child. She's playing a game with one of her father's old toys. She'll tire of it soon enough. I doubt she'll even come back again."

But she did come back, every day. Each night Joseph worked, she would be at the store, teasing and taunting him. He tried his best to forbid her from the store, but Mr. Patterson and even David would have none of it. They took to making a big deal each time she came to visit, and they mercilessly teased Joseph when she was away, calling her "Mrs. Forsyth." Even his family caught word of it as the rumors flew around the small community. He felt he was the laughingstock of Macomb and he only hoped she would grow tired of her game soon and put an end to it.

After a couple of weeks, she did not show up one night. Joseph was relieved, or so he thought at first. Then he was surprised to find he was a little disappointed. He realized he missed her, and that in some small way, he actually enjoyed her visits. Why hadn't she come to see him? Where was she? Had she already found someone else to shower her attention on?

He was surprised to find a new emotion growing: jealousy. He couldn't believe it. Jealous of what? They had nothing between them. They would never have anything. She was a stupid, spoiled, girl playing a stupid game, and she had somehow managed to turn his world upside down. He had plans for his life, plans that he had worked so hard for. She was pulling him away from them. He couldn't allow any more of this foolishness. If she stopped coming, that would be just fine. If she appeared again, he would give her a piece of his mind. It was time to stop this little charade.

She didn't appear for a week. He was satisfied that she was finally done with him. Even the Pattersons were slowing down on their teasing comments. Then one night, she appeared again. Joseph noticed she was a little paler than usual.

"I thought you had given up on me, Miss Hastings."

"Oh no, Joseph Forsyth. You won't get away from me. I've been ill, quite ill. The doctor thought I might not make it."

Joseph was alarmed. She had almost died? He hadn't even heard. He hadn't gone to see her. What was he thinking? Go and see her? What on earth was going on in his mind? He hated all this confusion and all these emotions. He had to put an end to it.

"I'm glad you have recovered. I have meant to have a word with you."

"A word about what?" she asked, taking a teasing and innocent tone.

"A word about your . . . visits."

"Yes? What about my visits?"

"I know you've been enjoying yourself at my expense. I need all of this to stop. You are a young woman from a respected family. It's not proper for you to visit me. Look what happened to you! All of this frolicking about the county and you took ill. It isn't proper. I couldn't . . ."

"You couldn't what, Joseph Forsyth?" Her eyes danced.

He ignored the question. "Also, you are interfering with my work. I have much to do and all of this has become . . ."

"Distracting?" she asked. "So you have been thinking of me, Joseph Forsyth. Don't pretend you haven't."

"I . . . It doesn't matter what I've been thinking. This has to end. It's not proper. I must ask you to stay away."

She laughed. "I'm not going to stay away, Joseph Forsyth. I'm going to marry you. Didn't you know that?"

Marry him? What was she talking about? She was looking at him, laughter in her eyes. Who was this girl to say such things to him? He felt his heart wrench; his head was dizzy. He was losing control.

"Enough of this!" he shouted at her. "Enough, Lucy! You are playing a game with me. I can't stand it. I need you to leave me alone. You need to leave. You need to leave now!"

She stepped forward and she kissed him. He stepped back in surprise, but she put her arms around him, pulling him closer and pressing her lips against his. He had never kissed anyone in his life. Her lips were warm and she smelled like flowers in the spring. He tried to fight for a moment more, then he threw his arms around her, pulling her even closer.

He loved her. The thought flew through his mind and hit home hard. *He loved her.* When had that happened? He loved her and he wanted her and he had to have her. He felt the world around him spinning. Everything had changed in a moment. Everything had changed for good. The center of his life had shifted and was now focused on this trembling young woman in his arms. He lifted her up and twirled her around. She laughed and held tight to him, her face buried in his neck.

"I love you," he whispered. "I love you, Lucy Hastings."

He set her down and she looked up, laughing again. "I know that, silly. It's about time you admitted it to yourself."

"What will the town say? What will your father say?"

"I don't care what Macomb says and my father will do what I want him to do. He's as wrapped around my finger as you're going to be."

"We have to tell him. I have to have permission to court you."

"You're right as always, Joseph Forsyth. Come to my house on Sunday after church. You can talk to my father then. He won't be happy, but he will come around. Besides, it's my brother you should worry about. Or have you forgotten?" She reached up and kissed him again, then she turned, giggling, and walked out of the store.

He heard more laughing. Mr. Patterson was at the counter. He had seen the whole thing.

"Well lo and behold, the love bug has finally bitten young Joseph Forsyth. I didn't think such a thing would happen in my lifetime."

Joseph felt sheepish. He shrugged and nodded in embarrassment.

"Oh, my boy, you are going to create a scandal that will keep tongues wagging in Macomb for years to come. A poor Irish immigrant courting a Hastings girl. Oh how the gossip will fly."

He didn't respond. Pete was right. Lucy was far above his station. He remembered Oliver bragging at the harvest festival about his family tracing their roots all the way back to the Mayflower. They were an old family in America and he was the newest and most hated kind. He didn't care. He wanted this girl like he had never wanted anything. He would win her as he did everything, with hard work and by never giving up. He had time to consider things before Sunday. He would convince Oliver Hastings no matter what it took. But a nagging uncertainty lurked in his mind. *Besides, it's my brother you should worry about. Or have you forgotten?* He had never forgotten Warren Hastings. He never would.

On Sunday, Joseph attended church with Charlotte and Jane at the Methodist Episcopal Church in Pope's Mill, which met in the local schoolhouse. He was nervous throughout and couldn't focus on the prayers or the sermon. Today was one of the most significant days in his life. He had faced so many challenges along the way, but somehow, this one seemed almost insurmountable. Perhaps it was because he wanted this more than he had ever wanted anything.

How had this happened so fast? And for a young woman he hardly knew. He didn't know how, but he felt more alive than he had ever felt. He wanted to have this woman, to build a life with her. To build a family and add them to his circle of protection. He could imagine Charlotte and Jane playing with his own children, all the family spending time together while he worked and took care of them. He smiled. A real future. Something he had only dreamed about.

Church finally ended and he took the family back to the farm, laughing away with Charlotte about her stories of her school years, although he wasn't really listening very well. As he dropped them off at the farm, Charlotte hugged him and gave his arms a squeeze.

"I'm so happy, Joseph, and I wish you the best of luck. You deserve happiness."

"What about you, Charlotte? What about your happiness?"

He saw sadness pass through her eyes. "Joseph you've given me everything a son could ever give. You've been a brother and more to Jane. You've given us a home and food, protection from the world. What more could I want?"

"How about a husband? A real husband."

"Oh, Joseph, of course I would love that. But I made my bed. I thought Robert was more than he is. I am grateful that he gave me a beautiful daughter and that I've been blessed with a wonderful son. There are many in this world who do far worse." She reached up and kissed him on the cheek. "Thank you, Joseph. Thank you so much. You have given us happiness. Now go find some of your own."

Joseph stepped back up into the wagon and was soon on his way toward the Hastings property. He had traveled this road thousands of times, but today, it seemed to take forever. Finally, he saw it in the distance and he gradually made his way through the entrance and up the drive.

He stepped down from the wagon and dusted himself off. He wore his best Sunday clothes, although even his best was of poor quality compared to what the Hastings family could afford. No matter. He made his way up the stairs and knocked on the door. How different this visit to the Hastings house was from all his other trips here.

The door opened and he explained that he needed to see Mr. Hastings. When asked why, he said he needed to talk to him about Lucy. The surprised butler hurried off a bit uncertainly. Joseph stood in the familiar entryway. His clothes felt hot. His heart was pounding in his chest and his hands were clammy. Soon the butler returned and led him down the familiar hallway to the library.

Oliver Hastings was standing behind his desk, arms folded. He was by himself and his eyes searched Joseph as he came in. Joseph felt slightly amused. *Finally, I have surprised Mr. Hastings.*

"Hello, Joseph."

"Hello, Mr. Hastings."

"My butler told me you wanted to see me. He said it was about Lucy. I assume he was mistaken."

"No, sir."

"What possible business could you have with Lucy?"

"Yes, I'd like to know that as well!" Joseph heard the familiar voice of Warren and turned to watch him storm through the door, his face beet red. He marched over past Joseph to stand with his father, eyes blazing.

This was the moment. It was probably best that Warren was here as well. He had to tell them and better to get it all done in one go-around.

"I'm in love with your daughter. I seek your permission to court her with a purpose to marry."

"What in the hell!" shouted Warren. "You little mick bastard! I'll kill you right now!" Warren started forward but Oliver restrained him.

"Shut your mouth, boy. I'm the master here and she's my daughter, not yours." He turned to Joseph. "Explain yourself and do it quickly."

"Sir, I saw your daughter when I last came here to deliver the rent. Since that time, she, of her own accord, has visited Mr. Patterson's store where I work. I did not encourage this, and in fact, I discouraged her, but she wouldn't have it. She has told me she loves me and I love her too. I know you will be very unhappy about this, but I want to court her. I'm seeking your permission, sir."

Joseph could see Oliver's face reddening with anger. "What do you mean she's been going to see you! She told me she was visiting her friends in town. Where is the damned driver! I'll have his head! How dare you see my daughter without my permission!"

"Sir, I told you she came to me, not the other way around. I had no choice in the matter. I want to assure you that these meetings were always in public and always proper. Still, I have found I have feelings for her. I know I'm not what you would consider an appropriate match for Lucy, but you have worked with me. You know the measure of me as a man. I have saved up money and am ready to purchase property. I have livestock and a trade. I have taken care of my father's family this many years with no help from anyone. I will give Lucy a good life."

"You won't touch my sister, you son of a bitch!" Warren charged across the room and flung himself on Joseph. They grappled for a few moments and then Joseph threw Warren to the ground and lay on top of him, holding him down with both hands.

"Enough! I told you to keep your calm, Warren. Joseph, release him!"

Joseph felt Warren stop struggling beneath him. He let up and Warren rolled away and pulled himself to his feet. He looked barely able to contain himself, but under his father's glare, he walked back slowly behind the desk.

Oliver Hastings didn't speak for long moments. He was looking at Joseph thoughtfully. Finally, he responded.

"I can't say I didn't think I could be more surprised. I don't know what's going on, but I'm going to get to the bottom of it. I want you to wait in the entryway. I'll speak to Lucy and find out if what you are telling me is true. From there, I'll decide what I will do about this." He rang a bell and soon the butler returned and escorted Joseph back to the entryway.

In a few minutes, he saw Lucy come down the stairs. Her face was pale but her eyes brimmed with happiness when she saw Joseph. She wasn't able to stay and speak with him, but she flashed him a smile on the way by. Soon, Joseph could hear shouting down the hallway, and he knew Oliver had learned that what he told him was true.

The shouting went on for some time and then finally subsided. Hours seemed to pass as Joseph sat nervously, waiting for an answer. After what seemed an eternity, he finally saw Lucy coming down the hallway, led by the butler. She was even paler and her eyes were red from crying. She glanced at Joseph for a moment and then she was led up the stairway without saying a word. The butler soon returned and instructed Joseph to follow him.

They were back in the library. Mr. Hastings was now sitting behind the desk with Warren behind him. It reminded Joseph so much of the first time he had ever set foot in here as the sixteen-year-old son of an Irish immigrant drunk. The memory made him feel small and vulnerable. He tried to gather his inner strength. No matter what was said here today, he would not give up.

"Well, Joseph, I've talked to Lucy. Today is a day of surprises for me. She tells me that you speak the truth. She did go to see you without my knowledge. She does love you. She does want you to court her. Now what am I supposed to do with you? That's the question."

"I know what you're going to say. I want you to know, Mr. Hastings, that I will not give up. If it takes years, I will come and I will ask you again and again. I will do whatever it takes to prove to you that I am worthy. So long as Lucy wants me, then I will persist."

Oliver chuckled. "Yes, I know that about you, Joseph. Everyone knows that. I saw it all those months you worked for me. I've never seen anyone work harder than you.

"I had nothing when I came here to New York. Did you know that? Oh sure, my family can be traced back to the Mayflower, but my direct line was always the second son, not the first. My family has moved from Massachusetts to Vermont to this bit of nowhere in New York because we didn't inherit the land or money of our fathers. I came here with a little money and nothing else. I built this farm up bit by bit with my own sweat. I bought other lands. I invested in the mine and the mill. I am who I am today by my own hard work. Yes, Joseph, I know what a hard worker looks like when I see him. I know what it feels like to be a new family in this town. Not one of the founders. You have my permission to court Lucy. You may begin immediately."

"What!" shouted Warren. "Have you gone mad, Father? This bastard will never touch my sister! You would let an Irish pig in our family? I won't stand for it!"

Oliver rose from his desk, angrier than Joseph had ever seen him. "You'll stand for it and more! Don't ever raise your voice to me again, you worthless pile of manure! I raised you to be a Hastings. What did you become? Drinking and womanizing with your friends. Riding around for sport on the farm when you should have been working! Terrorizing the workers and playing your games with them until they hated us all! I've had enough of it! I've made arrangements with Phinneas Ericks in Morristown for you to live with him. He is a lawyer. You will read law with him at my expense. You will stay there until you have a trade and until you have proven your worth. I am done giving you everything. It is time to earn your keep in this world!"

"Father, you don't mean it. I . . . I spoke in anger and in haste. Don't send me away."

"It's for your own good, boy. Now I need to speak to Joseph alone. You are dismissed."

Warren tried to start again, but Oliver raised his hand and cut him off. Warren turned and started to walk out of the room. He paused in front of Joseph.

"This isn't over, you mick bastard. I'm not done with you by a far piece." He turned and bowed to his father and then stormed out of the library.

Oliver turned back to Joseph. "My apologies for my son. He is a weak man. So as I said before, Joseph, what am I to do with you?"

"You said I may court Lucy."

"Ah yes, Lucy. You may court Lucy if you agree to my conditions. How much money have you saved to purchase property here in Macomb?"

"About two thousand dollars."

"Excellent. You will pay me that amount and I will sell you your farm."

"What farm? Do you mean the farm I'm on? I hadn't intended to buy it."

"If you want to court Lucy, then you will buy *that farm.* And to pay off the rest of the land, you will come to work for me as my general foreman. I need a man of your integrity and work ethic. What's more, the other workers will respect you. You are one of them. You must come to work for me for four years. That way I can keep an eye on you and make sure you are taking care of my daughter in the manner she's accustomed to. I will pay you a fair wage. You will work as hard for me as you have for yourself. When the four years are up, you may do as you wish. You will own the property free and clear and you should have a good savings as well."

"And your farm will be more productive than ever," observed Joseph.

"I don't get nothing for nothing. That's my bargain. Are we agreed?"

Joseph considered it. He wanted Lucy more than anything. There was nothing wrong with the farm he lived on, but he had wanted to get out from under Hastings's thumb, and now he would be under it in every possible way. He was tired of living his life under everyone else's control. But what choice did he have? If he agreed, he would have his land and he could take care of his father and his family. He could start his own family with Lucy. He would have the woman of his dreams.

"Agreed."

"Smart, Joseph, smart. You've always been smart and you've always been good for your word. You have my blessing to court my daughter, and when the time is right, you may marry her." Oliver stood and crossed the carpet to Joseph. He extended his hand. They shook hands and the deal was struck. Joseph had what he wanted, but as with every part of his life, he had years to pay for it.

Oliver left Joseph in the library. A few minutes later, he heard rapid steps and Lucy came flying into the room. She ran into Joseph's arms and held him tightly, kissing his neck and lips. He held her just as tightly, forgetting Warren, forgetting Oliver and the agreement. He had Lucy. She was his forever. He held her in his arms, loving her, holding her. He would protect her and take care of her. They would have children and a life together. A life on their own land. A life his mother and father had never known. He would give this life to Robert's family too. He would provide for them all.

CHAPTER 14

The Hastings Property

Macomb, New York

Saturday, April 13, 1861

Joseph rode through the southern fields at the extreme end of the Hastings property. He was testing the soil with a long, iron rod. The ground was still too hard. The first six inches would give, but beneath that the ground was still frozen. A few more days of sun and rain, and the fields would be ready to be plowed. As he rode, he stopped to talk briefly with the field hands, making sure that they had food and water and all of the tools they needed. He also checked that they were working diligently, although he rarely found anyone shirking. Joseph led by example, and he knew and was proud that the hands respected and even loved him.

Joseph smiled. He had accomplished so much in one year. Since his engagement, Joseph had worked harder than ever. He was a married man now with a baby on the way. The summer before he and Lucy had married, he had built a new house on the farm, *his farm*. The new house was only one story but was the perfect starting home for Lucy and him.

He rode back slowly to the Hastings house and ate dinner with Oliver, going through the day's findings and discussing timetables for the plowing and planting season. Since Joseph had taken over, productivity and crop yields had increased by twenty percent. Oliver was very pleased.

"Are you and Lucy coming for dinner on Sunday night?" asked Oliver.

"Yes, I think so, so long as she's feeling up to it."

Lucy was three months pregnant and had severe morning sickness. She found traveling difficult. During the day, she stayed at the main farmhouse, and Charlotte, who had grown close to Lucy, took care of her.

"What do you think of the news?" asked Joseph. There was only one item of *news* these days, the election of Abraham Lincoln and the rapid secession of a number of the southern states in response.

"I assume they'll get it all sorted out in the end. The southern states need our manufactured goods and our commerce. There hasn't been any fighting so far, and I'd think there would have been by now if they were truly at it. I do wish they would be done with it though and stop these games. It's bad for business."

"What do you think of this Lincoln character?"

"Tall and ugly so they say," joked Oliver. "Well, that's stating the obvious though. I don't know quite what to make of him or why he has the southerners' dander up so much. There's been plenty of northern presidents after all. It's this damned new party. If the Republicans would just keep their mouths shut, particularly about slavery, the whole situation would sort itself out.

"Even with that said, I don't know why they hate Lincoln so much. You'd think they'd be happy to have a westerner and not a Yankee for a president. The West depends on the Mississippi and Missouri and that means depending on the South."

"Perhaps they are worried about the slaves then?"

"Bah! He's said he wants nothing to do with the slaves. I don't understand their dependence on slaves in the first place. I can hardly get work out of my hands and we're paying them. I can't imagine a man working productively for free."

"Well, whatever the reason, it seems we're in a fine pickle. If it comes to fighting, how do you figure it affects Macomb, sir?"

"It will affect us plenty, Joseph. Every fool boy your age and younger will want to sign up to fight. Short or long, they will be gone for months or more. That will mean labor costs will go up across the board. We can try to pass those costs on at market, but I don't know if that will work or not. People can only stretch their wallets so much. Eventually, they have to make do with less. We will face lean times I wager." He turned to Joseph with shrewd eyes. "Now tell me for certain, Joseph, that you won't be tempted to join."

Joseph had already thought long and hard on the subject. "No, I can't join. I have a wife and a child on the way. I have my farm and my folks and my sister to take care of. Too many eggs in the basket for me to leave behind."

"You're forgetting your commitment to me. Four years, Joseph."

"I haven't forgotten and that's part of my calculation as well. I don't break my word."

"Wise man you always were, Joseph. You've always been the same as me. Pity you weren't my son."

Joseph didn't respond to that but merely nodded. He couldn't disagree more. Oliver and he were nothing alike. Oliver was a businessman first and foremost. Every decision he made was calculated to his own profit, no matter the effect on others. Joseph depended on his own hard work and on the respect of others, rather than their fear. He changed the subject.

"Speaking of sons, what news of Warren?"

Oliver laughed. "I'm sure you're very concerned about your brother-in-law. I've had very little word from Warren, just a terse letter or two.

Phinneas has written me and told me that Warren is progressing well. He's a bright boy, always knew he was. He just needed to grow up. I'd like to hear from him more, but that will come in time. Eventually, he'll realize I did him the best favor I could ever have provided him. I gave him the gift of his freedom and a requirement to take care of things by his own hard work. A man needs that. He will thank me someday."

"Wouldn't it do you both good to reach out to him a little more? Go visit him?"

"Warren's not like you. There's a hole in his heart that will take time to fill. He thinks the world owes him a living. No, Joseph, if anything, I'll have to wait for him to come back to me."

They completed their business and Joseph left the house well after dark. He saddled his horse (a wedding gift from Oliver) and rode the twenty-minute trip back to his own farm. The night air was still quite cold and he wore gloves and a heavy jacket to guard against the chill. Soon he was home, and after tending to his horse, he opened the door to the main house to greet his family.

Lucy and Charlotte were standing in the kitchen, cleaning the dishes from supper. Jane was sitting at the table playing with her dolls. She saw Joseph and came running up to hug him.

"Joseph, come over and have tea with me," she demanded. "Tina and Lisa have waited for you here all day, and you never came over to visit!"

Joseph smiled and laughed. "How inconsiderate of me, Jane. I must apologize to your dolls for my bad behavior. Give me a few minutes and I'll join you."

Joseph walked over and kissed both Lucy and Charlotte on the cheek. "Where's Father?"

"He's up at the tavern I'm sure. We haven't seen him all afternoon," said Charlotte.

Joseph grunted. "Another day of hard labor I see."

"Now, Joseph, don't start . . ."

"I know, I know. I gave up on Father a long time ago. But I can always hope." He turned to Lucy. "How are you today, my dear?"

"The same as yesterday and every day it seems since this baby started growing inside me. Charlotte does her best to take care of me, Joseph, but it's hard business. It would be nice if we had a more comfortable chair for me. And even better a nurse to help me."

"Lucy, dear, we've been through this. I can't afford to hire a nurse for you. I'm sorry."

"Couldn't we go live with Daddy again for a while then? Just until the baby comes? Joseph, you don't know how difficult it is. Charlotte has done a wonderful job here, but she has so much to do. If we stayed at Daddy's, then there would be people to take care of me and you would be that much closer to me every day. We could have lunch together. I could watch you work in the fields."

They had been through this discussion at least a dozen times already, although this was the first time that Lucy had brought it up in front of Charlotte. Usually, she only complained in private. Joseph couldn't agree to move. He was afraid if he did, he would never be able to leave Hastings's house again. "I told you, dear, we have a nice place here and Charlotte is doing as much work as a real nurse would anyway."

She switched tracks quickly. "What about the chair? Do you remember the one I showed you from Patterson's catalogue?"

He remembered the chair. It was a handmade, overstuffed chair from one of the most expensive manufacturers in New York City. The cost was equivalent to two months' salary. "That chair is very expensive too, dear. That's why I made you a nice chair to sit in. Isn't it comfortable enough for you? I know how to make you more comfortable." He stepped forward and put his arms around her. She pulled back and turned away, pouting.

"I just want a few nice things, Joseph. I gave up the big house and everything I had for you. Don't you want to take care of me?"

Joseph sighed. They had been through this so many times. "Of course I want to take care of you, my dear. Isn't that what I do every day? Isn't that why I work so hard? I tell you what. I have a bonus coming up at harvest time. If there is enough, I will buy you that chair."

"Oh, Joseph!" She threw her arms around him and kissed him. "You *do* always take such good care of me!"

"Quit all yer hugging and carrying on!" said Robert. Joseph turned to see his father coming through the front door, obviously very drunk. "I've got big news, boyo. There's a war on now."

"What do you mean?" asked Charlotte.

"A telegram arrived tonight. Those southern bastards fired on one of our forts down there. Hundreds killed they say. Now there'll be hell to pay. Joseph, you have to go give them a lesson."

"I won't be joining up, Father. I have too much to take care of here."

Robert looked up with surprise in his glazed-over eyes. "You'll join, boy. No boy of mine will be a coward. You won't be hiding behind the women's skirts. I'd go myself if I wasn't too ill."

"You're drunk. Go to bed and sleep it off. We'll talk in the morning."

Robert stepped forward with fists clenched. "Don't you give me any lip, boyo. I'm still young enough to tan your hide. What do you mean you're too busy here? All you do is run off to your wife's land all day long while I stay here and keep an eye on things. Look at this house. Look at this poor farm. If any of you had listened to me and we'd done things my way, we would have a proper life by now. Now you won't even fight like a proper man. You're a disappointment to me, Joseph, and make no mistake."

Joseph exploded. "How dare you call me a disappointment! I've done everything for you! When I came here, you had no job, you were behind in rent, you were a drunk, and your wife and baby were starving! I worked long months for free to pay your debts! I've taken care of you and your family for years now, all with my blood and sweat! I've sacrificed everything for you and you dare to challenge me now? You bastard!"

"I didn't ask any of that from you, Joseph. If you can't step up and care for your family in hard times without putting on airs, then I guess we've worn out our welcome. We'll be gone in the morning." Robert stumbled past Joseph to the bedroom and slammed the door.

Lucy stood in shock, not speaking. Charlotte came over to Joseph and put her arms on his shoulders. "I'm so sorry, Joseph. He didn't mean those things. He has a lot of pride. It's hard for him to accept charity from others, even from you."

"Do you realize how much I've given up for him, for you? Everything I've done since I came here was for you. And now he spits in my face?"

"I'm sorry. I'm truly sorry. He's drunk and he doesn't know what he's saying. He'll apologize in the morning. He will feel terrible about what he said tonight. He won't even remember it. He loves you, dear, you know that. He's so proud of you even if he has a hard time saying it. Go home, Joseph. Go home and things will be better in the morning. I love you, dear. We all do."

Joseph hugged her and hugged Jane. He left with Lucy across the yard to their own home. In bed later, he lay awake long into the night, tears running silently down his face.

The next morning, Joseph rose early and rode into Pope's Mill to find out the news. He arrived at Patterson's store and found it filled with locals buzzing with gossip. He was greeted by a number of people as he came in, and he had some difficulty making it to the front to find Pete and David.

"Joseph, can you believe it?" asked David. "A war! A real war. We received another telegram today. They are calling for volunteers. We are going to go down and whip them good!"

"*They* might be going down, but *you* won't be," said Pete. "Not with a store to mind and kids to care for. You'll be staying here and taking care of business, as I'm sure Joseph will be too."

Joseph nodded. "Where's Casey? His head's always been filled with romantic nonsense of going off to battle. We better talk to him or he will be joining, responsibilities or no."

"I haven't seen him today," said David. "Maybe we should ride out to his place and find him."

"No need," said Pete. "He's walking through the door right now."

Casey came scrambling through the crowd, elbowing people out of his way in his excitement. Joseph smiled. Casey loved adventure, or at least the idea of adventure. They would have their work cut out talking him out of it.

"Did you hear? Did you hear, boys? It's war! It's war! Let's all join up together. We'll whip 'em good and be back for harvest!" There were cheers from the crowd. Casey was beloved in Macomb, as loved for his lazy but gregarious good nature as Joseph was for his quiet, hard work.

"Now, now, Casey, let's not lose our heads," said Pete. "They might be asking for volunteers down in Washington but they haven't asked for them here, although I don't doubt they will soon."

"When they do, we will all join together! What do you say?"

David was silent. He was never the strongest of the three, and without Joseph, he probably would have followed Casey, regardless of Pete's concern.

Joseph walked over to his friend and put his arm over his shoulder. "We won't be joining, Casey, and neither will you. We all have farms and family. We're not young bucks anymore, full of piss and vinegar and without a worry in the world. Someone has to stay home and take care of things while the boys go out to battle. There's plenty who will join, don't you worry."

Casey pulled out from under Joseph's arm and took a step back. "We are young men, Joseph, least ways David and I are. You were an old man when you moved here, in mind if not in body. We can't let a bunch of our friends go off to glory while we stay here in safety. What would people think of us? We would miss everything!" There was a murmuring of agreement from the crowd.

"I won't go and I don't believe anyone with a family should consider going. We have responsibilities to our children, our farms, our town."

"You're a coward is what you're saying," replied Casey.

The store was silent. Joseph was shocked. His father's drunken words echoed in his ears. "You don't mean that, Casey. I'm no coward."

"Casey, don't say any more," warned David. But his cousin ignored him.

"If you refuse to join, if you stay here and let others fight for you, then I call you coward, Joseph Forsyth. I never thought I would say that to you but I do. You've given your soul to Oliver Hastings. All you care about now is profit and land and livestock. You have become a greedy coward."

Joseph lunged forward and struck Casey across the face. Casey fell backward hard, hitting the ground. Blood spurted from his nose. He covered it with his hand and tried to rise.

Joseph looked out at the gathered crowd. "Is that how it is? Does anyone else call me a coward? Does anyone else call me a money-grubber? I have worked hard in this town for years now. I've never asked for anything from anyone else. I've only asked to be allowed to work hard and take care of my family. Now my family needs me more than ever. I have a child on the way and two families to care for. Is that a coward?" Nobody answered. The room was dead silent. Finally, Pete Patterson stepped around the counter and put his hand on Joseph's back.

"Nobody is calling you a coward, Joseph. Nobody doubts your worth. Young Casey just has his blood up. For those who join the cause, we will all respect them and wish them well, but there are many with responsibilities who will need to remain behind."

Joseph felt terrible. Casey was one of his closest friends, but he was out of line. Casey would be a fool to join up. He would be leaving his children and his wife behind. Still, it was his choice. Joseph reached down to help Casey up. His friend shrugged off his hand and refused to look at him. Joseph stepped back and Casey eventually stood up and stormed out of the store, refusing to look back.

"Don't worry, Joseph. He'll apologize when his blood cools," said Pete. "You've shown common sense today. Something that's missing from many minds right now." Pete looked meaningfully at David.

"As for you, son of mine, you will follow Joseph in this, do you understand me? Would you leave your wife and kids to go off and get yourself killed? Who would take care of them after that happened? We've plenty of young men to take this responsibility. You will remain behind and take care of business here."

David looked at his father and then back at Joseph. The disappointment was clear in his eyes. "Yes, Father. I know you're right, but it doesn't feel too good. I want to go on this adventure."

"It's no adventure, boy. It's days of endless marching with death waiting at the end. There will be plenty of death for everyone soon. I want you home and I want you safe."

The door to the store crashed open with a loud bang. A dusty youth came in, out of breath. It was Brandon Honeycomb, Joseph's neighbor. He looked around frantically and finally spotted Joseph.

"You have to come with me right now!"

"What's wrong?"

"It's Lucy."

Joseph ran out the door and mounted his horse, taking off at a gallop and following Honeycomb. He could barely keep up and his eyes burned from the dust kicked up in front of him.

He made it home in just a few minutes and he jumped down, quickly tying his horse off and running into Robert's house where Lucy was staying during the day. He could see the fear in Charlotte's eyes the moment he came in. Even Robert was pacing back and forth. Charlotte ran into Joseph's arms.

"What's wrong?"

"It's the baby! Doctor Pierce is with her right now. She collapsed about an hour ago. She was bleeding. Oh, Joseph! There was so much blood and I couldn't stop it. I sent Jane next door to get Brandon. He went and found the doctor. Thank God he was home! Thank God Doctor Pierce was home."

Joseph rushed past her into his father's bedroom. Doctor Pierce was sitting at Lucy's side. He was wiping her forehead with a wet cloth. She was unconscious. Her body was rocking back and forth and she moaned in pain. A towel lay on the floor, covered in blood. The doctor looked up when Joseph entered and their eyes met. Joseph knew the news was terrible.

"Is she losing the baby?"

"I don't know, Joseph. I don't know yet."

He felt a twinge of relief. The baby was still alive at this point, at least as far as the doctor could tell. "How is she doing?"

"Joseph, there's more at stake here than just the baby. She's bleeding terribly and I can't stop the flow. If I can't stop the bleeding, I will lose the baby . . . and I may lose her. I've only seen this situation a couple of times."

"What happened the other times?" asked Joseph.

The doctor shook his head.

Joseph felt his world closing in. Everything he had worked for was falling apart before his eyes. He fell to his knees and closed his eyes. For the first time in a very long time, he prayed.

Three days passed. The bleeding slowed but wouldn't stop. Joseph didn't leave Lucy's side. He held her hand and whispered loving words to her, but she wouldn't wake up. The doctor spent hours each day with her, trying every treatment he could think of. Nothing helped; her fever would not go down.

Guests were constantly present in the house, including Oliver. The visits were a burden on Joseph. He was exhausted, and while he appreciated the well-wishes and prayers of friends and family, he wanted to be by Lucy every second in case there was any change. If she slipped away, he had to be there. He would never forgive himself otherwise.

Joseph spent hours praying in the dim light next to the bed. He held Lucy's hand and begged for God to save her and save their child although he had stopped believing in God when he lived with the O'Dwyers. Back then, he had spent months praying desperately, asking God to rescue him, to bring him back to his family. God had never answered. Eventually, Joseph had concluded that there must not be a God, or if there was, He didn't care about him.

Since that time, he had tried to control life by hard work, by kindness to others, by taking care of others. What had his reward been? The loss of his mother; his virtual enslavement with the O'Dwyers; another enslavement to Oliver Hastings, first to save his father and then as the price for Lucy. Now he reached out to God again, asking for a miracle. Not for him, but for his Lucy.

Lucy. His feelings for her were complex. He had held her up so high. She was the beautiful and charming daughter of the wealthy Mr. Hastings. She had pursued him and won his heart. He had sacrificed to gain her hand. Then when they married, she almost seemed to lose interest. She still could be witty and bright, but now she seemed to spend so much time unhappy. She had wanted their own house, so he spent countless hours and resources building it. She had wanted nice furniture. He dipped into his savings to make sure she had the items she wanted. Then packages had begun arriving, dresses and bonnets from New York. He talked to her about the expenses, but each time he did, she would grow hurt and weep, telling him how cruel he was. She knew just what to say to make him feel wretched.

She had said all she really wanted was to be a mother. When he found out she was pregnant, he had breathed a sigh of relief. She was indeed happy for a short time. But then she began to talk about the baby's room and all the things they needed. They couldn't possibly let their child endure secondhand clothing or makeshift furniture. More packages arrived. Joseph was surprised one day as he reviewed his savings to learn they had spent half of it in the past year. He worried about the future. How could he make Lucy happy? And she deserved so much to be happy.

How terrible to have such thoughts now. His darling wife might die and all he could think about was money. What was wrong with him? Maybe Robert was correct. Was he really doing all of this for himself? Out of selfishness?

He heard footsteps. Doctor Pierce had returned. "How is our patient?"

"She's still the same. Her fever hasn't broken. She hasn't regained consciousness."

"Have you been putting the cold compresses on her forehead?"

"Yes, every hour."

The doctor grunted. "Give me a few minutes, Joseph. You might want to go get some rest in any event."

"No. I won't rest until she's awake."

The doctor looked at him for a moment. "Suit yourself, but I need a half hour uninterrupted now. Go get something to eat at least. I'll let you know when I'm done."

Joseph rose reluctantly and left the room. His legs felt heavy and his body ached everywhere. His head was in a fog. He desperately needed to sleep, but he simply couldn't until he knew she was all right. She must wake up or she must . . . No, he wouldn't think of that right now.

He came out to find Charlotte and Jane at the table. They were sewing. He could still smell the lingering fragrance of bacon and eggs. It must be morning still. Midmorning at the latest.

Charlotte looked up at Joseph with concern. "How is she, dear?"

"The same."

"Can I make you some breakfast? I just finished the dishes but I can make you some more."

"That would be nice."

She grabbed a heavy iron skillet and a basket of eggs from the shelf.

"Joseph, you need to get some sleep."

"I know. I know that. But I can't. You understand, don't you?"

"I do. Listen, Joseph, I wanted to talk to you about Robert."

"I don't want to talk about him."

"Oh, Joseph, you must. Please! He feels so badly about what he said. He had the drink in him. You know how that makes him go on so. He never means what he says, no matter how horrible it sounds at the time."

"You would know best. He has said enough to you."

Her face flushed. "Joseph, you're hurting me. Your father is a good man. He loves you and he loves me. He's ill. He can't always handle his drink. He's been through a lot. I don't know if you realize how much. He talks so proudly of Ireland, but he's told me many things privately about his old home. He had a terrible time there."

"We all have difficulties. That is no reason to stop working and drink your life away."

"You're right, dear, but remember, he's not strong like you. You have to be strong for all of us, Joseph. I need you. Jane needs you. Now Lucy and the baby need you. Where would we be without you? Please, you have to forgive Robert. He's miserable right now."

At that moment, Robert came through the front door. He saw that Joseph was there and he started to turn to walk back out.

"Wait," said Joseph.

Robert turned back around. "How is Lucy?"

"Still the same."

Robert grunted. "I don't know what you want me to say, Joseph. I had too much to drink the other night."

This was Robert's apology? He had too much to drink? He felt himself growing angry. He looked over at Charlotte. Her eyes pleaded with him. He felt the fight leaving him. He was so exhausted. What was the point in arguing with Robert in any event? He had important things to attend to.

"What's done is done," he responded.

Robert gave a slight smile. "Well that's settled then. I can't handle all this fighting, pour me a little bit of whiskey, Charlotte. Now that's a good lass."

Joseph envied his father at that moment. How delightful to drown all his worries, all his responsibilities in a bottle. He envied his father and he hated him. He hated his weakness. He hated everything he had done to him. What he had forced him to sacrifice on his behalf.

"Joseph, come here!" It was the doctor.

He rushed back into the bedroom, fearing the worst. There was Lucy, covered in sweat, but her eyes were open and she was smiling weakly up at him. His heart filled with love. He rushed to her side and gently put his arms around her, kissing her forehead and holding her head against his chest. "Is she . . . ?"

"She's going to be fine."

"And the baby?"

"The baby should be fine too."

Joseph felt Lucy stiffen in his arms. He pulled back and saw the pain in her eyes.

"What's wrong?" he demanded.

"She's going to be fine, Joseph. She's just having some ongoing pain. The important part is the fever has broken. She's going to be just fine now."

Joseph knelt before her and held her gently. Gone were the doubts and the frustrations. His Lucy was going to live. Their child would live. All of the horror of the last few days hit him and he wept, holding her close to him. He had his family. He had his home. Life had its frustrations, but this was what really mattered. Joseph could hear the doctor leave the room and they were alone. He held her for the longest time, just the two of them.

Six months later, Lucy gave birth to a healthy little girl: Mary Jane Forsyth.

CHAPTER 15

Union Military Hospital Camp near the Jerusalem Road

Saturday, January 9, 1865

Rebecca felt at peace. She had left her nighttime prayer vigil with renewed strength and purpose. She knew she would persevere and she would keep her faith and honor. Although she had not slept, she felt refreshed and awake.

She made her way to the hospital tent. She saw Thomas far across the way, chatting with some orderlies. She nodded politely to him. She noticed she did not feel the butterflies this time when she saw him. She thought of her husband and her daughter. She was honoring them. Rebecca smiled to herself and began her routine with her patients. She wanted to check on Joseph first, but she held herself back. She would conduct her rounds in the usual order. She would not let her anxiousness or her passions overcome her.

She took her time with each patient, enjoying her duties, satisfied with her resolve. Finally she reached Joseph. She checked his forehead. He still had a fever although it didn't seem to burn with the same intensity as it had the previous night. Was he recovering slightly? So few ever survived the infections. But then Joseph seemed to have some special grace.

"Hello Rebecca." She heard the voice. She felt the feelings wash over her again. She had felt so strong, so sure of herself, but now she felt everything crumbling away again. *God please help me!* She did not look up but mouthed a short greeting and tried to concentrate on Joseph.

"His fever seems better today."

"I noticed that myself."

"So you've already seen him?" She looked up just for a moment and caught his eye. He was staring at her again. His eyes seemed different today. Less intent. Was there pain there?

"I was by this morning before breakfast. I had a few moments, so I looked in on him."

"Thank you."

"You're welcome of course." She felt a hand on her shoulder. The touch was reluctant at first but grew in intensity. She felt herself trembling. She leaned forward, trying to pull away but his hand followed her. She looked up again. The pain in his eyes was deeper now. She watched him for a moment, lost in her own emotions.

She shook her head. This was wrong. He was married. She shouldn't have these feelings. He was sinning, and so was she. She had to stop this.

"Please, Thomas. Please don't. You're a married man. I'm a widow. Such things are not proper."

He pulled his hand back. She could see his reaction turning to anger. "I don't know what you're saying. I'm just trying to help you."

She looked back into his eyes. "No, that's not true."

She could see the despair. "No. No it's not. I've tried so hard to keep this hidden, to stop myself, but I can't anymore, Rebecca. I . . ."

"Don't say it. Please don't," she begged him. She tried to pull away again but he held her. His hand moved up to her chin and he drew her face back up to his.

"I love you, Rebecca. I've loved you for so long. I love your faith and your spirit, I love your hard work and compassion, I love your pain. I'm swallowed up in you. I've tried to fight this for so long. I can't take it anymore."

How could he say such things? Was he trying to destroy her? She felt the tears well up and stream down her face. She was shaking. Thank God they were alone here among the wounded. She must speak now. She must turn him away. She tried desperately to find the words, but she couldn't bring herself to say them.

"I don't know what to say. We shouldn't be talking this way."

"Do you love me, Rebecca?"

"What?"

"Do you love me?"

"Yes." She heard the words coming out of her lips and was surprised. Did she love him? She had worked so closely with him for so long. He was a wonderful man and surgeon, so different from anyone she had ever known. But he was married. What a terrible woman she was. She deserved retribution. She felt the truth and couldn't hide it anymore. She turned to him.

"I do. I do love you, Thomas. So much. But I'm not worthy of you or of anyone."

He took her hands. "Don't say such things, dearest. I'm the one who is not worthy."

She pulled away. "Please. I can't talk about this. I can't . . ." She turned and quickly left the tent. She was so thankful he did not try to follow her. She was reeling. She had to try to figure out what to do. She ran to her tent and fell into her cot, sobbing uncontrollably.

She tried to pray, but the words wouldn't form in her mind. *He loved her*. Even worse, she loved him back, loved him desperately, she realized. She thought of her husband. What would he say, watching her from heaven? He could never understand these feelings. What would their little daughter say? She tried to pray over and over, tried to recover her strength again, but she couldn't this time. She was lost. *He loved her.*

She buried her face in her pillow, riddled with shame, and cried until exhaustion overwhelmed her and she slept.

CHAPTER 16

Macomb, New York
Monday, August 29, 1864

Joseph rode down the dusty lane in the early August morning, anxious to get through his rounds at the Hastings property before the heat grew intolerable. The past few weeks the sun had burned relentlessly and the humidity pressed down on everyone and everything.

Mary Jane giggled in the saddle in front of him. She had begged to go with him, as she often did, and since he had a light day that day, he had decided to bring her. He held her tightly with his left hand and held the reins with his right.

He loved his daughter more than life itself. She was his little angel, his savior. He remembered his despair before she was born, a despair from too many years of sacrifice, of taking care of everyone but himself. Since she had been born, the feeling had melted away. He still was taking care of two families, his own and his father's, but now none of that mattered. He had his little girl and she was all he truly cared about.

Mary Jane was three years old that summer. She was tall for her age and had the same curly, dark hair as her mother. She looked just like Lucy and had the same charming personality. Joseph took her with him whenever he could, and she was a darling of Macomb like her mother before her.

Each night he would play dolls with her or take her over to spend time with Jane. He would also take her for walks at night around their farm, showing her the stars, talking to her about his mother, about the print shop, and about the world. He had never known he could love someone as much as he loved her. He also had learned fear: a fear that something might happen to her someday. She was so small, so fragile. He had heard other fathers and mothers describe this feeling, but until someone had a child, they could never know how profound that fear was.

He continued down the road and eventually reached the Hastings farm. He rode all around the property in the early morning, checking on the workers and inspecting the crops. He was worried about the oppressive heat and the impact on the harvest. They needed a rain soon before any more damage was done. At each stop the workers talked to Mary Jane, and she would smile and laugh with them. Everyone loved Mary Jane.

After he finished the inspection, he stopped by to see Oliver and go over some of the farm financials. Mary Jane ran into her grandfather's arms. Oliver smiled and laughed. He loved Mary Jane as much as Joseph did. He brought her into his library and then put her down to let her play on the carpet while Joseph and Oliver talked.

"How do the crops look, Joseph?"

"Not good. We need rain soon. This summer has just been too damned hot."

"Too hot and not enough people to tend the crops. Not enough people and not enough money to pay those left behind."

Joseph agreed. "It was bad enough when we lost the first round of workers when the war started. The draft has taken most of those left behind." The draft had begun in 1863 and many young men, including workers on the Hastings property, had been called up. A draftee could pay three hundred dollars to avoid having to serve, but that was an impossible number for most farmhands to afford. The result was far fewer farmhands available.

This created a double problem. First, they had to cut production because of fewer available people, and second, the wages of the hands went up as competition among the local farmers increased for the limited available labor. Additionally, the quality of the workforce had thinned, so the production value of the workers as a whole had decreased. Joseph had done his best. Because he was respected and because he worked so hard, the farm drew a better share of the available workers, and continued to perform well.

An even worse situation was the loss of friends and family on the battlefield. Although Macomb was small, with less than one thousand people in the entire township, they had already lost more than a dozen men to the war. Just as hard to bear were the sons and brothers and fathers returning with an arm or leg missing, now struggling to work their farms and maintain their dignity. Thank God Joseph's closest friend in the service, Casey Ormsbee, was still safe and unwounded.

The war had dragged on and on, year after year, with no end in sight. The enthusiasm of a quick victory was shattered in Virginia at a place called Bull Run, where thousands were killed and wounded on both sides. The southern armies fought with incredible bravery and skill. In the East, the army of Northern Virginia under Robert E. Lee crushed the Union army in battle after battle, and twice invaded the North, leading to fears that the South might win the war, and might even take over the northern states. In the West, the story was different. There, the Union won battle after battle, eventually clearing the Mississippi River and driving deep into the southern states. Even Robert E. Lee was stopped in Pennsylvania in the summer of 1863 at a small crossroads town called Gettysburg.

Finally in 1864, the Union appeared to be winning, and all northerners celebrated the promotion of Ulysses Grant, who had won most of the victories in the West, to overall commander of the Union forces. Grant shifted his direct command to the East, and with the Army of the Potomac, had moved south against General Lee.

Grant and Lee crashed together in a series of battles: The Battle of the Wilderness, Spotsylvania Court House, the Battle of North Anna, and then the terrible slaughter at Cold Harbor. The casualties mounted like never before until it seemed the whole North would be bled dry of their youth. Now Grant was often cursed as Grant "the Butcher," and the talk increased again of granting a peace treaty to the South, and letting them go. Finally, the armies had settled into a static siege south of the city of Petersburg, Virginia. The casualties had begun to lighten, but the war seemed no closer to conclusion. Joseph turned again to the business at hand.

"How does the harvest look this year?" asked Oliver.

"We will be down almost fifty percent from our yields in 1861. However, the prices of all the crops have gone up. Overall our profit is down about thirty percent."

"Another year down thirty percent. I don't blame you, Joseph. I know you've pulled every ounce of productivity out of the people we do have. They respect you and they work hard for you."

"I do my best."

"I know you do. You've been more than a son-in-law to me. You've been a son. And you've met your commitments to me. Your four years are almost up. Have you thought about what you would like to do next?"

"You know, I've always wanted to open a print shop of my own. I want to build a shop at my farm or maybe at Pope's Mill. It wouldn't be a full-time job, but between the shop and the farm, I should be able to make a go of it. I might have to travel to Morristown and Ogdensburg some for business, but I could make a go of that on Saturdays."

Oliver seemed disappointed. "I was hoping you would stay on here, Joseph. You have been so valuable to me." He paused a moment. "I've been thinking on this for a while. Why don't you stay on at the farm for another two years as my foreman? I need you. Now more than ever. If you agree, I'll buy all of the equipment and you can run the print shop right here. I'll split the profits with you fifty-fifty. At the end of the two years, you can keep the equipment. Of course, I would keep paying you as we have already agreed. I would even entertain an increase."

"That's a generous offer," responded Joseph, "but I need some time to consider it."

"Of course, take your time. Your current commitment isn't up quite yet, in any event."

Joseph finished his business and departed from the property with Mary Jane. As he rode home, he considered Oliver's offer while his daughter sat contentedly in the saddle in front of him, humming softly and playing with a doll.

He was ambivalent about the offer. Oliver had treated him fairly over the past four years, but he could never forget that his father-in-law had forced him at three different times to work for him. Oliver may have softened toward Joseph after he married Lucy, but he was still a hard businessman, focused on profits and his bottom line. He was not being generous with Joseph now. Oliver knew Joseph could get the maximum income from the land. Joseph was tired of serving at the will of another. He had worked his entire life to break free of these bonds. He was close, so close now to being independent.

On the other hand, Joseph did not have sufficient money to buy the printing equipment on his own. He had put all of his savings into the purchase of the farm. He had saved up some money after that, but it was before the marriage. Since that time, Lucy's constant purchases assured that he was not able to add to those savings, instead they dwindled down to an alarming level. He talked to her over and over about her spending, but she would not let up. She would become focused on something she wanted and she would talk to him constantly about it for weeks or even months at a time. She would sulk and fall into depression, making Joseph's life miserable until he finally relented. Then she would finally be happy. Unfortunately, the happiness never lasted. After a few weeks she would find a new thing that she *had* to have, and the cycle would begin again.

As he rode on, Joseph felt desperate. He tried to keep this emotion in check. He tried to keep his head down and work as hard as he could. He had done everything to make Lucy happy and to provide a home for her and for Mary Jane. No matter how hard he worked, it seemed there was always another problem, another barrier in his way. How had it come to this?

He was surprised he had not considered the problem of capital for the new print shop sooner. What had happened to him? He had been so organized and deliberate when he came to Macomb. He realized he had been drawn along by the tide of events these past four years. He had done everything he could to keep Lucy happy while slowly losing faith that he could ever rebuild his savings and accomplish his dreams. He had instead buried himself in his work, in solving the many problems of the war, and of course in Mary Jane's life. Now he was faced with another two years of commitment. He was already twenty-six and would be twenty-seven in September. His life might be half over or worse by the time he was done. When would it be his time to live on his own? To work for himself and make his own decisions?

Joseph arrived home, these thoughts still deep in his mind. He rode up to the main house and dismounted, carrying Mary Jane, who had fallen asleep in the saddle, on his shoulder into the house. He opened the door as quietly as possible and passed into the main room where Robert, Charlotte, and Lucy sat at the table, eating a late breakfast and sipping coffee. Jane was playing on the floor nearby and Mary Jane awoke and ran over to join her. Robert was regaling the women with a tale about his youthful days in Ireland when he and a neighbor boy had been caught stealing eggs from the home of a Catholic priest and were threatened with a beating. Robert told the story in overdramatic fashion as if the future of the Church depended on this event, and the women laughed and teased him.

"Joseph, you've just come in at the best part, lad. I was about to tell them how I escaped the clutches of the evil Father Mulrooney, who had plotted to return our whole fair island to the evil clutches of Rome."

"I've heard this story more than a few times, Father." Joseph looked at all of them at the table, his anger rising. "Are any of you planning on getting anything done today? There's plenty of chores out there for all of us."

"Now, Joseph, don't get all plumped up like a rooster," said Robert. "Charlotte and Lucy just finished with breakfast and will be doing the dishes soon. I was planning on repairing the fence on the south side of the property. There's a couple posts that are leaning a bit."

Joseph and Robert had reached an unspoken agreement after their blowup three years before. Robert still drank as much as ever, but he had stopped criticizing Joseph. He had even taken to doing some light work around the farm, although it never amounted to much. Joseph kept the peace for Charlotte and Jane's sake. Jane was of school age and spent a good part of each day at the local school.

"Joseph, Robert is right, we've all been busy all morning. Why are you in such a foul mood today?" asked Lucy.

"I don't want to talk about it right now."

"Come on now," said Robert. "We're all family here. We've no secrets."

"Leave him alone," said Charlotte. "If he doesn't want to discuss it, then let's leave it be."

"Well, he doesn't have to come home all in a huff and start accusing us of idleness," said Lucy.

"Please leave it alone," said Joseph.

"Maybe you're the one who wasn't working hard enough. How can you get any work done while you're playing with Mary Jane?" asked Lucy.

"Now, Lucy . . ." said Charlotte.

"Let her say her piece! What are you driving at? All I do is work! How could you accuse me of anything less? I've taken care of you and your every need since the moment we married!"

"Taken care of me! And what have I done? I bore you a beautiful baby and another on the way. I have cooked and cleaned and taken care of the house! I do all this with hardly a thank-you from you!"

"I never said you do nothing! But don't say I haven't done everything I am supposed to do and more. I've killed myself for this family without hardly a thank-you. All you do is complain . . ." Joseph stopped himself.

"Complain is it? How dare you! I've done everything I can to live with you and for you. You promised you would take care of me, Joseph. What do you do instead? You make me feel terrible because I want a few small comforts amid all this squalor! You don't love me, Joseph! You've never loved me! I have given you everything, and it's never enough!"

"Now calm yourself, lassie," said Robert. "Joseph's not always kind or giving, but he tries his best."

Joseph turned to his father. "I'm not always kind or giving? What haven't I given to you? I've sacrificed everything for all of you! And you sit here eating your breakfast and complaining about me?"

"Joseph, please," implored Charlotte. "Don't say anything else."

Joseph kept his eyes on Robert, ignoring Charlotte.

"All you have done these past years is sit in this house and drink while I do all the work. I have done everything I can for you, and you've done nothing for yourself. I'm tired of everyone looking to me for answers! I can't do all this on my own anymore!"

Lucy cried out and ran out of the house. Joseph started to go after her but Robert held him back.

"Let me go!"

"Boyo, you've done enough harm today. Leave the girl alone. Or maybe you won't listen to a drunk and a ne'er-do-well."

Joseph looked at Robert and then to Charlotte. Charlotte had tears streaming down her face. He saw that Jane and Mary Jane were also sitting quietly and watching him. Jane looked hurt and confused, as if her world had just been taken away from her.

"I'm sorry. I didn't mean to say all of those things. I have been working so hard lately."

"Joseph, like I said, you've said enough. I think you should just leave."

Joseph turned to Charlotte.

"Please, Joseph," she said. "Just go. Go into town, let off some steam. I'll take care of things here. It . . . it will be better when you come back."

Joseph walked out of the house, his mind in a cloud. He mounted his horse and started out very slowly toward Pope's Mill. Why had he said all of those things? He was usually so strong, so able to keep his mind to himself. Today he just exploded. He realized it wasn't any individual problem, but all the problems together. He had thought he would be so much further along in life now. He had worked hard for so many years. He had purchased land and he was immensely proud of that. However, that had been years ago. Since that time, since he married Lucy, he had been unable to save any more money, and had actually fallen behind. Now he faced more commitment to Oliver, and would that even make a difference? How would the next two years be any different than the last four? Wouldn't he simply work hard for those years and still be as far behind at the end, or even worse?

He had to talk to Lucy. He had to show her what had happened. Surely she would understand. Surely she would see that all the extra money she had spent on these things they didn't need would ultimately prevent them from having a better farm, a print shop, a better life.

But would she? He had talked with her over and over about this very question. She always became upset and accused him of not loving her, accused him of not taking care of her like he had promised he would. She also would bring up Robert and Charlotte. How could Joseph complain about what she spent when he was taking care of another entire family with very little given in return?

Joseph eventually reached Pope's Mill, dark thoughts still streaming through his mind. He headed directly to Patterson's. He needed to talk to Pete. Pete always had sound advice and was a willing ear.

The old storekeeper was at the counter when Joseph came in. David was not in the store. Joseph was relieved by this as it gave him a chance to talk to Pete alone. Patterson looked up and waved at Joseph, but then he frowned.

"Good morning, Joseph. What's the matter? You look like death itself."

"Troubles at home."

"Not you, Joseph. What trouble could you have? Is that wastrel of a father at it again?"

"Trouble of all sorts. I've gone and made Lucy cry, and I've hurt Robert and Charlotte as well."

"What happened?"

Joseph told Pete the whole story, including Mr. Hastings's offer and Joesph's feelings of helplessness. His friend listened for a long time without saying anything.

"Joseph, I don't know if I should say this to you or not. I've wanted to say it for a long time."

"What?"

"To hell with the lot of them."

"What do you mean?"

"I've never seen a bigger pack of beggars and ingrates. Your father does nothing and takes everything. He is the biggest waste of manhood I've ever seen. Now Charlotte is a fine woman, but she's as blind as you are about Robert. You both pour your love and time and money into that man, and it's a well with no bottom."

"Pete, you don't understand . . ."

"I'm not finished. Now that I've started, I'm going to have my say. Worse than him might be Lucy. Now don't get me wrong, Joseph, I love that girl. We all do. She was always a shining light all around this town. But if there's ever been a more spoiled creature in the town of Macomb, then I'm Jefferson Davis himself. Joseph, you don't see it. They all take and take and take from you. You are the hardest-working man I've ever seen. You've tried to do right by all of them. But enough is enough. It's time you put your foot down with all of them."

Joseph was in shock. He had never expected to hear this from Pete. He had been a father figure to Joseph. Always a supporter and a friend. Now he had attacked everything Joseph stood for, everything important to him. He felt angry and confused. Was Pete right? Had he done all of this for all these years—for nothing? He started to turn to walk away.

"Joseph, don't leave like that. I know that was hard to hear, but I said what needed to be said. If you never speak to me again, I guess that will be the price I pay. I won't take it back."

Joseph turned back to Pete. "I've listened to you for years. I'm not going to stop now. It's very hard to hear, but you are at least partially right. They've all sat around like a group of leeches all these years."

"That's the truth of it, Joseph. And it's about time you realized it."

"What am I supposed to do? They are still my kin. I love them all. I can't just walk away from them."

"Well, we have time to figure all of that out. But first things first, you can't sign up again with Oliver. How can you ever stand up to Lucy when you're under his yoke?"

"I don't have a choice. I don't have the money to buy the equipment I want, and the farm isn't self-sustaining on its own."

"Not with an extra family to feed it's not. But that's not something we can fix today." Pete reached down under the counter and pulled out a metal box. He removed a key and unlocked it; inside was a stack of bills. He started counting out dollars.

"No, Pete. I can't take money from you." Joseph started to back away.

"You're not *taking* Joseph, you're *borrowing*. Here's a thousand dollars. This should be enough to buy what you need. You take this and you pay me back at the end of two years. I'm offering the same bargain as Oliver, but without the bondage. Write out a note against your property. That's just protection in case something happens to you. We can make sure it's all legal later."

He grasped Pete's hand and pulled him close. "You've been a father to me, Pete. The father I've never had." Joseph wrote out a note to Pete describing the debt, the payment terms, and that his property would be collateral for the note. He gave the paper back to Pete.

"You've been a son to me too. You and David are the most important people in my life, besides Mrs. Patterson of course."

Joseph took the money and placed it in his pocket.

"I can't thank you enough."

"Think nothing of it. You just bring it back when you're done with it."

"With interest."

"Now don't go fussing with that. If you want to bring a little extra at the end, that's your choice, my boy. I'm not asking for it."

He felt so relieved. Finally, a way out. Finally, a ray of hope. He heard the door to the store open behind him. He turned and saw Marie Ormsbee at the door, tears streaking down her face.

"Casey is dead," she said, then fell to the floor, her body wracked with sobbing.

Joseph ran to Marie, kneeling down and putting his arms around her. He held her, rocking her gently as she sobbed. He waited until she calmed down somewhat.

"Marie, what happened? What happened to Casey?"

"I just heard today. He was killed at some big battle south of Petersburg. There wasn't any other information. Oh, Joseph, what am I supposed to do? The farm has fallen apart since he left. I've barely made ends meet. His brothers have helped out as much as they can, but they have their own families to care for. I had hoped the war would be over by now. Things looked so promising in the early spring. He made it through all those battles, all these years, and now to die at the end!" She started sobbing again.

"I'm so sorry, Marie. I don't know what to say. We loved Casey. We all did. He was like a brother to me." He wanted to say more. He wanted to tell her that he would help her, that he could give her money. A few years ago that would be true, but not now. Now he had so little saved. His frustration grew even more. He could have helped and instead Lucy had accumulated expensive dresses and cookware, and the latest hats and shoes from New York. She was destroying him, he realized. She had taken away his freedom again as surely as he had become indentured to her. He wondered for a moment if Lucy and Oliver had planned this together? But no, that was too terrible to believe. Not of his Lucy. He turned his attention back to Marie.

"We will figure out what to do. You won't be forgotten. We will get some friends together and we will figure out ways to help you."

"Joseph, you are so kind, but what can you all do? I'm not the first wife to lose their husband these past four years. Everyone is stretched thin. I appreciate what you're saying, and I won't be so modest as to say no, but please don't upset yourself if there isn't much to go around. We will manage . . . somehow."

"Everyone loved Casey. I know people will help out any way they can. Let me get things set up with Pete in the next few days and then I'll stop by the farm." He reached into his pocket and peeled off a twenty-dollar note. "Here, take this. Get some groceries for the family."

She shook her head. "No, Joseph, I don't want that right now. That's very kind but we can get by for a bit."

He pressed the paper money into her hand. "It's okay, Marie. I want you to have it. This is just a little something to tide you over until I can get things properly organized." He pulled her up and she held tightly on to him for a moment.

"Oh, Joseph, what would we do without you? Casey was always so proud of you. He looked at you as another brother."

Joseph could feel his eyes welling up but he fought back the tears. "Get yourself some food now, Marie. I'm going to head back home and let Lucy know. I'll be back tomorrow and I'll come out to the house with Pete and David."

She hugged him tight for a few more seconds and then let go. Joseph didn't turn to Pete. He would fall apart if he did. Instead, he waved to the shopkeeper without speaking and walked out the door.

He mounted his horse and set off for his farm. He didn't know if he was ready to face Lucy, but he had to tell her about Casey. They had more important worries right now than a little family squabble. He tried to keep Pete's words out of his mind. He couldn't focus on that. When they had taken care of Marie, then he would have time to think everything over. For now, he had to provide for his friend's family.

He arrived back home in the early afternoon. He had hoped Lucy would be in the small house, but she wasn't, so he reluctantly headed to Robert's home. He opened the door and was surprised to see Charlotte and Lucy sitting at the table, both with faces red from crying. They must have already heard about Casey.

"Joseph, thank God you're home. You need to help right away!" said Lucy.

"I know, I already heard about Casey. Who told you?"

"What about Casey?"

Joseph paused. "What's going on? Is everything all right?"

"No, it's not," said Charlotte. "It's your father."

Joseph's heart sank. What could it be now? "What happened?"

"He was very upset after you left. He started drinking . . . drinking more than usual. He kept going on and on about how he would prove his worth to you. He kept drinking until he could barely walk but he wouldn't stop. Finally, he said he was going to take care of some things. We tried to keep him here, but he pushed us away and stumbled out the door. He's been gone for at least an hour. I have no idea where he went. Joseph, you have to go find him. You know how he can be when he's this drunk."

"Let him do what he wants. I have other problems to attend to."

"Joseph, please," Charlotte pleaded. "I'm so worried. He could die out there. I don't even know how he saddled up his horse. He was shouting the most terrible things. I've seen him bad before but never like this."

Joseph sighed. "Fine. I'll go find him, but I've had about enough of this. Our talk today isn't over. I'll wait until I'm done sorting things out with Casey, but after that, we will be having another talk."

"You still haven't told us what is wrong with Casey," said Lucy. She met his eyes. "Oh no. He's dead, isn't he? How horrible." She rose up and ran to Joseph, putting her arms around him. "I'm so sorry, Joseph. I'll do anything I can to help you."

He held her tight. She felt warm and comforting. He loved her so much, but she had hurt him and he could feel the distance that had grown between them even as she was in his arms. Well, that problem was for another time.

"I'll head back into town and look around for Robert. I'm sure he's just down at the tavern."

Joseph kissed Lucy on the cheek and then went over to hug Charlotte. She thanked him and then he turned back out the door for his second trip to Pope's Mill that day.

Darkness fell. Joseph was still in the saddle hours later, searching for Robert. He had checked the tavern at Pope's Mill, but his father wasn't there and nobody had seen him. He rode out to Casey's farm just in case Robert had caught news of his friend's death. He had not been there.

He then headed west along the shores of Black Lake and stopped at friends' homes, asking if anyone had seen him. He was starting to worry. Robert was certainly a sad soul, but he was also predictable. It was out of character for him to come up missing this long. The northern residents of Macomb had not seen Robert. As night deepened, Joseph headed home to see if his father had shown up there.

He was forced to pick his way slowly along the road in the darkness, and he arrived home an hour later. He hurried into the main house and saw immediately that Robert was back. His father was slumped at the table, barely keeping his eyes open. He had a cup of coffee in his hands. Charlotte stood behind him, a look of distress or even fear on her face. Lucy was not there and had presumably gone home at some point with Mary Jane.

"So you decided to come home after all, did you?" asked Joseph. "A fine chase you led me on today. Where on earth have you been?"

"I'll tell you that story, lad, if you'll shut your trap. I've been out earning my keep." Robert's words were slow and slurred.

Joseph looked up at Charlotte. "What is he talking about?"

"I don't know. He's gone on and on about earning his keep since he came home. I'm frightened, Joseph. I've never seen him like this."

"You've no reason to be scared, dear. I've done more in one night to earn for this family than Joseph has done in a year. You never were any good at making money, boyo. You're just like every tom fool in Ireland, breaking his back for the landlords while easy money is to be made for a sharp lad."

Joseph grew angry at the barb but there was no point in arguing with Robert in his condition. "What do you mean, easy money? What did you do?"

"I took care of things same as on the ship."

Joseph felt the blood run out of him. "What do you mean you *took care of things*?"

"I went to Morristown and found a good, old-fashioned card game with a few good lads from the old country. I made more money tonight than you've ever made in your whole life."

"What money? Where is your money?"

"I don't have cash, you ignorant whelp. I have a note. Now let me find it." Robert fumbled around clumsily in his pockets until he pulled out a crumpled paper. He handed the note to Joseph.

The letter in Robert's drunken handwriting promised to pay a Paulus Deary the sum of twenty-four hundred dollars within ten days.

"This note says you lost! Is this real? You said you won."

Robert blinked his eyes and held up an unsteady hand. "Now that doesn't sound right, laddie. Give me that for a moment. I was a little down for a while, but I made it all up. I made us a fair sum. I'm just like my boy. I can bring in the money when I need to."

What had Robert done? He had ruined them all. Twenty-four hundred dollars? Half the price of his farm. All gone in a night! Joseph couldn't breathe, he couldn't see. He sat down at the table. "What have you done to us? What have you done? You've ruined us all. You've destroyed us."

"Joseph, it must be a mistake," said Charlotte. "It must be. Please don't worry. Please don't."

He stood again, not looking at Charlotte. He had to get out of there before he killed his own father. He had to think. He walked out without saying another word and hurried to his home. Lucy was asleep. He left her a note that he would be back in the morning, then he remounted his horse and headed out toward Morristown. He arrived hours before dawn but he did not dismount. He rode his horse around the town in a daze, not thinking. Numb.

After dawn, he started searching for Mr. Deary. He found him before noon along with a couple of his friends who had been present the night before. They all verified the same story. Robert Forsyth had lost twenty-four hundred dollars to Mr. Deary. Joseph paid him nine hundred eighty dollars in cash as a down payment on the debt. He promised to meet with him again in the next week to work out the remaining debt. He then rode the weary miles home, more despondent than he had ever been.

CHAPTER 17

Macomb, New York

Tuesday, August 30, 1864

Joseph arrived home several hours later. He thought of confronting Robert but decided against it. He was still too angry and he needed time to calm down, time to think. Instead, he headed to the small house to get some rest. He came through the door to find Lucy waiting.

"Joseph, thank God! Where have you been? I've been worried to death!"

"I had to go find Father. When I did find him, I had to go back and clean up his mess. Something terrible has happened."

"What?"

He told her the whole story of Pete's loan and Robert's gambling. He could see her becoming more and more agitated.

"But why did you pay the money to this man in Morristown? What problem is it of ours what your father has done?"

"He's on the title to the property with me, Lucy."

"What?"

"I put him on the title with me to the property when I bought it. In case anything had happened to me, I wanted him to be taken care of. If he doesn't pay his debts, we will lose our land."

She slapped him hard across the face. "You're a fool, Joseph, a fool! You've destroyed our lives, giving everything up to him. I've had to go without and live in this little hut so they can live in the big house and have everything better than we do. You've never cared for me the way you care for your father. And now we are going to lose what little we have."

"I'm sorry, Lucy. I've tried to do my best for my people, including you."

"Well you haven't done your best. You've ruined everything! We are going to my father. He'll know what to do. We are going now, and you are going to do what he says. He will bail us out of this mess!"

All the way home, he knew it would come to this. He had no other way out of this disaster but to submit to whatever Mr. Hastings wanted. He was more trapped than ever, more under Lucy and Oliver's thumb.

"I need to rest for an hour or two, then I'll go with you."

"You can meet me there then. I'm going to go tell him what's happened."

"Please don't do that, Lucy. Please wait for me. I want to tell him myself."

"To be honest with you, I don't want to be near you right now. I'll take Mary Jane and I'll see you there after you've rested."

She swiftly gathered up Mary Jane and left, refusing to speak further with him. He was exhausted, but there was no way he would be able to sleep. He washed his face and hands, changed his dusty clothes, and headed back out to the Oliver Hastings property.

He was ushered into the library as soon as he arrived. Oliver was sitting at his desk with Lucy standing next to him. Her face was tear stained and Oliver's face was dark and foreboding.

"Joseph, what have you done?"

"I haven't *done* anything. I've taken care of my family, like I always do."

"You've destroyed your family! Unless you mean that bastard Robert. They aren't your family! Not the part that matters anyway. Now you've run up a debt that will take you years to pay. Years when Lucy and Mary Jane will go without so you can pay back that idiot Patterson for the sins of that bigger idiot, your father! Why didn't you come to me with this first? We could have figured out a better solution. And why did you borrow money from Patterson? I take it you had decided to go against me? To leave me here when I need you the most. When Lucy needs you the most. I've just finished telling my daughter she should simply come home and be done with you. But she won't! She's loyal to you. I can't imagine why, but she is. And after you stabbed me in the back!"

Joseph's mind reeled. How had he gotten himself into all this? Now Oliver was threatening to take Lucy from him, to take Mary Jane.

"You won't take my daughter and you won't take my wife! I have the right to decide my own future, Oliver. I appreciate the offer you made me, but I want to make my own way in the world."

"Who has ever stopped you? I've offered you a job here for a long time now. I have tried to give you opportunities. Is that such a bad thing? You may feel closed in because of your father, Joseph, but don't blame me for that. I've looked after your well-being."

"Because it benefited you."

"Of course it has. I'm not a fool. I do things in life that help me and help my family. That's the difference between the two of us, Joseph, and it always has been. I have never understood why you let your father stay on your property. Why you have let him freeload off your sweat. And now I learn you actually put his name on your land? Something he had nothing to do with. Look where it's gotten you. Now you're in debt from even more of his stupidity."

"You're right, Oliver. I should never have put him on the property. That happened before I married Lucy. You have to remember it's not just Robert, it's Charlotte and Jane. I would have left Robert to his own devices years ago, but I can't leave my stepmother and my half sister out in the cold. Surely you understand that?"

"I understand that, but you didn't have to give them half your property. You certainly didn't need to pay Robert's debts. If you hadn't borrowed money from Patterson in the first place, you wouldn't have had the money to give them. Then you would have come to me and we would have worked this problem out together."

Lucy had remained silent throughout the exchange. She stood behind her father, watching him, obviously hurt. It was clear what her position was.

"Well, whatever has happened, now it has to be fixed," continued Oliver.

"What do you propose?"

"I propose that you and Lucy come and live here for a while. I'll pay Patterson back and I'll pay the rest of this debt for Robert. In exchange he will deed you back the property. I'll give him ninety days to get off the property. I'll even give him another three hundred dollars so he can find a new place, *in another town*."

"And? I know there's more."

"The property will be sold to pay the debts. I'll give you the rest of the money and you can buy your printing equipment."

"Where would we live?"

"You would live right here, of course. We have plenty of room. You can keep working for me and you'll have a free home. With the money I pay you and the money from the printing press, it won't be long and you'll be able to buy a new place."

"Why couldn't you just loan me the money, and I'll pay you back?"

"I can't go back there, Joseph," said Lucy. "I hate that house. It's far too small and I could never live in the house where Robert lived."

"You're asking me to give up everything."

She came around the desk and stepped toward him. "Please, Joseph. There's room in the house here for all of us. This house is so beautiful. We have a cook and people to wash and take care of us. I would be looked after during the day and so would Mary Jane. There wouldn't be anything to worry about. Everything would be peaceful and nice. And it wouldn't really be any different than it has been. You've already been working for Daddy all this time! You two get along so well. You wouldn't even have to ride home at night anymore. You would be home."

"Look how happy Lucy is, Joseph. This is the right decision. You have put too much on her. She's been taking care of her own house, and half the time she's stuck taking care of Charlotte and Robert as well. She's not used to that kind of thing. She was raised a Hastings and Hastings don't serve others.

"Think about this. You would never need to leave. I told you you've been like a son to me. Why not stay here? I have all the room you would ever need. I know you want to start your printing business. I won't stand in your way. You can do it whenever you want—in the evenings or on Saturday. Just keep up your normal foreman duties."

Joseph didn't know what to do. He felt like he stood in his own grave with sand pouring in over him. "I need some time to think. Just a little time."

"Joseph, what is there to think about?" asked Lucy.

"Now, now, dear, you've a good man here. He needs a little time and we'll give it to him. He will do the right thing."

Joseph turned around and slowly walked out the door. He felt burdened as if he dragged heavy chains behind him. He had a way out now, a way to fix this terrible mess. But as always, he must give up everything to achieve it. When would all this end? When would he be able to live for himself, to live the way he wanted? He mounted his horse, the thoughts pressing heavily on his mind.

Joseph rode past his property and continued on to Pope's Mill. He was dismounting at Patterson's store when he remembered Marie. He had promised he would go see her. He had forgotten amid this new crisis. He would have to sort that out in the next day or so. For now, he had to talk to Pete. He entered the store and found his old friend at the counter with David, counting coins and scribbling notes in a ledger. They both greeted him but he could observe their faces change when they saw him more closely.

"What's wrong, Joseph?" asked Pete. "You look terrible."

"I am terrible. You can't imagine how terrible."

"What's happened?"

Joseph told them all of it, pausing now and again to answer questions.

"Why did you pay off Robert's debt? That was a fool thing to do," said David, echoing Oliver's words.

He explained the joint ownership of the land.

"I'm not going to say anything, Joseph," said Pete. "You know I've never understood your relationship with Robert. You are so wise in so many ways, but not in this."

"It doesn't help to be reminded over and over. So I'm a fool. I never thought I was, but I am. I thought I was doing some good in the world. Good for my family. Instead, I trusted a drunk and he has betrayed me. Again, he has betrayed me."

"Well, it's too late to fix it," said Pete. "What's done is done. What are you going to do about the debt? I'm not worried about what I loaned you. I know you'll pay me back. But I can't loan you more, Joseph."

"I understand." He wondered if he did. He saw the strange look in Pete's face. His friend didn't trust him anymore. Didn't trust him to make a good decision. He had just wasted Pete's savings, maybe his life savings besides this store. Wasted it on the gambling debts of a drunk. No wonder he wouldn't give him more. He told them about Oliver's offer.

"More years of slavery he wants," said Pete. "And now he wants you to live there too. If you move on that property Joseph, you'll never leave again. Those two will concoct plan after plan. You will live there the rest of your life working for Oliver Hastings. I'm not saying there's anything wrong with it, but it's not the dream you've ever had, my boy."

"What choice do I have? I've no money left. Not that kind of money. Lucy's spent everything I had saved. Now I owe twenty-four hundred more."

"Why doesn't Robert pay the rest of the debt?"

Joseph laughed. "Robert doesn't have a dime. He never does. He drinks every penny he makes when he does make any money. I've been slipping money to Charlotte all these years. Money for food and for Jane. They have nothing of their own."

"I've never seen drink own a man more than your father. Nor seen it destroy everyone around it."

"Well, he may have just ruined his own life. Oliver wants him off the property and I don't know what choice I have in the matter. I need to go see Charlotte. Poor woman. What's to become of her and Jane?"

"I don't know. But you can't save the whole world, Joseph. For too many years you've tried. At first I thought you were out of your mind, then I've stood back in awe as you did it. I thought you could do anything, Joseph. We all did. You are a remarkable man. I've never seen a man work harder, work longer. But you've let others cling on to you in a way I've also never seen. It's caught up to you now. Now you're going to have to make difficult choices. I wish I could help you more, but this time I can't."

"You've helped already so much, Pete, in so many ways. I have to go. I need to talk to Charlotte, and to Robert."

"You be careful with Robert. He's a smart tongue. You keep your emotions inside, but they come out in a storm. Don't make this worse."

"I won't harm him. Not in front of Charlotte in any event. Certainly not in front of Jane. But I have to talk to them. They have to know what's coming."

Joseph said his good-byes and rode back down the road to his own property. He was reluctant to see Charlotte and Robert, and reluctant to tell them what he must do—what was about to happen to them. How would they make it on their own? Robert would drink up the three hundred in a matter of weeks. The money would be gone and they would be without a home, without land, without a job. They would starve. He didn't know what to do. There was nothing he could give them, nothing he could do for them.

He approached his father's farmhouse hesitantly. He didn't know what to expect or how they would receive him. He knocked on the front door. The door opened and Charlotte appeared. She looked as if she had aged ten years in the past few days. Joseph tried to read her face when she let him in, but he had never seen her look like this. He had seen her sad, upset, even angry. Now she wore a tight, grim, emotionless expression. She waved Joseph in and he saw that Robert was inside, sitting at the table. Jane was fortunately at school.

Robert looked up and Joseph was surprised to see his expression. He had expected anger and defiance. Instead he saw fear and shame. "Please come over and sit down."

Joseph walked over and took a place at the table. Charlotte poured them all coffee and then took her place next to Robert.

"I'm ready to hear what you have to say, Joseph."

Again Joseph was surprised. He had never known Robert to accept any rebuff. He would blame everyone else, even Joseph, or he would be sarcastic and defiant. What was this change? For now it didn't matter, he had to say what he had come to say.

"Father, I have to ask you to leave the property and to leave me be. You have betrayed me again. Your drinking has betrayed me. I have spent my entire life trying to help you. In the meantime, you've treated me like I owed you for it. You've made me feel like I was ungrateful to you. I have had a lot of time to think about things the last few days. I have spent my life trying to win your approval. Trying to get you to acknowledge that I'm your son, that you love me, that you're proud of me. Instead, you have blamed, you have joked, you have drank, and you have sat around and let me take care of everything. Now you have done even worse. You have nearly destroyed me. It will take years to repair what you did in one night. I could maybe forgive that, but you already did this to me one time before. I love Charlotte and Jane. I . . . I love you. But I can't keep giving you my whole life, and get nothing in return.

"I have a way out of this. A way out that I don't want to take. Oliver has agreed to take Lucy and me in. He will pay all the debts. We will sell the property and I can use the rest of the money to buy some printing equipment so I can start a shop. But he is demanding that you leave in ninety days. He will give me another three hundred to give to you, so you have a start on a new place, a new life. I'm sorry. I'm sorry it's come to this. But it has, and I don't have a choice anymore."

"You're right, Joseph. About all of it."

Joseph couldn't believe his father's words. Robert had never admitted anything. Joseph was used to excuses, to bragging, to sulking. He had never heard his father admit his mistakes. "What do you mean *all of it*?"

"I'm a drunk and a failure. I failed at job after job in Ireland because I was in the drink. We only survived because your mother's parents helped us out now and again. They purchased passage for us to America and I gambled and lost our money on the way. You paid the price for my stupidity. Since you've come back, I've sat around and let you carry the burdens for all of us. Now I've done even worse, I've put us in a terrible situation. I'm a failure, son. I've always looked up to you. I've always admired your strength. But I've been jealous too. I haven't told you how I feel because I've felt bitter that you're a better man than me." Robert's voice broke and he closed his eyes. His body shook and tears rolled down his face. Charlotte moved closer and put her arms around him, holding him to her.

Joseph's heart melted. His father was proud of him. His father loved him. He had never said these words to him. Now he was admitting everything. Why did he have to wait? Why tell him now, when everything was falling apart? Joseph moved closer and put a hand on his father's back. He pulled Charlotte over close to him and held her face to his chest. She was crying now too.

"Father, thank you for finally telling me how you feel. But what are we supposed to do now?"

"I don't know. But I can promise you this. I'll never let another drop of drink pass my lips. I'm going to be a new man. I am going to work, and I'll earn back the money to pay off my own debts, to pay you off. I may have wasted most of my life, but I'm not going to waste the rest of it."

"I believe you. Give me some time to think about things. There has to be a way out of this. If we're both contributing, we should be able to make this work. I'll talk to Oliver. This has to change things. There has to be a way to save our land, our home."

But Oliver would not budge. Joseph argued with him for hours. He offered every possible plan he could think of, but his father-in-law would not relent. Joseph implored Lucy to change his mind but she refused. They wanted Robert out of his life, and Lucy wanted to go home. She wanted nothing else to do with the farm or with Joseph's family. How could he honestly tell her she was wrong?

Joseph left Oliver's house more frustrated than ever. His father had finally come around. He was willing to admit and face his mistakes. He was willing to quit drinking and help Joseph to pay off the debt. How could he abandon Robert now? At the moment when he was turning his life around? How could Oliver be so uncaring? Worse yet, Lucy had refused to even listen to the proposal. What had happened to her? She had pursued him with such persistence. She had seemed so happy, so in love with him. Since they had married, she had changed. Now all she did was complain about their circumstances. Maybe she hadn't changed, Joseph realized. Maybe this was the real Lucy the entire time, and she had only portrayed a different person to him and to the world before they were married. Perhaps this was all there truly was to Lucy. A spoiled, shallow, smiling doll, wanting nothing more than shiny objects and to be served and taken care of.

Joseph had to find another solution. He rode to Morristown in the late afternoon and tracked down Mr. Deary. He was in a local tavern having a drink with some other men. They all spoke with Irish accents.

"Ah, it's Mr. Forsyth. Good to see you again, lad. Did you bring me the rest of my money?"

"My time's not up yet."

"That it's not. But what can I do for you then?"

"I want to propose that I make you payments. I'm having a hard time raising all of the money now."

The men at the table laughed. "What do I look like, boyo? A bank? Your da lost that money fair and square. I have a note. Do you want me to involve the police in this matter? I want my money."

"What if I pay you interest?"

Deary's eyes narrowed. "What kind of interest?"

"I'll pay you ten percent per year until the balance is paid."

"Twenty percent. And I'll want it secured on your land. *And* I'll want another three hundred up front. Otherwise it's no deal, boyo."

"I don't have another three hundred."

"Easy enough then. I'll take it all instead."

Joseph was despondent. Where would he come up with another three hundred? The only person who could loan him that much money was Oliver, and Oliver wouldn't do so unless he met his terms. There must be some way out of this.

"Give me a few hours to think about things. Then I'll be back."

"That's fine, boyo. Take your time. But come back with the money or with agreement to my terms."

Hours later, Joseph returned home. His house was empty so he headed over to Robert's. They were still up.

"Joseph, where have you been all day?" asked Charlotte. "We've been worried about you."

"I solved the problem. We can all stay on the farm." He turned to Robert. "You will have to step up and take over things for a while. You have to keep your promise to me."

Robert nodded. "Of course I will, Joseph, but what do you mean by *take over things*?"

"I joined the army."

"What?" asked Charlotte. "What do you mean? Why would you do such a thing?"

"I had no choice. I had to come up with another three hundred to pay Mr. Deary. I don't have that much money in savings. I already borrowed money from Pete, and Oliver won't loan it to me. There is a new regiment forming in Morristown, the 186th New York Volunteers. They are paying three-hundred-dollar bonuses to join. It was this or lose the land, and lose all of you."

"What about Lucy?"

"I don't know. She wouldn't listen to me about you. She wants to go back and live in her father's house. She won't come back to the farm no matter what."

"You don't mean divorce?" asked Charlotte in horror.

"I . . . I don't know what I mean. I hope she will see sense and come back to me, come back to us. But I won't be with a woman who picks her father over her husband. I don't know what's happened to her. But she is ruining me. She has crushed me down so deeply with her pouting and her spending. I don't know how it happened, but it has. I have to stand up to her. I have to stand up for something."

"What about poor Mary Jane?"

"She'll be all right," said Joseph, his voice cracking. In all of this, the thought of going away from Mary Jane broke his heart. He loved his little girl so much. But what choice did he have? He could buckle under, surrender to Oliver, and live the rest of his life as just another servant at the Hastings house, or he could stand up for what he believed in. He may have made mistakes in the past when he took care of Robert, but now Robert was ready to deal with his problems. Now he was ready to help. Joseph couldn't turn his back on his father now.

Charlotte rushed forward and held Joseph. "Oh, Joseph, I'm so sorry. I'm so sorry for all of this. Now you are going away, going away from all of us and into danger. I couldn't forgive myself if something happened to you, and neither could your father."

"I took care of things. Now you need to do the same. You have to take care of this farm while I'm gone. You will have to work harder than you've ever worked. You can't drink. Give whatever help you can to Lucy if you are able. And take care of my little girl. Lucy will be angry with me when I leave. She will be angry at you too. But she will come around. I believe deep inside there is more to her than she's shown us of late. There's a vulnerable little girl who needs our love. At least I hope and pray that girl exists. In any event, I won't be here for her for a while. She will need you."

"We will, Joseph, of course," said Charlotte.

"Well, Father, you wanted me to join up in '61. Now you're getting your wish."

Robert frowned. "I was a fool, Joseph. I've been such a fool. You take care of yourself and you be safe. I'll take care of things here, and when you come home, we will work this farm together, father and son, boyo."

Joseph smiled. He embraced his father and held him tightly for a few moments. "I'm leaving in the morning. After I tell Lucy."

Jane was asleep and he wasn't able to tell her good-bye. He walked out into the darkness and headed to his home to stay for the last time. He slept alone in the dark and the cold, praying for his future and the future of his family.

CHAPTER 18

UNION MILITARY HOSPITAL CAMP NEAR THE JERUSALEM ROAD

SATURDAY, JANUARY 9, 1865

Rebecca woke later in the morning still exhausted. She was riddled with guilt. How had things developed so quickly between her and Thomas? She didn't understand her own feelings at all. She had certainly admired Doctor Johnston as a surgeon, even if he occasionally was arrogant and ordered her around. Where had these feelings come from? Where had *his* feelings come from? He had hardly spoken to her on personal affairs since they met. Then over a matter of days, he tells her that he loves her.

She was angry. Angry at him and angry at herself. She was a new widow who must honor her husband's life and his death for a suitable period of time. She had no right to think of another man in any light. Such thoughts were a terrible sin. Perhaps they could be forgiven, perhaps even understood, but not loving a married man. How could she have even let this happen to her? She would have to take swift action. She would pray and read the Bible. She would beg forgiveness for her soul. More importantly, she would speak to the hospital commander and request an immediate transfer, not only to another doctor but to another hospital. She must never allow such weakness and sin to transfer from the heart to the body. Her only chance at forgiveness now was outward propriety. What did her husband think of her, looking down from heaven, their little girl by his side? Yes, she must request a transfer.

The thought of leaving Thomas paralyzed her and filled her with dread and longing. Why did this have to go so far so quickly? Why couldn't they have simply progressed as friends, sharing a few thoughts to each other about their own lives while they continued to conduct their work together? Then they could have been together every day, every moment, for the rest of the war. Now she must leave him forever and she must do so swiftly.

What about Joseph? She couldn't let him down. She had worked so hard to keep him alive. Could she leave him without care? He was horribly sick with wound fever, in fact he might already be dead this morning. It was so rare for anyone to survive a wound infection. But she couldn't leave him. She decided she would stay until his end and then immediately request the transfer. She wasn't sure how she would convince the hospital commander to move her, but she would think of something. She could use the time nursing Joseph to come up with a suitable excuse. She could not bear to tell the truth or to come up with any reason that might harm Thomas.

Thomas. What would she do with him before she left? She must be strong. She would ask him to leave her alone for a day or two while she thought through their words. He would honor that. He was an honorable man. Her heart ached as she thought of sending him away. She tried to come up with some way to ease that pain. She closed her eyes, imagining her husband and daughter watching from heaven. She would simply keep their images in her mind when she saw Thomas. That would give her the strength to send him away.

She shook her head, trying to clear the cobwebs. She needed to check on Joseph first. If he was gone, it would be so much easier for her. That thought filled her with guilt as well. What had become of her? Of course she wanted him alive; she just needed to get away from Thomas. She needed to get to safety before it was too late.

She dressed quickly and headed out into the frigid morning air. The hospital recovery tent was less than a minute away. She looked around, hoping she would not run into Thomas on the way. She was relieved to see very few people were about and *he* was nowhere in sight. She entered the tent and her heart fell. Joseph was there still alive and kneeling over him was Doctor Johnston. She stopped and started to turn, hoping to sneak away and come back later.

"Rebecca." He had seen her. She turned back. He was watching her, his eyes piercing hers, searching and questioning. She felt her heart beating and her skin shivered. He was here. So close to her. She wanted to run but so much more deeply she wanted to see him. She found herself walking to him, first slowly and then swiftly. She noted there was no other medical staff in the tent. Words and thoughts flashed through her mind, whirling about in a confused pattern. She couldn't focus.

"Hello," she said, her voice faltering.

"Rebecca, I'm so glad you're here. I need to talk to you."

"Don't, Thomas. Please don't. I, I can't . . ."

He placed a hand on her arm and gave her a gentle squeeze. "Don't worry. I won't say it again. I do have many things I would like to say to you, but first, look at this." He motioned to Joseph.

"What is it?"

"I've been bathing his wound in iodine. I've been asking around to see if anyone had any ideas about how to treat the wound. I ran into Doctor Ericks. He was up at City Point recently and had a conversation with several doctors on General Grant's personal staff. There is a new experimental procedure. Wounds are being treated with alcohol or iodine after surgery. Some doctors are skeptical, because after this treatment the good pus is failing to appear. However, many doctors are saying that when they treat wounds like this, they are having a much better percentage of patients who recover without infection, and that infections are also being cured."

"Is it working?" Rebecca had never heard of this form of treatment before and she had been at the front for more than a year. She was excited that there was some possibility of hope for Joseph, but also professionally cautious about a procedure she was unfamiliar with.

"It takes a little time to be effective apparently. I treated him around midnight and again this morning as you arrived. I hope you don't mind me stepping in with your patient."

"He is our patient together." She stumbled over the word *together.* She was thrilled and repulsed by it. "This is very exciting news. Thank you for looking into it. Thank you also for staying up with him after I . . . left."

"I want to talk to you about that as well."

Rebecca felt sick. She didn't know what to do and was afraid of what she might say.

"Thomas, I don't think it's a good idea. I'm very sorry about what we said. Please understand I don't blame you."

"Rebecca . . ."

"Please, let me finish. You are a married man, Thomas. I'm a recent widow. We have crossed boundaries that should never have been crossed."

"We have only said a few words. There have been no actions."

"The words are just as terrible. The Bible makes no distinction truly, does it? We have already sinned beyond measure. I don't know how I found myself in this situation. I have always admired you—your work. I can only blame this situation on my emotional state."

"Don't blame yourself. Blame me. I'm the one who spoke the words."

She moved closer to him. She could feel her body ache. She was shivering. She had to keep her strength somehow.

"I will have to leave."

"What? You can't mean that." He moved closer to her, taking her arm in his hand gently. "Please, Rebecca, I won't utter another word. I will respect your wishes and we will get through this. We are a wonderful team. Look what we've done with Joseph. A miracle. I promise we can get through this."

She wanted to believe him. Maybe they could take a step back and continue to work together. She wanted that so badly, even as she dreaded it. She closed her eyes, trying to think. All she could feel was his gentle hand on her arm.

"Please, Rebecca. I need you. I need you here. The clouds are closing in on me. I try to fight against the pain. There have been too many bodies. Too much death. I can't sleep at night. You have been the only thing keeping me together."

His words surprised her. He was always so distant, so strong in his cynicism and wit. She realized all of that was an act. He was trying to cope all this time just like she was. If she was the reason he was surviving, could she take that away from him? Could she take this away from herself?

"I will stay so long as we remain friends. But there can never be another word."

He smiled, squeezing her arm. "I promise. I promise we will just be friends. I will find the strength somewhere. Your strength will be my inspiration."

She returned his smile, burning with elation and despair. They were lying to each other. She didn't have the strength to stop this from happening. She felt the passion carrying her away. Why couldn't she find the strength to fight this? She was trying, but it was too much. She had lost everything. She deserved a little happiness even if it was a sin. She knew in her heart that all of this might destroy her. Why was she being so deeply tempted at such a moment of weakness and vulnerability? It was in God's hands; she had no strength of her own. She prayed for strength, even as a part of her dreamed of Thomas.

CHAPTER 19

MACOMB, NEW YORK

WEDNESDAY, SEPTEMBER 1, 1864

Joseph arrived at the Hastings home early the following morning. He let himself in and turned to the right into the dining room. Oliver and Lucy were sitting at the long table eating breakfast. They both looked up and were relieved to see him.

"Joseph, we were terribly worried," said Lucy. "Where have you been?"

"I went to see the Pattersons to tell them what happened. Then I went and confronted Robert."

"You didn't harm him, I hope?"

"No, I didn't. He apologized and admitted everything. He's never been more straightforward. He promised to quit drinking and work hard to pay off the debt."

"Likely story," said Oliver. "He would promise anything at this point to avoid losing the farm. How did he take it when you told him he has to go?"

Joseph squared his shoulders. He knew how difficult this was going to be, perhaps the most difficult thing he had ever done. "I didn't tell him he has to go."

He saw Oliver's face go red. "What do you mean?"

"He's not going to go. I've decided."

"What do you mean, *you've* decided? I told you what we are going to do."

"Joseph, what are you saying?" asked Lucy.

"I'm not going to take you up on your offer, Oliver. I'm going to deal with these problems myself. Robert and I will deal with them."

"What do you mean?" asked Oliver. "What can that possibly mean?"

"I've talked to Patterson and I've talked to Mr. Deary. I have paid another three hundred on the debt. I've paid half the debt off to Deary, and Pete will give me time to pay on the note to him. I know he will. Robert is going to work the farm and make payments on a monthly basis. I'll send home what I can send as well."

"Send home? You're going away? What are you talking about?" demanded Lucy.

"I didn't have enough money to pay Deary. I knew you would never loan me the money unless I removed Robert from the property. So I joined the army for the three-hundred-dollar bounty."

"What the hell are you talking about, Joseph?" shouted Oliver. "You can't join the army. You have a family and responsibilities here. The four years you promised me aren't up. What about Lucy and Mary Jane? What about the new baby?"

"You left me no choice, Oliver. You forced my hand. I needed the money and I had no way to get it."

"You had all the money you needed and more! All you had to do was get that worthless bastard of a father off my land!"

"It's not *your* land anymore! Did you forget I bought the land from you? All you had to do was have a little understanding, but you wouldn't. You *had* to demand that Robert be kicked off my land. That he had to go away. That Charlotte and Jane would have no home and no future. You had to demand that I give up the only land I've ever owned, and come back here under your thumb. I won't do it! You've controlled me for too many years. Now your daughter has done the same. I don't control my own life anymore. I need some time away, time to regain who I am. I will send all of my pay home. The money can be split between Lucy and the debt on the farm."

"Sixteen dollars a month? Is that your private's pay? You make five times that right now with me. You're a fool, Joseph. As big a fool as your father. He ruined your finances and now you've ruined the rest of your life."

"I haven't ruined my life. I'm redeeming it. You have tried everything to keep me for your own purposes. I have worked to free myself year after year, but you won't let me go! You come back with more years, more obligations, more plans. I can't take it anymore!"

"What of your promise to work for me for four years? Now you're a promise breaker as well?"

"What am I, two months shy? I've paid my debts to you, Oliver, and make no mistake. If I did listen to you, I wouldn't have two more months; it would be four more years. What about after that? Another four years and then another plan, another obligation. I'm not you. I don't want to be you! I don't want to live your life!"

"You won't have my life now, Joseph. You've damned yourself. I won't give you another chance after this. I'll take care of Lucy and the children since you've chosen not to. I'm washing my hands of you."

"Oh, Joseph, how could you have done this to us?" cried Lucy. "Don't you love me anymore? What about Mary Jane? She needs a father. Now you're going to leave her and leave me pregnant? What if you're killed? You will leave me a widow and all alone? Father, fix this! Make him change it!"

"It's too late Lucy. Once he signed, he's stuck." Oliver shook his head. "I believed in you, Joseph. You were my son. My future. I gave my own son up for you. You are the biggest disappointment of my life. Get out of my house and out of my sight!"

"Oliver, you have to understand . . ."

"I said get out!" Oliver's voice rumbled through the house.

Joseph rose and turned to Lucy. "Are you coming?"

She looked at him and then looked at her father as if trying to determine what to do. "Why have you done this to me? You've ruined everything." Tears ran down her face. "You should go. Just go!"

Joseph turned and walked away, but he wasn't leaving just yet. He climbed the stairs and went to the room where Mary Jane slept when they stayed overnight. He found her playing on the floor. She ran into his arms.

"Daddy!"

"Hello, darling! Have you been a good girl today?"

"Uh-huh."

He picked her up and held her in his arms, closing his eyes and rocking her back and forth. He could feel the tears streaming down his face. How could he leave his little girl? He loved her so much. He had no choice, he had to leave or surrender and live the rest of his life under Oliver's control.

"I love you, darling. I love you."

"I love you, Daddy."

"I have to go away for a trip. I want you to be very strong and take care of Mommy and Grandpa. Can you do that for me?"

"Yes, Daddy."

She didn't understand. How could he explain to her he would be gone for months? That he might not come back. How could he tell his little girl he was off to kill other men or be killed? She would never understand that because it didn't make any sense. Thank God she couldn't comprehend how long he might be gone. He couldn't take it if she fell apart now.

"That's my wonderful girl." He held her closer, rocking her back and forth like he did when she was a baby. "I'll be home, home soon, dear. Home to you."

Joseph left the house and rode to Pope's Mill. He arrived at Patterson's store shortly after noon. The sun was out and the day was hot and terribly humid. Pete was in the front of the store putting away large sacks of flour.

"Joseph, how are you?" asked Pete, his face full of concern. "Did you talk to Robert? Is everything all right?"

"I did talk to Robert and I talked to Oliver. Things are not all right, but I've done what I think is best." He explained everything that had happened since he'd left the day before.

"The army, Joseph. Why on earth would you do that? I feel terribly now. I could have loaned you a bit more. Enough to stave off this Mr. Deary until we could figure out what to do."

"You've done enough already, Pete. I only hope you'll give me some time to pay back the debt I owe you."

"Of course I will, Joseph. You know that. Take the time you need. There's nobody I would trust more. But why? Why the army?"

"I have to stand up on my own again. Little by little I've come under Oliver's power. Oliver and Lucy, they've taken everything from me. Oliver won't let me go. He finds a reason each time to keep me for more years on his property. Lucy is the same or worse. She cares more about clothes and furniture than she does about me. I should have understood she would be that way from watching her grow up. She was always like a little princess, given everything she wanted in the nicest house in Macomb. How could I have expected she would be happy on a little humble farm? I was a fool."

"We're all fools in love, Joseph. The problem has been your nature. You've tried to take care of all of them and all they have done in return is taken from you. Joining the army doesn't make much sense for you financially. You could do better staying at home. But I think you're right. You had to stand up to them. You had to take back your freedom." He put his hand on Joseph's shoulder. "I'm proud of you. You did the right thing. Don't you worry. I'll keep an eye on the farm and on your daughter and Lucy while you're gone. Lucy will be fine. Oliver won't let anything bad happen to her. When do you leave?"

"Tomorrow morning. I have to report to Morristown to muster in tomorrow." Thinking of the army, he remembered Marie again. "Oh no. I've forgotten poor Marie. I need to get out to her property and take care of things."

"Isn't that like you, Joseph Forsyth? In the worst time of your life and you're trying to take care of someone else. Don't you worry about Marie. I'll take care of everything and make sure she's looked after as well."

"Thank you, Pete. I'm going to miss you and David. Please tell him good-bye for me. I don't have the heart to see him right now. You know how much you've always meant to me. You're the only real father I've ever had."

"I know that, Joseph. Thank you for saying it." He pulled Joseph in and embraced him, holding him for a few seconds. "You take care of yourself, young man. Independence aside, this is serious business. People are getting killed in this war as you know full well. I expect you home in one piece, do you understand me?"

Joseph laughed. "Yes, sir. That's one command I'm happy to obey if I'm able."

He bid his old friend farewell and rode home. He spent the rest of the day working with Robert on the farm, showing him the livestock and when to feed the animals, milk the cows, and when the crops should be harvested. Robert had never acted like this: he was serious and attentive, asking questions and writing down notes. Joseph felt a closeness to his father he had never felt before. He had always dreamed of this, of working with Robert to build a life for their family. Too bad it needed to come to this to finally bring him around.

That night, Charlotte cooked a tremendous feast of chicken, potatoes with gravy, hot buttered corn, and fresh-baked bread followed by a steaming apple pie. Joseph ate and ate until he was stuffed. They all did their best to enjoy the night, but it was hard to control their emotions, knowing that Joseph would be leaving the next day and that Lucy was not coming home tonight. Jane spent the evening next to Joseph, her hands wrapped tightly around his arm as if afraid that if she let him go, he would be gone forever. He had tried to explain why he had to go away and that he would be home soon, but she would not be consoled and she kept bursting into tears.

Joseph went to bed with a heavy heart. He hoped he had done the right thing. Had he acted too rashly? Should he have tried to negotiate with Oliver further? No, he knew Oliver wouldn't have changed his mind. Lucy and Oliver resented Robert, and Robert would have had to go, no matter what. Even if Oliver had relented on this point, he would have used it as just more leverage to chain Joseph further into debt with him. Joseph had done the right thing, the only thing he could do. He would serve his time in the army and Robert would work hard at home. They would pay off the debts of the farm and Joseph would come home when his service was at an end. Lucy would realize that Joseph and the children were more important to her than luxury, and she would come home to him. She had never fully trusted her father anyway.

What if she didn't come home? What if she refused? He couldn't think about that right now. He had too much in front of him.

The next morning, he rose early and saddled his horse. He brought one change of clothing, some bread and cheese for the road, and a pistol. He was ready to depart when a wagon came around the bend, driven by Pete and David.

"Thought you could use some company this morning. You'll need someone to bring your horse back in any event."

"Thanks, Pete, David."

He rode next to the wagon and they talked lightly about the past, telling stories about Casey, David, and Joseph, and all the trouble they would get into. "Mostly it was Casey and me in trouble," said David. "You were always too busy working and acting like an old man, scolding us for all our antics."

"Yes I did. For all the good it did me."

Pete's face darkened. "Now don't say such things. You're as good a man as I've ever known, Joseph. We can't always control the fate we're given. But hard work will dig you out of many a hole as they say. You give it a few years and you'll see where you end up. For now, you just keep yourself out of the way of those bullets!"

In the late afternoon, they made their way into Morristown. They rode down Chapman Street, the dust kicking up in the steamy heat. Finally they arrived at the muster office of the 186th New York Volunteers.

Joseph dismounted and removed his gear. He handed the reins of his horse to Pete. "Well, I guess this is it."

"I think I'll go with you," said David.

"That's funny. Pete would never allow it."

"I am allowing it, Joseph. He asked if he could go with you and I agreed." Pete looked into Joseph's eyes with deep pain. "This is my gift to you, Joseph. I'm sending my two boys out to war. Take care of him."

"You can't do this, Pete."

"I don't think I could stop him. He's gone on about nothing else since he heard the news. I wouldn't hear the end of it if I kept him behind."

Joseph embraced Pete again. "Thank you. This is truly the greatest gift you could have given me."

"You two quit your carrying on," said David. "I'm not a package to be passed between you. I simply decided that Joseph couldn't be trusted with such a weighty matter by himself. He needs looking after."

Joseph laughed. "So I do, my friend. So I do."

David and Joseph bid Pete good-bye and watched as the old storekeeper rode off slowly in his wagon, Joseph's horse trailing behind. They then turned and walked up the stairs of the muster office.

Joseph realized this was the start of a new chapter in his life. He didn't know what the future would bring, but he was happy to have a moment of freedom, a moment of control. Now he had his friend with him too, an unexpected surprise that made all of the shadows surrounding him less dark. He clapped David on the shoulder. "Let's get started then, boyo." They passed through the swinging double doors and into their new world.

A week later and they were no farther from Morristown than when they had begun. After spending the better part of a day filling out paperwork and receiving their issue of clothing and some ill-fitting boots, they were grouped in with another forty or so privates and marched out of town and into a nearby field. They were then issued tents and blankets, and their weapons—model 1863 Springfield rifle muskets.

For the next few days, they struggled to catch on to a dizzying set of regulations that governed every aspect of their life. They learned to march and obey commands, turning and presenting their weapons. They learned the bugle calls that woke them, called them to meals, and sounded them to bed. They were drilled in loading their weapons and then in firing them. Joseph found to his surprise that he had a steady hand and was an excellent shot, even though he had very little experience with a rifle.

"That's my Joseph. A natural hand at everything he's ever done," joked David.

They also had to get used to army food. Joseph saw quickly that the most inept soldiers were assigned the duties of cook. A local man complained and asked permission to go into town for a decent meal. He was roundly chastised by one of the sergeants, and made to stand watch all night as a punishment for his insubordination.

New recruits trickled in from all over St. Lawrence County. There was Nicholas, a tall redheaded boy from Ogdensburg who played the fiddle and loved to play practical jokes. There was Douglas from Morristown, a brown-haired, brown-eyed man of average height who was so nondescript that he was easily lost in the crowd, at least until he spoke. He was the son of a Baptist minister and he preached when he talked. Douglas carried a Bible with him and loved to lecture anyone who would listen that God would rain retribution down on the rebels because of slavery. James Sayer of Macomb was the son of a miner and had worked in the mines himself. He was short but wiry and strong, with dark hair and black eyes. He was quiet but would watch everything with deep interest.

All of the men became close through the days of dreary drilling and the need to cling together in an unfamiliar setting. Joseph found that just like on the *St. Charles* and in Macomb, men warmed to him quickly and looked up to him as a leader.

The regiment was under the command of Colonel Bradley Winslow. Joseph and his friends were assigned to Company D under the command of Captain McMullen. The men were able to elect their own noncommissioned officers. Joseph was elected corporal. He was quietly very proud of his selection, and the rank afforded him a little more pay to send home to the family.

He had felt a strange peace in the past days since he left. He'd wondered if he would feel regret over his decisions but he did not. He realized how badly he had needed to escape from all of the pressures of his world, from all of the people demanding all of his time, his attention, and his money.

A little distance gave him tremendous insight. He had come to Macomb to save his mother. When he found she was already dead, he had transferred that feeling of obligation to his stepmother, his half sister, and even his father. He had done everything he could for them. When the time came to marry, he had done the same for Lucy, for Mary Jane, and even for Oliver. He had constantly sacrificed his own needs and resources for everyone else.

They had all taken advantage of him, whether on purpose or not. He had enjoyed taking care of them, but he realized it was never enough. They had slowly taken more and more, until they took everything he had. Each in their own selfish way had grown to expect that Joseph would give them what they needed. He would always be there with gifts, with advice, with help. He had never asked for anything in return. They had grown used to giving him nothing.

Now all of that had changed. He had finally thrown them off and stood up for himself. He was pleased with at least some of the results. Robert had quit drinking and had agreed to work off his debts on the farm and take care of things in Joseph's absence. Oliver was angry at him, but Joseph had freed himself of his obligations to his father-in-law. He could live with Oliver's anger and disappointment. The only great struggle for him was Lucy. She had not come to see him again before he left. She had not written. She had chosen to stay with her father rather than support her husband's decision.

He was hurt by this and confused. Didn't she miss him? Didn't she want their family to be together? What about Mary Jane? Lucy must care that he was not able to see Mary Jane again before he left. Yet if so, why didn't she bring his daughter to him that last night? It might be possible that she simply didn't care how he felt, didn't care what was important to him. Could she really be that selfish?

He lay in his tent thinking over these problems. Still, he was content that he had stood up for himself. Lucy would come around surely. He would come home to a happy wife and to Mary Jane.

There would also be their new child—perhaps a boy this time to help someday on the farm. They would pay off the debts, and Joseph would save up money for the printing equipment. He could do all of this without Oliver, even if it took a lot longer. They would still see Lucy's father, but it would be as equals.

Joseph fell asleep with these reassuring thoughts in mind. The next morning they were woken up early and were soon in line for morning roll call. Captain McMullen announced they would be leaving that day. They would march to Albany over the course of the next few days. They would then catch a train down to Washington, then a ship to City Point, Virginia. Their ultimate destination was south of a city in Virginia named Petersburg, where the Army of the Potomac had been stuck for the past several months.

"Before we leave, I need to introduce another officer to you. This gentleman is from Morristown and has recently joined our ranks. It gives me great pleasure to introduce Lieutenant Warren Hastings."

Joseph looked up in surprise and shock. Surely he had not heard correctly. But there he was, his old enemy and the brother of his wife. Warren looked the same, except his moustache had just the beginning of some gray. He looked out over the company with pride and arrogance. His eyes moved along the line of men until they rested on Joseph. He smiled a knowing, secret smile.

He knew I would be here. He joined because of me. Joseph stared stiffly ahead, refusing to look at Warren. His mind reeled, trying to process what this meant. Why would Warren be here? Had Oliver tipped him off? Was it even possible that Lucy was so upset she had reached out to her estranged brother? He wasn't sure of the answers, but he knew one thing for sure: Warren was here for revenge.

CHAPTER 20

Union Transport Train

Monday, October 3, 1864

Joseph sat in the railway car looking out the window. The train was making its way through the Virginia countryside. He looked out the window in silence, watching the rolling hills and the pine trees pass by. He had expected to see miles of desolation. Most of the war seemed to have occurred in Virginia from everything he had read and heard. He did see the occasional soldier or encampment, but for the most part it seemed like the war had never happened here. Instead, other than feeling a little hotter, and the existence of more pine trees, he could have been traveling through upstate New York.

Joseph was still in shock over seeing Warren. He didn't know why his brother-in-law had joined the regiment or what he had in store for him, but he was gravely concerned. So far, Warren had made no attempt to speak to Joseph, but he knew that he had come to exact revenge. Joseph had looked over several times on the long train ride and found Warren staring at him a few rows away. His eyes were fierce and full of smoldering anger.

Fortunately, David was here. His friend knew all too well Joseph's history with Warren. David sat next to him the entire trip and kept an eye on the lieutenant. Joseph knew that David would be a witness to any altercation between them. He only hoped that the word of a private and corporal would be considered against that of a lieutenant if Warren tried to make a move against him.

"Mail call." A sergeant had appeared at the front of the carriage with a bag of mail. He began reading out names. David's name was called. He had a letter from his wife and another from Pete. David opened the letters and read them out loud, although he blushed and skipped over part of the letter from his wife. Joseph enjoyed hearing about home. They had only been gone a short time, but it already seemed an eternity.

"Joseph Forsyth." He looked up. The sergeant was holding a letter and he repeated the name. Joseph raised his hand and then quickly stood, moving through the narrow center corridor to the front, where he retrieved the letter. He expected correspondence from Robert or Charlotte, but it was from Lucy. His heart skipped a beat. He wasn't sure she would even write. What did she want to say? He walked back to his seat and sat down next to David. He showed the envelope to his friend and then silently tore it open to read.

Dear Joseph,

I haven't known how to write to you these past days. I am so hurt by your decision you can hardly know. We were building a life and a family together, and instead, you are throwing it all away and running away from your responsibilities, all for your father and his family.

Isn't our family more important? Is this about my father? I know he's not perfect, but he has only ever wanted the best for you. He has taken care of us with a job. He sold you our farm.

He was willing to help you start up your printing business. I know you feel like he was controlling you, but he didn't want to do that. He was concerned about you and so am I.

Joseph, you have to get away from Robert. You have no idea how much he takes advantage of you. That's why I went home to my father. That's why I wanted you to come stay there with me. I know you think this is all my fault, that I have spent too much money and bought too many things. Just remember if you weren't providing for two families, then all the things I wanted you could have provided me. I haven't caused these problems. Your father has. Joseph, don't you want me to look pretty? Don't you want our children to grow up with a decent house? With food on the table? That's all I ever wanted. Just to have nice things for the children.

I know what's done is done. You can't leave the army now. Please don't make even more mistakes. Please sell the property and require that Robert leave. I know it will be hard for you, and I'll miss Charlotte and Jane as much as you. But Robert will destroy our lives. He already has destroyed our lives.

Remember, I love you, and I only want what is best for our family.

Love,
Lucy

Joseph read the letter again and again, absorbing the contents. Why had she failed to mention Warren? Surely she must know by now that Warren was here at her father's request? Unless he was still keeping that from her. Oliver would know that Joseph would write Lucy and tell her. What benefit could he gain by keeping it secret? Or was Lucy pretending not to know so that Joseph wouldn't blame her?

Robert. Everything always seemed to come back to his father.

Joseph had spent his life dealing with Robert's mistakes. Lucy was blaming everything on Robert. Certainly his father had created the newest problem, although Joseph wouldn't have joined the army if Lucy's father had not been so heavy-handed. Lucy and Oliver wanted Robert out of Macomb and out of their lives; Joseph wondered whether their determination to get rid of Robert was based on what was truly best, or just what was best for them.

Joseph had given up so much for his father and Robert's family. Now Robert was finally committed to fixing his problems. Charlotte had written about how well Robert was doing. He hadn't been drinking since he made his promises. He was working long days on the farm. He was paying more attention to Jane than he ever had, and he was even eating more and putting on weight. Charlotte had thanked Joseph over and over in the letter. Thanks to Joseph and his belief in Robert, his father was becoming the man that Charlotte had always dreamed of.

How could he take that away now? He couldn't force Robert off his land and take away everything he'd ever had. If he did, he knew his father would take to the bottle again. Charlotte and Jane would no longer have his protection or his help. Why couldn't Lucy understand that? Her selfishness had convinced her that they would have been fine if it wasn't for Robert.

Perhaps Lucy had a point. If they weren't supporting Robert, their circumstances would be different. Was it fair for him to take away from Lucy to provide for Charlotte? He didn't know what to do. He had struggled with these questions for several years now. At first, he hadn't had any problems; there had been enough in savings to cover the shortfalls. Once the money dwindled away and he started having to cut back on spending, Lucy had begun complaining about Robert as the source of all their woes.

Joseph looked up and saw David watching him. His friend knew all his troubles. He saw compassion and understanding on David's face. Joseph nodded back, silently thanking his friend for understanding, and for being there for him. He rose and walked back down the corridor, passing through his carriage and several more until he was on a small balcony at the back of the train. He needed some fresh air and a chance to think about things.

He heard the door open behind him and turned around. It was Warren. Joseph started for the door but the lieutenant blocked him. He was smiling.

"Joseph. So good to see you. I was hoping we would have a moment to chat."

"What do you want, Warren?"

"I just wanted to find out how Robert is doing. He didn't look so well the last time I saw him."

"What do you mean?"

"Well I was finishing work one night and I strolled down to the tavern for a drink and some dinner. Imagine my surprise to see Robert Forsyth, quite drunk and playing cards. He was going on and on about you. Not very flattering things really."

Joseph could feel the anger rising, and also the surprise. Warren had been there the night Robert lost his money? He tried not to show his emotions. "What of it?"

Warren smiled. "I'm glad you asked. I was worried that Robert might besmirch the Forsyth family name the way he was going on and on. I thought the faster he left the better. I therefore introduced him to one of my good friends—a gentleman named Mr. Deary. I believe you've met him as well? He's a rather bright and talented card player. He sat down and played a few hands with your father. Just a few hands mind you. In no time he had completed his business and your father left the tavern. I'm afraid he was rather distressed when he did so, but I'm sure you'll agree with me that I was able to assure he left quickly and quietly."

Mr. Deary knew Warren? Warren had set up Robert? Joseph took a step forward.

"That's not all, of course. I also learned from Mr. Deary about your decision to join the army. I'm somewhat adverse to hard work as I think you know. The army sounded dreadful, but how could I pass up the chance to join you on this little expedition? And as a superior officer to boot. I'm sure you'll agree this was the opportunity of a lifetime for me. I remember when my father threw me off his land and sent me away. He picked you over me. I swore that day, and every day since, I would have my revenge on you. I've already ruined you financially, but I'm not quite sure that's enough. I'm sure I can arrange another disaster or two for you. Of course, what could really go wrong on a battlefield?"

Joseph moved forward and grabbed Warren's arms. He would throw him from the train. He didn't care what the result would be. Warren backed away, clearly surprised by Joseph's action. He tried to break free but Joseph was far stronger. He glanced around wildly, pulling Warren toward the rail.

"Joseph!"

He looked up. David was standing at the window. His friend opened the door, grave concern on his face. "What are you doing? People are watching."

Joseph looked through the window and saw dozens of soldiers watching him with surprise. He let go of Warren and stepped back.

"That's right, Private. No harm done. Thank you for helping me. I almost fell," said Warren loudly. He looked at Joseph with hard eyes. "Don't worry, my friend," he whispered. "We will take this up at the proper time. I promise you that."

October 26, 1864

The regiment detrained at Washington City and were fed. They caught another train south and then traveled by ship down to City

Point, Virginia. From there they marched to a staging area several miles behind the trenches of Petersburg where they were assigned to the IX Corps under General John Parke. Joseph hadn't known much about the Petersburg siege or the battle, so he was glad when Colonel Winslow addressed the men. Colonel Winslow was a tall, somewhat portly man with short brown hair and a nose ruddy with veins. He was aloof and had only spoken to the men a couple of times. Attending him were his second in command, E. Jay Marsh, and his third in command, Abram Stemberg.

"Men, we are here to help break through the rebels and finally take Richmond. The Confederate capital has stood for almost four years. We've sent army after army down here to capture it, but General Lee has found some way to stop us every time.

"Every time, that is, until now. Now we have our own general, General Grant. He won't quit. He has locked horns with Lee for months now and he hasn't stopped. Some criticize him for allowing too many casualties, too many deaths. I do not. This war won't be over until Richmond is taken and Lee is defeated. Whatever the cost, we have to get through those Confederates and take Richmond.

"Now you boys have never been in battle before. What's more, you've never seen a battle like this one. No one has. We will be leaving tomorrow for the front lines. There aren't open fields with rows of men standing like you've seen in the papers. The cowardly rebs hide behind trenches. They've dug deep down into the earth and they only come up when we attack them. We've dug our own trenches too. But we don't want to sit here all winter, do we, boys?"

There was a roar of agreement.

"That's what I thought. I've heard from General Parke that tomorrow we are going to break through. We are going to attack the Confederate line and knock our way through. Once we break the line, there's nothing stopping us from marching right into Richmond and winning the war. Is the 186th up for the job?"

Another roar rose, this one even greater than the last.

"Lads, all we have to do is break through that line and you will all be heroes. We break through the line and this war is over. These rebs have never seen anything like us. We are fresh and ready to finish this war.

"Now get some food and get some rest. We will be up and marching at dawn. I've ordered extra food for everyone tonight, including some corn on the cob I was able to requisition. Have a good night and tomorrow we whip them good!"

The regiment applauded thunderously and then the men dispersed to their tents. Joseph and David shared one together. The tent was an A-frame design that tapered up in the middle and then down in a triangular form to the ground. They set up as quickly as possible and then they organized their gear and built a fire nearby. As they tended to the fire, they were able to talk.

"Have you had any more problems with Warren?" asked David.

"No, not so far. But there will be. He is here to kill me if he can, I have no doubt. You need to watch yourself, my friend. You might end up getting hurt as well."

"We're in this together. What would my dad think if I let you get yourself killed? We'll keep an eye on Warren, the both of us. Joseph, I have a different question."

"Yes?"

"What do you think it will be like tomorrow? I mean, I've never been in a battle before."

Joseph felt the same fear. Hundreds of thousands of men had died in this war already. Perhaps worse were the stories of the terrible suffering of the wounded. A number of Macomb men had come back from the war with missing limbs. They were generally tight-lipped about their experiences, but the little they would say was terrifying to hear. He was so grateful that David was with him. Grateful and guilty. He knew his decision to leave was going to affect his family, but he had put his closest friend in danger as well. If anything happened to David, he would never forgive himself.

"We will be all right. We just need to stick close together and follow orders." Joseph smiled. "I don't think a bullet could harm a Patterson in any event."

David laughed. "Oh, I'm sure a bullet would go through me just fine. It's your thick head that would probably stop one."

Joseph looked at his friend for a moment. "Thank you for coming with me. You don't know how much it means to me."

David beamed. "I wouldn't let you go on your own. You know that. Not for this adventure."

They were soon joined by their friends, and the men stayed up late, laughing and joking, until an officer shooed them to their tents. They were awoken by reveille in the early morning light before dawn and assembled for roll call. After a quick breakfast, the men packed up their equipment in the silence and returned to form up in lines for marching, each company in line in alphabetical order. As the sun rose, they left the field where they had bivouacked and tramped down a dusty dirt road, heading north toward the lines at Petersburg.

The regiment marched for what seemed hours, punctuated by long waits as the lines in front of them started and stopped. Thankfully, the late-October day was cool. The men were very quiet this morning, Joseph noticed. He felt an anxiety he had never known before. As they moved along, he started to hear the distant din of artillery. He felt his heart beating hard in his chest and his hands went clammy and cold. He might die today. This could be his last day forever. What a fool he had been to join up. He had run away, he realized. He had been afraid to stand up to everyone in his life, and instead he had run away. He had thought he was finally taking a stand, but even his decision to join had been an act of avoidance, a half measure. Now he had put his own life in danger, and the life of his best friend. If he died, he would widow his wife and orphan Mary Jane. He had to survive.

The regiment reached a line of trees near the road, overlooking a field. They were ordered to leave the road and spread out along the edge of the field, taking up positions behind trees and whatever shelter the men could find. Joseph found a large broken stump and set up behind it, motioning David to join him. The stump provided complete cover for their lower bodies, and a comfortable place to rest their elbows and their rifles. From behind their cover, they could see out over the whole field to another line of trees in the distance perhaps five hundred yards away.

Captain Richard McMullen, the company commander, rode down the line, followed slightly behind by Warren and two other lieutenants. Captain McMullen shouted at the men to be prepared for a possible rebel attack. He informed them that they were on the extreme flank of the IX Corps position, and they were to hold no matter what came their way.

The cannon fire increased in intensity as the morning faded away to noon. Each man remained in position, alone with his thoughts. Joseph felt exhausted. The initial rush of energy had faded and seemed to drain him. He felt a bizarre mixture of anticipation and boredom. If something was going to happen, he wished it just would. The waiting was almost more than he could bear.

"Corporal, what are you doing there?"

Joseph turned and found Warren standing over him.

"I'm in position like the captain ordered."

"I have new orders. We need a few pickets for our right. I want you, Private Patterson, and a few others to come with me immediately."

What was Warren up to? Could he refuse? He looked around for the captain but he couldn't see him.

"Now, Corporal. That's a direct order!"

Joseph stood and brushed himself off. He called David over along with Nicholas, Douglas, and James.

"What do you need?" asked David.

"Lieutenant Hastings wants us to accompany him on picket duty."

"What? He has to be up to something." David turned to Warren. "What are you up to, Hastings? The captain ordered us to hold this line."

"The captain is consulting with the colonel and he left me in charge. We need pickets and I'm selecting all of you. I'm giving you a direct order and you will all come with me immediately, is that understood?" Warren drew his pistol, pointing it at Joseph.

Joseph raised his hand. "Enough, enough, no, we're coming."

Warren led the small group along the tree line and back to the road. He kept his pistol out in his hand. He looked back and forth for a moment along the road and then motioned for them to cross. Joseph took the lead and ran across the road into the trees on the other side. David, Douglas, Nicholas, and James followed. The tree line was similar on that side of the road except it curved to their left until the field eventually merged into the woods, a couple miles or so down the line. Warren ordered them to spread out and continue forward.

Joseph kept the lead position, walking cautiously and straining his eyes to see through the vegetation in front of him. They proceeded for what seemed an eternity, and Joseph was sure they were a mile or more from their position. He didn't know much about tactics, but he was sure pickets were not to be posted this far from a position. He kept looking back to Warren but the lieutenant still had his pistol in his hand and he was watching Joseph closely.

Joseph froze, raising his hand for the others to stop. In the distance, perhaps three hundred yards away, he could vaguely make out a gray form sitting against a tree. The Confederate was facing the woods to Joseph's right and he had not yet seen them. Joseph looked closely and could make out several more rebels among the trees. He shifted to his left and moved carefully behind a tree.

"What are you doing, Corporal?" demanded Warren.

"There are rebels up ahead."

"Excellent, you are to lead an attack."

"What?"

Warren smiled. "We *have* to make sure our line is protected. We've encountered the enemy. You will lead an attack immediately. I will hold here to observe."

"We have no idea what is out there. I'm not going to get these men killed. I won't do it."

Warren raised the pistol and pulled back the hammer, aiming directly at Joseph's head. "If you disobey I'll shoot you right now, Corporal. Nothing would give me greater pleasure. But I'll give you the chance to attack that position instead if you wish. Either way, Forsyth, you're not coming out of here alive."

"You son of a bitch."

"I told you, Joseph, I would have my revenge."

"Let me go alone. There's no reason the others need to come with me."

"No. You all go." He waved the pistol and turned to the others. "Get moving, all of you!"

Joseph rose and motioned to the others to follow him and to be as quiet as possible. He moved out, stepping slowly to avoid branches. He tried to keep trees in front of him as much as he could to avoid detection. In a few minutes, they had covered about a third of the distance to the rebels. They had not yet been seen. Joseph's heart threatened to jump out of his body. He looked over and caught David's attention. He gave his friend a grim nod.

A shot rang out, exploding in the quiet forest. Joseph cringed. The rebs had spotted them. Then he realized the shot came from behind. He turned and briefly glimpsed Warren, pistol in the air, smiling and nodding to Joseph before he stepped behind a large tree.

Joseph heard shouting in front of him. Warren had purposefully destroyed their surprise. Joseph peeked his head around a tree and saw scrambling movement as Confederates rushed to a line facing them. There looked to be dozens of them.

Joseph sat down with his back against the tree and placed his musket barrel up. He reached into his ammunition pouch and pulled out a paper-wrapped cartridge, pointing the ball end of the cartridge into the air. He bit off the opposite end of the paper, exposing the powder contained inside, and quickly poured the powder down the barrel. He dropped the cartridge in after the powder and then drew out his musket-ramming rod and dropped it quickly into the barrel, tapping the ball and powder firmly into place at the base of the barrel. He put the ramrod back and then pulled the musket up so his hands were in the middle, toward the butt. Joseph pulled back the hammer and placed a cap on the nipple. His musket was ready to fire. He heard the sharp rap of rifle shots behind him and the whistle of balls as they went past. He felt a strange calm come over him now that the moment had come. None of it felt real anymore. Time seemed to slow down.

Joseph turned and quickly raised his rifle, trying to find a target. Smoke clouded his vision from the rebels' first volley, but he finally found a gray figure frantically reloading. He was still two hundred yards out, but he took careful aim and fired. His rifle roared and bucked back. Joseph flung himself behind the tree. He didn't know if he had hit the target. He didn't want to know.

The musket fire increased. Joseph could hear the bullets ricocheting off the trees. Off his tree. He looked for his friends. David was behind a tree a few feet away. He was loading his rifle and he looked over for a moment and nodded. Nicholas was past David, holding his rifle with both arms and his head was down. He was shaking.

Joseph looked to his left. He saw a blue body on the ground, rolling back and forth slightly as blood spurted like a fountain out of a huge wound in the middle of his chest. He saw his face for a moment: James. He tried calling out to him but his friend didn't respond.

He turned back to the business of reloading. The bullets were raining down on his tree now, but he tried to concentrate. His hands fumbled with the rod as he tamped down the cartridge again then quickly turned the rifle around and pulled back the lever. He looked back over at David. Both were ready to fire. He nodded and then both turned around at the same time.

The rebels were coming. They were on their feet and moving among the trees. He took aim and shot a Confederate as the soldier darted between two saplings. This time he saw the shot hit home, and the bullet knocked the soldier off his feet. He could hear the reb screaming in agony as he hit the ground. He started to turn away as he saw rifles raised and flashes. Bark exploded in front of him.

Joseph looked over and saw with horror that David was on the ground, blood flowing out of a wound in his right arm. He had pulled himself behind the tree, but he was holding his arm and rocking back and forth. Joseph had to reach his friend. Resting his musket against the trunk, he rushed out from behind the tree and sprinted to David. Bullets flew by him but he ignored them. Somehow he made it without being hit. He flung himself down behind the tree and turned his attention to his friend.

"David, are you all right?"

"I'm hit but it's not bad. It hurts like the devil but it just passed through the side of my arm."

Joseph reached in his pocket and pulled out a handkerchief; he tied it around David's arm and pulled it tight. "There, that should help."

The roar of rifles drew closer. David looked up and smiled. "They're going to get us, aren't they?"

Joseph nodded. He looked around. Nicholas and Douglas were nowhere to be seen. James was still on the ground, no longer moving. "Yes, they're going to get us."

"Where's Warren?"

"I don't know. Ran away I guess."

"He could have had the decency to stay and fight with us."

"Decency has never been his strong point. I guess he got what he wanted though." Joseph peeked around their shelter for a brief instant. The rebels were within fifty yards and closing fast. He hoped they would be captured and that David would get medical attention as soon as possible. Joseph held his friend's head against his chest and closed his eyes, waiting, sure of the inevitable end.

A roar of rifle fire tore through the forest, louder than before. Joseph opened his eyes in surprise. The sound was in front of him. He heard a thundering scream and out of the trees ran dozens of Yankees charging hard and firing as they came. They passed Joseph and kept going. He saw a soldier knocked back and hit the ground near him but others kept coming. The sound of combat exploded but soon faded into the distance.

Captain McMullen appeared and, spotting Joseph, came over to the tree. "Corporal, what happened here? We heard the firing and came as quickly as we could."

Joseph looked around for Warren, but didn't see him. He thought of telling the captain what had happened, but he wasn't sure he would be believed. He decided to be careful. "Lieutenant Warren ordered us to scout this area, sir. We encountered the enemy in large numbers and were pinned down here."

"Excellent work, Corporal. If we hadn't found these rebels, they might have wandered into our flank. Where is Lieutenant Warren? I would like to give him my compliments."

"I'm not sure, sir. He was behind us and after the shooting started . . . I haven't seen him since."

"That's strange. Why wouldn't he be with you?"

"I don't know. Sir, permission to take Private Patterson back for medical treatment. He's wounded and needs attention."

"Permission granted, Corporal."

Joseph saluted then rose and, with the assistance of another solider, pulled David to his feet. His friend was conscious but very pale and he did not seem to be fully aware of what was happening. Joseph pulled David next to him and put his good arm around his neck, then half dragged, half walked him back toward the road.

He watched David closely as they went, hoping his friend would be okay until they were able to find the hospital.

"Well, I guess that's what the fighting's all about," said David, laughing weakly. "It doesn't look like I'm very good at it."

"You did great, David. Now just hold on and we will find someone to take care of this. Does it hurt?"

"I'm a far cry from hunky-dory, but it doesn't seem too bad. I don't suppose it will be enough to get me out of this mess. Now that I've seen a battle, I don't want to see any more of it."

Joseph agreed. Now that the fighting was over, he was exhausted and he could feel his whole body trembling. He also didn't know what had happened to the rest of his friends. He would come back and look for them as soon as he had David taken care of. "I don't like the fighting either. Hopefully they'll send you home. I think I'm stuck for a while."

"Joseph, look over there."

When Joseph noticed David's face had gone even more pale, he turned and followed his friend's eyes. Slumped against a tree was Warren. His eyes stared and his mouth was wide open as if in a silent scream. In the middle of his forehead there was a hole the size of a quarter. Blood had washed all over the tree trunk.

Warren was dead.

CHAPTER 21

THE HASTINGS HOUSE

MACOMB, NEW YORK

FRIDAY, NOVEMBER 18, 1864

Lucy sat on the front porch of the Hastings home, looking out over her father's property as field hands moved around busily with various tasks. She was terribly bored. Her life had transformed into a stunningly monotonous pattern. She rose each day and had breakfast with her father and Mary Jane. After breakfast, she would play with her daughter for about an hour, then the nanny would take over and Lucy would retire to the library to read, or she would sit out on the porch and rock silently, waiting for lunch. After the midday meal, there would be more of the same. On a rare occasion, her father would invite her into Pope's Mill to pick up some goods, or the family would have a visit from a neighbor or a friend, but for the most part, she sat day after day, alone and with nothing to do.

This was all Joseph's fault. She was still very angry with him. How could he join the army and leave her alone to fend for herself and to take care of Mary Jane without any help? What if he died and left her with nothing and as a widow? Didn't he love her anymore? Didn't he want to take care of her?

"Good afternoon, dear," said Oliver, coming out the front door onto the porch. "How are you?"

"Bored, Daddy. Bored to death. Mary Jane has acted up all day and I thought the weather was going to be nice today but it's too cold. Soon enough, I won't be able to come out at all."

"I'm sorry, dear. I have a surprise or two inside that I think will change your mood."

Lucy squealed in excitement. She loved surprises. She sprang out of her chair as quickly as her pregnant frame would allow and hurried into her father's arms. "Show me, show me, show me!" she demanded excitedly.

He led her into the library. Hanging on a cast-iron coatrack were two silk dresses, one a pale yellow and the second a dark blue. Both were covered in intricate lacework and with identical silk ribbons around the waist. The dresses had clever buckles in the interior of the back, allowing her to let them out several inches as her pregnancy advanced.

"Oh, Father, they are exquisite! Wherever did you get them?"

"I had them ordered from one of my contacts in New York City. They were originally imported from Paris. They were frightfully expensive, but my little princess is worth it."

She hugged him again and kissed him on the cheek. "Oh, Father, you're the best, the very best. Not like Joseph."

"Yes, Joseph has been very foolish. Very foolish indeed. Still, he's a good man. He's just stubborn, like your father. He will come around to things when he gets home. Robert will never hold it together. He never has and he never will."

"Robert has ruined all of our lives. Now because of him, I can't even see Charlotte or Jane. Why can't he just go away and leave all of us alone?"

"Men like Robert never leave those who will take care of them. They have to be forced out. I tried to help Joseph come to this realization, but he fought me. Now everything is worse. Men like Robert leave disaster in their wake."

"I just don't understand why Joseph would pick him over me. Over his daughter. Doesn't he love me anymore?"

"He does love you, dear, but he is easily influenced. Joseph is a hard worker and respected by other workers, but he's not a leader. He has to be led by the nose. We've let him get away once now, but we can't let him again. When he comes home we must redouble our efforts to break him away from Robert and bring him here.

"Don't worry, Robert will hang himself. It is just a matter of time. When he does, Joseph will fall apart and he will come to you and me to pick up the pieces. Then he will be all yours. He has all the right parts, Lucy. You picked a good man. He just needs to follow the right guidance, our guidance."

"What if he's killed? What will I do then?"

"You wouldn't be the only widow. There are plenty of them around. You are still young and still beautiful. If need be, it won't be difficult to find another man for you to marry. I'll take care of things if I have to."

She hugged her father. "Thank you so much, Daddy! You've always taken care of me."

"And I always will, dear. You deserve to be taken care of. Joseph didn't understand that, but he will in time. You will have dresses and good food, and a nice home, and people to wait on you. My daughter deserves no less."

"Daddy, I don't want Joseph to die. I love him. I love him so. He's been so good to me, even if he doesn't always understand the things I need."

"The war is almost over. He should be all right. No matter what, I will take care of you. It's good that there is a little time, otherwise

Robert might hold on and then things would be more complicated when Joseph arrives home. We must be patient."

"I hate being patient! Why did this stupid war even have to start? Why wouldn't Joseph listen to us and do what's best for him? Now I'm stuck, a mother alone, taking care of a child with no help!"

"Like I said, dear, it's all almost over."

The butler interrupted them. "I have a letter here, sir. A letter for Ms. Lucy."

"It must be from Joseph!" she exclaimed, running over to grab the envelope and tear it open. "It is from Joseph! It's dated November 1st. It's only two weeks out of date."

She read the letter, poring over the contents with excitement.

Dear Lucy:

I was so happy to receive your letter. I'm doing well enough here and I'm safe. David was slightly wounded in the arm but he was patched up right away and is doing fine. Poor James Sayer wasn't as lucky. I think you know him at least slightly. He was killed in a battle here a few days ago. I lost two other friends, Douglas and Nicholas. You didn't know them but they were brave and good boys.

We are settling in to a long siege of Petersburg. We tried some attacks, including one I was involved in (when David was wounded), but now things seem to have settled down and there isn't much going on. I miss our house and the farm. I miss Mary Jane and I most of all miss you.

I know you are upset with me and you feel I have done the wrong thing with Robert. I still believe I have made the right choices. He is my father and my blood. Jane is my half sister. I have given so much of my life to keep them safe. Now Robert is finally choosing the right path. I hear from Charlotte that he is working hard and hasn't had anything to drink. Charlotte misses you terribly, by the way, and so does Jane. She wrote me that she has tried to see you but you refuse. I am writing to ask you to reconsider. She doesn't have much in the world besides her parents, who she rarely sees, and of course Jane and Robert. You have been like a younger sister and a great comfort for her.

I am not upset with your father. I respect him greatly. He is a great businessman and I know he loves you and also cares for me. I only wish for him to allow me my own life. I know he wants me to work for him, and he wants you and me to live with him. I need my own space Lucy, my own life. I have worked too hard to live by someone else's leave.

Please hug Mary Jane for me. I miss her so much that it hurts me to think of her.

There is one more thing I must tell you. I have hesitated for days now to write to you about this. I don't think you are aware of this, dear, but Warren joined our regiment as a lieutenant. He served in my company and was one of my commanding officers.

Lucy, my dearest, Warren is dead. He was killed during the fighting on the Boydton Plank Road. I know that although he has grown distant from you and your father, this will be a terrible blow to both of you. I want to tell you that he died bravely and did not suffer.

I count the days before I see you again. I will suffer with you concerning Warren's death. Please consider again whether you could see Charlotte.

I love you,
Joseph

Lucy's hands trembled. How on earth had Warren joined the same regiment as Joseph? Why did he join when by all accounts he had a successful law practice in Morristown?

"What does Joseph have to say for himself?" asked Oliver. "Has he come around yet? What's wrong?"

Lucy silently handed the letter to Oliver, who took it from her and pulled his reading glasses out of his coat. He placed them on and began reading. Lucy watched his face closely, knowing what was coming. She watched the color drain out of his face and her heart fell.

"Well, he is dead then," said Oliver. "I have always feared the worst for my boy. Now it has come to pass. At least he died a soldier's death. Excuse me." Oliver turned and walked swiftly into the library, closing the door behind him. Lucy sat alone in the silence. Soon she heard the distant sound of sobbing coming from the next room. She felt hot tears coming to her eyes and rolling down her cheeks. She hadn't spoken to Warren in years. No matter, he was her flesh and blood, and now he was gone forever. She felt sorrow and guilt, terrible guilt for letting him stay away without reaching out. Now it was too late and she could never see him again, never apologize or ask his forgiveness. She knew what was true for her was a hundredfold more for her father. Oliver had spurned his son in favor of Joseph. Now Joseph had defied him and left them alone, and Warren was deceased.

The next few days were very difficult for Lucy. She grieved for Warren. She had never been close to her brother, but now there was no chance they would ever be close. She realized in the back of her mind she had always expected she could smooth things over between Joseph and Warren, at least over time.

Worse than her own grief was the general gloom that had descended over the Hastings property. Oliver would not come out of the library except to sleep. He was taking his meals there and he kept the door closed. Lucy had tried knocking on the door to see her father, but he wouldn't respond. She had already felt isolated and alone; now everything was that much worse. When she was alone, she thought more of Joseph and she would grow even sadder. She had tried wearing her new dresses to cheer up, but it hadn't worked. She didn't even feel like poring through her catalogues. Her time with Mary Jane had become intolerable for her. The child's incessant demands were driving her to distraction. She solved the problem by limiting her interaction to an hour in the afternoon. The nanny complained because she was supposed to have a break in the morning and the afternoon, but Lucy solved the problem by offering an additional day of wages a week if she would give up her morning time.

She also felt terribly clumsy and weary from the pregnancy. She knew it was still a few months before she would deliver, and she was impatient for the time to pass as quickly as possible. If Joseph were here, he would entertain her and keep her busy, yet another reason for her to be cross with him.

She woke up one morning to a clear, crisp sunny day. The air was cold but it was so bright and beautiful she just had to get out. She knew just where to go. Ever since reading Joseph's letter she had wanted to see Charlotte. She missed her very much and now she had a reason to visit her. She ordered her carriage to be brought out, and after breakfast she was driven down the dirt road toward the Forsyth farm, the wagon crawling along slowly to assure she was not overly jostled.

She had not been on the property in a number of months. She was shocked by what she saw now. The big house was clean and sparkling in the sunlight. The fences lining the road were in perfect repair. Lucy and Joseph's smaller house also showed signs of maintenance and the trim appeared to have been repainted. Who could have done all of this work? It must be Robert, she realized in surprise. Could Robert really have done all of this work in Joseph's absence?

She stepped down from the carriage and walked up the three wooden steps to the porch. She felt very apprehensive. She had not spoken to Charlotte or Jane in months now. What if Charlotte yelled at her? Lucy would not allow it. She would simply place the blame at Robert's feet. After all, Charlotte's husband had landed all of them in this situation and caused Joseph to go away. Certainly it wasn't Lucy's fault that any of this had happened.

She stepped forward and knocked on the door. The door opened. Charlotte was there, looking at Lucy without emotion. Then her face changed, softening. She stepped forward and pulled Lucy into an embrace. "Oh, my dearest girl! You've come to see me like I have prayed you would each day. Oh how I've missed you! Look how far along you are. How wonderful!"

Lucy felt warmth flowing through her. She missed Charlotte very much as well. She felt wonderful to be here with her. "Where is Jane?"

"She's at school. Please come in and have some coffee or tea."

Lucy stepped into the house. Again she was amazed at the improved condition. Several pieces of furniture had been replaced with newer items that looked hand built but of excellent quality and craftsmanship. Everything was clean and well ordered. Gone was the ramshackle moody depression of the place.

"Where is Robert?" she asked, fearful that she would be confronted by her father-in-law.

"He's in town purchasing some supplies. He won't be back for several hours I don't think. Please sit down."

Lucy felt relieved that she would not see Robert. She took a seat at the table while Charlotte heated up a pot of water. They chatted about the weather and other inconsequential things until Charlotte was able to finish brewing the tea, then she also sat down, offering Lucy some chocolate cookies to go with her drink.

"How have you been, Lucy? I've been so worried about you."

Lucy's eyes filled with tears. "Oh, Charlotte, things have been so difficult! You don't know, but Warren is dead."

"What? How?"

"He joined the same regiment Joseph did. We didn't know. He was killed in battle."

"I'm so sorry, Lucy. It's very strange that Joseph didn't tell me. How was he killed?"

"I don't know. Joseph didn't tell me anything specific. He did write that Warren fought bravely and he didn't suffer."

"I'm so sorry, dear, about Warren. I know how difficult that must be for you. I know you weren't very close, but he's still your brother." They talked about Warren for a few minutes, and then Charlotte asked how Lucy was doing without Joseph.

"I'm not doing very well at all. I miss Joseph terribly. I'm still very upset with him. He left us all, Charlotte. He left us all here alone."

Charlotte looked at Lucy for a moment, her eyes searching. "You remember that you forced him to do this, correct?"

"What are you talking about? He didn't have to do anything. He should have stayed here."

"Your father didn't give him a choice. He was forcing Joseph to choose between his blood family and his married family. The only choice Joseph had was to go away. He needed the money too."

"He would never have needed money if it wasn't for Robert, and he could have just agreed with what Daddy offered."

"You're right, Lucy, at least about Joseph's father. Robert is at fault here, most of all. Joseph has always stood by Robert. His father didn't always earn that right, but now he has."

"I saw how nice the farm looks. Is it possible Robert did all of this?"

"Yes he did. Every last part of it. All of Joseph's faith and patience have finally paid off. Robert hasn't touched the drink since that terrible night. He works so hard every day. He has worked this farm harder I think than even Joseph did. I wish your husband could be here to see it. He would be so proud. He will be so proud when he returns."

Lucy was surprised. Perhaps Robert had turned things around. What did that mean to her? She could hardly forgive him. He had ruined her life and taken so much of what should have been hers. Still, if he was doing well now, Joseph would never send him away. That would mean returning to this dismal farm again after Joseph returned. She didn't want that. She wanted Joseph to come live with them at the big house. Then her father and Joseph would both be there to take care of her. She wasn't sure what she would do, but for now, there was no reason to be rude, she needed Charlotte as an ally. She made her most charming and happy face, and beamed at Charlotte.

"I'm very happy for you, Charlotte. I'm glad everything is going well here now. If only I had my Joseph back."

"He will come back and everything will be like it was before. He's one of the bravest, strongest men I've ever known. I know he'll be all right."

Lucy felt her eyes filling with tears. She felt so happy to see Charlotte again, even if she was so closely tied to Robert. "It's so wonderful to see you again, Charlotte."

"I hope we can start seeing each other all the time again. I have a favor to ask of you. My parents are coming to visit after the first of the year. I would love to have you and Mary Jane come and spend the night. My parents would love to meet both of you and I know Jane would be delighted to see Mary Jane. I would too. I've missed her so much."

"Certainly, I would love to come see them, and I know Mary Jane would love to see Jane."

"Wonderful. I'll let you know as we get closer to the date. Also, I'd love to see you and Mary Jane on Christmas if possible."

"I would like that too. I'll see what I can arrange and I'll come see you as soon as I can."

They embraced, holding tightly on to each other for a few moments. Lucy felt warm and happy; she felt a lightness as a tremendous burden was removed from her.

She left Charlotte's house as the sun was beginning to go down. She had enjoyed herself more than she had in quite some time. As she rode in the carriage on the way home, she realized she had missed her afternoon time with Mary Jane. The nanny would be furious with her. Oh well, she was being paid to take care of things. Lucy would just make up something about the delay and apologize. Besides, she had desperately needed a break and an excursion away from home.

She arrived back home just as the sun was going down. When she entered the house, she could smell dinner wafting from the kitchen. Warm baked bread mixed with the aroma of baked chicken and buttery mashed potatoes. She was famished and happy that dinner was already nearly ready. She made her way into the dining room. The place at the head of the table wasn't set. She needed to talk to her father. She stepped past the table and to the door of the library. She knocked several times but there was no answer. Finally, she sighed and turned the doorknob apprehensively.

Inside the library Oliver sat at his desk. His clothing was disheveled and his face was lined with wariness and grief. He looked up and his face grew angry.

"What are you doing in here, Lucy? I told everyone I wished to be left alone."

"Father, I can't take this anymore. I know you're upset about Warren, but what about me? It's been days now. Remember Warren left you and I never have. I deserve your loyalty and your attention too."

"Warren didn't leave, Lucy. I sent him away. I sent him away in favor of *your husband*. Now Joseph has left me and Warren is gone forever."

"I know it's terrible about Warren, but Joseph hasn't left us forever. I went and saw Charlotte today and I have an idea, an idea that will make everything all right again."

"What do you mean?"

"Robert has done really well these past few months Father. You should see the farm. I've never seen it so well cared for. Charlotte says he hasn't had anything to drink since *that day*."

Oliver grunted. "That is good news for Charlotte. But what does that have to do with us?"

"I was thinking on the way home, Father. What if you offered to pay off the rest of the debt on the property and give the property to Robert? Then Robert would have the farm completely for himself."

"That would be good for Robert, but why would Joseph agree to that?"

"You could make Joseph your partner in this land."

"Why would I want to do that?"

"You don't have to make him a full partner, but what if you gave him a thirty-percent or forty-percent interest in the land? You could also offer to buy the printing equipment he wanted. If he owned the land with you, he would want to live here, and he would work even harder to take care of the property. He will end up with this land in the long run in any event through me, but why should we live somewhere else in the meantime? That way we could all live here together and Joseph would have what he wanted too."

Oliver's face brightened. "You're right, Lucy. If Joseph feels he's part of the farm, he would work harder than ever. Robert would have his own farm and Joseph wouldn't have to support him anymore. You would be here on the property with the grandchildren. You may have come across a solution after all."

Lucy beamed. She knew she had indeed come up with the perfect answer. With Joseph having a share of the land, they would not only be able to live here but there would be more money available to them. They could live in the big house and she would have servants to take care of the children and her every need. She would have two men making sure she was happy. Robert and Charlotte would have their own property, and with Robert now working hard, Joseph wouldn't have to divert their money or his time into taking care of his father. She would also still be able to be friends with Charlotte and to see Jane. Everything would be well again, even better than before. Finally she would have her nice things and her Joseph to herself.

Men were so funny. They were so strong, but at the same time, so easy to manipulate. A few tears or a smile and they did everything she wanted them to do.

She ran over and hugged her father. She was genuinely happy. "Thank you so much, Daddy. Thank you for everything."

She ran out of the room and past the dining room where dinner had now been laid out. Her hunger forgotten, she ran up to her room and sat down immediately at her desk to write Joseph. She poured out her heart to him in the letter, telling him in every way that she loved him and that she hoped he would accept her new idea for their future. She was sure he would come home.

CHAPTER 22

Company D, 186th New York Volunteers

In the Trenches near the Military Railroad and Jerusalem Road

Petersburg, Virginia

Sunday, January 1, 1865

Joseph woke up shivering in the rain. Up and down the long trench, he could see his company and regimental mates, each suffering in the freezing downpour under the soaked wool blankets and uniforms. A wooden step ran raggedly along the base of the trench, allowing soldiers to step up and fire out of the trench. Joseph ascended and carefully peered over the edge and across the barren land between his trench and the Confederate entrenchments across the way. The fields were completely empty, and where crops once grew there were only craters from cannon fire and churned-up mud. A few twisted and blackened stumps grew in macabre shapes out of the slime—all that was left of majestic pine and oak trees that once dotted the valley. He could not remember having passed a new year in more wretched conditions, even that first difficult year with the O'Dwyers.

Joseph hadn't thought of the O'Dwyers in a very long time. He wondered what they were doing now. Had they adopted a different child or brought on another apprentice? He thought no better of Michael than he ever had. His printing master was a shrewd businessman and a cheat. He had treated Joseph in a heavy-handed manner. Joseph still felt Michael had wanted to adopt him primarily to have a steady laborer. Michael was in many ways similar to Oliver. How strange that both of them had wanted to treat Joseph like a son. Then again, perhaps it wasn't so strange. Perhaps strong men who sought to dominate others were always drawn to men who won the admiration of others through honesty and hard work.

Joseph then thought of Aimée O'Dwyer. He felt a twang to his heart. He did miss her. She had loved him in her way. He had been the child she would never have, and she had put her hopes and dreams for the future in him. But she had known that his family was trying to contact him. She had known that Michael held back the letters, known and done nothing about it. He could not forgive her for that, even now.

Across the way, Joseph knew the rebels were even more miserable than he was. Petersburg was besieged, and only a trickle of supplies was reaching the Confederate lines. Those men were not only freezing, but starving and sick with disease from lack of medicine and fresh clothing. Joseph had personally witnessed the occasional line of captured enemies. The rebels were dressed in tatters with rags wrapped around their feet. Their bodies, once assuredly strong and muscular, were now no more than skeletons. He wondered how they endured, how they went on. He loathed them for their stubbornness, even while he respected and admired their resistance. Would he act differently if these trenches were outside Macomb? If the cannon were lobbing shells into his town, onto his farm? If his family might be raped or killed if the city fell? He understood their spirit and their resistance, even while he hoped and prayed that they would soon surrender.

Yes, he prayed, something he had forgotten he had the ability to do until very recently. Since he had joined the army and seen the horrors of war, he had felt a closeness again to God. Death is much closer in war. He could feel its presence around him all the time. Death had come for his friends, killing every one of them besides David when Warren forced them to attack a much larger force. Despite this, or perhaps because of it, he could feel God's presence around him, inside of him. He had seen terrible things but he had also seen the miracle of survival. War made the beauty of life much more vivid.

He observed movement down the trench line. David was returning from the latrine. He spotted Joseph and a wide grin filled his face. Joseph didn't know what he would do without David. He was ever the optimist, laughing and joking among the misery. Between Joseph's quiet hard work and David's laughter, they were a very popular pair in the company and the regiment at large.

"You look like you're having a nice time," observed David. "Is it wet and cold enough for you? Is your blanket suitably moldy and worn out? Is there enough mud for your boots?"

"Actually, it's the rats I prefer the most. They keep me company."

David laughed. "You would. Any idea what time it is?"

"It must be about ten or so. It's been light for a few hours."

"Well I hope you're having a glorious new year so far. I wonder what the master plan is for the day."

"Probably another day of rain, cannons, mud, bad food, and lack of sleep. Maybe if we're lucky, they'll throw in some death and terror to spice things up a bit."

"I wonder what my dad's doing right now."

"You know what he's doing. The same thing he's been doing for the past thirty years. He's stocking the store and standing in the store and cleaning the store and painting the store and thinking about the store."

David laughed again. "Rather predictable, isn't it? My dad is very boring, but I wouldn't mind being home to help him right now."

"Nor would I. And I'll trade you. You can have Robert and I'll take Pete."

"Sorry, not interested in that exchange. Still, your father has been doing pretty well, hasn't he?"

"He has. According to Charlotte, he's been doing very well. I didn't know he had a full day's work in him but he's been at it day after day for months now."

"The drinking?"

"He hasn't touched it. I'm proud of him. I had given up on ever seeing my real dad, the one I always wanted to know. Now, there's a real chance. If I can only convince Lucy to soften her heart, when I get home, there is a chance to finally have a real family. A real father."

"I'm happy for you. I just hope he can keep on the right path. He has hurt you too many times. He didn't deserve this chance, although I must admit he seems to be taking full advantage of it."

"He won't have another. I've given as many chances as I can, and more." Joseph wondered if that was true. Would he truly turn his back on Robert if he drank again? Would he be able to? He knew he had to. If he was going to have a life and any happiness, he either had to have a sober Robert, or no Robert at all. No matter what happened now, he had to stick to his guns. He had sacrificed so much to give his father this last chance. This had to be the final time.

"Corporal, you have a letter."

Joseph looked up. A sergeant was walking along the trench, handing out correspondence. He handed the envelope to Joseph. The letter was from Lucy, the first he had received from her in months. He tore it open; it was dated November 25, almost six weeks out of date.

Dearest Joseph,

I cannot describe for you how difficult it was to hear of Warren's death. He was always a hard man to love, but he was my brother and Oliver's son, and now that he is gone, there is no way to ever resolve all of the past.

His death brings home for me just how important it is that you come back to me so we can have our life back together. I miss you so terribly, my dear, and so does Mary Jane. We will have a new baby soon, a bigger family to share together.

I have wonderful news that I hope you will also welcome as warmly as I have. My father has offered something truly generous that would solve all of our problems. He wants to give your farm to Robert and let him take it over, clear of any debts. I saw how Charlotte and Robert are doing so well now. I know he can manage the farm on his own and take care of Charlotte and Jane the way you always hoped he would. He's not demanding that Robert leave anymore or that the land be sold. He wants Robert to have a life here, a life near us.

That's not the best part. He wants to make you a part owner of the Hastings farm! He is getting older, Joseph, and he needs your help now more than ever. He wants us to come back and live here and you can run the farm together. He said he would buy you all the printing equipment you want as well.

Joseph, this would be the best thing in the world for us. I could be with both of you every day. Our children would have their grandfather and would grow up with all their needs taken care of. We would have a wonderful house and security for the future. You could work the farm and the print shop, and when Daddy passes away, the whole farm would be ours. We would be the richest couple in Macomb.

Please, please consider all of this. This is everything we ever wanted. Your father and his family would be nearby and safe, and they would have their own land and their own future. We would have a much nicer property and house to raise our children in. I would have everything I always wanted and so would you, Joseph.

I can't wait to hear back from you. I know you will be as excited as I am about this news! All of our dreams are finally coming true. I love you with all of my heart.

Love,
Lucy

"What news from home?" asked David.

"Not too much. Lucy went and saw Charlotte. It sounds like Robert is still doing very well."

"That's great news, my friend." David clapped Joseph on the back.

Joseph concealed the true details of the letter from David. His mind was reeling. Perhaps Lucy was right. This seemed to be the perfect solution. If Robert were given the Forsyth farm with no debt, his father would have everything he needed to take care of Charlotte and Jane for good. They would be nearby and he would be able to see them frequently. This would also solve his own debt problems because Pete would be paid back and so would Mr. Deary. He would have a fresh start. Even more significantly, Oliver was offering him a partnership in the largest and finest farm in Macomb. He would instantly be a wealthy man. He would have a fine house to live in, and a printing press purchased for him. Lucy would have every comfort and would finally be content.

Despite all of this, he couldn't help feeling trapped. This felt like a deeper and subtler form of servitude. He had spent so much of his life working for others under terms he was forced to accept. Now Oliver was offering him everything he had wanted, but it would be on Oliver's property, in Oliver's house, working with Oliver every day. Joseph had wanted his own land, to be his own master.

Did it make a difference? He would be a partner after all. Probably not an equal partner, but he would share in all of the bounty of the Hastings property. In time, Oliver would retire or pass away, and all of the property would be his and Lucy's.

He felt divided and unsure of himself. What should he do? How could he refuse? He had already defied them all by joining the army. A decision that he admitted to himself was hasty and ill-advised. In trying to free himself of all his obligations to Oliver, he had left Lucy alone and run away from his problems. If he refused this offer now, Lucy would never forgive him. Would she even come with him or would she refuse to leave her father and simply live there on the property with Joseph's children? He didn't have to decide immediately, but eventually, he would have to write her back. That letter would determine his destiny.

"Corporal Forsyth, you're wanted down the line."

Joseph looked up. It was the sergeant again. "What is it?"

"I don't know. Captain McMullen wants you."

Joseph looked at David for a second, then nodded to the sergeant and followed him. What could the captain want? He couldn't imagine he was in trouble. He hadn't done anything he could think of. He wondered if there was an assault in the works? If so, why weren't all the noncommissioned officers summoned at the same time?

The sergeant and Joseph slogged through the mud toward the command post. Joseph nodded at a few friends along the way. The captain's post was about fifty yards down the trench from where David and Joseph were encamped. He had dug out a small niche that provided enough space for a cot and a small desk. He sat at the desk going through some papers. The sergeant cleared his throat to get the captain's attention.

"Oh yes, Forsyth, I want to talk to you for a few minutes." Joseph saluted and the captain returned the gesture, then waved him over toward him.

"What can I do for you, sir?"

"Well, first, I want your assessment of the situation. How are the men?"

"The men are fine, sir."

"Really? Be honest with me."

"They are tired. They want this to be over. I think they were better out in the open, when we were moving and fighting. The trenches are safe but almost worse."

"I agree, Corporal. I'd rather be done with it regardless of the result. Waiting and hiding and delay are poor for morale."

"Do you know when we will attack again, sir?"

"I don't. The orders are to hold tight for now. They are trying to starve them out it looks like. Nobody wants another Cold Harbor."

The captain was referring to the battle immediately preceding the siege of Petersburg. On June 3, 1864, following a few days of skirmishes, Grant had hastily ordered massive frontal assaults on prepared Confederate positions. Over ten thousand Union men were killed or wounded, which was for many the final straw in months of slaughter. When the army made it to Petersburg a few days later, another frontal attack was ordered; the men involved had refused to execute the attack. Joseph had assumed another such plan was in the works. Why else had the captain called for him?

"Is there anything else, sir?"

"Yes, Corporal, there is. I have some good news for you. Orders have come down for each company in the regiment to grant a few leaves. You have performed well under my command. You carry out orders without question. You are liked and respected by the men. I have a two-week leave available for you if you want it. I know you have a baby on the way."

A two-week leave. He couldn't believe it. Leave was exceptionally rare. Two weeks. He would lose many days in travel, but he should be able to get home and have a week with Lucy and the rest of the family. There was so much he could accomplish in a week, so much he could fix. "Thank you, sir, thank you very much. That would mean so much to me."

"Excellent. Here is the paperwork. You can leave after roll call in the morning. I only warn you not to be late in returning. There has been an increase in desertions lately, and they are dealing harshly with those who are absent without leave."

Joseph saluted again and then was dismissed. He tucked the leave in his pocket and worked his way through the slippery mud back to David. His friend was watching expectantly, wondering what was going on.

"What did the captain want?"

"You'll never believe it. He's granted me a two-week leave."

"You're kidding? You lucky bastard. Are you going home?"

"Of course. I'm not going to tour Virginia. I should have enough time to spend a week with Lucy and Mary Jane."

"Don't forget Robert and Oliver. Are you sure you want to visit?" chided David.

"I left hastily. You know I've regretted my decision. This is a chance to clean up the mess I made. Before it's too late."

"Always with the dark talk, Joseph. We've made it through unscathed so far. And don't forget you dragged me into this in the first place. They should have given me the leave. And a medal for agreeing to come along and watch out for you."

"I'll enjoy Macomb for the both of us. Besides, someone has to stay here and keep everyone else in line."

"I can't believe you're going home. You better go see Pete. He will never forgive you if you don't."

"I will. First thing. Well, maybe second thing . . ."

"How are you going to deal with Oliver? And with Robert?"

"If Robert is doing as well as Charlotte writes, I don't think I'll have to deal with Robert at all. There are things I need to say to him, but if he has truly quit drinking and is working hard, that's what's important. Oliver will be tougher. But Lucy wrote me with a new proposal that might just work."

"What proposal?"

Joseph handed Lucy's letter to David, who read it carefully. David whistled in surprise at the contents. "What do you think of this?"

"I don't know. I have wanted away from Oliver for so long. This would tie me to him forever. Still, if I was a part owner, I would at least have a say in things, and Lucy would be so much happier at home."

"Happy with the expensive furniture and the servants, you mean."

"That's enough of that." Joseph felt hot anger whenever anyone criticized Lucy. The feeling was confusing because he knew there was more than a grain of truth to what David said.

David put up his hands defensively. "I gave up long ago trying to give you family advice."

"Good decision. I do appreciate you, David. I can never thank you enough for coming with me. I don't know where I would be without you."

"I tried to join at the beginning, remember? If you had listened to me, we would be heroes by now, and already home and out of this mess."

"Sure, heroes, like Casey."

"There you are with the dark thoughts again."

"I won't have dark thoughts when I get out of here. I'll feel much better when I've straightened things out at home."

"I'm happy for you. Just remember not to give up everything. You might feel joining was the wrong decision, but I disagree. You needed to put some distance between yourself and all of them. It's time they start appreciating you. Don't let them pull you back in and take everything from you."

Joseph put his hand on David's shoulder. "You're a great friend, David. You've always looked out for me and so has Pete. I know you're right. Whatever decisions I make now, I need to take care of myself and not just everyone else."

Before the light failed, Joseph sat down in the mud and, holding his paper the best he could, scrawled out a note to Lucy.

Dearest Lucy:

I have the very best news, dear. I have been granted two weeks of leave and will be leaving in the morning to come home. I should have at least a week to be with you. I'm not sure if this letter will arrive before me, but I will send it in the morning.

I hope your pregnancy is going well and that little Mary Jane is happy. I miss both of you terribly and cannot wait to see you and our little girl, and of course our new baby.

I know the loss of your brother must weigh heavily on both you and your father, but I hope we will be able to move on and recover. I have given great thought to your proposal and I believe we will be able to start fresh when I'm home. I'll discuss this with you and Oliver when I arrive.

This distance has shown me how much I need you in my life. I know you feel the same. I love you, dearest, and I will be home to you soon.

Joseph addressed the letter, sealed the envelope, and placed the letter in his inside breast pocket to mail in the morning. Late afternoon turned to evening. The darkness came early to the winter sky. Soon, small fires were burning all along the trench, set low to assure they didn't create silhouettes and expose the men to sniper fire. David and Joseph spent the evening drinking coffee and eating their rations around the fire with a few of their closest friends. Everyone wished Joseph the best for his leave. After a few hours, the fire burned down and the men began to nod off. A watch was set, but only a single guard for the whole company. The Confederates hadn't attacked the lines in months; there was no reason to worry. Joseph fell asleep, dreaming of going home.

CHAPTER 23

Macomb, New York
Monday, January 16, 1865

Robert Forsyth worked his frozen fingers back and forth by lantern light in the early morning. Dawn was still an hour or more away, but he had to finish milking the cows and then feed the other livestock before he moved on to the rest of the daily chores.

He felt pride and peace as he went about his work. These past few months had been so different than the rest of his life. He had worked harder than ever before, harder than he had thought possible. More amazingly, he had quit drinking.

He felt the electric surge burn through him when he thought of alcohol. He felt the excitement and the regret. He missed drinking so much. He had loved it, every part of it. Sitting with his friends at night by a warm fire at the tavern, enjoying drinks and reminiscing about Ireland. Having a few drinks at the table while Charlotte made dinner and Joseph sat talking to him about the day.

He shuddered and shook his head. He couldn't think about that. Every time he thought of drinking, he could taste it, smell it, feel it warming his body and his freezing fingers. He loved to drink but it had destroyed him, destroyed his family. This was his one chance—a chance Joseph had given him at considerable cost. He couldn't fail.

He felt the self-loathing wash over him again. He had lost thousands of dollars in a drunken card game, trying to prove what a big man he was. He had forced his own son to join the army to try to recover from his sins. And that wasn't the first time. Twice he had placed his son in bondage because of his stupidity. He had never accepted responsibility for the first time, not truly. He knew at some point he would need to tell Joseph what really happened and ask for his forgiveness. That would be such a difficult thing to do, but he knew he had to do it.

He returned to his work. Mustn't dwell on all of that. The best way to make up for his mistakes was to work hard, work hard like his son, and make enough money to pay off all the debts. He would be worthy of his son for the first time in his life. How difficult it was to face a son who has always been better than him, a man respected while everyone thought him a fool.

He kept at his work. It would be a very busy day. Charlotte's parents were supposed to be arriving today. They would be staying for a few weeks. Charlotte was so excited to see her mother and father, who were only able to visit from Albany every couple of years. More significantly, Lucy and Mary Jane were coming over for dinner.

Robert had not seen Lucy since before Joseph left. Charlotte had seen Lucy a couple of times recently, including at Christmas, but Robert had stayed away, figuring that the more time and distance he gave the better. He was apprehensive about what she might say to him. He hoped she would find it in her heart to forgive him so the family could begin the process of healing. Charlotte needed Lucy in her life, and Robert needed Joseph.

He finished his morning chores as the sun came up and he returned to the house. Charlotte was already awake and had breakfast waiting when he arrived. She greeted him with a kiss. Jane was still asleep and wouldn't be up for another hour or so.

He smiled at Charlotte. She had changed so much in the past few months. Their relationship had been volatile and unhappy for so many years. Since he had stopped drinking, they had hardly fought. She was attentive and affectionate. She laughed at his jokes and stories. Jane was so much happier too.

His whole life was so much better now. Why then did he feel like he was on a runaway wagon heading down a steep and windy road? He loved his new life but he longed for the old one. Emotions washed over him every day. He thought that things were getting easier, that the old yearnings were lessening, but lately they had returned full force, perhaps even stronger. He felt them overwhelming him at times and he was afraid he would lose control and give in to them. He had too much to lose now.

"Are you going into town to sell the sheep today?" Charlotte asked.

"Yes."

"I wish that could be another day. We have so much to do already."

"I know, my lass, but I have a ready buyer and I don't want to lose the sale. If this works out the way I think it might, I'll have a large chunk to pay down the debt and get us moved along."

Charlotte came back over and put her arms around him. "I'm so proud of you, Robert. Joseph will be too. I never knew where he got his hardworking nature from until I learned it came from you. You've shown them all, Robert. You've proven that Joseph's trust in you was well placed."

He smiled and he felt the guilt again. Was the trust well placed? Could he keep this up? He just had to keep busy, keep working hard, and try not to think too much. If he kept working hard, the urges would eventually go away, at least so he prayed.

The morning passed quickly and then turned into afternoon.

Robert was mending a portion of the fence running along the front of the property when he spotted the Hastings' carriage coming up the way. He felt a surge of nerves. Lucy and Mary Jane were coming. Would she refuse to talk to him? Did he deserve less?

The carriage turned into the drive and stopped in front of the house. Charlotte came out of the house with Jane. Mary Jane flew out of the door of the carriage and into Jane's arms. Charlotte hugged them both and then moved forward to assist Lucy. Lucy stepped down slowly. She was very pregnant but dressed nicely in a yellow silk dress. She hugged Charlotte tightly for a few moments and then looked around until her eyes settled on Robert.

Robert walked over slowly, feeling sheepish. She watched him without any expression. He was about to say something when Mary Jane spotted him and ran to him, laughing.

"Grandpa!"

He picked her up in his arms and swung her around. "Ah what a fine and beautiful lass we have here." He laughed and held her close to him.

"Hello, Robert," said Lucy.

He set Mary Jane down and turned to his daughter-in-law. "Hello, Lucy. How are you?"

"I'm fine. Very pregnant and glad to see your wife. I . . . I saw the farm when I visited the last couple of times. I've never seen it look better, even with Joseph."

He smiled at her. She didn't have to say that. He felt a little of the fear ease away. She might still have things to say, but she was trying; she was making an effort. They finished their greetings and went back into the house where it was warmer. Lucy sat down and the girls ran upstairs to play. Charlotte had baked some rolls and she went to work buttering them and making some coffee.

"Robert, I don't have any more sugar here. Could you go out and get some from the larder?"

"Of course, deary. Just get settled in and I'll be back in no time." He walked back out the front door and to the left. Joseph had built a separate storage shed for both houses that contained dried meats, flour, sugar, and other items that could be stored in larger quantities. Robert opened the door and went inside. He began digging through the bags looking for the sugar. As his hands fumbled through, he felt something hard. He wrapped his fingers around the object and pulled it out: a bottle of whiskey. He dropped the bottle onto a sack and backed away. What was this doing here? He realized he must have stashed it away in the old days so he could have a nip or two on a day that Charlotte drove him out to do chores.

He picked the liquor back up and examined the contents. There was almost a full bottle of rich, brown whiskey. He turned the container slightly to the right and left, watching the liquid slosh around inside.

He felt a rush of excitement course through his body. He hadn't held a bottle in all this time. He uncorked it and closed his eyes, drawing the bottle up to his nose and taking a deep breath. The smell was strong and wonderful coursing through his body. He ached for just a sip, just a little of the flavor. He opened his eyes and looked around. He was in the shed. Nobody was outside or looking for him. He closed his eyes again and put the bottle to his lips. He arched it back and let the liquid slosh against the tip of his tongue. He didn't take a drink but just felt the flavor burning on his tongue. The taste was overwhelming. His breath quickened and his hands started to shake. He missed this so badly. He drew the bottle back up and took a quick sip, a small one, then he corked the bottle and put it away.

He found the sugar and picked it up, then walked quickly out of the shed and toward the house. He had done it. He had drunk just a little bit, not enough to harm anything. He felt wonderful and at peace. He could handle this. What was a small sip now and again? He realized his mistake before had been drinking too much. He didn't have to give up the whiskey if he just had a little taste now and again. Why hadn't he thought of this before? He whistled a little as he opened the door to the house.

"Robert, thank God you're back. Come here quickly!"

Robert looked and saw Charlotte standing over Lucy. Lucy was holding her stomach. Sweat rolled down her cheek and her face was contorted in pain.

"What's wrong?"

"The baby is coming. Robert, you have to get her home! Go get the wagon!"

Robert flew out of the house and hitched his horse to the wagon as quickly as he could. Within twenty minutes, he was back out in front of the house. As he was stepping down, Charlotte appeared on the porch, gingerly leading Lucy. Robert leapt down and then helped her up onto the baseboard. Charlotte placed a pillow beneath Lucy and then covered her with several thick blankets.

"You have to take her home very carefully, Robert. Take your time. The baby's not coming right away, but it's coming today. The important thing is to avoid bumping as much as you can."

Lucy looked over and smiled gratefully at Charlotte. "What about Mary Jane?"

"Don't worry about her. She can stay with us for a few days. My parents will want to see her. You just go have that baby and we will come see you as soon as we can."

"Thank you so much, Charlotte. And thank you, Robert."

Robert blushed. "You're welcome."

Charlotte came around and hugged Robert. "That's my man, taking care of us. Get her there as soon as you can. What time will you be home?"

"I still need to sell those sheep. I'll be home after dark I'm thinking."

"Take care, dear, and please be careful."

Robert drove the wagon very slowly, avoiding the worst holes and bumps in the hard-packed dirt road. Lucy held on as best she could, but she was overcome with pain that seemed to come in waves. Robert was in a panic. He knew nothing about babies or what might be coming. He only hoped he could get her home before the true labor began.

"Are you all right, lass?"

"I am, Robert." She touched his arm. "Thank you for taking me home. I . . . I'm glad things are going well for you and Charlotte. I know we haven't always gotten along well, but I know you are very important to Charlotte and to Joseph."

"Don't you worry yourself about such things right now, lass. You have a baby to bring. We're all doing much better now. Soon, our boy Joseph will be back, and all will be well with the world."

"I miss him terribly, Robert. I don't know why he went away."

"That was a rash decision and a bad one. Joseph's not perfect, but he's a good boy and a hard worker. Don't you worry yourself. He'll be back soon enough. He'll come back and take care of you and the little ones. We can all live back on the farm again."

She smiled at him through her pain. "Yes, it will be nice to have him back."

After what seemed forever, the Hastings property finally came into view. He turned down the drive and began calling to the workers, getting their attention. One of the field hands ran up to the wagon and then turned and ran for the big house after Robert explained what was going on. Before he pulled up, Oliver appeared on the porch with several members of the house staff.

"What's going on?" demanded Oliver.

"It's Lucy's time. I brought her back for you."

Oliver's face paled. He turned to one of the servants. "Saddle up a horse and fetch the doctor!"

"Yes, sir." The servant ran off while several others helped Lucy from the wagon.

Oliver turned to Robert. "Thank you for bringing her back. Where is Mary Jane?"

"We thought we could keep her for a few days while the baby is coming."

Oliver grunted. "I suppose that would be helpful. Tell Charlotte thank you."

"I will. I have to go. I'm selling some sheep today up at Pope's Mill. I can't be late."

Oliver nodded by way of farewell and soon Robert was back on the road, driving the wagon much more quickly now as he made his way back up to Pope's Mill.

He arrived at Pope's Mill in the late afternoon and met up with Jacob Mertin, a local farmer who had come out and inspected Robert's flock several days before. The sheep were Robert's great pride. Joseph had left a sizeable flock behind, and Robert had taken charge of caring for them and selling them. He had worked very hard over the past months and now he had an interested buyer. They only had to figure out the details of the price. Robert was hoping to get three hundred to three hundred twenty-five dollars. He would then send this money on to Mr. Deary, thereby making a substantial payment toward the existing debt.

He found Jacob and they shook hands. They took a walk together to discuss the terms of the sale.

"So have you considered a price, Robert?"

"I have done a little thinking about the sheep, boyo, but why don't you tell me what you are willing to pay for them. As you know, it's a fine flock. I have other parties interested, but I would like to sell them to you."

"They are in good shape. I was thinking three hundred and fifty dollars. What do you think of that?"

Robert couldn't believe his luck. The first offer was more than he had even hoped to get. He kept his face passive. "That seems low to me. These are prime sheep in excellent shape. How's about four fifty? That seems a bit fairer."

Jacob whistled. "That's a might high. I'll tell you what, I'll split the difference. How about four hundred?"

"Deal." Robert shook hands with Jacob, who reached into his pocket and counted out the money. Robert had never seen that much cash in his entire life. He pulled a bill of sale out of his pocket and filled in the numbers. They both signed and then shook hands again, exchanging the bill for the money. Robert quickly tucked the cash into his pocket and then bid Jacob good-bye.

Robert was fortunate. This would go very far toward paying off the debt, and was far more money than he was expecting to get. The market must be even tighter than he'd thought. He hopped off a wooden sidewalk and waltzed down the dirt street, whistling an Irish tune while he thought of how excited Joseph would be. He must write him as soon as he got home.

He stopped in the street and looked up, staring at the building in front of him. Without realizing it, he had walked over to the Pope's Mill tavern, his old drinking grounds. He knew he had to get home, but he remembered the small drink from that morning. He felt the same excited burst of nervous energy. Why not have another little drink? He had done so well with the sheep. He deserved it. He would just have a single drink of whiskey and then go home and celebrate with Charlotte. She would be so proud of him and so happy.

Robert entered the dim tavern and blinked his eyes, adjusting to the darkness. He was surprised by the stench of the place. He had never noticed that before. A strong mix of sweat and stale beer. There were several men he didn't recognize sitting at the bar. The bartender, Alexander, nodded to Robert when he recognized him. Robert had never gotten along too well with Alexander. He was disappointed;

none of his friends were here. No matter, he had come for a drink and he would have one and get back home.

"A whiskey," he ordered.

Alexander grunted and poured Robert a drink in a smudged glass. Robert paid and picked up the drink and passed it to his lips, sipping slowly at the fiery liquid. He felt that same electric sensation he had felt earlier. He raised the glass again and drank the rest in one gulp. He felt the warmth flow down his chest and into his stomach. Robert experienced that rich, satisfied peace again. He regretted drinking all of it in one quick gulp. Maybe he should have one more. Two drinks would certainly not make him drunk. He was celebrating after all.

"Give me another."

Alexander poured a second drink and Robert drank that down more slowly over a few minutes. He was surprised to feel the alcohol affecting his body. He felt almost drunk after just two glasses. The feeling was delicious.

"What brings you in here after so much time? I thought you had quit the place?" asked Alexander.

"I've given up the drink, boyo," said Robert. "Today is a special occasion."

"I'm sure," laughed Alexander mockingly.

"You don't know your head from your arse, Alex."

"I know you well enough to know there's no special occasions. Unless it's drunken Irishman day today."

"A special occasion it is indeed. I'll have you know I sold a flock of sheep today for four hundred dollars. That's more money than you earn in five years I'll wager, laddie. So don't go shooting your mouth off to me."

"That's a lot of money. Maybe you should be buying us all a drink," said one of the men at the bar.

Robert looked up. The two men sitting at the bar were now looking at him. He strained his eyes, trying to figure out who they were. He couldn't remember ever seeing either of them before, which was unusual. Macomb was hardly on the way to anywhere. They were both looking at him expectantly.

"Sorry, lads, I only buy for my friends." They grumbled a bit but then seemed to lose interest and returned to their own conversation. He ordered a third drink and sipped it over another half hour or so. When he was finished, he flipped a coin to Alexander by way of a tip, nodded to the strangers, and made his way out of the bar.

He felt a little unsteady on his feet. He didn't know what was wrong with him. It must be the cold air. He could normally drink five or six whiskeys before he felt anything. He must be becoming a weakling in his old age. An Irishman had to be able to hold his drink. Night had fallen while he was inside. He pulled an overcoat out of a saddlebag and then mounted his horse and started making his way home, whistling a happy tune.

He was home in a half hour. He dismounted and nearly fell over. He felt even more unbalanced after the ride home. The cool air and the riding seemed to have drawn the whiskey through his whole body. He took his time stabling his horse so he could catch his breath and clear his head. When he felt composed enough, he closed the stall door and walked up to the house. Taking a deep breath, he opened the front door and went inside.

Charlotte looked up and smiled when he came in. She was over the stove with her mother, juggling some hot muffins out of a pan. A roasted turkey, big and well browned, spilled out of an iron pan resting on a back table. Two pies also cooled above the turkey on a higher shelf. The house smelled wonderful and he felt his stomach grumbling in hunger.

Charlotte's father, John Johnson, sat at the table and nodded to Robert when he came in. Her father had never approved of Robert, and the relationship had always been strained. Charlotte's mother, Pleasant Johnson, was assisting Charlotte with peeling some apples for a pie. Jane sat on another chair with Mary Jane on her lap. Mary Jane saw Robert and jumped off Jane's lap, running to see her grandpa.

He picked up his granddaughter and twirled her around, hugging her closely. She was a wonderful joy to him. He had missed her terribly the past few months, and he was so happy she was back in his life now. He was still angry at Lucy for pulling her away from the family, but he needed to keep the peace for Joseph's sake and for Charlotte. Lucy would come around in time, Joseph would return home, and everything would be back to normal.

Mary Jane returned to Jane, and Charlotte came over to kiss him. He turned his head and kissed her on the cheek, afraid she might smell the whiskey on his breath. She held him closely for a second and then turned his face to hers and kissed him again on the lips.

He knew immediately that something was wrong. She pulled back and looked at him with surprise, then he saw her cheeks flush red and the line appear in her forehead. The stress line always appeared when she was angry.

"Robert, you've been drinking!" she whispered in a strained voice.

"Ssshhh, they'll hear."

"I'll be a lot louder if you don't answer me. You've been drinking, haven't you?"

Robert put on his best smile and tried to pour all of his charm into the response. "Now, lass, don't go overboard with me. I had a little celebration drink after I sold the flock tonight. It was nothing. Besides, wait until you hear the great news. I sold the sheep for . . ."

"What do you mean it was nothing? You promised me you would never drink again. You promised all of us you would never drink again!" Her voice rose and he saw both of her parents look up. They had obviously overheard her words.

"Hush now! We've family over, dear. It was a little mistake I won't repeat. Let's talk about this later."

"I don't want to talk about this later!" she screamed. "I want to talk about this now! I was just telling my parents how wonderfully you've done. They wouldn't believe me after all I've been through. Then you come home tonight, the first night they can see you, and you're drunk!"

"Shush your mouth, lass," Robert said, growing angry himself. "I'm not drunk, not by a long way. I told you I had one drink. If you would listen, I'll tell you why. I've made a wonderful deal on the flock, enough money to . . ."

"I don't care about the sheep, Robert. I care about your promise to me. I made a promise to myself at the same time. I promised myself I wouldn't put up with you anymore if you ever drank again. Now what am I supposed to do?" She burst into tears. Jane, watching her mother closely, also began to cry without understanding what was truly going on.

Robert felt his heart tearing apart. He knew he had broken his promise to Charlotte, but surely this wasn't the end of the world. He wasn't drunk. He had just had a few drinks. He wasn't intending to ever get drunk again.

"You bastard," said her father. "I've sat back and watched this long enough. You've destroyed Charlotte's life and her happiness." John rose from the table and Robert wondered if he might try to take a swing at him. He readied himself just in case. Robert turned his attention back to his wife. He needed to talk quickly and get things under control before the situation got out of hand.

"Charlotte, I'm sorry, dear. But let's not talk about this in front of the children. Look, you've upset Jane with your crying."

"I've upset her? How dare you blame me for this! You come home with drink on your breath after you promise never to do it again. Don't try to say I caused this!"

"I'm not saying that, lass, but please, let's keep a level head here. I made a mistake. We all do sometimes. I won't blame you for your anger. But look at all I've done these past few months. Look at everything we've built and are building. Don't throw it all away because of a small mistake."

He could see in her eyes she was wavering. He had hurt her, but she didn't want to leave. She didn't want this to be the end. He knew it would be okay. Time to turn on his best charm and persuade her. He stepped forward and put his arms around her. She pushed away from him but he held on to her. He felt her resistance crumble and he pulled her close.

"It's going to be all right, lass. I won't do it again. I promise I won't do it again."

She was still crying, but she held on to him. "Please, Robert. Please don't disappoint me again. I can't take it anymore. I need you. I need you."

There was a knock at the door. Who would be here at this time of night? Lucy must have had the baby. Charlotte wiped her eyes and moved toward the door. Robert caught John's eyes. He could see the anger. Charlotte might give him another chance, but he wasn't sure her father would. Still, there was always time to mend the fences.

Behind him he heard the door open. Charlotte was talking to someone. A voice he didn't recognize. Then he heard a scream. He turned in surprise.

CHAPTER 24

Union Military Hospital Camp near the Jerusalem Road

Thursday, January 19, 1865

Rebecca moved among the wounded, checking bandages and watching for infection. She left Joseph for last. He had survived another ten days. A miraculous week of vigilance. They had bathed the wound several times each day with alcohol. His fever remained and so did the infection, but it had not spread and he was still alive.

Rebecca had survived the week as well. The week had been tremendously difficult as her heart ached for Thomas, but she controlled herself and kept a safe distance. She knew if she gave in to her heart, she would have to leave him forever. Only by keeping her strength could she continue to be near him.

She had to stay by his side. She had lost everything else. She missed her husband terribly, but he would never be coming back. She missed her child even more. Everything had been taken away from her in life. All she had left was Thomas.

Thomas and Joseph. Joseph whom she had never really met, never talked to. Her stubborn insistence on trying to save his life had brought Thomas out of his distant shell and into her life when she needed him so desperately. She felt the guilt burn through her again. He was a married man. She had no right to him, and she was committing the deepest sin even by thinking of him. What could she do? She felt she would die if she left him. So she would be strong and she would focus on keeping Joseph alive. Joseph deserved to live. He could go back to his wife, whom he so clearly loved. She would make that happen no matter what.

Thomas would be leaving some day too, to return to his wife. No matter how strong she was now, he would leave her, and she would be heartbroken and alone. Even in strength she would not gain him. She could only save her soul, not her heart.

She finished with her patient and headed toward Joseph. She was interrupted by an orderly.

"I'm sorry to disturb you, but there is a telegram here for one of the patients."

"Who?"

The orderly read the name again. "A Joseph Forsyth."

Rebecca was surprised. Why would Joseph receive a telegram? He was a corporal, certainly not important enough to receive military communications. Private communications by telegram were exceptionally rare.

"I'll take that, thank you."

She took the telegram and examined the front. The message had come from City Point, Virginia, the headquarters of the Army of the Potomac. It had been forwarded through various other channels and appeared to have originated in his home state. She turned to the message itself, reading it quickly.

Rebecca dropped the telegram and nearly fainted. She was trembling and she could feel darkness covering her again. How could this have happened to her, to him? She picked up the telegram again and ran out of the tent. She had to find Thomas.

She looked in the operating and mess areas before finally heading to his personal tent. She opened the flap and found Thomas sitting at a small desk, writing out a report by a dim lantern. He looked up and showed surprise. She had never come to his tent before. They had only spoken a few times in this past week.

"Rebecca . . . please come in." He stood and motioned for her to enter. "What's going on?"

She ran into his arms and buried her face in his chest, sobbing. He put his arms around her, a little hesitantly at first but then firmly.

"What's wrong, Rebecca?"

She couldn't answer for more than a minute. She kept her eyes closed and just held Thomas, letting it all out. All the grief and pain and anger of these past months.

"Dear, what is it?" he whispered.

Finally she calmed down enough to answer. "Read this. I can't believe it."

Thomas took the telegram and quickly scanned the contents. "Oh, Lord no. How terrible. I'm so sorry."

He dropped the paper and held her closer. She drew into his strength, smelling his familiar scent. He was strong and kept her near him. She felt new emotions welling up. Her heart was racing. She needed him so badly. She had tried to resist, but now he was here holding her, taking care of her. She could feel him trembling a little as well. She knew he felt the same emotions. She wanted him. She had done everything to stop it. Now she needed him more than ever. She raised her head slowly, and looked into his eyes.

He pulled her to him. She closed her eyes, her body aching. His lips touched hers. First, just a brush, then deeply. She burned with passion. She felt herself slipping away. They kissed deeply and she clung to him with her body and her heart. He pulled her over to his cot and pulled her down, lying on top of her. He kissed her neck, his hands running down her arms and beneath her back. She was falling, melting beneath him. She prayed a last desperate prayer to

God. She could fight this no longer. She felt his warm breath on her neck as he kissed her over and over. His fingers grasped at the first button of her dress.

"Doctor?"

She froze. A voice from outside the tent. One of the orderlies was there. Thomas rose quickly and composed himself, placing a finger over his mouth to caution Rebecca.

"What is it?"

"May I come in?"

"I'm . . . I'm just dressing. I'll be out in a moment."

"I have exciting news for you and Nurse Walker. Your pet patient. You know, the miracle one? His fever has broken and he's awake."

Rebecca bolted up, conflicting emotions whirling through her. Joseph was awake. He was going to survive! She felt intense regret. Why had they been they interrupted? She wanted Thomas so badly. Couldn't they have just another few minutes together? A small part of her was relieved beyond measure. Were her prayers answered? Did God send the orderly to interrupt them before she fell into the deepest sin? She shook her head, trying to focus. She would sort these things out later. For now she had to go see Joseph. She had saved him. They had saved him.

The telegram! She picked it up off the ground and folded it carefully, trying not to dwell on the contents. Sadness overwhelmed her again. She had saved him, but would it matter? She had brought him back to live a life of pain and sorrow. A world she knew only too well. How would he survive?

For now he was alive. Thomas gestured for her to wait, and then he gave her hand a small squeeze and left the tent. She waited several minutes and then followed, looking around to make sure nobody was watching her. She made her way to the hospital tent excited to finally meet a conscious Joseph and dreading the news she must tell him.

CHAPTER 25

Union Military Hospital Camp near the Jerusalem Road

Thursday, January 19, 1865

He dreamt of home. Joseph walked through the sunny, humid summer fields of Macomb. In the distance, he saw Mary Jane and Lucy sitting on a blanket, a picnic spread out before them. They laughed and waved at him. He smiled and started running to them, but something was wrong. He felt his strength draining away from him, pulling him down.

He looked up again. Lucy was screaming. Confederates had appeared around her and they were firing at him. Cannon explosions erupted around them, blowing the rebels into pieces but showering Lucy and Mary Jane with shrapnel. He tried to run faster, but it was as if his legs were deeply embedded in mud. Finally, he arrived at the blanket. Lucy was still there but her head was bowed. He touched her shoulder and she looked up. Beneath her, Mary Jane was lying, her head on her mother's lap, blood everywhere.

He sat upright in bed, shouting. He didn't know where he was. He felt dizzy immediately and fell back hard onto a mattress. A mattress. Where was he? His head was a fog. Where had he been when he went to sleep? Certainly not here. He turned his head to the right. There were other men lying on cots, covered in brown blankets. What was this place? It looked like a hospital. How had he ended up in a hospital? He lifted his hands and felt around his body. His arms were fine. He wiggled his toes. He ran his hands up his stomach and to his chest. He was surprised to find bandages on his upper left chest. He slid the hands upward farther and felt lightning hot pain burn through his body. He had been shot, he was sure, but when and how?

He closed his eyes, trying to calm down. Trying to remember. He recalled the trenches, the muddy ditches before Petersburg. He had been there with his regiment, with his company. David was with him. They had been there for months. Long, boring months marked by wet, cold, disease, and occasional death.

His leave! He had been granted leave by the captain. He was supposed to depart in the morning. He had gone to bed. Then the dream, the strange dream of the rebels attacking at night. He had struggled to find David in the fighting. They had tried to escape but no! They hadn't made it. The rebels killed David before his eyes, and then they shot him. Shot him in the chest.

Was that real? He had thought it all a dream, but where was David? Where was his friend? He tried to lift his head to look around, but the dizziness engulfed him again and he had to lie back. He felt nauseated. He turned his head to the right and retched, vomiting on the mattress and over the edge.

"Joseph!" He heard a woman's voice, a voice he didn't recognize. He laid his head back and kept his eyes closed for a moment until the dizziness went away. When he opened them, there was a woman above him, a woman he didn't know. She was smiling at him with a look of relief and something else he couldn't place, as if she did know him.

"Joseph, you're awake! I can't believe it. How do you feel?"

"Dizzy. Weak," he responded. "Who are you?"

"I'm Rebecca Walker. I'm your nurse. This is Doctor Johnston. He saved your life. It's a miracle you survived at all."

Joseph opened his eyes again and saw there was, in fact, a doctor standing over him as well.

"I didn't save your life. Nurse Walker did. I thought you were lost when you came in. You had a terrible wound. She insisted I operate. Against my better judgment, I did. Afterward, your wound became infected and I thought you were surely going to die. We treated you, and by some miracle, you survived. You are a very lucky man to be here."

"Where is David?"

They exchanged glances. "Who is David?" she asked.

"David is my best friend. He was a private in my company. I was with him."

He saw her face cloud. "I don't know, Joseph. We don't know anything about your friend. I do know a large force of Confederates attacked your regiment in the trenches. There were many casualties and many people killed. I don't know if your David was one of them. I can ask about that, but it's going to take some time to find out."

Joseph shook his head. "He's dead. I know he's dead. I watched him die. He was murdered when we were trying to escape the attack. I can remember it. I thought it was a dream, but it's real. I know he's gone."

"I'm so sorry, Joseph." The woman's face showed true grief and compassion. She placed her hand on his arm and gave it a squeeze.

"How long have I been asleep?"

"A long time, Joseph, weeks."

Joseph couldn't believe it. He felt like he had been sleeping for some time, but hours, not weeks. "I was supposed to have leave. I was supposed to be home for two weeks."

He saw Rebecca's face darken but then she recovered and touched his arm again. "Don't worry about going home right now.

You need to recover and rest. When you're feeling better, you'll be released and then we can make arrangements for your future."

What did that mean? Was he going back to his regiment? Would he be fit to fight again? He closed his eyes and tried to rest. He was struggling with all of his thoughts, and after some time, he was still not asleep. He also noted the nurse and doctor had not left his side, but obviously thought he was asleep.

"When are you going to tell him?" the doctor asked.

"I don't have the heart to. How can you tell someone something like this?"

They obviously did know David was dead. They hadn't told him immediately because they were afraid of how he would react. Joseph was prepared for the bad news. He would wait until he woke up and then they could tell him. They continued talking.

"That's not the worst of the news. Thomas, I have to go."

"I know."

"You do?"

"We both know. I'm so sorry it's come to that, but I can't let you stay, and you can't let yourself either."

"Oh, Thomas, how will I live without you?"

"You will live, Rebecca. You're the strongest woman I've ever known, the strongest person. You will make it. You've held out and held up all this time."

"How can I leave Joseph though? I have to wait and tell him."

"You've done enough. I'll tell him when he wakes up. He might be out for hours. I don't know if I can take it that long. If I was alone with you again . . ."

"I *know* I can't take it, Thomas. I . . . I have to leave now."

"I'll stay here and keep a watch over him."

"Thank you. Thank you for everything. I'm so sorry it's come to this." Her voice dropped to a whisper. "I love you. I will always love you."

Joseph heard the rustling of fabric and was sure they were embracing. They might have said more, but he was already drifting off to sleep. He thought he might have imagined all of it, but when he woke up what felt like hours later, the doctor was still there by his side, although the nurse was gone.

The doctor brought him some water. "How are you feeling?"

"I'm . . . I'm fine. When I was falling asleep, I heard the two of you talking. I thought I heard that the nurse was leaving. Why would she leave?"

The doctor looked surprised and confused for a moment. "It's nothing. She was supposed to transfer ages ago to another hospital, but I had kept her here for a while. You just happened to catch our good-bye." His voice cracked and Joseph was sure there was much more to it. Still, this wasn't his business.

"What about the bad news? I heard you talking about that too."

The doctor hesitated again. "Unfortunate that you overheard anything, but you would know soon in any event. I have rather difficult news for you. Perhaps the most difficult."

"I already know. David is dead. I told you that."

"That's not the news, Joseph. As I told you last night, I don't know what happened to your friend. This is the news I am speaking about." He handed Joseph the telegram.

Joseph took the paper and began slowly unfolding it. He felt a strong terror washing over him. What could this possibly be? Finally he had the telegram open and he read the contents.

> *To Corporal Joseph Forsyth:*
>
> *I regret to tell you that on the night of January 16, 1865, your home was burned to the ground. Your father and his wife, her parents, your half sister, and your daughter, Mary Jane, were all inside and died in the fire. We suspect this was murder. We are looking for two strangers who were seen following Robert home*

from the Pope's Mill tavern. I'm so sorry for your loss. I hope you are able to come home to us immediately. Lucy will need you.

The telegram was signed by Sheriff Marion Pope, a man Joseph barely knew from Macomb. A second telegram had been added from the army, granting him an immediate thirty-day leave to begin the moment Joseph was released from the hospital.

Joseph's hands trembled. This couldn't be true. There had to be some kind of mistake. How could his family be dead? The people listed in the telegram didn't even make any sense. Why would all of those people be together in one place? Charlotte hadn't seen her parents in a long time. It was possible, he supposed, that they might have visited, but what would Mary Jane be doing at the house? Lucy hadn't allowed them around in months. Why would Lucy have not been in the house if Mary Jane was there?

Then he remembered with horror that he had encouraged Lucy to work things out with Charlotte. If she had done so, then Mary Jane could well have been at the house visiting, even spending the night. Could all of these things have happened together? What about the reference to the tavern? Robert had quit drinking. He had promised, and Charlotte had written how well he was doing. Joseph shook his head. *Of course he could have started drinking again. Your father was a weak, drunken fool.* He admitted this to himself fully for the first time. He had been a fool to trust him. Now his family had paid the ultimate price. It was possible that the telegram was incorrect, but he knew in his heart that it was the truth. His little girl was gone.

He rolled out of the cot and hit the ground hard. He had to get up. He had to get going now and find out what had happened. His whole body was numb, his mind was numb. He felt the earth swallowing him up. He tried to rise, but the dizziness returned and he fell back down.

"Joseph, stop it! You're too weak to move. I know this is the worst possible news, but you have been at death's door. If you try to leave now, you'll be dead in a few hours. You must rest. I'm so sorry for your loss, Joseph. I don't have words to express how sorry I am. But it won't help if you die too. You need to rest up. In the meantime, I can see if I could get a telegram through for you to let them know where you are and when you will be able to go home."

Joseph could hardly hear him. His life was over. Everything was gone. His father was gone. Charlotte, who had been the only mother he really had ever known, was gone. Beautiful little Jane. Worst of all, his little Mary Jane was gone. His heart and his soul was that little girl. How could she be gone from the world? How could he be left behind without her? He closed his eyes and rocked back and forth, sobbing, feeling the darkness wash over him, begging to die.

Joseph awoke again. He realized he must have passed out. The memories flooded him again. Mary Jane dead. Robert had betrayed him again, this time destroying everything. *He's lucky he's dead or I'd kill him myself.* He felt a huge hole in his heart. The emptiness there stunned him. How could he go on without his little girl? Perhaps he wouldn't. Perhaps he would simply end things. As a soldier, he had seen death. He had seen life fade away. Death was no stranger. He couldn't think about such things. For the present, he had to get home and find out what had happened. Had his family been murdered? What was Robert's involvement? He had to be there for Lucy. Poor Lucy, losing her brother and now her child and her closest friend.

The doctor came back to check on him along with an orderly who brought a plate of food. Joseph realized he was starving and gratefully took the plate. He sniffed the contents that seemed to be made up of some sort of hot cereal. He began hungrily scooping the stuff into his mouth as the doctor tried to work around him and check his wound.

"How long will I need to be here before I can leave?" asked Joseph.

"Weeks at least, perhaps a month. You have had a very near miss. I know you must be extremely anxious to go home, but you won't be going anywhere for some time to come."

"I can't wait that long. I need to leave now."

The doctor looked at him with compassion in his eyes. "I understand, but it would kill you. Like I said, I will see if I can get a telegram through for you. I can also write down anything you want me to send and I'll get a letter out right away. Just let me know when you want to do that."

Joseph finished his plate and set it down next to his cot. He felt exhausted just from the effort of eating. He placed his head back against the pillow and closed his eyes. "Tomorrow would be fine, Doctor. I still need to rest. Thank you so much for everything you have done for me."

"Of course. Although again, it was Nurse Walker who saved your life. All I did was follow her lead. She is an amazing woman."

Joseph nodded again and drifted into sleep. He rested for a week and a half, waking up for short periods of time to eat. He visited now and again with Doctor Johnston, asking questions about the doctor's life and about Rebecca. He learned from the doctor how Rebecca had fought for his life, and his admiration for her grew. He wished she had remained behind so he could have thanked her properly.

Gradually, he felt his strength returning. He felt more awake, although still terribly weak. As he regained his consciousness, his senses came alive. He noted the terrible stench of the place and the endless coughing and moaning. The hospital tent was kept stiflingly hot by a series of iron stoves. Lanterns burned day and night, allowing the medical staff access to the patients around the clock.

Finally, he felt he was ready. He waited all day, continuing to rest as best he could. As the evening passed to night, the sounds in the hospital faded somewhat and so did the traffic. Now there were only a couple of orderlies walking periodically among the wounded. They would stop and talk at the corners of the tent for a few minutes at a time.

At such a moment, Joseph turned over and rolled as quietly off his cot as he could, biting his lip to control the pain in his chest. He ducked behind the cot and watched the orderlies as they chatted, looking out one of the tent entrances. He crawled slowly in the opposite direction, turning periodically to keep his eyes on them and make sure they didn't see him. After what seemed forever, he was finally able to crawl to the opposite side of the tent near one of the other entrances.

Joseph found some wooden dressers. He carefully opened one of the drawers and reached inside, pulling out a handful of cloth cut into strips for bandages. He also found a stack of uniforms and carefully examined them, pulling out a relatively clean jacket and some boots. Tucking the bandages and the jacket under his arm, he carefully put on the boots (fortunately, they had not taken his pants). Then he took a final look over at the orderlies and ducked quickly out of the tent and into the night.

He was immediately hit with overwhelming cold. The stark contrast between the stifling tent and the freezing night startled him. At least the air was clean and fresh. Making sure nobody had spotted him, he pulled the jacket on over his bloody shirt and buttoned up the front. When he was finished, he turned over on all fours and tried to pull himself to his feet. He couldn't do it. He was surprised by his weakness. He had always been so strong, the strongest person he knew. Now he couldn't stand on his own two feet. He felt some of the dizziness swimming in his head, but he fought off the feeling. He had to get home. He would have to battle through the weakness.

He spotted a wagon a few yards away. He crawled through the frozen grass and finally found one of the wooden wheels. Using the wheel as a lever, he pulled himself slowly to his feet. He stood with the help of the wheel for a few moments, steadying himself. The dizziness returned but gradually faded.

He saw movement in the darkness. He made out the shape of Doctor Johnston heading to the tent. He must be coming back for late-night rounds. He would quickly discover Joseph was missing. Once that happened, they would find him and return him to his bed, probably restraining him. He would not have another chance to leave for a long time.

Joseph turned away so he would not be recognized, and pushing himself off the wheel, he started walking slowly away from the tent. He could see a line of trees in the distance, no more than fifty yards away. If he could make it to the trees, he might hide and then make his way to a train. He had his telegram with an official pass and he had a little money still in his trouser pockets. He just had to get away from the hospital.

He walked away as quickly as he was able. His legs were so weak and threatened to buckle with every step. He was sure he would be spotted. He listened attentively, waiting to hear the cries that would mean Doctor Johnston had discovered him missing. Finally, after what seemed an eternity, he made it to the trees. He took a couple of steps into the woods and then turned, holding on to a tree for dear life. He felt dizzy and worried he would pass out at any moment. Still there was no cry of alarm.

He saw movement at the tent entrance of the hospital. Doctor Johnston was there, looking out from the tent, his head moving in all directions. He was clearly looking for Joseph. He walked out of the tent and then along the perimeter. He disappeared in the darkness, only to reappear a few minutes later back at the entrance. He then pulled out something and fumbled around. After a moment there was a spark and a light. He was smoking a pipe.

Why hadn't he called the alarm? Why had he searched alone and then stopped? Then Joseph understood. He was letting him go. The doctor had been very worried about his health, but now that Joseph had made his decision, the doctor was respecting his choice. Joseph felt gratitude and warmth fill him. He silently thanked the doctor and sat in the darkness, watching him smoke his pipe until the light slowly faded away. The doctor tapped out the pipe, then with a final look out into the darkness, he turned and returned inside.

Joseph made his way along the woods, pausing every few minutes to rest. He finally found the main road and began walking into the darkness, hoping he was going the right way. He walked all night, resting frequently. He fell several times in the darkness and lay on the frozen ground until he found the strength to rise again. He was starving and felt a terrible thirst. Somehow he kept going, the thought burning through him. He must get home. No matter what, he had to find a way.

Dawn came. He was still on the road, barely walking, supported by a crutch he had fashioned out of a branch. He hobbled along, halfway out of his mind, his chest burning in pain. Finally when he thought he could go no farther, he saw buildings in the distance. He made his way slowly forward, finding a little extra strength. He was stopped by a sentry at the entrance to the little town. He showed the soldier his pass and was ushered in. He hobbled on and came to a small hotel. He purchased a room on the first floor and a little bread and water. Only when he was inside the room with the door closed did he fall onto the bed, his bread untouched. With shaky hands, he poured a drink of water out of a pitcher near his bed. He took a few small drinks and then tipped the glass back, drinking deeply. He set the glass down and collapsed in the bed, darkness overwhelming him.

◆ ◆ ◆

Joseph arrived in Washington City in the District of Columbia three days later. The sun was out in the early morning, and although the weather was still cold, Joseph enjoyed the bright warmth as the sun shone down on him. He couldn't remember the last sunny day he had experienced.

He felt a little better now, although he was still very weak. He had lay for a day and a half in his hotel room, drifting between sleep and consciousness, trying to remain awake long enough to eat a little bread and change the bandages on his wound. When he had woken up, he had felt much better and had enough strength to stand and walk without the crutch. Even his wound looked slightly better.

Now after a day and a half of travel, he had arrived in Washington. He would need to find a train traveling to New York or Philadelphia, and then to Albany. He knew it might still be three or four days before he arrived home. He had passed through Washington on the way to Petersburg and was still in awe of the huge city. The Capitol Building stood on a rise, towering over the nearby buildings, the dome still under construction, but further along than when he had last been here.

He made his way down Pennsylvania Avenue heading for the B&O Railroad Station on New Jersey Avenue and C Street. He paused to purchase some roasted nuts from a street vendor. He had to walk several miles to the train station, which was nearer to the Capitol Building in the distance.

As he walked, he thought through his plan as he had many times along the journey from Virginia. He had sent a letter to Lucy and Pete telling them he was coming. When he arrived back in Macomb, he would immediately go to Lucy and make sure she was able to go on. After that, he would meet with Pete and the sheriff to find out what happened and if they knew anything more about the men who had supposedly followed Robert home. Hopefully, they would have found them by that time. If not, Joseph would decide what to do next. He was sure that this was a murder, and sure too that Robert was the cause.

"You don't look in shape to be walking anywhere, Private," said a voice nearby.

Joseph looked up and nearly fell over in surprise. Abraham Lincoln was standing in some gardens, looking out to the street and apparently had just addressed him. He had no idea he was close to the White House but the building stood in the background. Lincoln wore his customary black suit and tall black hat. He was attended by a solitary guard with nothing more than a pistol.

Joseph didn't know how to respond so he merely nodded.

"That's no response, son. I said you look about to fall over. You're as white as a sheet. Where are you off to in your condition?"

"I'm on my way home, sir," answered Joseph, unsure what to say.

"What's your name and where are you from?"

"I'm Joseph Forsyth and I'm from Macomb, New York."

"I'm not familiar with Macomb. Where is that?"

"It's in upstate New York, near Ogdensburg and Morristown on the Saint Lawrence."

"Ah, an upstate New York man. A good fighter I would suspect. What are you doing in Washington City?"

"I'm going home on leave. There's been . . . there's been trouble at home." Joseph's voice cracked as he said it.

Lincoln's eyebrows furrowed. "What kind of trouble?"

"There was a fire. Most of my family was killed. My . . . my little girl was killed. They think it might have been murder. I have to get home."

Joseph saw sorrow flash across Lincoln's face. "How terrible. How are you traveling, though? You look too weak to walk."

"I was wounded. I'm pretty weak, but I can't waste time. I have to get to the train station right away."

"I understand, Private. Well, I can help you, but first you should come inside and have a meal, take some rest."

"I don't have time, Mr. President. I'm . . . I'm sorry, but I have to go. My train is leaving in a few hours."

"If you have a few hours, then you have time. Don't worry, son. I'll get you some food then I'll have you taken to the station. There will be plenty of time to get there. For now, come inside and I'll show you around. You can have a hot meal and we can chat awhile."

Joseph was anxious to leave and felt very nervous in Lincoln's presence, but a hot meal and a ride to the train station would be very beneficial. He was still very weak and had limited money. He nodded his agreement and followed the president and the guard through the garden and then to the White House itself.

They entered the house through a large door. There were dozens of people moving around the house at various tasks. Joseph was also surprised to see a few men actually lying down in the hallway, asleep under their coats. The house was wide open to the public apparently.

"Waiting to meet with me," explained Lincoln. "Sometimes people will stay here for days."

Joseph was shocked at the lack of protection for the president. His own regiment devoted an entire company as the provost guard for the colonel, and yet the president of the United States had only one guard, and people were allowed to wander freely through his home.

"It seems strange everything is so open," commented Joseph, and then he mentioned the provost guard in his own regiment.

Lincoln laughed. "Well, I'm supposed to be here for the people, and I'm sure your colonel is far more important to the war effort than I am."

Lincoln led Joseph into his office. Joseph could see the unfinished Washington Monument out of the window. There was a small writing desk near the window and a big table in the middle of the room piled with various maps and books. Lincoln waved Joseph over to this large table and had him sit down, clearing a spot for him from among the heap of documents. He ordered food and coffee. Within a few minutes, a large tray of sandwiches was brought in along with coffee and an assortment of cakes. Joseph was starving and quickly wolfed down several sandwiches and a finger-sized piece of vanilla cake.

"So, Joseph, tell me your story."

"What part?"

"All, if you wouldn't mind."

Then Joseph found himself telling his entire life story to Abraham Lincoln. He told him about the voyage to the New World and his indenture. He told him about the O'Dwyers' cruelty and deception and then his escape and voyage down the Saint Lawrence. He told him of his father's drunkenness and debt, and Joseph's own labors to dig Robert out. He explained his hard work, his pride in buying land, his courtship of Lucy, and his subsequent frustrations. He told him of Oliver's heavy-handedness and Warren's lust for revenge. Finally, with broken words, he told him of his wounding, of David's death, and of the terrible telegram from home.

Lincoln sat for a long time after Joseph was finished. He could see the grief in the president's face, a face already creased and preaged with care. Finally, he spoke.

"That's a sad tale, Joseph. I'd like to tell you it's one of the saddest I've heard, but I can't. No, this war's given me too many such tales and worse. I've heard of whole families wiped out, every son killed in a battle. Farms have been destroyed, futures disintegrated before their eyes. Still, you've had more than your fair share of grief."

"I've done my best, but it doesn't seem to ever be enough."

Lincoln laughed. "Now that is something I can certainly relate to. I've done my best in this war, yet many people despise me and want to see me down the road as soon as possible. I thought they had me licked this last election, but somehow I hung in there. I suppose they will get their wish eventually. I would grant that wish to them now if I could, but there is too much work left to do. I have to finish the job as they say. But enough about me, it's you I want to discuss.

"Joseph, there's nothing you can do about Mary Jane. I've lost two boys. Edward when he was just four, and Willie here in Washington back in 1862." Lincoln's voice cracked when he mentioned Willie. "Losing a child creates a hole you will never fill. That loss must be borne, and borne for good. I wish I could tell you there was some way to make it better, but there isn't. I miss both my boys so much and there's nothing I can do about it.

"In terms of your father, there isn't anything more you can do. You've done your best for him. You fought for him and his family in a noble and honorable way. My own father used to say no matter how much you whittle, a tree is still a tree. You did what you could, but Robert remained Robert. He's gone now, hopefully to a better place. I believe in God and I believe in forgiveness. I hope Robert did as well.

"This war has taught me many things, but one more than any other: You can't do anything more for the dead but grieve them. That part will come by and by, but the question for you, Joseph, is what you will do for and with the living. What will you do with Lucy and Oliver? They seem well-intentioned, but they want you to live their dream, and they seem set on making sure you have no choice but to do it. What will you do with them?"

"I don't know what to do. Lucy just lost her little girl, our darling Mary Jane. Oliver was trying to make me see that Robert would never change. I ignored them both and I cost all of the people in that house their lives. It's my fault. How can I tell them no now? They were right and I was wrong."

"I don't see it that way. You did your best with Robert. Lucy's and Oliver's actions had more to do with steering you than steering you clear of Robert. Remember that when you see them again."

"What should I do?"

Lincoln laughed again a final time. "I don't meddle where love's involved. You'll have to figure that out for yourself, my boy. But think on my words. You've given your whole life to everyone else. You need to start living for yourself a little as well. There's nothing wrong with that. No matter what, Lucy will probably remain difficult. I have a tremendous amount of experience with a difficult woman. It hasn't been the death of me . . . not yet anyway."

Lincoln rose and shook Joseph's hand. He called in a worker and directed that Joseph be taken by coach to the train station. A first-class ticket was to be purchased for Joseph, at Lincoln's expense.

He looked at Joseph one more time. "Farewell. I wish you the best, my boy. I'm glad I met you. I wish you the best of futures."

Joseph smiled. "I wish you the same."

CHAPTER 26

MACOMB, NEW YORK

SUNDAY, FEBRUARY 5, 1865

Joseph walked up the muddy drive to the Hastings house just as darkness was falling. He was exhausted and freezing from the steady rain and wind. He dreaded this moment, this moment of coming home. He had yearned for this homecoming all those months at Petersburg. He had imagined Mary Jane running into his arms, Lucy standing proudly behind with their new baby. Oliver next to her, also beaming proudly; a new, mutual respect between them. Robert and his family, invited and honored guests, standing nearby.

All of that was gone. Mary Jane was gone. He would never see his little girl again. She wouldn't run into his arms or sit on his lap. She wouldn't giggle at his teasing or kiss him on the cheek. She wouldn't grow older and marry, beginning her own family. She was gone along with Robert and Charlotte, along with Jane, his only sister. Part of him was gone forever with them. Now he had to concentrate on what was left and the hard road ahead. The first step of that journey lay before him, up the stairs and inside the Hastings house.

He climbed the stairs slowly, reluctantly. He had traveled so far for this moment. He reached out and turned the doorknob, then stepped into the house. There was no one in the front room, this room he had sat in so many times, waiting to pay his rent, to negotiate for his father's debts. He walked through the room and turned to the dining area. The dining room was lit and prepared for dinner. Two places were set. A couple of servants were busying themselves with the dishes, lighting candles, and setting the silverware. Joseph watched them for a few moments, then heard footsteps coming down the stairs. He turned to look up the steps and there was Lucy. She was holding an infant. Her eyes were tired and her face was worn with stress lines. She looked ten years older. He could see all the pain and the sadness he had felt himself mirrored in her expression. She looked up and stared at him for a moment, as if he were a ghost, then she hurried down the stairs and pulled him to her, holding the baby with her left arm while she held him close.

"Oh, Joseph! Oh, Joseph, you're here. You're finally here. I hadn't heard from you all this time. Where have you been? You must know—you must know our little girl is gone. She's gone forever." Lucy burst into tears that grew into racking sobs. Joseph put both his arms around her and held her close, sharing her wrenching grief.

"What happened? Why was she at Robert's house? Is it true this was a murder?"

Lucy calmed down eventually and explained everything she knew. She confirmed that she had reconciled with Charlotte and that she had been invited to stay the night with Mary Jane to visit with Charlotte's parents. She had begun labor and had left Mary Jane at Robert and Charlotte's when she went back to give birth. She had delivered their new baby the same night as the terrible fire. She didn't know anything more about the murders, just the rumor that two men had encountered Robert at the tavern in Pope's Mill and were seen leaving the tavern and following him home.

Joseph told her about his wound and about David. He told her about Nurse Walker and Doctor Johnston and their efforts to save his life. He told her of his escape, the difficult journey, and about meeting the president. She listened, asking questions here and there.

"How terrible about David. Your memory is correct, Joseph. He was killed. Pete heard a week or so ago. He took it very hard."

"I haven't seen Pete yet. I will have to go see him tomorrow and meet with the sheriff."

"That will be a hard meeting. I feel so badly for Pete. Now, Joseph, it's time to meet your new little girl. I know it's so difficult, but we also have to take time for her. Yes, another girl. I named her Lorinda."

Joseph took the baby from Lucy and held her in his arms. She was still tiny with a tuft of black hair. She was asleep. She looked just like Lucy, the beautiful, innocent Lucy everyone had loved. Joseph held her closely while Lucy watched, tears falling again down her cheeks. He felt a flurry of conflicting emotions. This child, like his return home, was supposed to be a celebration. Now he felt guilty. He felt if he loved this child now, he was somehow betraying Mary Jane. He needed to grieve for her first, to have time to let her go. He handed Lorinda back to Lucy. Like everything else, he would have to do his best with this while he recovered from the tragedy.

"Well, our conquering hero returns."

Joseph heard the voice and turned to the dining room. Oliver stood, both hands on his hips, staring at Joseph with a hard expression, the expression Joseph remembered from the early years when he was a lowly field hand trying to pay off his father's debts. Joseph nodded in return.

"Come with me, I wish to speak with you alone."

Joseph looked at Lucy, whose face had paled. She averted her eyes, refusing to look at him. Joseph had dreaded this confrontation perhaps even more than seeing Lucy for the first time since he'd enlisted. But this was another step in the long journey to healing. A step he must make. He turned and followed Oliver into the library. Oliver closed the door behind them and then walked over to his desk, sitting down and offering a chair to Joseph.

"We heard you were wounded. Are you recovered?"

Joseph told Oliver briefly about his injury and treatment. Oliver also asked about Warren. Joseph gave him the same answer, deliberately shielding him from the truth. He felt Oliver's eyes boring into him. He was sure Oliver felt there was more to the story than he had told him.

"Well, what is done is done with Warren. I've lost my only son. He was arrogant, and he struggled at times to put in a hard day of work, but I had hope for him. He just never measured up, bless his soul. I always held out hope that he would finally grow up. Now I'll never know, but that can't be helped. I have to figure out the future.

"I've been angry with you, Joseph, angrier than I've ever been at anyone. I knew it was a mistake to trust Robert. I knew he would fail. I never imagined it would result in the tragedy that occurred. However, when you make mistakes, you have to live with the consequences.

"Joseph, it's not easy to say these things to you but they must be said. You have many wonderful qualities: hard work, honesty, integrity, a natural ability to make common folk love you. What you lack is judgment of character and you've too much softness sometimes toward others. You let Robert and his family walk all over you. You spent your money and the fruits of your labor on them. I know they were family, but you kept on taking care of them long after you should have. I finally had to step in and demand you send Robert away. I had everything taken care of until you acted like a spoiled young boy and defied me. You defied me and ran away from your responsibilities. You left that Irish drunk on your property, picking him over me. You left my daughter here in grief and sorrow. You left my farms unattended and left me scrambling to find a decent foreman.

"Look where it got you. You put your trust in your fool of a father and he got himself and everyone around him killed. My precious granddaughter was killed. It's only a miracle that I didn't lose Lucy and Lorinda as well. If I had, I would have killed you myself. Killed you for destroying everything in my life."

Joseph clenched his jaw, but remained quiet.

"Instead, I have decided to give you this one last chance. I'm going to forgive you. I've thought long and hard about this. I'm going to still make the offer to let you buy into the property. I will name the price and the shares of ownership and you will agree. Don't test my patience with a negotiation. You will live in the house here with Lucy and Lorinda. I'm not investing in the print shop. Don't ask me to do it. I always thought that was a wasted investment, but I was willing to indulge you. That time has passed. I've wasted enough time and money.

"From now on, you will listen to my advice. I will try to teach you how to read people since you so clearly lack the capacity yourself. You will stay on the property and you will not leave. You will live here in the house with me and Lucy and Lorinda.

"Those are my terms. My final terms. If you disagree, then you will leave my property and you will never come back. Lucy will stay here with the child. You will stay out of our lives. If you try to fight me, I will pull in every favor, pull every string, to drive you out of Macomb forever. I can make that happen. I can ruin you in this town forever. Do you understand me?"

"I understand you. I can't answer you today. I need to see Pete tomorrow and find out what the sheriff knows about the murders. I need a little bit of time."

"You've always been a man who wanted a day to answer. Well enough, I'll give you a day. Tomorrow night I want your answer. You won't stay another night in my house, another second on my land, if you say no. Think hard on this, Joseph. Once you decline, I will never let you back in. There will be no reconsideration. Remember, I cut my own son out of my life. I can certainly do the same to you. I won't join you for dinner tonight. I don't want to see you again until you have your answer. I told you before you were like a son to me. Now you have the chance to act like one. Go back to Lucy. Take your day. Make your decision."

Oliver waved his hand by way of dismissal. Joseph rose and walked out into the dining room. Lucy was already seated and dinner had been served. Joseph sat quietly through dinner, hardly touching his food. He was angry at Oliver. There were so many things he had wanted to say. However he knew that there was much truth in what his father-in-law had said. David's death. The death of his daughter. Perhaps the deaths of all of them were on his hands. He had defied Oliver and trusted Robert. He had left Macomb, taking David with him, running off to the army because he couldn't solve his problems at home. Now he had to face the consequences. He had one day to decide his future.

The next morning, Joseph set out early, borrowing a horse from Oliver's barn. He rode the long, familiar road to Pope's Mill. He had another difficult reunion ahead of him. He had not seen Pete since he left for the army, when he departed with Pete's son, who would never return. What would Pete have to say to him? Would he blame him as Oliver had? He had every right to.

Before he made it to Pope's Mill, he had another terrible milestone to reach. He rounded a familiar bend and came into sight of his farm.

The little cottage he had built for Lucy was still there, strangely out of place without the farmhouse. The barn was also standing but was partially burned down and blackened in many places. The farmhouse was gone entirely.

He rode slowly onto the property, moving ever closer to the site of the farmhouse, where much of his life burned away. As he neared, he saw the remains of the fire. There was very little—a few blackened timbers crisscrossed in the burned soil. The stone steps leading to the cellar still stood, smeared with soot but recognizable. Joseph didn't dismount but remained by the ruins for a long time, memories flooding him. He wept silently in the early morning rain. His future had died here with Mary Jane and his family.

Why had he written Lucy, pushing her to make up with Charlotte and his father? Why hadn't he just followed Oliver's advice and thrown Robert off the property in the first place? Then Mary Jane would be alive. They would all be together at the Hastings house. Robert and Charlotte would be gone, living somewhere else. He would have lost the relationship with them, but they would be alive, Jane would be alive. Joseph thought again about taking his own life. The pain was so great he didn't know if he could live with it any longer. Everything was his fault. Still, he had Lucy and the baby. He had to go on for their sakes. Eventually, he turned his horse and moved away. There was much to do. More difficult reunions and even more difficult decisions awaited him.

He made it to Pope's Mill at about noon. The little cluster of houses and buildings was busy. A number of people recognized Joseph and grimly greeted him. He understood. What do you say to someone who has lost his entire world? He rode on and made his way to Pete's store, then dismounted and entered.

He couldn't help but smile. There was Pete, stocking the store shelves, whistling a quiet tune to himself. Pete had been such a rock in his life. He imagined if he came to the store forty years from now, Pete would still be there, forever sweeping and stocking. Pete looked up at the sound of the door opening and spotted Joseph. He dropped a jar of jam that fell to the floor, exploding in a red mess. He walked swiftly over and threw his arms around Joseph.

"You're home. You're safe. Thank God. Thank God in heaven. Joseph, I'm so sorry. So sorry for everything that's happened to you."

Joseph held the embrace for a moment then pulled away. "Thank you, Pete. Thank you so much. I'm sorry about David. It's all my fault he's gone."

"Don't you say that. Don't you even think it. David knew what he was getting into from the first. Don't you remember he wanted to join with Casey all those years ago? You helped me stop him. You gave me three more years with my boy that I might have lost if you hadn't been here to influence him. No, Joseph, don't you ever blame yourself for David's death.

"It's hard. It's very hard to live without him. But I have my other son: I have you, Joseph. You've always been a son to me. Since the moment I met you, I've respected and loved you. I remember when you came in the first time, a scrappy Irish lad on the run, trying to find his father. I was so worried for you because I knew Robert and I knew what you would find. But what did you do? You didn't run again like most boys would. You didn't give up. You rolled up your sleeves and you worked off his debt. You worked sunrise to sunset and beyond, day after day until you had your own land. You did everything you could for your father, and for so many other people in this town. You were a great friend to David, and a great friend to me."

"Thank you so much, Pete. You've always been like a father to me as well." Joseph was so thankful. He had expected more anger and blame, but his friend had treated him with compassion and understanding, even after Joseph's decisions had contributed to David's death. He was surprised by the difference between Pete's reaction and Oliver's, but it brought home the stark distinctions between the two men.

"How is Lucy?"

Joseph told Pete about seeing Lucy, and about his confrontation with Oliver.

"So he's given you a choice to follow his orders or leave the family forever. Son of a bitch. Do you think Lucy would really stay with him?"

"I don't know. She refused to come with me last time. She has always been a little afraid of her father. Oliver has so much power. Even if I tried to take her with me, he would fight me with everything he has."

"Oliver's not as high and mighty as he thinks. Folks around here are tired of his sharp dealing and putting on airs. You might find more support if push comes to shove than you think."

"Thank you for saying that. I'm not sure I believe you, but you are kind to say it."

"Believe what you want, Joseph, but it's the truth. You are respected and loved by so many people. Oliver may have money and power, but he doesn't have the support of the people. That said, I have my own proposal for you, and I hope you won't find it as heavy-handed as Oliver's."

Joseph was surprised. What did he mean? "What proposal is that?" he said.

"I told you you're like a son to me, Joseph. Now I've lost my only son. I would like to have you come live with me, you and Lucy and the girl. We could sell your land and pay off that Deary scoundrel. You could keep the rest; you wouldn't even need to pay me back. You would work that off in no time. Eventually, you could come in on the store with me. You've always been such a hard worker. With David gone, I need a helping hand. In time you could take over the store. I would be able to slow down. I know you've had this offer before, and more than once, but I'd like to think you would find that future a much gentler and better one than you would with Oliver."

Joseph hadn't expected this at all. Now he was more confused than ever. It was so difficult with his grief and guilt to see clearly what to do. Still, he was tremendously grateful to Pete. He was offering Joseph a way out, an alternative to the future Oliver was pressing on him.

"Thank you, Pete. Thank you for everything."

"Of course, my friend, my son."

They left together to see the sheriff and they went to the tavern and interviewed Alexander. Alexander confirmed that Robert had been drinking, and had told him and the strangers about the sale of the flock. He also had seen the strangers slip out just a few minutes after Robert left. Alexander had never seen the men before. The sheriff had interviewed numerous other people, but other than one person who confirmed that the men were seen traveling south the night of the fire, nobody had any additional information. The sheriff considered the fire a murder and said he would continue to investigate, but if the men had drifted into town and just as quickly left, it was very unlikely he would ever find them.

Joseph thanked all of them and then departed. The day was getting long and he had to be back to the Hastings house for dinner. He rode away and set back for home. What should he do? Should he go after the murderers? Nobody knew their names or what they looked like. He knew nothing about police work. How could he find them? It was even possible the men were unrelated to the fire, that the fire was an accident, although Joseph felt in his heart that wasn't true.

Should he take Pete up on his offer? If he did, he might well lose Lucy. Not only that, but Oliver might come after him and even after Pete. Oliver could divert his business away from Pete's store and encourage others to do so. It was the kind of vindictive thing he would do. Joseph had already badly affected Pete's life; could he risk bringing more misery down on him? Also, although it was hard to admit because Pete's intentions were so noble, would he simply be trading one slavery for another? Throughout his life it seemed others wanted him to work for them, wanted his hard work and his stability. Some of the offers were well-intentioned, some were not, but were the results the same?

What about Oliver? He didn't want to live on Oliver's land. He didn't want to spend his life doing what Oliver wanted. He would be more under his thumb than ever if he chose to return. But if he didn't agree, he would lose Lucy. He would lose his life and his new little girl. He had already lost Mary Jane and his father's family. Could he survive losing his wife and new child as well? Did he owe Oliver for putting his faith in him? For spurning Warren in favor of him?

He had less than a half hour left to decide. The rest of his life came down to the next few minutes. He let his horse walk slowly, his mind pondering these difficult questions. Finally, as he turned into the drive at the Hastings house, he made up his mind.

Joseph arrived at the house just in time for dinner. He hugged Lucy and the baby, and then a servant took Lorinda away so that they could eat in peace. Oliver joined them at the dinner table. They discussed the sheriff's investigation and Joseph told them about seeing Pete. He did not mention Pete's offer. They did not discuss Oliver's deadline during the dinner, although there was tremendous tension in the room. Lucy obviously knew what had been demanded and Joseph caught her searching his face, looking for clues of how he would answer.

After dinner, Oliver invited Joseph into the library. "I want Lucy to come with us," said Joseph. "She clearly knows about the issue at hand, and this decision involves her as much or more than the two of us."

Oliver considered this for a moment and then nodded his head in assent, waving Lucy into the library as well. He closed the door and took his accustomed place at his desk.

"Well, Joseph. You've had your day. I assume you have made the right decision."

Joseph looked at Lucy, then turned to Oliver. "I will not agree."

Oliver's face instantly turned red. "You bastard! I have given up everything for you! I moved mountains to help your situation! I gave you my daughter, offered you my inheritance! You dare to turn me down! This isn't a game, Joseph. You have already cost me dear, dearer than any man has ever dared. Think carefully on what you say, as I said, there will be no coming back."

"My mind is made up."

"Joseph, how can you say that?" demanded Lucy. "I'm your wife. We have a life here. A home and a family."

"We can have a home and a life elsewhere. I have another plan. A future I can see, that makes sense to me. You are my wife. Lorinda is my child. You are supposed to be a part of me. I have made up my mind. I'm asking you to come with me. Come with me now."

Oliver jumped out of his seat, taking several steps toward Joseph. "You won't be taking her anywhere! I told you that if you refused me, she would be staying here. The baby will stay here as well. If you've made up your mind, you have no place here. Get out of my house and get out of my presence before I take matters into my own hands!"

Joseph ignored him, his eyes on Lucy. "Lucy, listen to me. It doesn't have to be this way. Your father doesn't own you. We are husband and wife. We have lost so much, but we had a home together, a life together. We can have that again. We have Lorinda and we have each other. Forget this house. Forget the servants and all of the money and fancy clothes. They don't mean anything! You are what matters. You and me and Lorinda."

Lucy hesitated as if not sure what to do. Finally, she turned to her husband. "Joseph, you're asking me to trust that you will make the right decision. You trusted Robert and you left me here and ran away to the army. I suffered terribly here and you didn't even care. Then you encouraged me to reconcile with Charlotte and Robert. That decision cost Mary Jane her life. Listen to Father. He might be heavy-handed sometimes, but he has always been right. He sacrificed Warren for you. We have lost so much family because of you. Don't you love me? Don't you want to take care of me? Joseph, I can't go back to the chores and the dirt and the constant worry about money. I was lonely without you these past months, but I did have my father and I had the security of his house, of people here to help me."

"You mean servants. You mean clothes and expensive food and carriage rides."

"What's wrong with those things, Joseph? There's nothing wrong with nice things. I tried to do things your way, to sacrifice and live that way. Where did that get us? Where did working with your father and trusting your father get us? My father was right all along. We should have stayed here from the beginning. If we had, Mary Jane would be alive. We would have both our children. Warren would be alive too. Joseph, don't you see what you've done? How you've let everything fall apart with your trust and your decisions?

"Please, dear. Please don't leave me and the baby. I can't go with you if you leave. I'm not strong enough. I lost something when Mary Jane died. Something I don't think I'll ever get back. I need this. I need all of this. If you stay, we will have a perfect life. The best life that is left to us. Someday this land will be ours. We will have safety and security. Please, Joseph!"

"Who are you?" he asked. "I don't know the woman I married. You are trying to blame me for Warren's death. I didn't want to tell you this, but I have to now. Warren put a gambler up to taking Robert's money when he was drunk. Then he joined the army and tried to have me killed. He led me to an ambush and ordered me to attack a heavily defended position. David was wounded and my closest friends in the company were killed. Warren was killed in the same attack. Killed by a stray bullet even though he was far back from the action. Do you understand? He would have killed me if he had the chance. Warren was a monster.

"You blame me for Robert? Robert was his own man. I did my best for him and Charlotte. You're right, I trusted too much, gave too much for too long. But I'm not the only one to blame. Your father forced my hand. If he had worked with me without demanding Robert leave, then I would not have had to join the army to pay the debts. I would have been home when all of this happened. Your father pushed me instead of allowing me to make my own decisions, just like he has always pushed me, always manipulated me. Has he told you the price I've paid to him? The months of work to pay my father's debt? The extra months after Warren *attacked me*? The price he forced me to pay in order to marry you? Your father pushed and pushed me until I broke. I should never have left for the army, but what choice did I have?

"And what about you? Before we married I owned my land free and clear. I had savings and a future. After we married, you spent and spent. I asked you to stop, but you wouldn't listen to me. If I said no, then you would mope and brood, forcing me to give in over time. You would never let up. We ended up with no savings. No money for our future, no money to pay my father's debt. You forced me to work and work, for what? For nothing. All so you could have silk dresses and furniture from France. What will all those possessions do for you, Lucy? Do they make you happy? You're the least happy person I've ever known. Will they make you happy in the future? Will they bring Mary Jane back? You had a part in all of this too, dear. It's time to begin accepting that, instead of just looking pretty and complaining about how difficult life is without servants."

Joseph turned to Oliver.

"And you. The great puppet master. Sitting in your big house and running everyone's lives. Wringing every ounce of sweat out of your field hands and servants each day. Paying them as little as you can. Holding back your crops to change the market. Running tenants off your land without a care in the world for them. Using your connections and your money to threaten and influence people so you can make even more money. You want me as a son. I am not like you, Oliver. I will never be like you. I don't care about having all the money in the world. I don't care about dominating others and controlling them. I just want my own land, my own family, my own life.

"I will never work for you again. If Lucy will not come with me, then I will go my own way. I don't care about your opinions anymore. I don't care if you think I caused this tragedy. I will make my own decisions, I will control my own destiny, I will take care of my own family and build my own future. There is nothing you can do to me, nothing you can take from me. If you want to come after me, then try. I'll be waiting."

Oliver was so angry, he was shaking. He reached into his drawer and pulled out a revolver. He aimed the pistol at Joseph and pulled back the hammer.

"Father, no!" screamed Lucy.

"You leave this house this instant! Do you hear me! You leave this house and you never look back. If you come onto this property again, by God I will shoot you dead. You will never see my daughter again or my granddaughter. Now get out of this house before I kill you!"

Joseph turned to Lucy. "Are you coming? Now is the time to decide. Will you put all of this stupidity away and come *live* your life? Live a life of contentment and simplicity, a life we control and can enjoy. You are my wife. We have our daughter and our future together. Please, Lucy. Your father doesn't own you. Let's leave this place. Let's start our future again."

She stared back and forth at Joseph and Oliver, tears streaming down her face. She couldn't speak, couldn't move. Finally, she shook her head.

Joseph watched her for a moment more, then he stepped backward slowly out of the room. He walked through the dining room and out the front door. He untied his horse, mounted, and rode slowly off the Hastings property, never to return.

CHAPTER 27

Union Military Hospital

City Point, Virginia

Friday, April 28, 1865

Rebecca Walker moved among the wounded, tending with her usual care. There were no more new casualties. General Lee had surrendered on April 6, and General Johnston on April 26. There were still plenty of soldiers recovering. The fighting had intensified with the breakthrough at Petersburg on April 2, and for the days that followed when General Grant had chased Lee. With Lee's surrender, Rebecca was now treating both Union and Confederate wounded. Still the nation was in deepest mourning. President Lincoln had been assassinated on April 15.

She marveled at the facilities at City Point, which were far larger and more sophisticated than what she had faced at Petersburg. She had enjoyed her time here these past few months, away from the dirt and the constant din of battle. Away from all the pressures. Away from Thomas.

"Rebecca." She froze. As if her thoughts had conjured him, she heard his voice. She turned slowly and there he was, standing in a new uniform, thinner than ever—her beloved Thomas. She felt the familiar deep ache immediately. She had worked so hard to dull it these past months. Yet here he was and the feelings were as strong as ever. Thank God she had found the strength to leave him.

"Hello, Thomas. What are you doing here?"

"I'm going home. I wanted to see you before I did."

"Home." She thought of her own home. There was nothing there. Her husband was dead. Thomas would return to his wife and family. He would have children and practice medicine in his small Pennsylvania town. He would leave her forever.

"How are you?" he asked, the words coming softly. He was watching her. She could tell he was saying good-bye forever. He was soaking up her features, storing them for a lifetime.

"I'm fine. I have been so busy. The work never stops here. But the doctors are kind and I've made friends."

"No, I mean how are *you*?"

"I'm still here, Thomas. The pain is starting to fade a little. I don't spend every second thinking of the past. I can see a little light in the future. Not much, but it's a start."

He moved closer. "I wish you hadn't left me. We could have made things work."

She laughed. "Could we have? We were an instant away from giving up everything. I wanted you, I want you now, but I couldn't be with you. I couldn't stand you returning home and living the rest of your life with this stain on your soul. No, that's not honest. I couldn't stand being with you and then losing you to her forever."

"I would have given up everything for you."

"Would you have? At the end, could you really do that for me? These have been terrible times, dear. You have been away from home almost a year. I was here. You fell in love with me. I love you for it. You saved me when I didn't know if I could go on. But in saving me, you nearly destroyed both of us. You have a wife at home who you love. You can go back to her now without living the rest of your days in guilt. I did the right thing, even if it felt like it killed me to do it."

"Joseph left."

"What do you mean?"

"He ran away from the hospital one night. He wanted to go home. He didn't care if it killed him. I can understand wanting something so badly regardless of the price you will pay."

He moved closer and took her hand in his. She felt the old thrill, his touch burning her. She couldn't do this. She had barely escaped. She pulled her hand away.

"I'm sorry, Thomas. I can't. I want you to go home in peace. I love you, my dear. I will always love you. I want you to go home to your wife. Have a beautiful family. Take care of the sick. Grow old. And remember me each day. Remember our sacrifice. I will always be there for you in your heart."

He pulled her close again and held her tightly. She held on to him, enjoying their last touch. He pulled away slowly. "I love you, dearest."

"I love you too, my Thomas."

He turned slowly and walked away. She watched him every step to the door. He turned for a moment and looked back, smiling and waving good-bye. Then he was gone. She closed her eyes for a few moments, remembering him. She thought about all of their many months working together, her growing affection, the surprise when she learned he cared about her. She relived their one moment of passion and the bittersweet interruption that saved her from terrible sin. She whispered a prayer for him.

Then she thought of Joseph. She said another prayer for him. She knew his pain. The loss of a child, the loss of your family. She prayed he was still alive, that he was home, that he was safe. She felt in her heart that he had made it back to Macomb, that he was moving forward in his life, no matter how great the burdens.

As she turned away to the next patient, she felt an overwhelming peace. She thought of Thomas again. She would always love him, but she had kept her promise to God and to her husband. Now she could move on with her life, wherever she was led.

CHAPTER 28

Macomb, New York

Sunday, April 30, 1865

Joseph stood in the field looking down at Mary Jane's gravestone. Sometimes he would just sit at the foot of the stone, thinking of his little girl, talking to her about his life.

"I still think of you every day, dear. Almost every second sometimes. I'm so sorry I wasn't here for you at the end, that I couldn't protect you. I hope Charlotte is taking good care of you, and you and Jane are having fun in heaven." His voice broke and he had to stop for a moment.

"I haven't talked to your mother. I thought she would come, but she hasn't. Your little sister must be getting bigger. I wish I could see them both. I know you would want us to be all together, to be there for you. I just have to keep praying.

"You would be very proud, sweetie. I went into Ogdensburg this week. I bought my printing equipment. It's not much and it's used, but it's all mine. I used the leftover money from the sale after I paid back Deary and Pete.

"It's hard not having my own place anymore, but I've found a wonderful piece to rent. It's owned by Lawrence Hewett, and it's forty acres and a decent little farmhouse. I had to sell all the livestock too, but I was able to hold on to one milking cow and all the seed I'll require for the year. Pete told me he'd loan me a mule to plow the fields. If not, I can always hitch myself up.

"It's funny, dearest, but at one point I was doing pretty well in life. Before I married your mother. Don't tell her I said that! The funny thing is all that money, and the extra things, they don't add up to anything much. I'm happier now than I've ever been. Well that's not true. I'm content, but I miss you more than life itself and I miss your mother and your sister.

"Pete keeps bothering at me to come live with him. I told him no, just like I told your grandpa. I'm done with depending on people. Whatever happens in my life now, I do on my own. That's all I ever wanted, but I always felt a responsibility to others.

"I suppose you see your grandpa Robert up there in heaven. Tell him I'm still very upset with him. I'm trying to come to peace, but I can't. I gave him everything and he gave me nothing in return. In truth, he gave me less than that. He took everything from me. I spent my entire life trying to take care of him, trying to get him to love me. I've realized you can't change people. I've realized you can't always trust what they say; you have to look at what they do. Funny it took me this long to figure it out.

"I don't know if I have all the answers now. I make plenty of mistakes still; trust me. I do know that I'm not trying to force my hopeful view of the world on everyone anymore. I've become cautious. I watch and wait to see who people really are now before I let them in. I've lost something along the way, an innocence I guess I always had. It was a price that had to be paid. I can't let people take advantage of me anymore. I've learned to be a little more selfish. It takes a long time to teach me a lesson I guess.

"I pray every day that God will bring you back to me. I wake up and hope I'll hear your little feet, see you running across the room to jump into my arms. I know I'll never see that again, at least on this earth. I'll have to wait for heaven to see you again.

"Well, dear, I suppose I need to go now. If you see David and Casey, give them a big hug for me. If you can put in a word for me with Lucy, I'd be much obliged. I want our family back, although she will have to leave all those spoiled wants at the door.

"Then again, if Mr. Lincoln could handle a difficult woman, I suppose I could as well. Give him a hug for me as well. Tell him thank you. He'll know what I mean."

Joseph reached down and kissed the headstone. He reached into his coat and pulled out a doll he had bought at Patterson's. He placed it at the head of the grave, resting against the marker. He kept his eyes on the doll for a few moments longer, then walked away.

A few yards down he stopped again, his eyes resting on a different marker. He stood for a minute in silence, looking at the grave, his face showing no emotions. Then he reached into his pocket again. He then departed the little cemetery, leaving a necklace resting on the marker. It had a small leather rope with a wooden cross, worn and battered. He left it on the headstone of Robert Forsyth.

He arrived home as the sun was beginning to set. He went into the barn and milked his cow, then completed a few other chores by lantern light before returning to the farmhouse. He spent a few minutes starting a fire before laying out a frugal dinner of bread and cold meats. Just as he took his first bite, there was a knock at the door. He rose and crossed the entryway, unbolting the door and opening it.

Lucy stood there before him, Lorinda in her arms. She had nothing with her, and she looked exhausted and cold.

"Lucy, come in. What's the matter?"

"I ran away. I came here on foot. I don't know what's going to happen, Joseph, but I had to come."

He brought her in and pulled a chair over to the fire. He had hot coffee on the stove and he poured her a cup and brought her a blanket. When she was settled, he asked her to continue.

"Ever since you left, I have been wanting to join you. But I've been afraid. Afraid of my father. Afraid of living life without everything I'm used to. Joseph, I'm so sorry. I've been a fool. I wanted the things I have had since I was a little girl. I thought those were the most important things in the world, more important even than love. I thought if you loved me then you would give me those things. When you wouldn't, I was confused and upset. My father never told me no.

"After you left I've realized the most important thing in the world is our family. I've realized that Lorinda needs her father, that I need you too. I made my mind up a few days ago that I would leave and find you. I found an excuse to come into town. Pete told me where you were. I bided my time until today when Oliver left to look at a farm that is coming up for sale. I packed up a little food, scooped up Lorinda, and headed out the door.

"Joseph, I'm ready to live my life as your wife. I know you may not be able to give me all of the things I used to have, but I don't care anymore. I want to start our life again. Please take me back. Please, dear!"

She buried her head in her arms and began to cry. Joseph put a hand on her back and drew her head to his waist, holding her. He said a silent prayer and thanked God, and sent a thank-you to Mary Jane for good measure.

"Of course I will take you back, Lucy. That's all I ever wanted. As long as you understand that we have to work together. You will have to be patient. You will have to be content."

"I will do all those things. I promise. Oh, Joseph, what about my father?"

Joseph remembered what Pete had told him. "I'm not worried about Oliver. I don't think he will do a thing. If he tries, he will find half the town rising up against him. I have my own friends and my own support in Macomb, and I didn't have to buy it."

"Joseph, thank you, thank you! I love you, dearest. I love you so."

Joseph held Lucy for a long time in the flickering light of the fire. He was content. He had his wife back and his little girl. He had as much future back as he would ever have. He was sure Lucy would struggle. She had lived a lifetime of luxury. Perhaps she could never change. He would wait and he would watch. He would never give in to her pouting and complaining again. He could handle living with a difficult wife.

He brought Lucy some of his dinner and made sure she was comfortable. She nursed Lorinda and then placed her in a crib Joseph had built weeks ago, hoping he would be able to use it someday. He then helped Lucy to bed. She was exhausted and fell asleep within moments.

Joseph walked quietly through the house and back out the front door. He sat down in a chair he kept on the porch, looking out over the land and up at the stars. He wondered about life, all his adventures, and all those to come. He whistled an Irish tune his mother had taught him. He was finally home.

EPILOGUE

Joseph and Lucy Forsyth continued to live together in Macomb, New York. They had three more children together: Frances, Cassie, and Robert. The Forsyths migrated in 1879 to Nebraska, where Joseph continued to farm and also served as a rural mail carrier. The Forsyths never owned land in Nebraska, but were beloved in their community.

Joseph passed away on October 30, 1922. The author of his obituary noted that, "In common with all who knew him, he was honored for his many excellent qualities. He will be remembered as an inborn gentleman. His passing not alone places a heavy loss upon those who were bound to him by family ties, but their heartache is shared by friends to whom he seemed almost equally dear and who realize not only their own personal loss, but the great loss that has come to the community, in which, while he harried with us, he was ever a worker on the side of right."

There is a historical basis for the meeting with Abraham Lincoln. According to his obituary, when Joseph was traveling back through Washington after the fire, "while waiting for his train out, he passed by the White House. President Lincoln was outside the building and ordered the guard to admit Mr. Forsyth and the kindhearted president was very sympathetic, showing him through the building and on his departure giving him his blessing."

The mystery of the murder of Robert Forsyth and his family was never officially solved. However, an article from the Morristown newspaper was found in Joseph Forsyth's home after his death in 1922. The newspaper is quoted in part as follows: "The authorities believed at once that murder and arson had been committed, and great efforts were made at the time to locate the murderer, but nothing ever came of it and the mystery remained unsolved for years until a man named Gallinger was about to be executed in California for murder. He confessed to having murdered a whole family in this [St. Lawrence] county, but he could not name the location as the country was strange to him. As there had been no other family murdered in this county, the natural conclusion was that Gallinger was the perpetrator of the awful crime which was committed to cover up the robbery of the household."

JOSEPH AND LUCY FORSYTH LINEAGE

Joseph and Lucy Forsyth gave birth to Frances Estella Forsyth, at Macomb, New York, on February 25, 1870.

Frances married Ulysses Grant Shipman on March 15, 1894. Ulysses and Frances are reputed to both have suffered from disabilities, and had a very difficult and impoverished life together.

Ulysses and Frances gave birth to James Wayne Shipman in Wayne, Nebraska on April 21, 1903.

Ulysses died when James, who went by "Wayne," was a young man. Wayne spent two years in Nebraska working to pay off Ulysses's debts.

Wayne married Elinor Ann Ingles on January 27, 1931 in Nebraska. They lost their farm in the dust bowl during the Great Depression and eventually migrated to Washington State.

Wayne and Elinor gave birth to James Curtis Shipman on August 7, 1941. He was the fourth of five children. The Shipmans settled on the south hill of Puyallup before purchasing a quarter section of land in Alfa, Washington.

James attended high school at Onalaska, Washington, where he met his future wife, Janice Marie Davis, born February 21, 1942. James and Janice were married on January 27, 1962, after James served in the US Navy. They lived in California while James attended mortuary college, and then they moved to Long Beach, Washington, before purchasing Schaefer-Shipman Funeral Home in Marysville, Washington in 1973. James, who always went by Jim, was actively involved in the community along with Jan. He passed away on October 31, 2013, beloved by the people of his community like his great-grandfather before him. Jan still lives nearby.

Jim and Jan gave birth to Angie Lynn Shipman on February 4, 1968, and the author, James D. Shipman, on January 4, 1970. Joseph and Lucy Forsyth are the author's great-great-grandparents.

LINES: INSCRIBED TO MR. AND MRS. JOSEPH FORSYTH ON THE SAD DEATH OF SIX RELATIVES BY FIRE DURING THE WAR IN 1865

BY MRS. D. MCFALLS
1877

When time its mysteries unfold

And year by year away has rolled,

In that Great Day will be revealed

The past events. Those now concealed

From mortal ken, revealed at last—

The deep, dark mysteries of the past.

Then, only then, perchance the screen

May rise that clouded this dark scene

From mortal vision, wrapt in night,

No sound was heard, no ray of light

Betakening evil, husked in sleep,

No hand to save, no eye to weep,

No wild alarm no fire bells rang,

No hurrying feet or tramping clang

Along the way. All was still

Till the sad sight their bosoms thrill.

All that was seen when morning broke

Was fading embers and the smoke.

Then woke and started with a fright

The wile alarm: What of the night?

Where were the inmates? Had they fled?

Or fire consumed them? Were they dead?

From house to house the herald sped

With heart of fear, and thought of dread

To see if missing ones were there—

The aged ones and children fair.

The search is vain, hope dies away—

They must in smoldering ashes lay.

And now the mystery deeper grows:

How could it be that fire could close

Around them all, nor one awake

To tell the danger of their state?

But other hearts must wake and feel

Death's poignant grief around them steal.

Hearts that had fondly yearned for those

O'er whom the dark black embers close.

The mother with her infant child

Dreamed not of anguish deep and wild;

But when her first-born one should come

At morn, to that find happy home,

How joyfully she then could tell

That baby came! And all was well.

Oh! Drop the veil and hide the grief

For which no one could bring relief.

On tented field that father lay,

Nor dreamed as midnight wore away

Of scenes at home. His vision fled

To conquest's hour, and o'er the dead

Saw but the crown of victory.

Oh! Mortal vision, could'st thou see

The depth of grief awaiting thee,

Then all the war like dreams would flee

And wrap thy soul in misery.

The visions would not float away

To battle scenes and war-like fray—

To beating drum of sounding fife,

Or grand array of martial life.

A message! O, what does it bear?

Sad tidings from the loved ones there.

Great God forbid! I thought when peace

Returned and war would cease

To clasp the loved ones to my breast,

And feel, indeed that they were blest.

O! break the seal, and read it now!

I feel the warm blood flush my brow!

No clarion sound or battle peal.

His head, his heart, his senses reel.

A father, mother, sister, child,

Grandparents—and his brain grows wild!

O, who can tell how soon our bliss

May change to wild despair like this.

The morning skies—all clear and bright—

May set in deepest gloom at night,

And grief may rend these hearts of thine

Where fond affection's links entwine

So lovingly, that naught would seem

Could e'er disturb thy fondest dream.

And though some new made link may twine

Within this family chain of thine,

Yet other links may break away

And fondest hopes and loves decay.

I know how hard 'twould be to bear

Her loss—thy first-born blossom fair.

For mine had faded years ago,

Sad'ning my heart with grief and woe,

Feeling when that dear tie was riven

A stronger bond for me in Heaven.

And you, dear friends, as years pass by,

Will feel your sadden hearts draw night

That heavenly bourn, that future life—

Unknown to sorrow, grief or strife.

And now may God some balm distill.

Nor deeper weight of sorrows fill

Those wounded hearts. May future bliss

Bring joy and peace and happiness.

ACKNOWLEDGMENTS

I want to thank Amazon, Lake Union Publishing, my amazing editor Danielle, and everyone I have worked with at Lake Union for all their hard work and support.

ABOUT THE AUTHOR

James D. Shipman is a northwestern author and attorney. He graduated from the University of Washington with a BA in history in 1995, and from Gonzaga University School of Law with a Juris Doctorate in 1998. Mr. Shipman is a lifelong student of history, particularly medieval history, the American Civil War, and World War II. He has published a number of short stories and poems, along with *Constantinopolis.*

He resides north of Seattle with his wife and children. Mr. Shipman enjoys pottery, music, the outdoors, and spending time with his family. Connect with Mr. Shipman on his website: james-shipman.com.